Praise for
Promise Me Tonight

"A sensual yet endearingly tender love story—every romance lover owes herself this book!"

—*New York Times* bestselling author Eloisa James

"*Promise Me Tonight* by Sara Lindsey made me sigh with delight! This is one of the most charming debuts I've read in years. If you love Julia Quinn, you'll love Sara Lindsey!"

—Teresa Medeiros, *New York Times* bestselling author of *Some Like It Wild*

"An exquisitely enchanting debut by a dynamic new author who will instantly secure a place in romance readers' hearts. This novel is charming beyond belief, with vibrant characters, polished and fresh writing, and one of the most adorable heroines you'll ever meet. Read *Promise Me Tonight*, and get ready to fall in love!"

—*New York Times* bestselling author Lisa Kleypas

SARA LINDSEY

PROMISE ME TONIGHT

A WESTON NOVEL

A SIGNET ECLIPSE BOOK

SIGNET ECLIPSE
Published by New American Library, a division of
Penguin Group (USA) Inc., 375 Hudson Street,
New York, New York 10014, USA
Penguin Group (Canada), 90 Eglinton Avenue East, Suite 700, Toronto,
Ontario M4P 2Y3, Canada (a division of Pearson Penguin Canada Inc.)
Penguin Books Ltd., 80 Strand, London WC2R 0RL, England
Penguin Ireland, 25 St. Stephen's Green, Dublin 2,
Ireland (a division of Penguin Books Ltd.)
Penguin Group (Australia), 250 Camberwell Road, Camberwell, Victoria 3124,
Australia (a division of Pearson Australia Group Pty. Ltd.)
Penguin Books India Pvt. Ltd., 11 Community Centre, Panchsheel Park,
New Delhi - 110 017, India
Penguin Group (NZ), 67 Apollo Drive, Rosedale, North Shore 0632,
New Zealand (a division of Pearson New Zealand Ltd.)
Penguin Books (South Africa) (Pty.) Ltd., 24 Sturdee Avenue,
Rosebank, Johannesburg 2196, South Africa

Penguin Books Ltd., Registered Offices:
80 Strand, London WC2R 0RL, England

First published by Signet Eclipse, an imprint of New American Library,
a division of Penguin Group (USA) Inc.

First Printing, February 2010
10 9 8 7 6 5 4 3 2 1

In loving memory of the furry muses who have graced my life and my lap with their presence, especially Gillyflower, who always knew when I needed a break from writing and let me know by demanding to be fed, brushed, or generally adored, and Miss Mia Meowski, an angel kitty too good for this life, who never left my side during a deadline crisis. I still miss you every day.

Acknowledgments

My heartfelt gratitude to my incredible editor, Kerry Donovan, and my amazing agent, Kimberly Witherspoon, for believing in this book and in the books to come. Thanks to the fabulous folks at NAL, and to the wonderfully talented Dana France for giving me the cover of my dreams. This book would never have been written without the support and encouragement of my fellow romance writers, especially Tessa Dare, Lindsey Faber, Courtney Milan, Elyssa Papa, and Stacey Agdern, who discussed and read this book more times than I think any of us care to remember. My dear friends Lizy, Alexandra, Jenny, and Kara—you nagged me for chapters, listened to me whine, and, the true test of friendship, you've forgiven all the unreturned e-mails and phone calls incurred throughout this crazy process. Most of all, I have to thank my family for standing behind my crazy dream, for loving me even when I'm at my most unlovable, and for being by my side every step of the way. I would be lost without you, and not only because I have a terrible sense of direction.

The Weston Family Tree

Lady MARY BRANDON *m.* OLIVER *Viscount Weston*
1752-   1747-

HENRY 1772-   ISABELLA 1778-   OLIVIA 1779-   CORDELIA 1788-   IMOGEN   RICHARD 1792-   PORTIA 1796-

Promise Me
Tonight
BOOK 1
featuring
James Sheffield 1772-
Viscount Addison

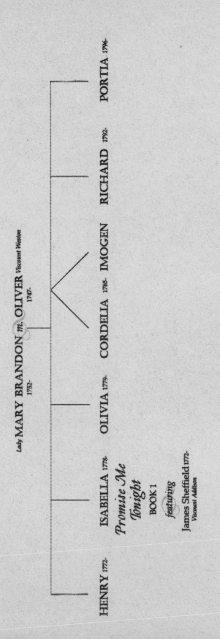

Prologue

Seconds always seem inconsequential. After all, sixty of them exist in a single minute. But then, minutes are equally fleeting when considered in terms of all the hours in a day. Days, too, fly past, turning into weeks, then months, each small, each insignificant, really, in the sum of years that make up a lifetime.

But a single second can change everything. A tiny moment in a vast web of time can forever alter the fabric of a life. At ten years old, James Sheffield knew this to be true. It had taken only a second for the last breath of life to leave his mother's body after hours of fruitless labor with a stillborn child and for Death to stake his claim. The gloomy pall that lingered over the house after his mother's passing had lasted for months, but just a moment was necessary for James to ascertain that the fall down the stairs, whether by accident or design, had broken his father's neck.

And, as he stood and watched his father's coffin lowered into the ground to rest alongside the one containing his mother and infant sister, a second was all James needed to decide he would never again risk the hurt of losing someone he loved. Even at his young age, James knew there was only one way to protect himself, and that was never to love again. So he wrapped up the remaining shards of his shattered heart and buried them somewhere so deep and dark that no one, including him, would ever be able to find them.

Chapter 1

~~Dere~~ *Dear Mama,*
I am ~~gowing~~ going to marry James. It will be ~~nise~~ nice. We will live near you. I am ~~hape~~ happy. I love you.

Love, Isabella
(Mises Danyels helpd me with the speling.)

From the correspondence of Miss Isabella Weston, age six

Letter to her mother, Mary, Viscountess Weston, expounding on the benefits to be found in marrying the boy next door—August 1784

Weston Manor, Essex
July 1792

Perched precariously on the banister of the long portrait gallery so as to better observe the party in progress one floor below, fourteen-year-old Isabella Weston was faced with the devastating sight of her true love dancing with another woman. She turned her head to look at one of her younger sisters, Olivia, who, safely seated on the floor, was craning her head to peer through the carved marble balusters.

"Can you believe how that—that *hussy* is dancing with

James?" Izzie demanded. "Honestly, she should be ashamed, dancing like that with a man who is not her husband."

Izzie, of course, fully planned on dancing with James Sheffield that way, but she would be married to him when she did—or engaged, at the very least. Of course, since she'd been planning the wedding since the day they'd met, Isabella felt they *were* practically engaged.

She'd been only six when they'd met, but one smile from James had been all it took for her to tumble head over heels in love. Of course, she hadn't really known at the time that it was *love*—just that she wanted him more than she'd ever wanted anything before. She wanted to take care of him, to share her family with him, to fill his world with laughter and brightness, and to banish the shadows from his eyes. And though she'd been young, Izzie had been nothing if not determined, and she'd determined right then and there that someday when she was all grown-up, James Sheffield would be hers. Now she *was* all grown-up, or *almost*, and the sight of James with another woman made that "almost" *almost* unbearable.

"Oh, Izzie." Livvy sighed, sounding far older than her twelve years. "Not James *again*!"

Isabella shrugged. "I can't help it. I love him."

"I know. Believe me, *I know*. I would get far more sleep if you didn't. But he, well—" Olivia bit her lip and tugged at a lock of golden brown hair. "He's older."

"James is *not* old. He just turned twenty in May. Hal"— she waved a hand at the crowd below that included the girls' older brother, Henry—"will be twenty in September, and he certainly isn't old."

"I didn't say James was old. I said he was *older*. And he's Hal's best friend . . . and our neighbor. To him you're nothing more than a little sister, and even if he *is* aware of your feelings, I'm worried that—"

"Aargh! I just saw *that woman* touch his—" Izzie waved a hand in the vicinity of her backside, nearly toppling over the railing as she did so. As much as she wanted to squash *that woman* like a bug, she had imagined doing so in a more metaphorical sense. And, of course, such a fall might well break her neck and, if it didn't, her mother might kill her anyway for appearing *en déshabillé* in front of the guests. Not that her thick flannel nightgown and wrapper didn't cover every inch of her from the neck down, because they did, but it wouldn't be *proper*.

Along with snakes, spiders, and apricot jam, Izzie loathed the word "proper." Henry tormented her with the former; her mother with the latter. But it was her mother's sort of torture that made her quake in her boots; propriety and Izzie had never gone together.

Izzie hopped down from the banister and plopped herself beside her sister. "Now, what were you worried about?"

"Nothing," Livvy muttered.

"Do you know who she is?"

Olivia rolled her eyes, and without bothering to ask for clarification as to the "she" in question, replied, "I believe the woman dancing with James is the rather notorious widow who finally convinced Lord Finkley to walk down the aisle again."

"Oh dear," Isabella whispered, torn between fascination and dismay.

After his wife had passed away some fifty years earlier, Lord Finkley had spent his time with a parade of young mistresses and society widows, each of whom had hoped to seduce the wealthy elderly man into matrimony. None had succeeded . . . until now. This meant that James was in the hands of the most cunning female England had seen in a half century or of an evil sorceress—or both. Either way, Izzie didn't like it one bit!

"I had expected something more of the woman who finally trapped Lord Finkley."

Olivia shook her head. "You're just jealous, and you know it."

"The way she's acting is disgraceful," Izzie huffed. "Do you *see* the way she's throwing herself at him? Why doesn't her husband *do* something?"

"Because he's in the corner, snoring his head off, and has been for the last hour?" Livvy suggested. "Truly, I don't think James minds. She *is* quite beautiful," she added, rather unnecessarily in Izzie's opinion.

"I suppose. If you like the tall, skinny, far-too-much-bosom-on-display sort."

Of course, even though she would have liked to, Izzie couldn't blame the woman for throwing herself at James. He was too handsome for his own good. She could spend— drat it, *had spent*—countless hours cataloging his physical perfections, the first of which had to be his hair.

It was the color of vintage brandy, highlighted with gold where the sun had kissed it. He wore it just a bit longer than the current fashion, and it curled up at the ends where it met his collar.

Then there were his eyes, beautiful green eyes fringed by lashes that were most unfairly longer and darker than hers. *Her* lashes were a scant shade darker than the straw-colored hair on her head, and didn't that just figure. Vanity, thy name is Isabella Weston.

He had a nicer nose than she did, too. Aquiline, she believed was the word, and it made him look quite fierce and arrogant in a way she secretly found thrilling. Her nose was very average in comparison. It wasn't even fashionably *retroussé* like Olivia's. And wasn't that the height of unfairness? Isabella felt that as the first daughter born in the Weston family, she ought to have had first pick of nice noses.

Lady Finkley had a rather elegant nose, Isabella noted unhappily. It was a trifle on the long side, though, she decided as Lady Finkley leaned close to James and whispered something in his ear that caused him to throw his head back with laughter.

Isabella ground her teeth as the clock in the gallery sounded half-past eleven. James and Henry had promised to bring sweets up to her and Livvy before midnight since the girls were too young to be allowed downstairs for the ball.

Olivia yawned. "I'm sorry, Izzie, but I can't stay awake any longer. They've probably forgotten about us in any case. I'm for bed. Good night."

"Mmm-hmmm," Isabella mumbled, never taking her eyes off the scene below.

"Common courtesy demands that you wish me good night in return."

"Mmm-hmmm."

Olivia gave a loud huff. "The things I have to put up with," she muttered under her breath. Izzie heard her, but she was too preoccupied to give her sister a worthy parting shot. Livvy heaved a disgusted sigh as she stood and padded off toward the bedchamber they shared.

The things I have to put up with, indeed, Isabella thought as she watched James walk with Lady Finkley around the perimeter of the ballroom, her arm wrapped about his and his hand resting on the small of her back. Izzie grimaced. She knew exactly how powerful that touch was. It was so magical that from the very first time she had held his hand, she'd never wanted to let go. She did, however, want Lady Finkley to let go. In fact, she just plain wanted her to *go.* Finally, after two immeasurably long turns about the room, Izzie's wish came at least partly true when James escorted Lady Finkley over to her comatose spouse.

Izzie tracked James as he moved through the throng of guests, pausing when she caught sight of her parents dancing together, gazing at each other as if they were the only people in the room. It was sweet, she supposed, that they were still so much in love, but it was also rather embarrassing. It was a trifle discomfiting, too, given that Isabella's baby brother, Richard, had been christened just that morning—thus the reason for the celebration downstairs—and her mother had said, with a pointed look toward Isabella's father, that she did *not* plan on there being any more christenings at Weston Manor until she was a grandmother. However, the looks she was currently giving her husband told an entirely different story!

Not really wanting to follow where that train of thought

led, Isabella's eyes sought out James once more and found him with Henry, who was standing in the crush of people by the refreshments. She should have known. Her mother often said her eldest child had been born with a bottomless pit in place of a stomach. Unfortunately the same could be said of Lord Blathersby, whose sole interest in life—besides food, of course—was his sheep, which meant that Henry often got stuck speaking with the ovine-loving gentleman. From the pained look on her brother's face, he'd been trapped for some time now. *Poor Hal. But*, she thought in true sisterly fashion, *better him than me!*

James Sheffield had always considered himself a good person, but he spent several moments savoring his best friend's suffering expression before going in to rescue him from the most boring man in Christendom.

"Took you bloody long enough," Henry grumbled as they made their escape. "I've been trying to get your attention for ages, but you were too wrapped up in the luscious Lady Finkley to pay any notice. Not that I blame you. Had similar thoughts myself. Bloody unfair, though, that you got to play Casanova while I was stuck with old Blathersby and his sheep."

"Blathersby and his sheep." James laughed. "Never fear; I've heard it all before and on multiple occasions." He shook his head. "Come, it's nearly midnight, and we promised Izzie and Livvy we'd bring them some sweets."

Henry grimaced. "Lord, it completely slipped my mind. Good thing you remembered. You know how Izzie gets when she's angry."

James nodded and hustled Henry over to the crowd waiting to get at the dessert table.

"What a devilishly dull affair," Henry remarked as they waited in line. "First the christening this morning, and now this. It was good of you to come. You could have been off weeks ago."

"Of course I came," James replied, a gruff note creeping into his voice. "Neither of us would have been comfortable leaving until your mother was safely delivered, and delaying our trip for another month made no real difference. The Colosseum isn't going anywhere, and it was important to your mother that you be here for Richard's christening."

"And you," Henry insisted.

"Only to make sure I keep you out of trouble," James teased, but his chest was tight with emotion. The Westons were the closest thing he had to a family since he'd been orphaned at age ten and sent to live with his grandfather, the Earl of Dunston. The best that could be said of the earl was that his main property, Sheffield Park, neighbored Weston Manor, home to Viscount Weston and his family.

They had taken him in as another son; their warm, bustling home had been his refuge. When he and Henry had gone off to Eton, Lady Weston had kissed and clucked and wept over both of them, a performance she had repeated when they'd headed to Oxford.

She had cried when they'd graduated earlier that year, but James figured that was primarily because Henry had spent more time "rusticating" than he had at school. James had taken a first in literature, partly to please Lady Weston, who was more than a little enamored of a certain Elizabethan playwright. Henry had joked that morning that if his father had not had some say in the naming of his children, the family's newest addition might well have been christened Hamlet or Falstaff. Yes, the Weston children were fortunate to have such a father. James had once thought himself lucky in his own sire, but—

He shook his head. He didn't want to think about it. Not tonight. Not ever, really. Far better to focus on the present, and—

"Put it back on the plate, Hal. These are for Izzie and Livvy," James scolded as they filed past the refreshments table.

"When did you grow eyes in the back of your head?" Henry grumbled through a mouthful of cake.

"I've known you since we were ten. Don't you think a

decade of friendship gives me some insight? Besides, you eat everything within reach."

"I'm a growing lad," Henry retorted.

James chuckled. He was tall at six feet, but his best friend had at least three inches on him and was built like a brawny prizefighter.

"If you grow any bigger, I am going to sell you to a traveling Gypsy circus."

"Remind me once more why we are friends."

"Aside from the fact that no one else is going to put up with you?" James joked, turning to look back at Henry. "For one thing, you would never have graduated without my help."

Henry laughed. "I still can't puzzle out how you went to all those boring lectures."

"Self-control?" James suggested.

Henry grinned and shrugged his shoulders. "I doubt it would have made a difference. I was never much good at lessons."

James couldn't argue with that. Intellectual pursuits were not, admittedly, Henry's forte. Bedroom games—actually, games and sports in general—were where he excelled. Still, James was certain Henry was smarter than he let on; his best friend certainly wasn't lacking in imagination, he reflected, remembering all of the scrapes Henry had gotten them into.

He was smiling as he made his way up to the gallery, Henry right behind him, but his amusement faded when he saw Isabella standing at the top of the stairs, one foot tapping impatiently, her arms crossed.

"Finally!" she exclaimed. "I was beginning to think you weren't coming."

Standing as she was, the braces of candles flanking the staircase illuminated her from behind, casting a golden glow all about her and gilding her unruly blond curls into a halo. She looked like an irate angel.

"What happened to Livvy?" Henry asked.

Izzie gave them both a pointed look. "*She* got tired of

waiting, figured you had forgotten us, and decided to go to bed."

Henry looked down at the plate and glass in his hands as the clock chimed the quarter hour. "I'm sure she's still up. I'll go take this to her. Wouldn't want her to think we forgot. She can be nearly as bad as you." And with that said, he took off down the hallway.

"What does he mean, 'She can be nearly as bad as you'?" Izzie muttered, sitting down.

"Er, have some cake," James said quickly, shoving the plate of sweets at her. He waited until she'd downed three gingersnaps and a piece of cake before deeming her mood restored enough for him to safely sit beside her.

"So, did you enjoy the dancing?" he asked.

"Not as much as you seemed to," she said, a hint of bitterness shading her words.

"Beg pardon?" James leaned closer to her, certain he'd misheard her.

"I simply remarked that you seemed to be having a grand time dancing with Lady Finkley." She stared down at her plate. "Is she your lover?"

"W-what?" James sputtered. "Izzie! That—that is totally inappropriate. You shouldn't even *know* about—"

"Lovers?" she supplied, gazing up impishly at him as she licked her fingers.

"Yes, blast it! You shouldn't know about those sorts of things, and you certainly shouldn't ever speak of them."

"Then she isn't?" Isabella queried.

"No!" James exploded, and then lowered his voice. "Dash it all, this isn't proper. And it certainly isn't any of your business."

"Oh."

The softly uttered syllable contained a definite note of dejection. She looked away, and James thought he saw her shoulders tremble. He instantly gentled his tone. "Izzie, look at me. Come on. *Izzie.*"

She kept her eyes glued to the plate in her hands. He took it from her and set it aside, then placed a finger under her chin, raising her head until he could look into her eyes.

"My God, you're *jealous*," he said incredulously. She swung her head away but made no attempt to deny it. James cupped his hand around her cheek, turning her face back to his, and felt wetness on the silky, soft flesh pressed to his palm. He watched a single tear trickle down her pale cheek, then another and another, turning her lashes into dark golden spikes.

"Sweetheart," he pleaded, though he hadn't a clue what he was pleading for. Direction, he supposed. And he had learned from past experience that uttering an endearment was the safest way to break the silence in situations like these. Of course, he had never been in this particular position before, and he hoped never to be in it again. It was damned uncomfortable!

Bloody hell. Isabella had always dogged his heels when she was younger, but he'd had no idea she fancied him in that way. She looked miserable and defeated, so unlike her usual sunny self, and it killed him to be the cause of it. He slung his arm around her shoulders, hugging her close. She burrowed her face into his shoulder, soaking his jacket with her tears.

"Don't cry, Izzie," James begged. "Please, don't cry."

"I-it's j-just that you were s-smiling and laughing with her, and I just w-wished so badly that I was older and could wear a beautiful gown and be the one dancing with you." The words were muffled as they poured out against the soft, black wool of his coat. He murmured nonsense into her hair, soothing her as he would an upset child, but it only made her cry harder.

"Hush, now." James cupped her face in his hands and wiped her tears away. "I am not nearly so good a dancer as to be worth all this fuss."

The small smile she gave him made James feel like the king of England—utterly grand and slightly mad. As James stared into her watery eyes, for a moment, it seemed as if he saw his soul gazing back at him; the thought terrified him, and he pulled his hands away as if burned.

"Someday," he said gruffly, "when you're older and have that beautiful dress, there will be so many men wanting to dance with you, you'll wonder why you wanted to dance with *me*."

"That is *not* true!" Isabella protested fervently. "I will want to dance with you for the rest of my life. Only you. I know it. I *know*, and I won't change my mind. I *won't*."

"You *will*," James insisted.

"Never." She sniffed and shook her head mutinously. "I lo—"

"I hope you are not so foolish as to think yourself in love with me."

She flinched at his tone.

He hated that he was hurting her, but it was best to end this infatuation now. "What you feel for me isn't love—affection, admiration even, but not love. And if you're smart, you will save your love for some lucky man who deserves it and will love you back. I am not capable of love."

"But surely, when you were younger . . ."

"That was a long time ago. I have had some years, and no small amount of help from my grandsire, in which to conquer that weakness."

Isabella shot to her feet. "Love is *not* a weakness—"

"For God's sake, lower your voice." He stood and looked down at her. "So young and innocent," he murmured. "Izzie, I hope you will never find love to be a weakness." His voice was weary and bleak. "But I promise you it can be."

She shook her head mutinously and jabbed a finger at his chest. "And I promise you I will still want that dance."

James sighed.

Izzie glowered, her bottom lip thrust out and quivering, and he knew the fight was up. "All right, don't glare at me so. If you still wish it, when the time is right, I will certainly claim that dance."

Isabella's face brightened, and her eyes lit with sudden hope.

James felt a moment of trepidation, but he told himself it was foolish. Izzie would likely fix her attention on some other gentleman and forget this entire exchange within a fortnight. And if she didn't, it wasn't as though a dance with her would change anything.

"Do you promise?" Isabella demanded.

"Promise what?" Henry asked, his sudden presence startling them both.

"James was just going to promise to dance with me at my come-out ball," Isabella replied.

He hadn't been about to do any such thing, James wanted to protest, but he didn't want Henry to know what had transpired. For one thing, it would embarrass Izzie. For another, he wasn't certain how Hal would react.

He might take it as a great joke; Henry was generally an easygoing fellow. When it came to his family, though, Henry was all seriousness—fierce, protective, pistols-at-dawn seriousness. Of course, James had done nothing to encourage Izzie, but Henry might not care. And James really didn't want to get laid flat because of some innocent fancy. From their sparring sessions at Gentleman Jackson's, James was painfully aware that Henry had a bruising right hook.

"Izzie, your come-out ball?" Henry frowned. "That's years from now and—"

"I promise," James said quietly, his eyes never leaving Isabella's.

"Good." Isabella gave James a smile that had him wondering if a dance was truly all he had agreed to. He wasn't sure why, but he had the eerie feeling that he had just given himself into the custody of a girl with eyes the color of a summer sky and a smile that filled his heart in a way that scared him down to his toes.

Chapter 2

If you will please let me come to Eton, I promise to be very good. I will be quiet as a mouse. I will invite you to all my tea parties. Or just send James Sheffield home. I miss him. A lot. But Henry Weston, my brother, can stay there. Thank you.

From the correspondence of Miss Isabella Weston, age seven

Letter to Jonathan Davies, headmaster of Eton College, which, as the sender learned some years later, had never been posted, thus clearly explaining why no admittance letter was ever forthcoming—September 1785

White's Gentleman's Club, London
May 1797

"You really want to know what brought me back to England, Hal? Guilt, pure and simple."

James pulled a creased piece of paper out of his waistcoat pocket and reached across the table to hand it to his best friend.

Henry glanced at it, then looked up, puzzled. "It's the invitation to my sister's come-out ball."

"Exactly." James sighed.

Henry shot his friend a bemused look and shrugged his shoulders. "It's damned fine to see you, of course, and my mother will be over the moon that you're home, but it really wasn't necessary for you to come to Izzie's ball."

"Oh, but it was." James grinned as he reached over to flip the invitation to the back where Isabella had scrawled the words "You promised" followed by a multitude of exclamation points. Henry's expression slowly changed from bafflement to amusement.

"Lord, I had forgotten about that completely."

"I would your sister had your memory."

Henry laughed. "I wouldn't be overly concerned. It will be difficult for Izzie to make sheep's eyes at you through a crowd of her admirers."

At James's confused look, Henry burst out laughing. "Have you not heard? My sister has been named the next Incomparable. She didn't come out last Season because my mother was confined again, but Izzie spent the winter in Bath with my aunt and caused quite a storm. All those matchmaking mamas with their turbans tied too tight were up in arms because a girl not officially out got more notice than their milksop daughters." He gave an annoyed snort.

A succession of images danced through James's mind as he remembered the hoydenish girl: Isabella galloping astride in Henry's old shirt and breeches, crying when she got stuck at the top of a particularly tall tree, her face covered with light freckles and sticky blackberry juice after an especially fruitful day of berry gathering.

He raised a disbelieving eyebrow at Henry.

"I'm not hoaxing you, I swear." Henry laid a hand over his heart. "Morgan even offered to sell me his grays if I would introduce him to Izzie! Can you believe it? He swore he would never part with them. And Stimpson! *He* said he would give me all his time in the ring with Jackson if I could get him on Izzie's dance card! Wait a tick—I could give him *your* dance and split the time with you."

James felt something suspiciously like a growl building in his throat and quickly took a large gulp of brandy. What had happened to Henry's protective instincts? This was ridiculous. It wasn't that he was jealous, of course. He was simply feeling protective. A good thing, too, since Henry seemed inclined to sell his sister to the highest bidder!

He stopped himself. That was unfair. Henry hadn't accepted these offers, and even if he had, an introduction to Morgan or a dance with Stimpson wasn't going to seal Isabella's future.

Still, he decided to have a word with each gentleman—just a friendly chat—where he would make it clear that if so much as an improper finger was laid upon Isabella Weston, the culprit would answer to him—preferably with pistols at dawn.

"Look, Hal, I didn't come all this way *not* to honor my promise. I gave my word to Isabella that I would dance with her, and I will."

"But—"

"No." Then, before Henry could resume his talk of Isabella's suitors and their various bribes, James inquired after the rest of Henry's family.

"Everyone's fine, just fine," Henry said. "Although I can't think why you bother asking, because Mother must have written you much the same in her last letter."

"She did," James admitted with a grin, "but I never know if the important information is there. I think your mother could expound for fifteen pages on *Othello* and forget to mention that the house had burned down or that your butler had the plague."

Henry laughed. "To the best of my knowledge, neither of those things has come to pass. Weston Manor remains intact, and Caldwell is in excellent health. With regard to *Othello*—that's the one with the boor, right?"

"Moor," James corrected. "But I daresay a man who strangles his wife is a boor, at the very least."

"Eh?"

James opened his mouth to explain, but Henry shook his head and held up a hand. "Don't bother.

He was still smiling later, after the men had left the club and were walking toward the family town house. His grandfather wouldn't be in residence since he rarely left

Sheffield Park, which was for the best given that, as the past several years spent in Ireland had evinced, James had no desire to be in the same country as the earl, let alone in the same house.

When they reached the hotel, James turned to Henry, who was continuing on to his own bachelor lodgings, and found himself reluctant to bid his best friend good night. "I'll see you tomorrow at the ball, then?"

Henry nodded enthusiastically. "Between the party and having you home, Mother will be so distracted, she won't have any time to lecture me." He surprised James by grabbing him in a fierce, brief hug that came close to crushing all of his ribs. "It's good to have you home," he said gruffly.

"It's good to be home," James said automatically. As he watched his best friend saunter off down the street, he realized just how true it was. "It's good to be home," he said again softly.

The Weston Town House, London
The Following Evening

Isabella paced back and forth in her bedchamber, stopping every so often to peer in the full-length mirror and reassure herself that she looked her best. She wore a round gown of white lawn, drawn in below her breasts by a sash of aquamarine silk the color of her eyes; the sash was tied behind her in a double bow, the ends of which fell as low as the short train. The neckline and the cuffs of the short, puffed sleeves were trimmed with delicate alençon lace.

Her hair was dressed in loose curls and ringlets, held back from her face by a white satin bandeau embellished with pearls and fabric rosettes. A double strand of pearls, a birthday present from her parents, completed the ensemble. Yes, all in all, Izzie was very pleased.

She *did* wish the neckline were the tiniest bit lower, but her mother had held firm on that point. She tugged down on the material. There, perhaps that was a bit better. It seemed a shame to conceal what she had learned were two of her more alluring assets. Her cheeks had no need of pinching; the knowledge that she was finally going to see James had suffused her countenance with a soft pink flush.

Five years. She hadn't seen him in five interminably long years. It seemed impossible, but it was true. First, the European tour meant to last one year had stretched into two, and then James had gone to Ireland to deal with the property he had inherited from his mother.

She'd learned from Henry that James was turning the estate into a foundling home, a noble cause surely, and one that made her love him all the more because it was so in keeping with his kind, generous nature, but she wished it wouldn't keep him so far away.

But now he was home—thanks to her rather brilliant foresight in garnering that promise—and it was time to introduce one James Sheffield to the new, improved and oh-so-adult Isabella Weston so they could get on with living the rest of their lives together. And the sooner the better, which was why she was going to make sure James Sheffield fell head over heels in love with her at the ball. And if she had to use some persuasive tactics . . .

Well, she wasn't averse to the idea of hauling him into an alcove and kissing him senseless. She wasn't sure exactly *how* to kiss someone senseless, but it always worked in novels. No one would blame her for throwing herself at him. He always had been too handsome for his own good. Just the sight of him caused her heart to flip-flop around in her chest.

Oh, she wished she could sneak out of her room and go find him that instant, but she had been warned—not exactly on pain of death, but on pain of something her mother promised would be extremely disagreeable—not to budge from her room until she was fetched for her so-called grand entrance. Izzie thought "grand" worked as a description only when used to measure the extent of the mortification she would suffer.

Her stomach pitched when she thought about soon having to curtsy and descend a long staircase while—under the intense scrutiny of everyone in attendance—wearing a dress with a train certain to trip her up and heeled slippers sure to catch in the aforementioned train.

The little supper she had managed to consume before getting dressed formed a hard ball in the pit of her stomach, and she suddenly felt overheated. She closed her eyes and was assaulted by a vision in which she tripped on the second stair and tumbled down the rest of the way, coming to rest in an ungainly heap at the base.

Isabella devoutly hoped her neck would prove to be broken, since that would be vastly preferable to having to stand up and face everyone.

She could do this, Izzie told herself. She'd managed her presentation to Queen Charlotte without making a cake of herself. Tonight was supposed to be enjoyable. And it would be . . . so long as she didn't fall on her face.

She wished her sister Olivia were present to distract her, but Izzie had been given her own room now that she was officially "out." She had complained to her parents that the arrangement meant that Livvy would also get her own room—a room that was actually a bit larger than the one Isabella had moved to—and *she* wouldn't be out for at least another year.

That had been a mistake. Her mother had lectured her for nearly an hour on the bitter fate of all the starving children in England who would happily share the scullery maid's quarters with a dozen other children if it gave them a roof over their heads. Izzie was of the opinion that the scullery maid's room couldn't possibly fit more than six or seven of even the most emaciated children, but she wisely forbore to comment. She did, after all, get the point.

A knock at the door jarred her out of her reverie. A glance at the clock confirmed her suspicion that it wasn't yet time to go down, but she welcomed *any* diversion.

"Come," she called out.

Henry entered the room, looked her up and down, and then motioned for her to turn around in a circle.

"Well? Do I look all right?"

"Damnation, Izzie, I'm going to have to fight them off with a stick," Henry growled, enfolding her in a hug.

"Really? Ouch!" she exclaimed as something in Henry's coat—something that felt like a rock—smashed into her ribs. "What in heaven's name is in your pocket?"

Henry quickly let her go. "Sorry," he said sheepishly. "I forgot that was there, but it's a good thing, actually, or I might have forgotten to give it to you, and it's the reason I came to your room in the first place."

"And what is 'it'?"

"Your birthday present, naturally."

It wasn't at all natural, as Izzie's birthday had been in March, but Henry hadn't been home then, and Izzie wasn't going to quibble over the particulars when there was a present in the offing.

Henry reached into his waistcoat and pulled out a small velvet box. "I do realize it's a bit late, but this seemed like the proper time," he said, handing the box to her.

Isabella opened the box, and her eyes grew wide.

"Henry, I, uh, well . . ."

For the first time in her life, she was actually speechless. She took a deep breath and pasted a smile on her face.

"Oh!" she exclaimed with what she hoped sounded like happiness. "How lovely! It's a . . . large gold ball . . . on a chain!"

Henry laughed. "It's a good thing you're not a gambler, Izzie. Your face gives everything away." He reached into the box and unfastened a tiny clasp on the side of the ball. The two halves opened, and a chain of six miniature portraits spilled out: her parents; Henry; Olivia; identical twins, Cordelia and Imogen; Richard; baby Portia. It was her family, and she could cup them in the palm of her hand, look at them whenever she wanted, and take them with her wherever she went.

"Oh, Henry!" she sniffed. "It's wonderful! Thank you!"

"Well, don't cry," he admonished.

"However did you manage it?"

"Livvy. The chit's useful to have around at times. When

she's not buried in a book, she's always sketching or working at her watercolors, so you never noticed a thing. I took her paintings, along with that set of miniatures Mother commissioned when Richard was born, to an artist in London. The hardest part was keeping it a secret."

"You did an excellent job. I am quite overcome."

"I'm glad you like it. Does this mean you'll forgive me for abandoning you during your first Season?"

"Where are you escaping to this year?"

"Ireland. There are some new hunters I want to look at, and after, I figure it's time I finally saw the orphanage, now that it's nearly finished."

"James is returning to Ireland straight away, then?"

Henry nodded. "Mother would have my head if I didn't stay in town for at least another fortnight, but James is leaving tomorrow. You know he doesn't like to stay in the same general vicinity as the earl any longer than he has to, and Sheffield Park is too close to London for comfort. I am surprised he came at all."

"Of course he came. He promised me he would."

"You and your promises," Henry laughed. "Now I had best be getting downstairs. Mother will doubtless invent some new torture for me if I am not in place for your entrance."

"She is still going to force you to dance with Miss Merriwether," Izzie warned.

Henry groaned. "She's made me promise three times today."

"Now, now," Izzie chided. "Miss Merriwether is very nice."

"Yes," Henry said. "Nice." He said the word with utter distaste, as if it were such a terrible thing to be nice, and then moved to quit the room. "I'll see you downstairs."

He opened the door just as she remembered she had a favor to ask.

"Henry?"

"Yes?" He turned back to face her.

"Will you tell James I have saved the dance just before supper for him?"

He grunted his assent and was halfway out the door when she thought of something else.

"Henry!"

"What?"

"Thank you again for my present. And for being my brother."

He strode back into the room and wrapped her up in one of his huge, engulfing hugs.

"I love you," she murmured.

"I love you, too." He dropped a kiss on her head and left.

Alone once more, Izzie glared at the clock on the mantel, silently willing the hands to move faster. She gazed down at the portraits in her hand, her heart flooding with happiness at the sight of all the beloved faces and her mind overwhelmed by her brother having given her such a thoughtful gift.

He hadn't always been so considerate. When he and James had come home during school holidays, all Izzie had wanted was to be with them. Naturally, they had been intent on escaping her. Izzie was nothing if not persistent, though, and she had usually managed to find them out wherever they were hiding.

They had never looked very happy to see her, though James had been far better at concealing his annoyance than Henry. With James's intervention, Izzie's presence had been tolerated, which was yet another reason why she loved him.

Sometimes she had gotten to play the damsel in distress, the princess locked up in a tall tower guarded by a ferocious dragon—boring, that. And once in a very rare while, if the boys were in a good mood, she had been promoted to pirate or Indian brave or, her absolute favorite, the bold, dashing highwayman. Those had been glorious days.

Izzie had always loved playing dress-up and make-believe. It helped her hang on to the childhood world still inhabited by most of her siblings, a world she was reluctant to leave. Tonight was the beginning of that journey into

the perilous and unknown waters of adulthood, a prospect
at once exciting and frightening. But James, her anchor,
waited for her downstairs, and adulthood was just another
adventure, wasn't it? And tonight she would be a queen—*a
pirate queen*—beautiful and regal and perhaps a little bit
reckless and wicked.

A rapping at the door startled her into the present. *Now*
it was time. With one last loving glance, she folded up the
miniatures, closed the clasp, and placed the necklace back
into its velvet home. She set the box down on her dressing
table since she was already wearing her pearls. They were
more fitting. The pearls were a symbol of adulthood, and
though her family would always be with her, would always
be part of her, tonight was a step she had to take alone.

Izzie followed the footman to the gallery and stood just
out of sight of the top of the stairs. The murmuring of the
guests greeted her ears, a steady, low sound punctuated every so often by a lady's high-pitched twitter or a gentleman's gravelly laugh. She took a deep breath, and then
nodded to their butler, Caldwell, who was serving as the
majordomo. He rapped his staff against the oak banister
until the crowd quieted.

"The Honorable Miss Isabella Anne Weston," Caldwell
proclaimed, his voice booming out.

Pirate queens never trip, Isabella told herself as, smile
in place, she moved into position at the top of the stairs
and looked out over the guests. The sight that met her eyes
was comfortingly familiar: a bright, colorful array of rich
satins and silks set off against the darker, jewel tones of the
men's formal dress. This lush background was ornamented
by the flutter of feathered headpieces and the flashing glit-
ter of sparkling gems and shiny buttons, highlighted when
the candlelight reflected off them. And somewhere down
there was James.

Chapter 3

I am sorry I tried to get out of lessons by pretend-ing to be sick. I know it was wrong, but doing sums is so very boring. I should not have lied, though, because now I am sick and I would rather be doing sums. Nurse says I have got my just deserts, but she is wrong. I have not had any cake or even a cup of chocolate; only willow bark, which is very bitter and not at all sweet.

From the correspondence of Miss Isabella Weston, age eight

Letter to her governess, Mrs. Daniels, apologizing for a feigned illness, which soon turned uncomfortably real— April 1786

James was standing with his back to the stairs, talking with some old friends, when Caldwell made the announce-ment. Thus he had a perfect view of several grown men's jaws dropping in unison. *What on earth?* he thought, turn-ing around, and then he felt his own jaw drop as the air whooshed out of him and he beheld a vision. The loveli-est woman he had ever laid eyes on was floating down the stairs like an angel, but no angel had a mouth like that, and he was tempted to lay far more than eyes on her.

Dear God! Was it possible *that* was actually *Isabella*? He shook his head, trying to reconcile his memories with the stunning woman before him. She was easily the most beautiful woman he had ever seen.

He took an involuntary step forward, needing to see her more clearly. She was more than beautiful. She was bloody gorgeous, though not in the classical sense. Her long-lashed aquamarine eyes were almost too big for her face, giving her an air of wonder. Above them were highly arched brows, the same rich gold color as the curls piled atop her head. It wasn't just her hair that shone, either; she was radiant, glowing with innocence and promise.

But there was nothing innocent about her mouth, a perfect peach rosebud. Her bottom lip was slightly fuller than the perfectly bowed top one, giving her a perpetual, irresistible pout. That pout was complemented by the slight point to her chin that hinted of stubbornness and mischief and gave a vaguely elfin cast to her countenance. She was, in a word, enchanting. She certainly had all the men in the ballroom under her spell.

When Isabella reached the bottom stair, her father took her hand and led her into the opening dance, drawing a collective sigh of admiration and envy from every male present. They leaned forward to watch her whenever the dance brought her close, drawn to her like moths to a flame.

Or dogs to a bone, he thought, looking at the faces of the men around him. Morgan resembled nothing so much as an enamored puppy dog. And Stimpson was practically slavering; James followed his line of vision to where Isabella's breasts threatened to spill from her bodice.

Dear God, Isabella had breasts. She had changed, grown up.

She had *breasts*.

The realization jolted him, struck him, left him reeling. He felt rather as he did upon leaving Gentleman Jackson's after a particularly grueling session in the ring—outsmarted, battered, and not quite steady on his feet.

He didn't like it.

Not one whit.

"My God," he overheard Stimpson say laughingly to the

men around him. "Even without the dowry, it'd be worth getting leg-shackled to have *that* waiting in your bed."

James saw red. He wanted nothing more than to smash that bastard's face in and beat him to a bloody pulp. He didn't even realize he had drawn back his clenched fist in preparation, when he felt a hand tugging insistently on his sleeve.

He whirled around, ready to vent his anger on whoever had dared to interfere, and was shocked to see it was Henry. He was so shocked, he let himself be dragged to the opposite end of the ballroom before he dug in his heels.

"Bloody hell, Hal, did you hear what he—"

"I heard." Henry nodded grimly. "I heard and, like you, I would like nothing better than to rearrange his face, but you can't start a fight. My mother would kill us."

James felt some of the tension seep out of his shoulders. "You are right, of course. I don't know what I was thinking."

"You weren't," Henry stated bluntly, winning a smile from James. "And neither was Stimpson." James's smile faded. "But then again, to give her credit, Izzie *does* seem to have that effect on men."

James looked over at Isabella, who had just finished the opening minuet and was now surrounded by a crowd of gentlemen jostling to get to her dance card before it filled up.

Henry rolled his eyes. "Thank God as her brother, *I*, at least, am immune to it."

James's face grew positively grim. "What the devil are you about? Surely you are not suggesting *my* reaction is anything other than brotherly?"

"Oh no. Of course not," Henry said quickly.

Too quickly.

"Look, Hal, I have known Izzie since she was in pinafores, and—"

"Oh, that reminds me," Henry interjected.

"What does?"

"Supper."

James didn't bother wondering how Henry had made the mental leap from pinafores and James's brotherly feelings, or lack thereof, to the upcoming meal. With Henry, any and all thoughts eventually led to food, one way or another.

Henry went on. "I remembered that Izzie asked me to pass along a message. She's saving the dance just before supper for you. And now I am going to see if Miss Merriwether has saved a dance for me."

"Why would you dance with Miss Merriwether?"

Henry shot him a look of pure exasperation. "Didn't you know? I've fallen madly and passionately in love with her. We're planning on eloping to Gretna Green tonight." He threw his hands in the air. "My mother put me up to it! She likes the chit for some reason and, as always, made *me* promise to dance with her."

He sounded so put-upon, so abused, that James had to laugh. "Better a mousy old maid than a wanton widow," he contended. "During our dance, Lady Ellwood slipped me a note proposing an assignation during the ball."

"Lucky bastard. Why don't *you* go make nice with Miss Merriwether while *I* see to the other lady's needs?"

"Rumor has it she's on the hunt for a husband," James cautioned.

"She's all yours," Henry said quickly.

"That's what I thought." James smirked. "But should you change your mind, the lady will be waiting in the conservatory at midnight."

Henry blinked owlishly. "But the town house doesn't *have* a conservatory."

"Precisely," James said. "Enough of that, though. We mustn't keep Miss Merriwether waiting."

Henry glared at him and then stalked off toward the wall where the chaperones and spinsters were holding court.

As his dearest friend departed in search of his wallflower, James's eyes involuntarily sought out Isabella on the ballroom floor. His countenance darkened when he found her gaily dancing a cotillion with Marcus Debenton,

Earl of Brantley, heir to the Marquess of Ardsmore . . . and one of the most determined rakehells in England. Damnation, hadn't Henry warned her away from such men?

James looked around for Isabella's father. Surely he would put an end to such an improper acquaintance. He found Lady Weston first, or rather, she found him.

"James!" She hugged him tightly. "Oh, it's so good to finally have you home!"

He nodded distractedly, still focused on the dance floor. Brantley held Isabella's hands a touch too long, he noted with a grimace. And his gaze was straying from her face down to—

That was it. He was going to pound the blighter into the ground.

"Ah, don't they make a striking pair?" Lady Weston sighed.

"He is not a fitting person for her to know," James ground out.

"Do you mean Brantley?" She laughed. "I have known him since he was in short coats; his mother and I have been friends since we were girls. We always wondered if they might suit . . ."

"Trust me," he said through clenched teeth, "they won't."

"Of course not." She grinned knowingly and patted his arm.

Bloody hell, she couldn't think *he* was jealous. First Henry, now Lady Weston? Had everyone in the family gone mad?

"Don't you mind about Brantley. I assure you, he is as harmless as a kitten."

James gave an incredulous snort.

She ignored him. "In any case, *he* is not the reason I sought you out."

"Let me guess. You were going to remind me that, as a gentleman, I have a duty to make sure that even the plainest wallflower gets to dance."

"Exactly." She beamed at him, looking for a moment

more like Isabella's older sister than her mother. "Don't fret. You will get to dance with Izzie later."

James scowled, but when the time came to claim his dance with Isabella, he found himself unexpectedly eager. She was surrounded by a horde of fawning fops, one of whom was improvising an ode to her "bright orbs hued like placid seas, and lips as red as ripe cherries."

James didn't know what the poor fool was about, spouting such trite drivel. And it was inaccurate to boot, since there was nothing the least bit placid about Isabella, and her lips weren't really red at all, but more of a soft coral.

James shouldered his way through the crowd of men, making sure his elbow "accidentally" connected with the ribs of the amateur poet, until he reached Isabella. He half expected her to throw her arms around him in a crushing hug, the way she had always greeted him as a girl, but she simply said his name and held out her hands to him. The smile lighting her face was all the invitation he needed; his name on her lips was a homecoming.

All the other occupants of the room disappeared as he grasped her dainty hands in his much larger ones. The action sent a jolt of intense awareness rippling through him; it snatched at his breath and raced along his body, leaving him light-headed. He felt as if there were millions of tiny champagne bubbles shimmering and dancing in his blood, and he had to call upon every last ounce of self-control to keep his face neutral and repress the outward signs of his overwhelmed senses.

And then he felt her tremble and knew she felt the connection, too. That knowledge nearly sent him over the edge. Triumph swept through him, along with a powerful surge of possessiveness, surely the vestige of some primitive, masculine instinct. Her hands shook slightly, as if in unconscious question; he tightened his grip, his body answering what his mind had yet to accept.

He bent his head and gazed down at her upturned face. Time suspended as their eyes met and held.

His eyes roamed over her face, searching each feature, learning her all over again.

He looked away first, frightened by the nameless feelings coursing through him.

"I believe this is my dance," he finally said, his voice oddly rusty to his own ears. Her hands still rested in his, and he could feel the pulse at her wrist hammering away.

His body responded, his blood pounding in long, slow thuds. Her chest rose and fell rapidly, causing parts of her anatomy to bounce around, and the sight was wreaking havoc on parts of *his* anatomy that had no business responding at this particular time and place, especially to this particular female.

He had definitely been too long without a woman. That was the only explanation for such behavior, although, when he thought back, it hadn't really been all that long. But why else would he suddenly believe that Isabella, who was like a sister to him, had the most perfect bosom in the world?

In the time he'd been away, Isabella had managed to grow glorious breasts that were very notable, especially on her slender frame. He almost wished they weren't quite so noteworthy—*almost*, mind you—since he hadn't liked the leering glances some of the men had given her. Not, he was sure, that their leering glances looked much different from the one he himself was currently directing at her chest.

Bloody hell, he was ogling, even fantasizing about Isabella Weston's breasts, and he wasn't sure he could stop.

Worse, he wasn't sure he wanted to.

James forced himself to take a step back, both mentally and physically. He released her hands and held out his arm to escort her over to the dance floor. He eyed her up and down, taking in her dress and hairstyle, and couldn't find fault anywhere. Well, he *did* wish her neckline were higher since it really was too low, but in all honesty, she looked exquisite.

As he led her onto the dance floor, James was aware of the envious glances thrown his way. He laughed inwardly, delighted to be the chosen one and thrilled to be stealing her away from all the besotted idiots and incompetent poets. Isabella must have felt the reverberations of his chest against her arm, for she stopped suddenly and looked up at him.

"What?" she asked suspiciously. "Oh dear. Is it my hair?" She reached up and patted around her head. Her efforts released a few unruly curls from her coiffure and sent her scent wafting through the air. She smelled like honeysuckle, and he ached to take her mouth, to see if she tasted as sweet as she smelled.

Dear God in heaven, where had *that* thought come from? He felt uncertain and off balance, as if something elemental had changed, but he didn't know what it was or how to right it. He had read once about a desert phenomenon where, all of a sudden, a man's footing could give way, disappearing without a second's notice, sucking him farther and farther down into the sand.

That was what this felt like. He hadn't been given time to prepare, had been taken unawares, and now he was drowning in Isabella: the sight, the scent—the very feel of her.

"James?"

He shook his head, knowing even as he did that it wouldn't be enough; with Isabella beside him, his mind would never be entirely clear.

"James!"

"What?"

She glared at him and gesticulated wildly about her head.

"Oh, no. Your hair is fine. You look lovely. Actually, more than lovely." His voice quieted, deepened. "I think you're the most beautiful woman I have ever seen." The words tripped off his tongue before he realized what he was saying.

Isabella smiled at him, her face aglow with pure delight, and she looked even more beautiful than she had just a moment before. *Bloody hell.* He was in serious trouble.

Then she suddenly straightened, seeming to come to some sort of resolution. The natural glow dimmed and was replaced by a calculated, seductive smile and a flirtatious bat of her lashes. "I would wager you say that to all the young ladies."

Nary a one, he silently corrected her, breathing a sigh of relief he had gotten off so easily. "Only the pretty ones," he replied with a devilish grin, bowing as the music began.

"Heartless bounder."

She curtsied, gazing up at him coquettishly.

"Impertinent baggage."

The subtle flirtation, the give and take, became part of the dance. The delicious anticipation built each time they came together, only to break apart and then reunite again.

Gazing down at Isabella while attempting to concentrate on the dance, James was perturbed by how totally different he felt with her. There were remnants of the easy, teasing camaraderie of old, but there was a new, heightened awareness that James knew was born of desire.

As their hands touched, intense heat leapt through the layers of gloves; he wondered if they would scald each other if they touched skin to skin. This pulse, this living energy between them, had been growing steadily from the moment he had taken her hands in his.

James couldn't tell whether he was more exhilarated or terrified, because although he was at a ball dancing with a girl just out of the schoolroom, a girl whom he had always regarded as a little sister, he couldn't remember a time when he had been so happy or had wanted a woman more.

As Izzie had so carefully plotted, when the dance ended, James escorted her into supper. He was the perfect companion, making sure she was seated comfortably before solicitously gathering a plate of tempting morsels for her to eat . . . and then he brought her a glass of lemonade when all the ladies around her were drinking champagne. She thought he had been aware of her as a woman during their dance, but he couldn't have made it plainer that he still saw her as a child. Her stomach, and her hopes, plummeted.

In her quest to get James alone, Izzie had planned to feign some sort of illness, figuring that he would gallantly escort her from the crowded, overheated dining room. With her stomach in knots, though, there was no need for pretense; as soon as Isabella tried to eat, her stomach rebelled and her head spun. She began to sway in her chair and felt James's hand grip her shoulder, steadying her from behind.

She twisted in her seat to look up at him. "I think I'm going to be sick," she blurted out, horrified by the admission.

James looked horrified as well, and the ladies seated on either side of her quickly edged away with alarmed, faintly pitying expressions. Fortunately, the cacophony in the room prevented Isabella's announcement from spreading any farther.

James assisted her up from her chair and quickly steered her out of the dining room. Actually, he half carried, half dragged her, as Izzie was too busy concentrating on not casting up her accounts in front of the cream of London society.

As they made their way from the dining room, she was grateful for the strength of his arm beneath hers. James was like a pillar in her life, she mused, always there to support her, steady and strong. In truth, he was more like her cornerstone; her love for him was the foundation on which she'd built herself. Now all she needed was for him to feel the same way about her.

Despite her stomach staging a very angry revolt, Isabella reflected it was a good thing it was James hauling her out of the dining room and not some other gentleman. No one would think twice about her being with James; he was practically a member of the family. Little did they know that Izzie fully intended to make the gentleman in question a family member in truth and that she harbored some rather salacious fantasies about being dragged off somewhere by him!

James deposited her onto a bench in the hallway and pushed her head down.

"Breathe in and out," he commanded. "Slowly, now. In and out. Just like that. Good girl."

Izzie focused on the sound of his voice, the deep rumble

soothing her even as it seduced her. The nausea faded away and was replaced by flutters of anticipation. She slowly sat up.

"I think I'm all right now," she said with a sigh of relief.

"You *think* you're all right now," James muttered. "You think you're *all right*? You nearly fainted—something we both know you have never done in your precious life—but you're all right?" He raked a hand through his hair, setting it on end.

"Please, you needn't shout. Truly, I feel much better."

He sagged down onto the seat next to her. "You scared the devil out of me."

Izzie had to look away to hide her smile; it felt lovely to be the subject of so much infuriated anxiety. "I apologize," she replied solemnly. "It certainly wasn't something I planned." Well, she hadn't planned on *actually* getting sick.

James turned an accusing eye on her. "You haven't turned into one of those vain, simpering misses who has her laces drawn so tight she can't breathe properly?"

He looked so appalled that Izzie had to laugh. "No, and I pray I never shall. I fear I didn't have all that much to eat today, what with the preparations and all." And with your proximity wreaking havoc on my nerves, she added silently.

"Well, that should be easily remedied." He stood and held out his hand. "Come, I'll take you back to the dining room and you can stuff yourself to your heart's content."

She shook her head. "I can't," she said glumly.

"You can't eat? Why in God's name not?" he demanded.

Izzie bit her lip in annoyance and then explained. "It's ridiculous, I know, but everyone will be watching me. Young ladies are not supposed to display hearty appetites."

He thought for a moment, then grinned and snapped his fingers. "I know just what to do. I can sneak a plate of food out here to you."

"I suppose that might work," Isabella mused. "But I can't eat in the hallway."

James frowned, obviously vexed that there was a flaw in

his plan. "All right," he said, after a moment's thought, "I will meet you in the library in five minutes."

"Bless you! Some champagne would also be welcome," Izzie said as she stood and trailed a hand down the sleeve of his coat, watching in amusement as he stumbled back a step. He turned to leave, shaking his head as if to clear it, and Izzie wanted to cheer.

"James?"

His expression was wary as he pivoted to face her. "Yes?"

"Please tell my mother that, should anyone ask, I tore the hem on my gown and will rejoin the party shortly."

He nodded and moved to go.

"Oh, and James?"

He halted and raised one brow in silent question, clearly torn between amusement and apprehension.

Isabella flashed him her most seductive smile, the one she'd practiced for hours in front of a mirror. "This gown doesn't allow for a corset."

His eyes nearly crossed as he muttered something under his breath and set off for the dining room. As soon as he was out of sight, Izzie leapt up and danced her way to the library, her entire body thrumming with excitement.

Soon it would be just the two of them.

Alone.

In a room with a lock on the door.

A lock she meant to employ.

The evening was shaping up quite nicely, if she did say so herself.

Chapter 4

Mrs. Daniels tells me I am doing very well in my music lessons. This is her way of saying I am better than Olivia. When I told this to Mama, all she said was, "Pride always comes before a fall." I think having another baby is making her very confused. Who ever fell playing the pianoforte?

From the correspondence of Miss Isabella Weston, age nine

Letter to her aunt Katherine, Marchioness of Sheldon, detailing the hazardous effect being *enceinte* has on the brain— November 1787

Attempting to open the library door while simultaneously balancing two overladen plates of food and a flute of champagne was as difficult as one would expect from a task associated with Isabella, James thought peevishly. It was a good thing he knew there was brandy on the other side. A man liked to be rewarded for overcoming a challenge.

After a bit more juggling, he managed to open the door ... and nearly dropped everything.

Isabella was perched on the long table in the center of the room, swinging her legs back and forth and, God help him, he would swear the neckline of her gown had dropped another inch.

James swallowed hard, trying desperately to think of

something other than throwing the bloody food and champagne aside, leaning her back on that table, and tossing up her skirts.

He took an unconscious step forward and she hopped down off the table, putting an end to that momentarily disturbing and uncomfortably arousing fantasy.

Thank God!

Isabella hurried forward, took the plates from him, and went to set them on the table. Then she came back toward him, but rather than taking the glass of champagne, she brushed past him, heading for the door.

James pivoted, wondering if—hoping, even—she had read his mind and was fleeing the scene with her virtue intact.

Instead, he watched with growing helplessness as she locked the door; the dull thud of the bolt sliding home twisted his stomach into a tighter knot. The traitorous organ a foot above it—the heart he had thought was dead—clenched when she turned back and smiled at him.

"I shouldn't like someone to stumble upon us while I am—" She paused.

Being ravished? James's disloyal mind supplied.

"Stuffing myself to my heart's content," she finished, relieving him of the champagne. She sashayed back to the table, and James couldn't tear his eyes from the gentle sway of her hips.

He licked his dry lips and forced himself to look away and head over to the sideboard; if ever there was a time to drink, James felt certain this was it.

He tossed back a snifter of brandy without even tasting it, then poured another and walked over to Isabella, who was seated once more on that blasted table eating a strawberry ice—trust Izzie to skip straight to dessert—her eyes closed in an expression of bliss that did nothing for his composure.

He needed to put some distance between them. Fast.

He walked over to the bookcases, so befuddled that it

took him a moment to realize the shelves directly in front of him were empty.

"They're reserved for my mother's book," Isabella supplied, then shrugged. "If she ever finishes it."

James nodded. Second only to her husband and children, Lady Weston's grand passion was writing a collection of critical essays on Shakespeare's female characters.

"She wanted to save this entire section," Izzie continued, "but my father contested that having more than three shelves full of one's own book in one's own library was somewhat self-aggrandizing."

She set aside her ice and came up beside him, her nearness further fraying the tangled ribbons of his senses. Then she leaned in to point at the books below the empty shelves, and her hand brushed against his stomach. He stifled a groan.

"This set of the *Complete Works* was my father's wedding gift to my mother."

She trailed her fingertips lovingly over the fine leather and gold bindings, a gesture he felt on every oversensitized inch of his body.

"This set," she said, reaching to the shelf below and pulling out a crimson volume, "was his present to her when Henry was born." Her arm grazed his midsection again, a bit lower this time, and he let out a gasp. He thought he saw the corner of her mouth quirk into a smile, but it disappeared so quickly he decided he must have imagined it.

"It really is exquisite, isn't it?" she murmured, gently fanning out the leaves of the book.

He gaped at her, then frowned. Was it possible the chit was deliberately teasing him?

"Have you never seen a fore-edge painting before? Look, now you see it. . . ."

James forced himself to focus on the delicate image revealed on the exposed edges of the pages.

"And now you don't." She closed the book and the scene vanished, replaced by ordinary gilt edging. She replaced the volume on the shelf, tormenting him with yet another whisper of a caress. "Now this set . . ."

James followed her gaze down to what was sure to be yet another collection of Shakespeare's works. Then he imagined where her next touch would land and hurriedly stepped back, raking a hand through his hair.

"Really!" he huffed in exasperation, more for his inability to control his own body than for any dislike of bookbindings or the Bard. "How many *Complete Works* could a person possibly need?"

"Ah," Isabella interjected, "but we're not talking about a person. We're talking about my mother. Some women like jewels, but—"

"Your mother likes books," he finished for her. Then, unable to help himself, he reached out and brushed an errant curl back behind her ear. He'd removed his gloves when he'd gone to fetch supper, and now he was touching her, skin to skin. A little sigh of contentment escaped her lips, and it hit James like a fist to the gut. He quickly pulled his hand away. Damnation, this was *Isabella*!

The problem, James thought, was that she didn't look like herself. Well, she did, but she didn't look like the Isabella he had carried in his head during the past years. That Isabella had been a child, which this Isabella most definitely was not.

This Isabella was a goddess, and if he remembered his mythology correctly, goddesses were always dangerous to mortal men. He needed to put things back on proper footing, but how?

"So . . . " He searched for something—*anything*—to say. "Did you miss me?"

The moment the words left his mouth, James could have kicked himself. *Did you miss me?* What kind of asinine question was that? Could he sound any more like a bloody idiot? And why did he care?

"Yes, I missed you." The words emerged as a choked whisper.

James felt something sweet and unexpected bloom in

his chest, all because this little slip of a girl, a girl he had known since she was in pinafores, had missed him.

"D-did you miss *me*?" She tried to keep the question light and teasing, but James heard the wobble in her voice, saw her beautiful eyes glistening too brightly.

"I didn't want to." He realized the truth in the words as he spoke them. "I didn't want to," he said again, taking an involuntary step toward her, then another, and another, until he was face-to-face with her. He knew he should back up, return her to the dining room, and then make his farewells and leave—leave until this madness had passed.

She was a child, and younger sister of his best friend, for Christ's sake. The only feelings he should have toward her were those of a protective older brother. Anything else was inappropriate and dangerous. Yes, James knew he should walk away, but he had an awful suspicion he wasn't going to.

"Y-you didn't want to . . ." Her voice shook as she watched him.

James swallowed hard, and then nodded once.

"B-but you did?" It was half question, half statement.

He stared down into her aquamarine eyes, dewy with tears. They were at once the eyes of the woman she had become—the most beautiful, most desirable woman he had ever encountered—and of the adorable, irascible girl she had been. He had never been able to lie to the child, and he found it just as impossible now.

He *had* missed her. He had missed her wit, and her sunny smiles, and her delight in the absurd. He had missed their conversations, and the looks they shared when Henry said something particularly daft, and the way she had always shown up no matter how hard he and Henry had tried to hide from her.

More than all of that, though, he had missed her—some indefinable quality that was *Isabella*.

Dear Lord, he was becoming a half-wit. Yes, he had missed Isabella. He had also missed Henry, Lady Weston, and the rest of the family. There were a lot of people he had missed, including his tailor, his boot maker, and Lucy, the lovely little ballet dancer who had been his mistress before he'd left.

Of course he had missed Isabella; she was practically his little sister. It would have been strange if he *hadn't* missed her, James rationalized.

Isabella was still looking up at him expectantly, anxiety and hope written clearly on her face.

"Yes," James said easily, now that he had figured out his feelings. He smiled down at her benevolently. "Of course I missed you."

The expression of pure joy that burst across her face was dazzling. Her happiness wrapped itself about him and yanked hard at his insides.

"Oh, James," she cried, throwing her arms around his neck. Then she pressed her mouth to his and he froze. Her eyes had fluttered closed, and she was kissing him without a whit of skill, frantically rubbing her lips against his, and he, James Sheffield, acknowledged rake, was instantly harder than the oak bookcases lining the room.

Some part of his brain, surely the rational part, sounded alarm bells at the staggering *rightness* he felt at having her in his arms, her mouth pressed to his. God, she was sweet!

No!

No, no, no!

This was *Isabella*!

He pushed her away, his breath rushing in and out of his lungs, and struggled for control.

Think of Henry, he told himself.

Think of—

He groaned when she slipped herself right back into his arms, pressing kisses all over his face. He was trying to find the strength to pull away again, when Isabella returned to his mouth. He couldn't stand it. He was only a man, and he couldn't resist her any longer. One kiss, he told himself. One good kiss, and then he would stop. Resolved, he angled her head back, deepening the kiss.

Isabella made a noise at the back of her throat, and just

like that, the rational part of James's brain ceased to function. All his noble intentions of gently ending the kiss and escorting her back inside crumbled and were swept aside by an overwhelming flood of lust. One of his hands skimmed down her back to cup her bottom.

Her lips parted in shock, and he seized the moment to slide his tongue into her mouth. He sensed her surprise as he teased her tongue with the tip of his, tasting champagne and strawberries and something perfectly, uniquely Isabella.

He memorized the tantalizing combination, knowing the kiss was all he would ever have of her. He couldn't stop himself from wanting her, though, in all fairness, he couldn't imagine a man alive who wouldn't want her, but he would never have her. Of that he was certain. Because he had missed her and because he did care about her—as much as he allowed himself to care about anybody—there could never be anything more.

Aside from her being his best friend's little sister, Isabella was a woman who deserved to be loved, and James had no intention of ever loving, of ever being that vulnerable. . . . Love meant trusting another person entirely. Love meant the possibility of loss. And James had already suffered enough loss for one lifetime. He wasn't willing to risk hurting that way again.

And as for marriage and children, they played no part in his future. The Sheffield line and as far as he knew, the earldom, would end with him. It was a fitting retribution against the man who had taken him in solely to ensure the continuation of the earldom, a proper payback for all the times his grandsire had berated and belittled him.

Revenge tasted sweet.

As sweet as the soft warmth of Isabella's mouth.

He couldn't have both, and his choice was already made.

But he couldn't pull himself away from her.

He was a selfish ass, and he wasn't going to give up this little glimpse of heaven.

*   *   *

Heaven.

Isabella was in heaven.

On second thought, she doubted even heaven could feel as perfect as this.

Surrounded by the heat and strength radiating from James's body, she felt safe and cherished. Here was the man she had loved practically forever, and he was kissing her, sending feelings she had never even imagined coursing through her.

Good heavens, his tongue was in her mouth and his hand was fondling her bottom! She knew that these were liberties she should not allow any gentleman to take, but she didn't care.

This was James—*her James*—and she was his. She tentatively, instinctively touched her tongue to his, savoring the spicy male taste of him. He groaned against her mouth and kissed her passionately, without restraint, as he kneaded her bottom, holding her firmly against him.

Isabella moaned at the feel of his hardness pressing against her belly. She was out of control, past any sense of decency. Her hands fisted in his hair as his mouth did wicked things to hers. As if from a great distance, she heard little mewling animal sounds and was shocked to realize they were emanating from her.

An urgent, tingling warmth pooled deep in her belly, then radiated outward, making every inch of her body yearn for something that seemed just out of reach. She pressed closer, rubbing her breasts against the hardness of his chest, trying to assuage the ache.

James broke the kiss with a strangled growl. She could feel his breathing, heavy and hot against her cheek. His chest rose and fell as he drew in deep gulps of air, fighting to regain some control. She didn't want him in control. She wanted him as wild and undone as she was. Her hands tightened in his hair as she let out a distressed whimper.

"Shhhh." He soothed her, sliding his hands up to massage her nape. Her head rolled back, and James lowered his lips to the silky spot beneath her chin. She gave a hum of approval, and he continued to nibble and lick his way down her neck to the swell of her breasts.

The ache in her breasts intensified, and Isabella arched her back, feeling restless and unsatisfied. The air in her lungs seemed to expand, making breathing difficult.

"James?" His name was a question and a plea.

He answered by trailing his hands down from her neck to cup the ripe bounty she offered. She started at the first light touch of his hands, but he brushed his lips softly against hers in reassurance. The tension drained from her body as his knowing fingers began to learn her shape through the barrier of her gown. The gentle caress was too much and not enough.

A flash of sanity intruded when she felt the sash on her dress loosen around her ribs, then slither to the floor, but she was distracted when he took her mouth again, his tongue thrusting deeply in a way that had her squirming against him.

"Sweet," he murmured, running his tongue around the sensitive shell of her ear. "Sweet, let me touch you. I *need* to touch you."

Isabella could barely comprehend the words, lost as she was in a swirling, sensual fog. "Yes," she panted. "Yes."

She didn't know what she was agreeing to—and she didn't particularly care, just as long as he didn't stop. She would die if he stopped. In her wildest dreams she had never imagined the feelings he would evoke in her, the flames he would ignite.

It was the feeling of cool air whispering across her shoulder blades that jolted her back to reality, penetrating the sultry haze that had enveloped her. She opened her eyes, realizing with mounting horror that she was standing in the library, her dress falling down around her waist, with the party guests mere rooms away.

Oh dear.

She was fairly sure this would rank highly on her mother's endless list of situations that well-brought-up young ladies should never, ever find themselves in. It might even place in the top three. Being found naked in a gentleman's bed would be worse, she supposed. Or standing in the packed ballroom and announcing at the top of her lungs that she was insane and barren. But this was bad.

Very bad.

Not at all proper.

This was wrong, she told herself.

But, oh dear God, it felt so heavenly right.

James was nibbling on the spot where the line of her throat met the curve of her shoulder, and his hands . . . his hands were on her breasts, gently squeezing and rubbing, and her nipples were hard as pebbles against his palms.

She had to stop this; really, she did. Her hands slid into his hair, intending to draw him away, but his mouth slid downward, engulfing the tip of her breast. Sanity retreated, her eyes fluttered closed, and the hands that should have been pushing at him were suddenly grasping at him, holding him captive.

He took the silken mound further into his mouth, suckling strongly, and then lightly bit the tip of her breast, a gesture that sent golden sparks bursting behind her closed eyes. Just when she thought she couldn't take any more, he moved to lavish the same attention on her other breast.

Isabella gave a soft, keening wail, grabbing and kissing every part of him she could. She knew she was close to something wonderful, but she couldn't begin to understand all the feelings building up inside her. She let out a frustrated moan.

James lifted her up to sit on the desk and stepped between her thighs, reached underneath her skirts, and ran his fingers up her calf, caressing her through her silk stocking, an action that caused gooseflesh to break out all over her body. She froze, then shivered as his hand moved higher, past her garter, to stroke the sensitive skin of her inner thigh.

His other hand came up to cup her cheek, drawing her in for a kiss, and she eagerly opened to him. Her body relaxed as their mouths met and mated in a dance so natural, so perfect, she never wanted it to stop.

Her hips arched up, instinctively rocking to the rhythm established by their thrusting tongues. He took his hand from her face and wound it around her back, supporting her and gathering her closer. His other hand drifted to her center, his questing fingers searching out the place where she ached with some unknown need.

He stroked up and down, feathery caresses that had her squirming and gasping. She clasped her arms around his neck, trying to get closer. He groaned, and those wicked fingers increased their pressure and pace, driving her further, faster.

She clung to him, the air in her lungs rasping in and out, as rapid as his own breathing. She breathed him in, savoring the slightly sweaty smell of him, and braced her forehead against the hard plane of his chest where she could hear the racing beat of his heart.

Listening to that organ pound away—listening to it pound for *her*—filled Isabella with joy, adding to the physical pleasure building inside her.

The words of love she had bottled up for so many years struggled to burst free.

She couldn't contain them any longer.

"Oh, James, I love you. I love you so much!"

He froze, and then jerked away from her, stumbling back a few steps. He was staring at her as if she'd bewitched him and he'd finally managed to break free of her spell.

"Jesus!" He swore softly and fluently, a string of oaths so colorful and anatomically impossible, it would have made a sailor blush. She wanted to applaud and save up a few choice phrases to shock Henry with, but she couldn't.

Not now.

Not when her heart was breaking.

Izzie bit back a cry. The words that had exploded from her lips in the heat of passion now sent a chill snaking through her. It was obvious that he didn't return her feelings.

The cold settled in the region of her heart, turning it to

ice, then migrated down to the pit of her stomach. She felt fragile and unsure; one word, one touch could shatter her.

And still she ached for him—body, heart, and soul.

What must he think of her, allowing him such liberties? She'd been so foolish to believe he'd take one look at her and fall in love. That was the stuff of novels and fairy tales.

"I told you long ago that I was incapable of love. A wise woman would have heeded those words." His voice was hard and distant. She would have thought him entirely un-affected if not for the hands fisted at his sides.

"I can't help how I feel. I've loved you since I was a girl." Her throat was so tight with unshed tears, and she had to fight to get the words out.

"Well," he said coldly, "tonight is about growing up."

Isabella gasped, feeling his words like physical blows. The tears welled over and a choked sob escaped her.

At the sound, James jerked as if he had been shot. His head whipped around, and she felt his eyes on her. Her bodice was still down around her waist and when the heat of his gaze settled on her breasts, she couldn't help her body's response.

"Damnation. Cover yourself!" he growled harshly, before turning away again.

She gave a startled cry and began yanking her dress up, fumbling as she tried to tug it back into place. When she realized that it would be impossible to do up her own buttons, and that she would have to ask James for help, Isabella nearly decided to stab herself with the letter opener on the desk and end it all right there. Fortunately for the Aubusson rug beneath her feet, her taste for melodrama ran only so far.

"I need you," she said softly. She drew in a deep breath, and then let it out, along with her pride. She addressed him, or rather his back, with the little that remained of her dignity. "I need you to do up my gown."

He didn't move. In fact, her words seemed to have frozen him to the spot. Izzie glared at him. What was *wrong* with him? She had asked him to help her with her dress, the very least he could do, and he just stood there. He should be on his knees, kissing the ground beneath her feet, that she wasn't demanding that the banns be read. Many a marriage had gone forward for far less of an indiscretion than she had just participated in.

No, than *they* had just participated in. He had been the one who had undone the bloody gown in the first place, and he could damn well assist her in getting it back on! And it felt bloody marvelous to curse, even if it was only in her head! All urge to cry fled as self-righteous fury seized her, so intense she actually shook from it.

Isabella stamped her foot. Just like that, James tore into motion. He lunged forward, grabbed her shoulders, and spun her around. He was almost savage as he hauled the two halves of the dress together and began fastening the buttons and retying the sash.

Isabella was aware to her toes of the large, angry man at her back. His body fairly vibrated with tension, and she could hear the air racing in and out of his lungs, feel his hot breath against her nape. She shivered, wanting him despite herself, excited by the primitive savage she could sense lurking just beneath his highly civilized veneer.

Chapter 5

Unfortunately, there is no one else I can ask. So, my dearest, wisest, and most loving older brother, I hope you will answer my question and set my mind at rest. Can quarreling and the subsequent exchange of flowers get a woman with child? Every time our parents have a terrible row, Mama gets a huge bouquet and then we end up with a new sibling nine months later. Is this merely a coincidence? I had the most dreadful spat with the parson's son yesterday, but today he apologized and brought me some wildflowers. Am I fallen?

From the correspondence of Miss Isabella Weston, age ten

Letter to her brother, Henry Weston, questioning the probability of an outcome following a certain sequence of events—October 1788

"I need you. . . ."

A shock ran through James's body at hearing those words from her mouth. Emotions warred and clashed within him, battling for supremacy.

Anger, certainly, at her for kissing him at all, but mostly directed toward himself.

Desperation, from the pain of unfulfilled desire. Horror and guilt because, God forgive him, he had nearly taken

Isabella—who was practically a child, and not just any child, but one he was honor bound to love and protect as a brother—right there on a table in the library.

Self-loathing because, if he was being honest with himself, he still wanted to.

And excitement and hope and something else, some emotion he couldn't name but that tugged insistently at his heart, thrilled by the notion that she needed him.

"I need you to do up my gown."

James stared at her. *I need you to do up my gown.* Not *I need you.*

Disappointment rose up in his throat, which was bloody well ridiculous since he should have been down on his bloody knees and kissing the bloody ground; that was all she was asking of him. Unaccountably, it made him angry. Actually, it made him bloody furious! Then she had the gall to stamp her dainty little foot at him, and something inside him snapped.

He grabbed her shoulders, turned her about, and angrily began fastening her gown, erasing, with each inch of flesh that disappeared from his sight, the undoing that had been his undoing. As he slid the top button through its silken loop, his hands brushed the soft skin at her nape. He felt a shudder travel through her body. Just like that, he came undone all over again.

The hands that had wanted to throttle her only moments before gentled; he watched, fascinated, as his thumbs began caressing her petal-soft skin. It was as if his mind had no control over his body. Not that that was surprising. It was a different part of his body altogether that was dictating his behavior with Isabella.

As the thought ran through his head, Isabella let out a soft sigh, and turned into him, her head nestling against his chest. His arms automatically came up and tightened around her, holding her close . . . and then he realized what he was doing.

Bloody hell, it had happened again. She had made him lose control, and he didn't like it. Didn't like the way she made him feel. Or rather, he liked it too much, but he had decided long ago not to feel. Because feeling led to loving, and loving was dangerous.

He could not let himself fall in love. That, and only that, was what enabled him to step away from Isabella. It was an act of self-preservation. It was so tempting to take what she so sweetly offered.

Her lips, still swollen and rosy from his kisses, pouted to once again be covered by his own. Her lush body arched against him was the physical embodiment of every erotic fantasy he had ever had, but he cared about her too much already. She was a risk, a complication he couldn't afford.

She would hurt now, but she would heal. What she felt for him was infatuation, the remnants of a childhood *tendresse* mixed with a good dose of lust.

Lust for Isabella Weston.

It was strange, yet undeniable, and certainly preferable to love. Lust he could dismiss. Love was—

It didn't bloody matter *what* love was, because she wasn't in love with him. She couldn't be. It was some sort of bizarre womanly logic, which meant it had nothing to do with logic at all. He was older and, moreover, he was a man; it was, therefore, *his* assessment of the situation that was correct, and he was dealing with lust, not love.

Not love at all.

So he stepped away from her knowing, as he did, that it was the right thing to do.

"I apologize," he said. "That shouldn't have happened."

"You're apologizing for kissing me?" she asked incredulously.

He nodded. "And for the—" His gaze dropped to her chest, finishing the unspoken thought.

With the events of that evening, Izzie wouldn't have thought she had a shred of modesty left, but she felt a blush stain her cheeks. She realized the flush was also due in part to the angry flame his words had fanned.

"You're apologizing for kissing me," she repeated tightly.

He nodded again, looking a bit wary.

"I don't accept," she said.

"You don't accept what?"

"I don't accept your apology. I am not at all sorry you kissed me and touched me." Her tone was soft, but the words were deliberate, sharp arrows, flung to try to topple all his walls and defenses.

"I am not sorry at all, except that you stopped. It was magical, more than I ever could have imagined. I know you don't want to hear it, but I *need* to say it."

James shook his head, warning her to stop, but she ignored him. This was too important.

"I *love* you, James. Foolish as it may be, I do. It is more than love, actually. I almost feel as though you are a part of me. From the first time I saw you, I—"

"You were a child!" he protested.

"I *knew*." She caught his gaze with her own, holding it. "I love you. I always have, and—"

"Izzie, if you loved me at all, it was as an older brother. Come, enough of this nonsense."

"That is true," she said slowly.

"That it's nonsense?" he goaded.

She shook her head, sifting through his words, weighing them. "No, it is true that when we first met, I was too young to have the sort of feelings for you that I have now."

He moved to speak, but she held up a hand, silencing him.

"I can see that you don't want to accept what I am telling you right now, but my love for you *is* real. I *do* have these feelings, though, like me, they have changed and matured over time. First, it was the love of a child for the boy who rescued her from trees while her brother stood by laughing. Then it changed to the love of a girl for the young man who sneaked sweets up to her at balls and promised her a dance."

"I never thought I'd have to keep that promise," James muttered, tugging at his cravat.

"But you did, just as I knew you would, because you are honorable and thoughtful."

"Don't make me out to be some sort of saint, Isabella. I have as many faults and transgressions as the next man. Probably more."

"I don't expect you to be perfect. Heaven knows I'm not. But I do believe you're perfect for me." Her voice grew husky and dropped to a near whisper. "So now my love is that of a woman for the man she knows she is meant to be with."

He was so silent, so still, that she could barely see the rise and fall of his chest. She took a cautious step toward him, treating him as she would an unpredictable wild animal. Another step brought her within inches of him. He still hadn't moved, hadn't done so much as blink. Isabella found it rather unnerving.

She leaned into him, looked up at his beloved face, and did the one thing she had sworn she would never do. She begged. "Please, James. Love me. Let me love you."

She held her breath, waiting, wondering what he would say, what he might do. She was hoping he would just sweep her back up into his arms and start kissing her all over again.

"We should be getting back," James said after a long moment. "Supper will be ending, and people will begin to wonder where the guest of honor is." He held out his arm to her.

Feeling terribly numb, Isabella accepted it. A sense of unreality enveloped her. She had laid her heart bare. She had asked—no, she had *begged*—for his love, *pleaded* to be allowed to love him. Her lips were still tingling from his kisses and her heart was still pounding; yet he was ready to take her back to the party and wash his hands of her. How utterly depressing!

Still, Isabella reflected, she had made progress. The thought buoyed her flagging spirits. As wonderful as it would have been to have him fall on his knees and pledge his undying love for her, Isabella had known in her heart of hearts that it wouldn't be that easy. He was going to fight what was between them. Let him try. After only a few hours in her presence he had nearly made love to her in the library!

The remembrance of the shocking things he had done to her, the wonderful way he had made her feel, summoned all those urgent feelings again. An uncontrollable shiver sped through her. His entire body stiffened in response, and she heard his sharp intake of breath. She had *definitely* made progress.

Isabella smiled brightly up at James, throwing him off balance. "Despite what you say, James Sheffield, you're not past saving, and nothing you say will change my mind. I refuse to believe it."

"Believe it." His voice was harsh. "I'm warning you, Izzie. Don't try to 'save' me. You'll only get hurt."

They stood at the entrance to the ballroom, and Isabella pressed closer to his side, rising up on her toes to whisper in his ear. "You should know from what transpired tonight that I am willing to take risks when the reward is so very . . . touching. I must thank you, my lord, for your attentions. I am feeling very much recovered, quite ready to dance, in fact. I do wish Mother would allow the waltz; I am certain that dancing it with you would prove quite stimulating."

She watched with satisfaction as his eyes nearly crossed once again. He looked ready to drag her back into the library, and while there was nothing she would like more, perhaps some good old-fashioned jealousy would prove more effective than simply falling into his arms. In the Minerva Press novels she had read, the heroines were always making the heroes jealous, and it seemed to work for them.

She tugged excitedly at his sleeve. "Look, James. Over there." She pointed and waved at someone on the opposite side of the ballroom. "It's Marcus. Oops, I mean Lord Brantley." She giggled. Actually it was more of a twitter.

She hadn't known she'd had it in her. "I believe he is my next partner."

James shook his head. "You already danced with him once this evening."

"Oh, but Mother said it would be all right for him to partner me twice tonight, on account of our families' being so friendly. Don't be anxious. I am only holding you to one dance, just as you promised."

James scowled, but he reluctantly escorted her across the room, and Izzie forced herself to keep up a constant stream of chatter, telling him how nice Marcus was, how handsome, how intelligent, how cultured.

"He actually quoted poetry to me," she said delightedly. "Can you believe it?"

James's expression clearly stated that he could believe it all right. In fact, he looked as if he wanted to pound the man into the ground.

"And he is a marvelous dancer," she confided, when they were only a couple feet away from the man. "Mayhap even better than you."

Isabella didn't wait to see the smoke pour out of his ears. She just flitted over to take her new partner's arm and let him sweep her into the dance. She avoided James for the rest of the night, but she saw him hovering, felt his eyes on her the whole time, his gaze warming her from across the room. She couldn't wait to kiss him again, to feel all those amazing sensations he aroused in her, to make more progress. Progress, she decided, really was an excellent thing.

Chapter 6

My dear brother, I don't know why you persist in asking the question, "Or else what?" Or else a little bird will tell our mother about a certain book you have in your possession. A certain book of engravings that fell into the hands of your innocent, impressionable little sister. It is thrilling to know I shall be able to hold this over your head for the rest of your life! A life that would be shorter should our mother learn what treasures you keep hidden beneath your mattress . . .

From the correspondence of Miss Isabella Weston, age eleven

Letter to her brother Henry, reminding him that sisters are not above blackmail but, in fact, embrace it—March 1789

Isabella was forced to reassess her supposed progress when Henry returned from Ireland one month later without James in tow. It was the orphanage, she assured herself, and she would be lower than dirt if she were jealous of the poor little souls James was helping.

After two months, Isabella realized she might just be lower than dirt. She missed James like mad, so much she started speculating whether it would be possible to adopt every last orphan in Ireland. How could she make *progress* when they were in two different kingdoms? The situation was beyond vexing, and although the Season offered plenty in the way of amusements, it was *not* proving an adequate distraction.

It was nearly enough to make a person hate London, but it simply wasn't possible to hate the city where one could go to Gunter's for a white coffee cream ice every day of the week. White coffee cream ices, she had found, were good consolation for a lonely heart.

Oh, she had more than her fair share of suitors, but the mere thought of James made her heart race faster than it did in their presence. She had even let Lord Stimpson draw her into an alcove to steal a kiss to test whether her reaction to James would have been the same with any man.

That experiment had proven disastrous, and by disastrous she meant a kiss so wet and nauseating that when he called the next morning to propose, Izzie had to run from the room to avoid being physically ill. Since the incident with Stimpson could not in all fairness be compared with her interlude with James, Izzie realized she needed a reputable rake, someone she was certain had comparable skill in the amatory arts. Fortunately, she knew just the man for the job; if Marcus Debenton couldn't make her see stars, no one save James ever would.

She couldn't ask him straight out, though, since she was sure he would refuse. For all his misdeeds, Marcus was an honorable rogue, which meant he wouldn't kiss his mother's friend's daughter if his life depended on it. Actually, his life probably did depend on it. If Lady Ardsmore ever learned that her son had kissed Izzie, she would march him down the aisle of St. Paul's with a pistol at his back. In the end he would be either married or dead, which amounted to the same thing for a rake.

So subterfuge it would have to be, and Lady Galloway's annual masquerade ball presented the perfect opportunity. She knew Marcus would attend if only because hidden identities offered such potential in the way of seduction. She also knew she would be able to locate him as he reputedly dressed as a satyr every year; Izzie had heard more than one lady remark that it wasn't much in the way of a disguise.

Isabella chose her costume accordingly. A Grecian-style gown of white silk hugged the curves of her breasts and hips, then flowed sinuously down to the gold slippers on her feet. A matching gold domino covered the top half of her face, and a sparkling diamond brooch secured the gown over one shoulder, leaving the other daringly bare. She wore her hair loose, a riot of honey blond curls, topped by a coronet of wildflowers that transformed her into the perfect woodland nymph. As a satyr, Marcus should be unable to resist pursuing her. And he was. She hadn't been in the ballroom for a half hour when she felt a large, warm hand descend on her bare shoulder.

"My lady nymph," said the deep voice at her back.

Isabella turned to face him. "My lord satyr," she replied in a husky murmur, sinking into a curtsy.

He raised her up and peered more closely at her face. "Do I know you?"

"Not tonight," she purred, hoping the answer would satisfy him.

Apparently it did, for he whisked her into a boisterous country dance without another word. She was breathless and laughing by the time it was over and, she noted, Marcus had maneuvered them so that they were right by the balcony doors when the music ended.

He gently tugged on her arm, urging her to give up the safe confines of the well-lit ballroom for the danger and adventure of the night. She followed, though her eyes grew wide when she heard the languid sighs and low moans emanating from the dark corners of the balcony.

Maybe this wasn't a good idea.

As he led her down the balcony steps into the formal garden, she wondered if it had actually been a very bad idea. Going out on the balcony with a gentleman was slightly scandalous; the garden was, well . . . Izzie was beginning to think Marcus had more in mind than just a kiss, a suspicion that seemed to be confirmed when he whisked her around a tall hedge and drew her up against him.

She was at the point of no return, on the verge of crossing over. She could tell Marcus who she was and he would have her back inside in a flash, hopefully before anyone—especially either of their mothers—was the wiser. No doubt she would be soundly scolded, but her reputation wouldn't suffer. The longer she stayed in the garden, the more she played with fire . . . and the more she risked getting burned.

But she had to know.

She had to know if the feelings she had for James were real or just a habit. A habit could be broken. It wouldn't be easy, but she could do it—*if* her love for him was a habit. If it wasn't . . .

"You are awfully quiet, sweet nymph," he murmured against her ear.

There was nothing for it but to brazen it out. She had to know.

She pasted a sultry smile on her face and gazed up in what she hoped was an alluring manner. "I was unaware that talking was what you had in mind."

He laughed. "Beautiful *and* bold. I am a lucky fellow, indeed."

Isabella inclined her head in acceptance of his flattery.

"But," he continued, "as you say, speech was not foremost on my mind when I lured you out here. Satyrs and nymphs are known for communicating in another language entirely."

"Greek?" Izzie squeaked in the split second before his mouth came down on hers.

His chuckle reverberated through her body, but that was as close to tingling as her extremities were feeling. Actually, her toes were a little numb, but that had more to do with her modiste accidentally ordering the gold satin dancing slippers a size too small.

Oh dear. One of England's most accomplished rakes was kissing her, and she couldn't think about anything but her pinched feet. That she was thinking at all didn't bode well.

When James had kissed her, Izzie had barely been able to remember to breathe, let alone think.

She forced herself to concentrate on Marcus and the kiss. It was pleasant, she supposed, and certainly preferable to slobbering Stimpson, but there was no magic.

Not even a little bit.

One of Marcus's hands squeezed her breast.

How dare he?

Her slap took him off guard; he stumbled back, tripped, and landed on his bottom in the grass. He rubbed his cheek and stared at her in utter disbelief.

Isabella gave a disgusted huff and flounced back to the house, her shoes pinching her every step of the way. Fortunately, the ballroom was such a crush, she was easily able to persuade her mother that she had been dancing the entire time. Her reputation was intact, although the same could not be said of her feet. But the poor dears made an excellent excuse for a hasty departure, and Isabella was safely home before the unmasking.

After her second failed experiment, Izzie assiduously avoided any situations where kisses might be proffered. She stuck so close to whoever was chaperoning her, other matrons were heard imploring their charges to display such proper conduct. Much to Isabella's relief, when it became clear she was a model of decorum, the rakes and young bucks got bored and let her alone.

That was when the others began to swarm. Isabella's excellent breeding coupled with her remarkable beauty did not go unnoticed by men of a certain age—and some rather past that certain age—who felt the pressure to settle down, start a nursery, and preserve the family name. And so the proposals began.

Since her parents insisted it was only polite to allow a man to declare himself, Izzie was forced to sit through every offer of marriage, and each one was more monotonous and tedious than the last. She was treated to recitations of estate holdings, down to the very last acre, sheep, and silver epergne. She stifled yawns through family histories tracing all the way back to the Conqueror. And then there were the men who took her acceptance for granted and lectured her on her future duties, which, Isabella thought, explained a great deal about why they were not yet wed.

By the time the Season ended and the Westons returned to the country, Isabella had turned down a duke, the second son of a marquess, an earl, two barons, a Russian prince, three wealthy tradesmen, a preening poet, and a Scottish laird—eleven proposals and not one of them from James Sheffield.

She hadn't had so much as a letter from him.

And that stung.

She couldn't—wouldn't—let herself believe the attraction had all been one sided, but the fact remained that he had been able to walk away from whatever burned between them.

He had been able to walk away from her, while she had been ruined for all other men.

A bitter laugh escaped her.

Not exactly the sort of progress she had hoped for.

Not.

At.

All.

Before Isabella knew it, December was upon them and with it the dreadfully tedious undertaking of helping her mother address invitations to their annual Twelfth Night ball. Her mother always liked to work in the library, which had never bothered Isabella before, but she now found it terribly distracting. Her cheeks were perpetually crimson, causing her mother to ask repeatedly whether she needed to sit farther away from the fire.

And if she did manage to focus, it was only a matter of time before she caught a scent of the rosemary and bay leaves tied to the bunches of mistletoe hanging throughout the house. Thoughts of mistletoe naturally led to thoughts of kissing, and thoughts of kissing led, of course, to thoughts of James, and then Isabella got distracted all over again.

"Izzie!" Olivia hissed, kicking her under the table.

"Ow!" Isabella yelped, and jumped, nearly oversetting her inkwell. "What was that for?"

"Girls?" Lady Weston looked up. "Is everything all right?"

"Yes," Olivia said. "I was just warning Izzie that her penmanship was getting a bit sloppy."

"You *kicked* me!" Izzie protested.

"I was trying to be subtle," Olivia ground out.

"Oh dear," Lady Weston said, and made a clucking noise. She had come over to inspect the damage and was leaning over Isabella's shoulder. "Oh dear," she repeated.

Izzie frowned. True, her mind hadn't been entirely focused on the invitations she'd been addressing, but it wasn't exactly what one would call a stimulating activity. It was thoughts of stimulating activities that had distracted her in the first place. . . . With a sinking feeling in her stomach, Izzie glanced down at the paper before her.

"Oh dear," she blurted out, echoing her mother's distress. After copying out Baron Bridgeman's direction, Izzie had absentmindedly embellished the creamy paper with drawings of interlocking hearts and wreaths of flowers, all containing various permutations of her and James's names. Another invitation sitting in the finished pile bore no address at all; Izzie had filled the space instead with marriage vows. On yet another she had sketched herself and James locked in a passionate embrace.

Cheeks flaming, Isabella snatched up that particular envelope just as her mother was reaching for it to take a closer look. Izzie ripped the damning evidence in half and crumpled the pieces into a tight ball as she stood, walked over to the large fireplace, and threw them in.

"Olivia," her mother said, "I believe we've done enough invitations for today. Why don't you go upstairs? I am certain Mrs. Daniels could use your help in the schoolroom."

"But—"

"No." Lady Weston's voice was firm. "I need to speak with your sister. Alone," she added, when Olivia made no move to leave.

"Fine," Livvy huffed. "I'm only the one who noticed it in the first place," she grumbled, shutting the door behind her with more force than was strictly necessary.

"Actually, Mama," Izzie said, edging toward the door herself, "I think I am feeling a bit feverish. Perhaps I should go lie—"

Lady Weston gestured to a pair of comfortable wing-back chairs by the fireplace. "Sit," she commanded, her tone brooking no room for argument.

Izzie gave her mother a look that said she was not at all happy about it, but she did as she was told. Her mother tugged the other heavy chair to directly face Isabella, and then seated herself. She took a deep breath as if readying herself for what was to be an unpleasant conversation.

"My dear," she said, leaning forward to place a hand on Izzie's knee, "I know you have feelings for James."

"If by feelings you mean love, then yes, I love him."

"Darling, your affection for James has never been in question, but . . ."

"But?" Izzie prompted.

"But," her mother said with a sigh, "I cannot help wondering if you are so fixated on James that you have closed your mind and your heart to anyone else."

"There is no one else for me. Only James."

"You didn't give any of your other suitors a fair chance," Lady Weston protested.

"Yes, I did."

"Really? Name two."

"Stimpson and Brantley," Isabella shot back, though in truth she'd given each of them far more than what her mother would probably consider a fair chance.

"The former disgusted me," she continued, "and the latter evoked no warmer feelings than those one would expect from such a long-standing friendship. Just the sight of James makes my heart race and my insides get all quivery and—"

"And yet we must face the facts," her mother finished for her. "James does not seem to reciprocate your feelings."

"But he kissed me!" Izzie blurted out, then clapped her hands over her mouth.

"He did *what*?" Lady Weston squawked.

"Er, well . . ." Actually *she* had kissed *him*, but she would have to be on the rack before she would confess such brazen behavior to her mother.

"Isabella Anne Weston," her mother threatened.

"All right, he kissed me. I admit it." Izzie raised her hands in surrender. "It was the night of my ball. I was crying, and he felt sorry for me."

"Mmmm . . ." Lady Weston gazed at her, silently assessing. "And that was all, was it?"

Isabella flushed and crossed her arms over her chest in defiance. "Do you truly wish to hear the details?"

Her mother thought for a moment before grimacing. "No, I suppose I don't, but you may as well know that a gentleman may kiss a lady without his heart or any of the finer feelings being involved."

"Oh, there were *feelings* involved," Izzie muttered under her breath.

Not quietly enough, apparently, for Lady Weston flushed bright red. "I presume that this . . . uh . . . incident did not go much beyond kissing and that you are . . . er . . . all in one piece, so to speak?"

"Eh?"

Her mother looked pained.

"Mama?"

Lady Weston drew in a deep breath. "Yes?"

"I still don't understand what you mean about being all in one piece."

Her mother groaned. "This isn't something I should have to explain until your wedding night."

"Oh!" Izzie's eyes grew wide with sudden comprehension. "You wanted to know if James and I were like Venus and Mars."

"I beg your pardon," her mother said. "Did you say Venus and Mars?"

Isabella nodded. "Yes, like the pictures in the book I found in—well, it's not important where I found it, and I only looked at it because I thought it was so odd to find a religious tract in ... the place where I found it. Which is not important," she added again for good measure.

"I am afraid you've lost me. A religious tract?"

"That's just it!" Izzie waved her hands in frustration. "It wasn't religious at all, but the title was so misleading. *Godly Love*, I think it was called."

"Ah." Lady Weston nodded. "I believe I begin to understand. I can also imagine where you found it or, rather, whose possession it was in. I presume it has moved along with its owner to his bachelor lodgings so as not to corrupt any of my other children. Well, my other children aside from Olivia," she clarified, "since I can't imagine you kept such a find to yourself."

Isabella's blush proclaimed her guilt.

"Now, back to the subject at hand—I trust you and James were not like"—Lady Weston swallowed hard—"Venus and Mars."

"Oh no!" Izzie exclaimed with horror.

Her mother breathed a huge sigh of relief. "Thank God!"

"It was more like Juno and Jupiter."

Lady Weston buried her face in her hands and made a choking sound. Isabella couldn't tell if she was laughing or crying. Maybe both.

"Mama, if it makes you feel any better, I don't believe I have been compromised. At least not past redemption."

Her mother looked up, wiping tears of mirth from her eyes. "Believe me, darling, that makes me very happy, indeed." Then her face grew somber. "What does not make me happy, and I am certain has you rather miserable, is James's continued absence."

Isabella nodded glumly.

"Now, I know you don't wish to hear this, but maybe it's time to face that James does not return your feelings."

"But—"

"No, you must listen to me. In holding out for James, you have turned down many eligible suitors, men who may not have made your heart race, but who were all proposing marriage. Sometimes love is not the *coup de foudre*, as the French say; it is not always love at first sight. But love can grow between two people. Common interests and similar beliefs lead to friendship, which in turn can lead to love."

Izzie slowly digested her mother's words; they did not sit well. She squirmed in her chair, longing to voice her disagreement but knowing it was wiser not to argue.

"Dearest," Lady Weston continued, "it is not that I am asking you to give up on James entirely—indeed, nothing would give me greater happiness than having him become a son in truth—but I would urge you to take some notice of the other men whose acquaintance you make. You might meet a man who suits you admirably, with whom you could build a life and a family. You do want children, do you not?"

Isabella nodded. She *did* want children—James's children. But it was probably best not to voice that sentiment aloud. She somehow had a feeling her mother wouldn't appreciate it.

"So you'll try?" Lady Weston asked anxiously.

"Uh . . ." Izzie tried frantically to figure out what her mother was talking about.

"Just make a little effort. Don't dismiss a gentleman out of hand because he isn't James. I only want for you to be happy, but you must open your mind to the possibility that there is not a single, straight path one walks on through life. You must be willing to follow the twists and turns of fate to find happiness, nor can you simply expect it to find you. Do you understand what I mean?"

"Yes, Mama."

"Good. And will you promise to make an effort with your suitors next Season?"

Izzie sighed. How could she refuse her mother's earnest entreaty?

"All right," she agreed, praying fervently that something would bring James home before she had to make good on it.

Chapter 7

I do not know why people claim to love surprises.
It is all well and good to love a good surprise, but
I have yet to meet a person who liked a bad one. I
certainly do not, and I wish a certain person whose
name begins with "H" and ends with "enry," who is
home from school for the holidays, was not so fond
of leaving them in Livvy's and my room.

From the correspondence of Miss Isabella Weston,
age twelve

Letter to her aunt Katherine, Marchioness of Sheldon, following a week of most unpleasant shocks of the aquatic,
reptilian, and insectile nature—December 1790

Belmore Hall, County Kerry, Ireland
March 1798

"James," she whispered.

Hearing his name on her lips, exhaled on a shivery
breath, sent chills straight down his spine. His blood started
to pound in hard, slow waves. He groaned, turning over in
the bed to bring her closer. He was hard and aching, ready
to explode, but his questing arms met only air.

James abruptly woke up and realized he was alone.

Again.

He didn't know which was tormenting him more, the

guilt or the wanting, but Isabella Weston was going to be the death of him, one way or another.

He thought of going to see one of the tavern wenches in the local village, but a glance at the clock on the mantel, just visible in the light from the dying embers, made him decide it wasn't worth the effort. It wasn't as if it would help, in any case.

He hadn't been with a woman in more months than he'd like to count.

He wanted only her.

James rolled out of bed, his body still primed and ready, and shrugged on his dressing gown. As he stoked the fire, he looked up and caught a glance at his reflection in the mirror over the mantel.

He looked like hell.

He probably would have scared the girls at the inn, showing up looking like a man possessed.

Possessed.

It was an apt description of how he felt. That, or haunted.

The guilt haunted him, but not as fiercely as Isabella herself. His nights were filled with memories of the softness of her skin, the silkiness of her hair, the sweet, satin heat between her thighs.

The little witch was driving him mad, damn her, invading his dreams night after night.

He was the one who was damned, though, lusting after his best friend's sister.

Bloody everlasting hell.

With a muttered curse, James tightened the belt of his dressing gown and grabbed a candlestick off his bedside table. Lighting the taper in the fireplace, he quietly made his way downstairs to what had been his father's study, now an office of sorts for the orphanage.

Along with his bedchamber, it was the only room that hadn't been remodeled and redecorated when he'd turned the country estate into a refuge for, as his grandfather had put it in one particularly vitriolic letter, "every potential pickpocket and future doxy in Ireland."

James reached for the bottle of whiskey he'd stashed behind some particularly uninteresting books to keep it hidden from young boys bent on mischief, strode over to his father's desk, and slumped down in the chair.

He lifted the bottle to his lips, not bothering with a glass, and took a healthy swallow. Drinking away his troubles . . . He knew it was pathetic and juvenile, but even worse, he knew it was futile.

The fiery liquid wasn't strong enough to burn away the taste of Isabella. That was impossible. He worried sometimes that she had somehow imprinted herself on his very soul.

He shook his head. That was sentimental, womanly thinking. Lust was making him crazy, putting thoughts into his mind that surely didn't belong there. He would go to the village tomorrow, he determined. If he remembered right, there was a pretty little blond serving girl. . . . Maybe she could ease this desperate need, this fierce desire that had taken control of him, and then life could return to normal.

That was his last coherent thought before he was startled awake by the touch of a hand on his shoulder accompanied by a rather exaggerated clearing of the throat.

Disoriented, James blinked up into the concerned gaze of his steward. He closed his eyes for a long moment before taking a deep breath and opening them again.

"Tell me, Connor," James said. "Is there perhaps construction work going on outside?"

Connor shook his head. "I'm afraid no', milor'."

"Then this confounded hammering is in my head?"

"Afraid so, milor'."

James groaned, then clutched his head when Connor pulled open the heavy drapes, flooding the room with painfully bright sunlight. "What the—," he began.

"There's another of them urgent messengers for ye, milor', so it's best ye be gettin' sobered up now."

"An urgent messenger? Again? I don't bloody well believe it. I thought my last reply made it quite clear that— Well, I suppose it would be rude to show him the door without hearing whatever cock-and-bull story my grand-sire has cooked up this time. All right, Connor, tell the man I'll be with him shortly. I need a few minutes to clear my head."

James sighed as he massaged his throbbing temples. This was the fifth messenger his grandfather had sent since November. The first had informed James the earl was ill and commanded him to return to Sheffield Park. James had sent the man back with the reply that he was sure his grandfather would soon be well again; he was far too or-nery to die.

On that account, at least, he had been correct, because the messengers kept arriving with letters penned in the earl's bold hand, and James kept sending them back. He recalled a game he'd played as a child, tossing a ball back and forth until someone finally dropped it and lost. He was not going to lose.

Nor was he going to take out his frustration on the mes-senger, James reminded himself. He walked over to the window and felt himself relax at the sight of a pair of ado-lescent boys laughing and tussling on the lawn. Past them, one of the teachers he'd hired was dancing about in a circle with a group of young girls. They wore bright smiles on their faces, so different from the sullen, downcast expres-sions they had worn when they'd first come to live at Bel-more Hall.

As he watched them, he felt a flood of warmth around his heart. The house had seen too much sadness and then had suffered from years of neglect. Now Belmore Hall was full of life and light and the laughter of children, just as his parents would have wanted it. He had located his old nanny, Mrs. Fitzpatrick, and offered her a small fortune to live at Belmore and oversee the daily business of the foundling home. She had accepted with alacrity and taken over the running of the house so easily, it seemed she had been there for years. The children all adored her, as James had known they would, and between her and Connor, there was really nothing that required *his* attention. . . .

His work there was done, James realized abruptly. It had been done for some time, but he'd stayed because he didn't know what else to do. It was time to go—

James stopped himself. One couldn't *go* home if one didn't *have* a home.

Weston Manor was the closest he'd come to a home since the death of his parents, but now that was lost to him, too. Even if Lord and Lady Weston were unaware of it, he had betrayed their trust. The knowledge weighed on him heavily, and though he didn't deny himself the comfort of Lady Weston's letters, reading them always filled him with self-loathing.

Henry had tried visiting him once, months ago, but James had sent him on his way as quickly as he could without being rude. It was damned awkward having to look your best friend in the eye when you had nearly taken his sister's innocence. And heaven help him if Henry, or anyone else in the family, ever learned what liberties he'd taken that night. He would be soundly beaten, if not shot outright, and he deserved no less. A gentleman didn't do the things he'd done, not to a respectable young lady, without offering marriage.

After all the Westons had done for him—had been to him—this was how he repaid them. Oh, he could claim that Isabella had kissed him first, but he had kissed her back. He had urged her on, had taken all that she was willing to give and still demanded more. He had thrown aside a lifetime of principles, had forsaken the people to whom he should have been most loyal. And he'd done it all in a heartbeat because he had been so overcome with lust for one wisp of a girl.

Lord, what was it about her that incited such a response in him? She was beautiful to be sure, but James had been with his fair share of stunning women. He admired her clever wit, but as that quality was characteristic of all the Weston females, James knew it wasn't what made her uniquely attractive. In his mind's eye he flashed back to the instant at her ball where, right after calling him a heartless bounder, she'd gazed up at him, her aqua eyes sparkling with delight and her pale skin flushed with excitement.

Radiant. That was the only word to describe her. She exuded joy and life, both of which he'd seen snatched away at far too young an age. In order to protect himself, James had kept those twin forces, joy and life, and their offspring, love, at a distance. But being around Isabella made that difficult; her vitality called to him, drew him like nothing else could. She gave him glimpses of what life could be like if he allowed himself to truly feel again, and her smiles eased the pain of his past to where he almost forgot why he was the way he was.

And that was why he had to stay away from her, because if he let her, she would worm her way into his heart. She had that power. And then, if he were to lose her ... He simply wouldn't survive. His father was proof enough of that, and James would not end like his father. He wouldn't let his happiness depend on another person, no matter how much she might tempt him.

He forced his mind from thoughts of Isabella, for that way madness (and whiskey) lay. No, for now he would concentrate on dealing with the messenger, but it was a sad day when receiving a hate-filled missive from his only living relative was a welcome distraction.

He found the man in the entry hall looking most ill at ease, though it was hard to say whether that was due to the nature of his mission or the cluster of children inspecting him. He wasn't anyone James recognized, which had been the case with all his predecessors, but was hardly surprising given that the majority of the servants at Sheffield Park should have been pensioned off a decade ago, at least.

One could hardly expect a servant who had difficulty making it up and down the stairs to travel the six hundred miles from Essex to County Kerry. In truth, the journey was a perilous undertaking for anyone; the crossing on the Holyhead packet was rough at the best of times and then, assuming a safe arrival in Dublin, there was the anti-British sentiment which, if the newspapers were accurate, was growing more pronounced and violent by the day.

James noted the messenger's haggard appearance and took pity on him. "Children," he intoned, then waited until he had their attention. "I am going to take our guest into the study now. Please return whatever valuables you have lifted off him."

The messenger looked startled, and then astonished as, one by one, his watch, coin purse, handkerchief, and a host of other items were handed over amidst loud grumbles. James wanted to laugh, but he fought to keep his expression stern. "I have told you on numerous occasions that such impolite and criminal actions have no place at Belmore Hall."

"Yes, milor'," they chorused, all trying to look repentant and failing miserably.

James sighed loudly and rolled his eyes, eliciting giggles from the younger children, at least those who had been at Belmore long enough to overcome their fears of being punished and sent away.

"All right, off with you." James made shooing motions with his hands. "No doubt Mistress Fitz can assign you more chores and schoolwork to do, since your minds and hands are not busy enough to stay out of other people's pockets."

There was more grumbling as they quickly dispersed and James ushered the messenger into the study. "I apologize for their behavior," he said, closing the door. "Apparently thievery is a difficult habit to break." He shook his head. "Now, what urgent news brings you here? What Banbury tale has my grandfather sent you to pedal?"

The man shifted uneasily.

"Come, I am certain the earl gave you a message for me. You needn't fear being shot. All the other messengers left Belmore unscathed. I assure you, I am quite used to his rants."

"My lord, perhaps it would be better if you just read

this," the man said, pulling a letter from the inside pocket of his coat and handing it to James.

James motioned for the messenger to be seated, and then took his own seat. Anything written by his grandfather, he knew from experience, was best read sitting down. He picked up the letter opener on the desk and slid it under the wax, then paused.

That wasn't his grandfather's seal; it was Lord Weston's.

A wave of panic welled up and crashed down over him, and James's gut started churning. He could think of only two circumstances in which the Westons would send a special messenger, and both involved death. Either someone had died or was about to. With trembling fingers he set the letter opener and folded the piece of foolscap down on the desk. He couldn't bear to read it, because then he'd have to face whatever news it contained. His mind raced with unhappy possibilities, each scenario more horrible than the next.

Henry was surely at some shooting party or another, where any one of a thousand mishaps—a gun's misfiring or a riding accident, for instance—might have befallen him. Or had one of the little ones taken ill? Or what if something had happened to Izzie . . . ?

His heart seized and his brain went blank, unwilling to finish the thought.

Slowly, numbly, he reached for the letter and broke the seal. He read the first line slowly, and then read it again, struggling to come to terms with what was written:

I shall put it plainly as I know you won't wish condolences: Your grandfather has shuffled off his mortal coil.

James crumpled the paper in his hand as he rose and began to pace. Emotions flew at him, fast and wild, battling with one another for supremacy—surprise, triumph, anger, fear—but they were fleeting, and he was left feeling empty.

His grandfather was dead.

How many times had he dreamed about this day? Too many to count, he supposed, and he'd always thought the news would fill him with joy, or at least some measure of satisfaction.

He had never imagined this cold nothingness.

He must be in shock. . . . It was hardly surprising, given that his entire life had suddenly been turned on its head. *He* was the Earl of Dunston now.

Christ.

James sagged against the nearest bookcase, the enormity of the situation beginning to seep into his brain. In all the times he'd imagined his grandfather's demise, somehow he hadn't taken that extra mental step wherein *he* inherited the title. Then again, he had never truly been able to imagine a world without his grandfather.

The earl was—*had been*—such a tyrant, James almost felt a bit adrift knowing he was finally gone. It was as if his life had been a giant game of chess and his opponent had suddenly disappeared. He had won, but it was a hollow victory, and he didn't know what to do now that there was no next move to be made.

Baffled by his dark thoughts, for surely he should be calling for a case of champagne, James focused once more on the letter. The reading of the will was to be held at his earliest convenience, Lady Weston informed him, and she expected that his grandfather's solicitor, a Mr. Palmer if memory served, would await his arrival at Sheffield Park.

His arrival at Sheffield Park.

Sheffield Park meant seeing the Westons.

Sheffield Park meant seeing *Isabella.*

His chest seized. Oh God, he couldn't breathe. Cursing, he stumbled to the window and pried it open, desperate for air.

"Are you all right, my lord?"

"Fine," James gasped. "Bloody marvelous."

He took hold of himself. Straightening, he asked, "Do you know what date the funeral was set for?"

"I'm sorry, my lord, but I believe it's to be held on the morrow. You'll never make it, I'm afraid, but that was the latest it could be pushed back. I came as quickly as I could, but our crossing was delayed and—"

"Don't trouble yourself," James interrupted. "I wouldn't have attended in any case."

When James arrived at Sheffield Park, he was not in the best of moods. He had spent many long days traveling to the place he had the very least desire to be, and he was exhausted, both physically and emotionally. It was dusk when he finally dismounted and gave the reins over to one of the grooms. All he wanted was a meal, a bath, and his bed—and a drink. A stay at Sheffield Park definitely merited a drink.

He was not pleased, therefore, to learn that Lady Weston's expectation that Mr. Palmer would await James's arrival had proven quite correct . . . and quite literal. The man had taken up residence "as if he'd just inherited the title," a disgruntled Mrs. Benton bemoaned.

James calmed the agitated housekeeper, assuring her that he would have the will read as early as possible the following morning and, with any luck, the man would be gone before noon. However, when he awoke the following morning, which seemed to come all too soon, James realized that judging by the angle of the sun sneaking past the curtains, it was closer to midday. Poor Mrs. Benton would have to feed the solicitor luncheon after all.

"Mr. Palmer is waiting for you in the study, my lord," the butler informed James when he came downstairs.

The study.

It was the logical place for a settling of legal matters, but the mere thought of the room left him entirely unsettled. His heart was pounding in his chest as he opened the heavy oak door, and every muscle in his body was painfully tense, poised for a fight. All the ugly memories of the day he had arrived at Sheffield Park came flooding back to him.

Even after all these years, it remained the worst day of his life. Worse than the day when he had stood beside his

father and watched as his mother and baby sister were laid
to rest. Worse, even, than the day of his father's funeral,
only months after burying his mother. It was worse than
the days of the horrible crossing from Ireland to England
when he had cast up his accounts almost constantly; if the
choppy waters weren't wreaking havoc on his innards,
then it was his anxiety over leaving everything he had
ever known. He had arrived torn between trepidation and
excitement, his stomach all tangled and twisted up with
knots, which only grew worse when the sprawling house
came into sight.

A huge edifice of golden stone, Sheffield Park dominated the landscape. A large reflecting pond, actually closer
to the size of a small lake, stretched the length of the main
facade, doubling the immense structure. From a distance
the house was intimidating; up close, its size was staggering.
James looked up and up and up—the pale yellow brick just
kept reaching on as if it were responsible for holding up
the sky itself.

Mrs. Fitzpatrick, who had volunteered to escort him on
the voyage, was equally impressed. "'Tis a fine grand house
ta be sure." She gave him a bright smile. "An' jest think,
there'll come a day an' ye'll be laird of it all."

A surge of pride and excitement shot through James. He
was finally going to meet his grandfather. His father had
not spoken of the earl often, and never in glowing terms,
but he *was* James's grandfather, and he *had* arranged for
James to come live with him. In fact, he had demanded that
his grandson be sent to him immediately and that he be
treated with all the care and respect due to a future English
earl.

The knowledge that his grandfather wanted him and
was concerned about him had lit a spark in James's breast.
Throughout the journey he had kindled it, coaxed it into a
steady flame of hope that helped stave off the encroaching
darkness.

The sound of a throat being cleared recalled him
abruptly to the present, and James realized that Mr. Palmer

had gotten to his feet and had been holding out his hand for the Lord only knew how long.

"Forgive me, Mr. Palmer." James shook the man's hand. "This room holds rather strong memories. . . ."

"Say no more, my lord. Returning to Sheffield Park so soon after losing your grandfather—"

"James!" A large hand clamped down on his shoulder as, almost before he could identify the voice, Oliver Weston pulled him into a brief, hard embrace.

"How are you, lad?" Lord Weston asked softly, looking intently at James.

James shrugged and prayed devoutly that eyes were not in fact the windows to one's soul, because if they were, he was about to be dismantled for all the dark desires of Isabella he harbored there.

He was about to ask why Lord Weston was present, for surely he was past the age of needing a trustee, when he spied a second visitor and forgot how to breathe. As if he had conjured her up with his thoughts, Isabella rose and curtsied.

"My lord."

"Miss Weston."

James bowed and swallowed hard. Christ, his dreams hadn't done her justice. He'd hoped—God how he'd hoped—that if he saw her again, when he saw her again, the longing would have vanished. If anything, it was twice as strong. Need clawed at his gut and stirred his loins . . . and James decided that it would be prudent to quickly seat himself behind his grandfather's massive desk.

That cooled his ardor. All he needed was a paper in his hands and the scene would be set for that first meeting. He remembered thinking it odd that his grandfather hadn't risen to greet him when he had entered the room. He'd wondered if perhaps the earl had gout. James hadn't been quite sure what gout was, but there had been a neighbor in Ireland who had always remained seated, mumbling about his gout acting up whenever ladies entered the room.

Although James had been able to see his grandfather

only from the torso up, the man hadn't looked to be suffering from any sort of affliction, gout or otherwise. For a man then in his sixth decade of life, the silver-haired earl had appeared remarkably fit. His grandfather's thin, angular face resembled nothing so much as a bird of prey, mostly because of the beaklike nose that dominated it. Below that protruding feature were lips permanently compressed into a hard, disapproving white line.

James remembered it as if it had only just happened, how his grandfather had looked at him for a long, uncomfortable moment, his piercing, icy blue eyes sharp and alert, like a hawk scanning the ground for his next meal. Then, with an air of complete dismissal, the earl had transferred his attention to Mrs. Fitzpatrick.

"Are you *Irish*?" he'd asked, the word laced with disgust.

"Aye, milor'."

"Then you will go. My butler will see to it that you have the means to return from whence you came."

James had regarded his grandfather in dismayed shock. His mother had told him that some Englishmen didn't like the Irish, but he'd never expected to see such outward hatred. He'd assumed his mother had meant some Englishmen did not like the Irish in the way that he, for example, did not like green beans.

Everyone had their own preferences after all, and if one was presented with green beans at a house not one's own, one put on a good face and ate them anyway. His grandfather hadn't seemed inclined to put on a good face and eat his green beans.

James had looked up at his old nurse and seen the distress written across her face. He'd bravely squeezed her hand and nodded, trying to assure her that he would be all right, though he had been far from certain himself.

"You may go," stated the earl.

Mrs. Fitzpatrick had hesitated.

"Now." The word had sounded like a clap of thunder, reverberating throughout the large room. James's nurse had sent him an apologetic look, kissed his temple, and fled the room, taking with her his last link with home.

James bit his cheek and reminded himself that he was no longer that scared little boy. Every inch the lord of the manor, he rose to his feet.

"Lord Weston, Isabella, it is very kind of you to call, but as much as I would like to sit and visit with you, I am afraid Mr. Palmer and I have important business—"

"My lord," the solicitor interjected, "it was I who requested his lordship and Miss Weston come for the reading of the will. Their presence will soon be explained, and all will become clear."

James arched one dark brow. "How wonderfully mysterious of you, sir," he responded with blatant sarcasm. "I am all agog with curiosity. Let us commence." He sat down again and leaned back, crossing his feet on the desk.

Mr. Palmer frowned, but he adjusted his spectacles on the bridge of his nose and began to read. He droned on through a seemingly endless list of bequests and pensions for various ancient servants and retainers who had loyally served the Sheffield family, and then stopped and began to tug at his cravat.

"I am afraid . . . ," he began. "That is, this is a very difficult situation. . . ." He took a deep breath, and then said in a rush, "The former earl has left all properties, possessions, and monies not specifically entailed to his successor, that would be you, my lord, to Miss Weston. I shall act as trustee and executor for all the Sheffield houses, possessions, properties, and monies, and Lord Weston will serve as joint trustee until Miss Weston marries or reaches her majority."

A moment of heavy silence settled over the room as its occupants, aside from Mr. Palmer, slowly absorbed the momentous implications of the solicitor's pronouncement.

"I don't believe you, Mr. Palmer," Isabella whispered, her face drawn and pale. "There is no reason the earl should leave anything to me." She was trembling as she stood and faced James. "This is some kind of farce you have concocted, and I don't wish to hear another word."

"Miss Weston, please . . . ," the solicitor began.

"Did you know about this?" Isabella demanded, turning hurt, bewildered eyes first on her father, then on James.

Lord Weston sat as still as a statue, not a flicker of emotion crossing his face.

"I knew he hated me," James said. His voice was calm, conversational even, giving no hint of his racing thoughts. "I knew he never wanted me to inherit, but I had no idea he was so imaginative."

"It isn't imagination!" Isabella's voice rose as she stomped her foot in frustration. "Did you understand what Mr. Palmer said?"

"Yes," James replied coolly. "I understood. I have inherited a grand title and magnificent properties, but I am really nothing more than a poor relation, a humble supplicant. I must beg from your father and Mr. Palmer for every farthing I require to maintain the estates. I must obtain their approval every time a tenant's roof needs repair or Mrs. Benton feels the footmen are in need of new livery."

He gave a bitter laugh.

"And someday I shall doubtless have to prostrate myself before you, Isabella, and hold out my hands for whatever groats you are beneficent enough to toss my way. Will you be tight with the purse strings, do you think?"

"Stop!" Isabella cried, clapping her hands over her ears. "I won't hear any more. This is madness!"

"No, Miss Weston," the solicitor responded. "Although I most strongly disagreed with the late earl's choices, he *was* in his right mind when he made them. A claim of mental incompetence will not hold up in court. Your grandfather took the precaution of having several respected London physicians witness the will."

"How farsighted of him," James drawled.

"My lord, at my urging, the former earl did agree to give you a quarterly allowance for your personal use."

"A quarterly allowance?" James barked. "By God, that's bloody rich. Or not, as is now the case with me. A quarterly allowance." He shook his head in disbelief. "I suppose he didn't want the Earl of Dunston dressed like some damned vagrant."

"My lord," Mr. Palmer cautioned.

"What, does my *poor* choice of words offend you, sir?"

"There is a lady present, my lord."

"You're right." James tapped his forefinger against his chin as if in thought. "And this is one lady I certainly cannot *afford* to offend, as I am soon to be her charity case."

"My lord, please, there is a solution, if you will but listen."

"What, did my loving grandfather also leave me a loaded pistol?"

"James!" Isabella exclaimed in horror.

"Marriage," Lord Weston said suddenly, breaking his long silence.

The solicitor inclined his head. "You are very perceptive, my lord."

"Marriage?" Isabella repeated in a trembling voice. She sank down on the settee beside her father, her face grown quite pale. She stared down at her lap. "He would need an heiress of—of considerable fortune, would he not?"

"He needs you, my dear," Lord Weston said, placing an arm about Isabella's shoulders. "Marriage to you effectively cancels out the terms of the will, does it not, Mr. Palmer?"

"Indeed, my lord." The solicitor bobbed his head in agreement. "In fact, it was the late earl's wish that the two wed. He told me that he had long desired an alliance between your families and, though I am not precisely sure what he meant, he felt that marriage to Miss Weston would ensure that the present earl didn't make the same mistake that his father—"

"I believe I have heard enough, Mr. Palmer."

There it was, the real reason his grandfather hated him. The earl's words from that first meeting in this very study had been branded on James's mind.

"Listen well," his grandfather had said, "for I shall only say this once. You are the heir to the Dunston title. You are, of course, completely unworthy, given that your mother was an Irish slut, but, since she trapped my weak sod of a son into marriage, I have no other choice. It is my responsibility to see to it that you are in every way fit to assume the title when the time comes. That, and only that, is the reason your presence is tolerated here."

James had gaped at him, wondering if he could possibly have misheard the ugly words that fell so easily from his grandsire's mouth.

"It seems you have inherited your father's dim-wittedness as well. I shall have my work cut out for me. At least you *look* English. I suppose we must be grateful for small mercies."

It was at that moment that James had decided he hated his grandfather. A black rage had filled him, replacing the suffocating grief of the past weeks. He had clung to the anger, relished it. After all, it was all he'd had left.

He had cried himself to sleep that night, muffling the sound of his sobs in his pillow so that no one could hear. He had never felt more alone. That small spark he had cherished had been brutally extinguished, and all his hopes for the future had been savagely snuffed out, plunging him into darkness and despair.

And now despair loomed again. Despite his control, James had been shocked by the contents of the will, though he wasn't sure why he was surprised. His grandfather had tried to control every aspect of his life from the day he had moved in at Sheffield Park. The earl had dictated everything from what books James could read to how much dessert he was allowed to eat. Hell, James wouldn't have been surprised to learn there had been a limit to the number of times he could use the privy each day. Even six feet underground, his grandfather was still trying to rule him. The old man was tenacious, even in death.

James's voice was steely with determination as he said, "I will not play his games. As far as I am concerned, the title is dead. Do you understand? I will never, *never* marry."

James heard a gasp of dismay from Isabella, but he forced himself to ignore it.

The solicitor was not so inclined. "Please, Miss Weston, do not distress yourself. His lordship is overwrought. He doesn't know what he is saying."

"You presume too much, Mr. Palmer. I know *exactly* what I am saying. Upon my death, the Sheffield line will end and the earldom will become extinct."

"What will you live on in the meantime?" the solicitor countered. "I must tell you that your quarterly allowance will not prove adequate, and you seem ill disposed to ask Lord Weston or me for funds."

"There are men born into the world without rank and privilege, Mr. Palmer. Those men work, receive an honest wage, and rise or fall on their own merits. I have always thought a career in the army would suit me admirably."

"The Earl of Dunston in the army?" the solicitor exclaimed in shock. "Why, that's preposterous."

"I have made my decision," James stated firmly.

"Come, you can't mean to tell me you would prefer to risk death over assuming your rightful position and marrying this delightful young—"

"However cruelly you choose to phrase it, Mr. Palmer, my answer is still the same."

With a piteous sound like a wounded animal, somewhere between a moan and a cry, Isabella bolted for the French windows that led out onto a stone terrace and down into the formal garden.

An uncomfortable silence gripped the three men. They stared, hypnotized by the sight of Isabella's retreating figure, watching as she passed through the garden into the wooded acreage that lay beyond.

A loud crack of thunder jolted them back to the present. Lightning flashed and the heavens opened, loosening a torrent of rain. Once the rain started pouring down, James had fully expected Isabella to turn around and make for the house. As she kept moving deeper into the home woods, he swore.

"Damnation, what in bloody hell does she think she's doing?" James muttered, and then turned to the other men.

"Mr. Palmer, no doubt we shall be in touch sooner than either of us would like, but I believe you have said more than enough at present. If you will pack your bags, I will see to it that a carriage is made ready to take you back to London."

James faced Lord Weston. "I am sorrier than I can tell you that this happened. I'll go after her and try to . . . to explain," he finished lamely.

"Do you know where she's headed?"

"The folly, I think. I'll bring her back to the manor as quickly as I can. You might ask Lady Weston to see that there's a hot bath waiting."

"Foolish girl." Lord Weston shook his head. "Always so impulsive and headstrong. She may refuse to come back with you."

"I know." James sighed. "Right now I'm just hoping she hasn't the presence of mind to lock the door." And with that, he strode out the open doors into the freezing rain, calling himself ten kinds of fool.

Chapter 8

Why, why, why *do I always blurt out the wrong thing at just the wrong time? I don't think Mama minds that Mrs. Snopes will no longer be calling upon us, and her pet monkey truly did bear a remarkable resemblance to her late husband, and I did think having his likeness around would be a comfort. Papa says that someday this tendency to speak before I think is going to get me into real trouble!*

From the correspondence of Miss Isabella Weston, age thirteen

Letter to her aunt Katherine, Marchioness of Sheldon, on the gross impropriety of telling a woman her deceased husband bore a strong likeness to the family pet—June 1791

The folly, a small thatched cottage built by James's great-grandfather when such structures were all the rage, was situated in a small, wooded copse behind the walled garden. When James, Henry, and Isabella were children, the small room had served them as medieval castle, pirate ship, and African jungle. It was the place where they stored all their treasures and a safe haven from cross governesses, angry parents, and irate tutors. Later, James recalled, he and Henry had used the place for trysting with the village girls.

James was so caught up in his thoughts, he paid no mind to his footing and slipped on a patch of wet grass, just barely managing to keep his balance. He was wet and cold and feeling terribly guilty and angry, and he was *not* looking forward to being alone in such a small space with Isabella, especially since she must be as soaked as he was, and her garments would be clinging to—

He slipped again, and this time he couldn't catch himself. Bloody hell, he thought, wiping at the mud on his breeches. It was a reminder, and apparently a much-needed one, that lusting after Isabella Weston was dangerous—dangerous to his health, his heart, and his very soul. It was too bad, he reflected, as the folly came into view, that he seemed to have such a damned hard time remembering it.

Isabella was so wrapped up in her misery, she didn't even hear when he opened the door, which luckily for him, she had not thought to latch. She was huddled up against the far wall, her head down on her knees.

"Izzie," he trailed off, not really knowing what to say. She didn't lift her head, but he could tell by the sudden tension in her shoulders that she had heard him. He took a step closer.

"Go away," she said. "Just go away." When he made no move to leave, she uttered the one word that destroyed him. "Please."

He crossed the remaining distance between them and sank down beside her. He pulled her unwilling body into his arms, holding her on his lap as he had done so many times to comfort her when she was little.

Only she wasn't little anymore, and his body instantly reacted to her nearness. He willed himself back into control, strangely grateful for his chilled garments. He tightened his arms around her, murmuring into her wet hair, "God, Izzie, I'm sorry. I am so, so sorry."

He felt her shaking in his arms and lifted his hand to her cheek. Her skin was icy cold against his fingers, and her teeth had begun to chatter. James realized he had to get her back to the house before she became seriously ill. "Come on, sweetheart," he said as he rose to his feet, Isabella still in his arms.

The endearment, so thoughtlessly uttered on his part, seemed to shake Isabella out of her private anguish. She twisted about in his arms until he set her on her feet. She backed away toward the wall, her gaze at once longing and accusatory. She stared at him until it seemed she could no longer bear it and, with a shuddering sigh, she turned and rested her head against the wall, clearly exhausted by the day's trials.

James placed his hands on his hips and glared at Isabella's back. Damn it all to hell, he was tired, too, and wet and cold. He was also feeling incredibly guilty and all sorts of other emotions he didn't care to further investigate but knew he didn't want to be feeling. He walked over to her and placed a hand on her sodden shoulder. He felt her flinch at his touch but steeled himself against the pain that knowledge brought.

"Izzie, you're drenched. Look, I know you don't like me much right now, but you must let me take you home." She said nothing, and James's jaw hardened. "Fine then, if that's what it takes, I will carry you back to the bloody house." He made to pick her up, but Isabella whirled away.

"No. No! I am not going anywhere with you." Her voice was shrill, verging on hysterical.

"For God's sake, Isabella, you are chilled to the bone, and your teeth are rattling like Spanish castanets. You are going to make yourself ill, and I refuse to have that on my conscience. Come now, let's go back to the house where—"

"Your conscience?" Angry eyes the color of a stormy sea blazed up at him. "*Your conscience?* You don't have a conscience. You don't have a *heart*." She spat at him.

"Enough," he barked, but she was too far gone to listen.

"You don't have a heart, because people with hearts want other people, need other people, *love* other people. But not *you*. Not James Sheffield." He made a move toward her, but she backed away, swiping at the tears now coursing freely down her cheeks.

"No, you are independent. Self-sufficient. A *man*. I *need* you," she choked out, "but you don't need or want anything, do you? You just—"

"I said that's enough, damn you!" He lunged for her and hauled her into his arms. His fingers clenched in her tangled, wet hair, holding her face immobile. He pressed his cheek against her temple, and he could feel her breath coming in warm, harsh spurts against his throat. "You think I don't want you?" he asked incredulously. "You think I don't *want* you!" His voice was a deep rumble in her ear.

"Then, why?"

He didn't pretend to misunderstand her. She wanted to know why he wouldn't marry her.

"It's complicated," he said.

She arched an eyebrow, clearly less than impressed with his confession. He would have to tell her, then. He should have known. With her, it would always be all or nothing.

"Can we at least talk about this once we are warm and dry?" he asked.

There went the eyebrow again. He supposed that meant no. Damn. Luckily there was a fireplace in the folly, stocked with dry kindling, thank heavens, since he wouldn't have been able to gather so much as a dry leaf in the current downpour. He sighed and began searching for a piece of flint and a tinderbox. A few minutes of silent searching yielded them, and he set about making a fire; a cheery blaze was soon going in the fireplace. James had shed his jacket and waistcoat while building the fire. Now he began unbuttoning his shirt.

"What are you *doing*?" Isabella squealed.

"What does it look like I am doing? I will be damned if I will sit here in these wet clothes. And I will be damned if I will let you sit around in that gown. Take it off." He sat on the floor and tugged at his boots.

"Excuse me?"

James looked up from his task. "I beg your pardon, did you need my assistance?"

"No! I—I am not taking it off."

"Like hell!" James didn't particularly care that he was in the presence of a lady. He gave a vicious yank, and his second boot came off. "Get out of those wet garments, or I will do it for you." He rummaged around in an old chest and found several quilts. He threw one at her. "You can use it to cover yourself."

He turned his back to give her some privacy. He heard the intermittent thuds of her sodden garments hitting the floor, and then there was silence.

Oh dear Lord, she was naked!

He'd left his wet breeches on in deference to proprieties, though there was nothing remotely proper about any of this, but even the chilly fabric couldn't mute his body's re-action to the knowledge that Isabella was naked and within his immediate grasp.

Damn, damn, and damn again.

"You can turn around now."

He did. She had swathed herself in the large quilt so that only her head was visible and had seated herself with her back to the fire. Not so much as a toe was in sight, which was probably a good thing. A toe might have sent him over the edge, might have had him falling on her like a raven-ing wolf. He glanced down at his bare feet. Nothing there to inspire lust. He looked back at her. God, but she was beautiful.

Firelight played on the hair cascading down her back, making it gleam like burnished gold. The warm glow lit on her face, too, giving her the radiance of a Renaissance Ma-donna. His belly clenched just looking at her.

He forced himself back to the task at hand. "I need to explain why I said . . . what I said." He didn't want to repeat the hurtful words any more than he supposed she wanted to hear them. "It isn't you. It's me."

She laughed, a hoarse, ugly, hurting sound. "How original."

"I never meant to hurt you, Izzie."

"Did you take this out of a book somewhere?"

"I am telling you the truth. It isn't you. I made a decision long ago never to marry."

"How wonderfully convenient," she said, sarcasm coating each word.

Funny, his body thought it was pretty damned inconvenient, given that he couldn't have her without marriage, and yet he was only a quilt tug away from having her naked. Best not to think of that, he reminded himself. He needed to explain why he wouldn't—couldn't—marry her. She deserved nothing less than the truth.

The problem was, he didn't think he could tell her the truth. How could he make her understand his fears, with her family so healthy and loving and whole? She didn't know what devastating loss could drive a man to do; he hoped she never would. But he did. He knew it all too well, and he had promised himself never to be that vulnerable.

Because he knew how it would end. In his heart of hearts, he knew with deep certainty that he was, in every way, his father's son. The magistrate had deemed his father's death an accident, a tragic fall down the stairs, but James knew the truth. It was no accident. His father had wanted to die, and no matter what it looked like, James was certain he'd thrown himself down that staircase and killed himself as surely as if he'd put a bullet through his brain.

James couldn't tell her that, though. It was a secret he had kept for too long. Besides, he didn't think he could bear for her to look at him with pity or disgust. He'd have to try a different tactic.

"I won't marry, Isabella, because it wouldn't be fair to my wife."

He saw he had her attention now.

"The only reason my grandfather ever tolerated my presence was that I was his damned heir, the future of the bloody Sheffield line, but as you can tell from the contents of his will, he despised me. He despised the fact that my father fell in love with and married a woman who happened to be Irish."

His mother's face rose up in his mind. She had been so

beautiful, so loving.... He swallowed hard against the lump in his throat.

"Well, I am going to have the last laugh. He thought my mother's blood stained the family name? With me, that family name will cease to exist. Do you understand me? I will never, *never* have children."

He had dropped down to his knees beside her so she could see the truth written across his face. Family meant everything to Isabella. She wouldn't want him now.

Her eyes were huge in her face, a face that was still too damned pale, and he could see her fighting not to cry. He watched her draw in a deep, shuddering breath and attempt to pull herself together.

"So it's the—the children you're opposed to?" she asked.

He frowned, taken off guard by the question.

She took his silence as assent. "I have heard . . . ," she began, pausing to lick her lips, a gesture he felt all the way down to his loins. "Well, I overheard the maids...." Her face had turned bright pink. He was dying to know just what was going through that pretty little head of hers. Nothing good, he'd wager.

"I have heard there are ways for a woman to keep from getting with child." The words flew out of her mouth in a rush, and her face turned several shades darker, but her eyes never left his. He had been right. Nothing good. Because he could think of far too many ways to do what she'd alluded to, and the images were running through his mind in quick succession, threatening what little composure he had left. He buried his head in his hands.

"I don't know exactly how . . . I mean, I didn't quite understand what they . . . Is it true?"

"Yes," he groaned, "but they're whores' tricks. You shouldn't even *know* of them, let alone bring them up in conversation." Especially with a man who's ready to tear that quilt off you and show you just how they work, he thought.

"If I . . ." Her voice wavered. "If I agreed not to have children, would you marry me?"

His head jerked up to look at her. She couldn't mean it. The thought was ludicrous. He raked a hand through his hair. She was killing him, and he deserved it. If ever there was a woman destined for love and marriage and mother-hood, it was Isabella Weston. But she was serious, he saw. Deadly earnest. She was willing to give that up for him. If he'd still had a heart, it would have broken right then and there.

"I would never do that to you, Izzie," he said quietly, re-gret infusing every word. "As I said, such a situation would be unfair to any woman. You deserve to marry a man who loves you and will give you children."

"But I don't *want* to," she cried, tears spilling down her cheeks. "I love *you*. I want to marry *you*."

"Izzie, don't you want children? Honestly? Haven't you dreamed of holding a baby in your arms?"

"Well, yes, but it was ours—"

"That will never be. But you are meant to be a mother, Izzie. Don't say that you would sacrifice that for me. I would spend the rest of my life feeling guilty, and besides, despite what you think right now, you would come to resent me for it."

"I wouldn't. I *wouldn't*. Please, *please*, James. I love you. I love you so much."

She began to sob, heart-wrenching, body-wracking sobs, and he couldn't stand it. He reached for her and pulled her into his lap again, rocking her as he clumsily patted her hair. Oh God, she was ripping him apart with every jerk of her body, every cry that broke from her mouth. He had to make it stop.

So he did the only thing he could think of. In truth, it was the only thing he'd thought of since that night in the library. All he'd thought of in all the long, lonely nights since then. He slipped a hand under her chin and lifted her face to his. She was so beautiful and sweet, even with her face blotchy and her eyes red. And she loved him.

He lowered his head until his lips brushed hers ever so lightly. He heard her small gasp of surprise, felt her body tense. And then she twisted her arms out of the quilt, ran them up into his hair, and dragged his mouth down on hers. It was a kiss filled with desperation, fear, anger, and passion, undeniable passion—passion that clouded his brain and swamped his senses, shutting out everything that existed outside the two of them.

James knew he'd slid into dangerous territory. As he ran his hands over the silken curves of her shoulders, aware to his toes that there were a thousand other silky curves waiting to be discovered, warning bells clanged in his head. But as her tongue skimmed over his bottom lip, she made a little sound of pleasure at the back of her throat, and suddenly he couldn't care that what they were doing was the height of foolishness, if not outright stupidity. Apparently they had come to the right place, because as he lowered her to the floor, James realized why these secluded little buildings were called follies.

She was so weak where he was concerned, it disgusted her. He'd just told her that he wouldn't marry her, and still she wanted him. Wanted him with every fiber of her being, every beat of her heart, every dream in her soul. It was painful, this wanting.

She could tell that he wanted her, too. It was in his kiss. It was in the gentle sweep of his fingertips along her collarbone and in the ragged edge to his breathing. But wanting was different than loving, and it wouldn't make him marry her. She knew it with some sort of feminine instinct. She needed to make him love her, but she wasn't sure she could. There was so much hatred inside of him, so much of the lonely, hurt little boy still lurking beneath the surface he'd worked so hard to make impenetrable.

It scared her, it really did, because she wasn't sure he could ever love her more than he hated his grandfather. And yet she still wanted him—wanted every glorious second fate allowed her to spend in his arms. What that said about her character, she didn't want to know. All she knew was that she wanted James Sheffield. Desperately. She wanted his kisses, the way his arms felt around her, the soft feel of his palms cupping her cheeks, the wildness that he seemed to ignite within her with the barest touch of his hands.

She shivered at the feeling of his lips moving over hers, the warm, solid, utterly masculine taste of him. Everything he did with her, to her, was magical. Perfection. She only wished she could incite the same glorious feelings in him. Not for the first time, Izzie cursed her inexperience. All she had to go on were a couple of kisses, some overheard conversations between the parlor maids, and that book, *Godly Love*, she had stumbled upon in Henry's room. She'd spent sleepless nights imagining James doing some of those wicked things in that book, thoughts that never failed to send little streamers of warmth shooting through her belly. And now she was on her way to making fantasy into reality.

A reality where he had made her no promises, spoken no vows. And she didn't care. That couldn't be good. But being good paled in comparison to the feel of his weight stretched out on top of her body.

He settled more intimately against her, rocking his erection against the place between her thighs. She couldn't hold back the moan that slipped from her lips. He opened the quilt farther, kissing his way down her throat. Izzie held her breath in anticipation as he neared her breasts. He blew a stream of cool air across one, then the other, making her squirm. Then he began to lick—long, lazy circles around the outside of her breasts, nearing but never reaching her nipples, which peaked and pouted for attention.

"James," she begged.

He gave one last, long lick, then lightly bit down on one nipple, tweaking the other with his fingers. She cried out and bucked her hips up into his, overcome with pleasure. The place between her legs was throbbing now, aching for fulfillment. He suckled greedily, first at one breast, then at the other, and Izzie thought she'd die from the sensations rocketing through her.

It was too much and not enough.

It was the library all over again.

And more.

His fingers were burrowing under the quilt, unwrapping her. It seemed her modesty had gone the same way as her good sense, for she wasn't ashamed by his perusal of her body. She took the same delight in learning him, tracing the smooth muscles of his back, curling her fingers in the springy gold hair on his chest.

"Do you still think I don't want you?" he whispered against her ear, before once more claiming her mouth. "I don't seem to have any control with you," he muttered between kisses. "I want you so bloody badly, I'm ready to burst. But you don't have any idea, do you?" he rasped. "You can't begin to understand what it feels like. How I feel I'll die if I can't come inside you."

But she *did* know, Izzie thought. She wanted to tell him, to explain about the empty ache inside of her, but all she could manage was, "Yes." It seemed he understood after all, for he groaned and kissed her, his fingers moving down to the soft thatch between her thighs. *Yes*, she thought, as he traced up and down the wet entrance to her body. He stroked her slowly, gliding his finger up and down the cleft, then swirling it about her wet, aching entrance.

When he finally slipped one long finger inside her, she was beyond speech or thought. She was beyond herself, existing only in some otherworldly realm where sensation ruled. His thumb brushed the hidden bud at the peak of her sex, making her gasp and writhe against his hand.

"You're so tight," he groaned against her lips. He began to work a second finger inside her, stretching her as he rubbed his thumb in circles over the delicate spot where exquisite pleasure blossomed. It was too much; her body felt like a spring wound much too tightly. It was all so new, so fast, so very, very intense. She whimpered and dug her fingers into his shoulders, trying to convey her desperation.

"It's all right," he murmured, kissing her softly upon her temple. "Just trust me."

She did. Foolish though it might be, she trusted him with every part of herself, even her heart. He would probably break it, but it was his all the same—it had been for as many years as she could remember. Just like that, she relaxed, and with one more soft caress, he had her flying over the edge, crying out in pleasure, drowning in bliss.

For one long moment, her breath caught, her heart stopped, and time itself seemed suspended. It was an instant of exquisite peace and utter turmoil, of everything being perfectly right and oh so wrong.

She opened her eyes slowly. Dazed and dreamy, she gazed up at James. Her love. Her lover. A satisfied smile curved her mouth, but it faded when she saw the harsh set of his jaw, the tight line of his mouth. He was kneeling beside her, his palms splayed on his muscular thighs. His eyes were closed tightly and he was breathing hard; it actually looked as if he might be in pain. Concern for him chased away the sleepy languor stealing over her mind and body.

Gathering the quilt back around her, Izzie came up on her knees beside him. She reached out and tentatively rested a hand on one of his. His eyes flew open and he inhaled sharply. She drew back, startled by his fierce expression.

"James? What's wrong? Are you hurt?"

He shook his head. "Sorry," he grunted. "Just . . . give me a minute."

"Oh dear," she fussed.

"I'm not hurt," he ground out.

"You're not?"

"No. At least not in the way you mean."

She bit her lower lip and frowned. "I don't understand."

James drew in a deep breath, obviously preparing to tell her something unpleasant. Tears pricked at her eyes. She had done something wrong, she just knew it. What had been the most beautiful experience of her life had been so distasteful to him that he even hesitated to speak of it.

Her distress must have shown on her face, for he reached out and cupped her cheek in one of his large hands. "You know the way you just felt?" he said. She nodded. "Do you remember how you felt just before that?" She nodded again. "That's how I am feeling right now."

Izzie's eyes dropped to the large bulge tenting his breeches. It certainly looked uncomfortable. She remembered the frantic, nearly painful feelings that had coursed through her right before she had shattered. She wanted to give him that same release, to bind him to her with pleasure, just as he had bound her.

A thought occurred to her, so daring an idea that she felt her cheeks heat. Maybe she could touch him as he had touched her. Before common sense or some latent sense of modesty could intervene, she lunged for the buttons at the front of his breeches.

"Wha—what are you doing?" James choked out, his hands rising to grip her shoulders, effectively stilling her movements.

Izzie focused her gaze somewhere over his right shoulder, unable to meet his eyes. "I thought that, well, maybe I could . . ." She swallowed hard and took a deep breath. "I wanted to touch you the way you touched me," she said in a rush.

"Oh God," James groaned. His hands fell away from her arms and rose to cradle his head. "Oh God!"

Was that a note of eagerness she detected in his voice? The same desperation that had echoed in her pleading cries? Her curiosity had already gotten her into trouble once today. Surely that should be enough of a warning to make her snatch her hands back to her sides. Apparently not, she thought wryly as she watched her hands move, seemingly of their own accord, to slip the buttons from their holes.

His eyes closed and his breathing deepened, quickened, but he made no move to stop her. She felt bold and powerful and wicked, a pirate queen once again. She touched her fingers to his hot flesh, marveling at the way his sex jerked and moved in response. He moaned, a delightful sound, and she stroked him, learning and memorizing the intriguing combination of silk and steel.

"Izzie," he grunted, his head falling back, his arms dropping to brace his palms on the floor.

"Do you like this?" she asked in a sultry tone. At least, she hoped it was a sultry tone. The heroines in the Minerva Press novels always teased men in a sultry tone, and it always brought them to their knees.

Then again, she *had* brought James to his knees, Izzie realized, and she had to fight to suppress a giggle.

He still hadn't answered her question, so she lifted her hand away from him. "I guess you don't like it," she mused innocently.

"No. Yes. I do. Like it. Oh God. Please. Your hands. Touch me again."

She smiled and lightly curled her fingers around him. "What now?"

He didn't answer her, just covered her hand with his and began moving it up and down in a slow rhythm. He spread his knees apart to give her better access and clamped his hands down hard on his thighs. He was entirely in her power, *literally* in her hands.

And she loved it.

Loved that she could pleasure him.

Loved that he was helpless to resist her.

Simply loved him.

His skin was flushed, sweat glistening on his brow as she continued her slow torture. The strangled groans emanating from his throat only fed her excitement. She realized with a start that not all of the sounds were coming from him. The hot flames of his arousal had fed her internal fires, which though recently sated and banked, had come roaring back to life. His hips bucked erratically, thrusting his shaft through the circle of her hands.

His head fell forward as he covered her hand once again with his own, rougher, faster, showing her what he wanted. His face was drawn tight, contorted with pure, harsh need. His knuckles were white where his fingers dug into his thighs, and the corded muscles in his arms bulged with tension.

She felt the primal rhythm echo low in her belly, in the private place where he'd touched her so intimately. Her inner muscles contracted in time with his movements. The small bud he'd caressed began to throb. Her breathing hitched. She was close to that magical place he'd taken her. She could sense it, just out of her reach. She wanted, no *needed* to go there again. She couldn't bear this hovering on the brink, this desperate desire.

Still stroking James, Isabella slipped the fingers of her free hand down between her thighs. Softly, shyly, she touched herself, marveling in the pleasurable sensations that shot through her body. Her hand moved faster, matching his pace, and her urgency grew. Golden streamers of warmth burst and unfurled, racing through her blood, setting her whole body awash with heat. Her eyes closed as, with a little cry, she reached the paradise she'd been striving for.

At her cry, James's entire body went rigid. He knocked her hand away and grabbed a handful of the quilt she was wrapped in. He was up on his knees now, his hips bucking quickly. Izzie gazed in rapt fascination as he covered his sex with the fabric, and then shuddered and thrust once, twice, thrice, before collapsing down on his knees, his breath rushing in and out of his lungs.

His sex was smaller now, she saw with interest. How vulnerable it looked, she thought, lying dormant against his thigh, as though trying to hide in its nest of curly, golden hair. James seemed vulnerable, too. He had come undone, lost control, and she felt a surge of protective tenderness well up in her chest.

She loved him so much, it scared her. He had been quite angry when she had said the words before. But that was before. Surely it would be different this time. It had to be. The words, the emotions, were expanding in her chest, threatening to choke and overwhelm her if she didn't say them.

So she did.

Chapter 9

I overheard my parents arguing about the don's threat to send Henry down from Oxford if his improper behavior does not cease. Sadly, no specifics were mentioned. My father said boys were bound to commit youthful indiscretions. Why, I wonder, does not the same hold true for girls? I daresay the female sex makes up the better half of most of these so-called indiscretions. I find it altogether vexing that I must be a model of discretion, while Henry, by virtue (or lack thereof) of being a male, may do what he likes. I hereby vow (pray do not tell my parents) to indulge in at least one youthful indiscretion to even the score for all womankind!

From the correspondence of Miss Isabella Weston, age fourteen

Letter to her aunt Katherine, Marchioness of Sheldon, on the grave inequalities of gender—April 1792

I love you. How could three small words make him feel so wonderfully alive and yet strike such dread into his heart? She was waiting expectantly and, damn him for the bastard he was, he couldn't give her the words in return. Swallowing past the lump in his throat, James raked a hand through his hair. Dear God, how had things gotten so out of hand? Or rather, how in bloody hell had his thing ended up in her hand?

He felt a slight stirring in his groin and quickly shepherded his thoughts to safer pastures. He didn't want to think about what he'd just done, ever, which was depressing, because it was easily the most damned erotic experience of his entire damned life. But it had been with Isabella, and it had been very, very wrong.

He was surely going to regret it later, once his body had stopped singing the "Hallelujah Chorus." It wasn't lost on him that despite his unwillingness and his flat-out refusal to marry her, he was certainly doing his bloody best to compromise her every chance he got.

He wanted her; that much was certain. But he didn't want to marry her. He didn't want to want her. "Want" wasn't the right word. He couldn't want her. And he couldn't marry her. He was already having enough trouble fighting off the feelings she roused in him, feelings he had buried and sworn off long ago, and marriage would surely send him hurtling over the edge of that cliff. The fall would kill them both.

So he forced himself to ignore the way her bottom lip trembled, to turn away from the sad reproach in her eyes. He said nothing, but rose to his feet and began buttoning his breeches. He listened for a moment and noted with no small bit of relief that the blasted rain had finally stopped.

He strode over to where he had placed their garments before the fire and felt the cloth. His shirt was still slightly damp. James shrugged and pulled it over his head. His jacket and waistcoat were still wet through, but he put them on. Her clothes were in much the same state, and he certainly wasn't taking her back to the house wearing only an old quilt, so he figured he should suffer right along with her. It seemed the gentlemanly thing to do. On further reflection, though, the time and place for gentlemanly behavior was long past.

He held out her gown and undergarments, and then watched in amusement as Isabella, holding the quilt about her as best she could, waddled over and snatched them from his grasp. He turned his back to give her some privacy, also more than a little too late, given what had just transpired. He occupied himself with the miserable business of putting his wet, muddied boots back on, and then stood before the fire. He stared into the swirling orange flames; the logs crackling in the grate provided the only sound in the room—well, aside from the rustling noises of Isabella dressing, but he was trying his damnedest to ignore that.

"Are you still planning on enlisting?"

Her voice seemed unnaturally loud after the long silence, and it startled him. He heard the unasked question: Would you still rather die than marry me?

James hardened his heart against the pain he was about to inflict. She would hate him for this, he knew. He hated himself for what he was about to do, but he had no choice. She deserved more than he could give her. She deserved to be loved with more than just his body, but that wasn't in his power.

"Yes," he said softly, infusing a lifetime of regret into the single syllable. She remained silent. He turned to face her. Her chin was high, her face composed, but he could see her entire body trembling.

"I'm sorry, Izzie. I can't marry you. I wish ..." He stopped himself. Wishes were futile. "I'll leave as soon as arrangements can be made." He refrained from telling her that she would meet someone else, or that she would forget him, though the former, at least, would most certainly come to pass. Of course, if he weren't already dead by that point, James might just have to kill the bounder. He wanted her so damned much. And, selfishly, he didn't want anyone else to have her.

She began to nod so slowly and evenly that he was reminded of an automaton he had once seen on display. Its movements had been similarly precise; its face, equally devoid of expression, had possessed those same haunting eyes that looked but did not see. Damn, damn, damn. He had come to the cottage hoping to make things right with Isabella. Instead, he had all but taken her innocence and, as if that weren't bad enough, he'd had to go and destroy her spirit as well. Perhaps he just ought to admit all that had gone on and let her father and Henry draw straws to shoot him. At the moment, a lead ball seemed less painful than having to watch Izzie move about like a broken doll.

She bent and picked up the quilt from the floor. She began folding it, her motions methodical as she smoothed out the wrinkles and lined up the corners. Abruptly she stopped, her eyes fixated on a spot on the quilt. Her eyes flickered up in his direction as she let out a shuddering breath. His momentary confusion departed in a rush as he recalled, with almost painful clarity, how at the moment he'd been about to climax, he had grabbed the quilt and spilled his seed against it.

Bloody hell. James strode toward Isabella and yanked the quilt out of her hands. He bundled up the sordid proof of his folly and stuffed it into the bottom of the trunk he'd pulled it from. He would come back later to retrieve it. With the aid of a few heavy stones, he planned on finding the offending article a new home at the bottom of the large reflecting lake in front of Sheffield Park.

Isabella said nary a word, simply watching while he straightened the room and banked the fire. She waited until he was finished and then walked to the door. He followed her out, stopping to glance around one last time for any glaring signs of the multitude of sins he'd committed since entering. Everything looked to be in order, however, so he closed the door. He wished it were as easy to walk away from the knowledge of what he'd done, to shut away the mingled memories of bliss and despair that threatened to swamp him.

James focused instead on walking, on putting one foot in front of the other, step after step after step. The fastest route from the folly over to Weston Manor was through the home woods, which meant there wasn't any sort of a path, so he concentrated on the wet leaves and grass underfoot. He devoted himself to spotting mushroom rings and not slipping.

He didn't let himself look ahead, not in theory or in practice, since Isabella was trudging along a bit in front of him. Perhaps it would have been better if he had allowed himself to look, he would later reason, since he might have seen the large tree root sticking out of the ground several feet ahead.

The large tree root several feet ahead that was directly in Isabella's path.

The large tree root sticking out of the ground that sent Isabella sprawling.

At her choked cry, James jerked his head up. He saw her fly through the air and land hard on the ground. He ran to her side, nearly tripping on the same root, and turned her onto her back. Her eyes fluttered open and she let out a little moan, and he remembered to breathe. Gathering her up in his arms, he began to feel for broken bones.

"Where does it hurt?" he asked.

Isabella shrugged and tears began to seep from beneath her lashes. He supposed that meant she hurt everywhere. Her face was pale, too pale, and there was a nasty scratch along her right cheekbone. She flinched when he touched her left wrist, and her whole body jerked when he probed her right ankle through the thin kid leather of her boot, soaked through with mud and rain. James rose, holding her tightly to him, and began to walk as quickly as he could while remaining sure of his footing.

Isabella wasn't heavy by any means, but by the time the honey-colored brick walls of Weston Manor came into view, James felt ready to collapse. Isabella was hurt and shivering, his wet garments were chafing him in places he really didn't want to be chafed, and his guilty conscience had had just about all it could take for one day. Clutching Isabella more firmly to his chest, he bounded up the stone steps leading into the formal garden; moments later, he hurried up a second set of stairs that led to the balcony.

Shifting Isabella's weight to one arm, he rapped on the glass panes of one of the doors that led from the great hall out to the balcony. Inside, a maid caught sight of James and his burden, and her eyes widened in alarm as she hastened over to let them in.

"She's all right," James told the frightened girl, "but she's had a fall. Have the doctor fetched."

"James, is that you?" Lady Weston's voice sounded from the neighboring parlor.

"Yes," he called out, "but let me just warn you—"

She swept into the room and her face blanched.

"There's been a bit of an accident."

"What happened?" she gasped.

"Izzie tripped when we were walking back. She may have broken her wrist, and her ankle twisted when she fell. It's possible that she hit her head, but I think she's just fainted from the combination of pain and cold. I've already told someone to send for the doctor."

Lady Weston stepped forward and laid a trembling hand on her daughter's damp head. Then she composed herself, once more the mistress of the house briskly taking charge. "First, we need to get both of you out of those wet clothes."

James swallowed hard. Those words, that sentiment, the idea of getting Isabella out of her clothes—that had been the point of no return. He sighed. Hindsight was ever perfect.

"Shall I call a footman to carry her up to her bedchamber?" Lady Weston asked. "You must be exhausted."

"I'll take her up." He was almost certainly never going to hold her in his arms again, and he would be damned if he'd let a footman take these last moments away from him.

"That would probably be best. Her new room is on the third floor, at the opposite end of the corridor from Henry's room. I'll be there in a moment. The maids should have already built up the fire in the bedchamber. I must tell Oliver that you've returned. He was about to go after you himself."

"I tried to get her to return with me to the house straight away, but . . ."

Lady Weston's lips turned up slightly. "I would imagine she was feeling less than receptive to you after"—she waved her hands about—"after what happened."

He shifted uneasily. "Look, I—"

She shook her head. "You don't have to explain," she said. "Not to me." She gave him a teary smile. "Although I had hoped you would be my son by marriage, I want you to know that, no matter what happens, you will always remain a son in my heart." She dabbed at her eyes. "Go on with you now. I'll be up as soon as I've spoken with Oliver."

James's eyes stung. He had braced himself for anger and recriminations, and instead had been met with understanding and unconditional love, neither of which he particularly felt he deserved. Now he was swamped with even more guilt and regret, and he had been doing magnificently well in accumulating those on his own.

He sighed again and headed for the stairs. As soon as Izzie was settled, he would head back to Sheffield Park and get warm and dry. On the morrow, he would pack for London and get about the business of leaving this all behind him. He would be gone within the week, and given the state of the war, with the bloody Dutch joining the Frogs and the damned Spaniards likely to do the same, he would be lucky to ever again set foot on English soil. Amendment: When he returned to Sheffield Park, he was going to get warm, dry, and roaring drunk.

He opened the door to her room and strode over to the bed, where he eased Isabella out of his arms and gently laid her down. He rubbed his thumb over her cheek and then leaned down to press a soft kiss upon her lips. Her eyes fluttered open just like a princess in a fairy tale. She smiled dreamily, but then looked about in confusion.

"James?"

"You fainted," he told her, "but you are going to be fine, just fine." He took a step away from the bed. He needed to get out of there. He couldn't face Lord Weston—not now, not yet. Hell, with the knowledge of Isabella's lush body branded on his mind, he wasn't sure he would ever be able to face him. Thank God Henry was away, on a hunting trip in Scotland. "The doctor has been sent for, and your mother will be here any moment and—"

"James?" she said again, fully awake now, her big blue eyes beseeching him, begging him to tell her that it had all been a bad dream. Lord knew, he wished he could. Swallowing past the lump in his throat, he bent and placed a last, light kiss on her temple, taking a moment to memorize the softness of her skin against his lips, the way she smelled so sweetly of honeysuckle.

"Good-bye, Izzie," he said. She closed her eyes, and he knew she had heard the awful note of finality in his voice. He turned and quit the room, heading for the servants' staircase. Saints be praised, he escaped undetected and made it back to Sheffield Park without further incident. It was, he noted, the first bloody thing that had gone right all day.

The sound of voices trickled into her consciousness, causing Isabella to stir restlessly. As she moved slowly through that dreamy state between sleeping and waking, three things became apparent. The first was that she hurt. Badly. And all over. She had never taken a beating, but Izzie was sure this was what it must feel like. Second, her left hand was rather alarmingly and uncomfortably wet, and she wasn't altogether sure she wanted to know the reason. Third, at least two of her sisters were in the room.

Izzie opened her eyes, shut them, and opened them again. She blinked rapidly to dispel the double image hovering above her face.

"Is she awake?" one of the faces asked.

"Her eyes are open, aren't they?" the other face retorted.

"Well, yes, but she doesn't *look* awake."

"Have *you* ever slept with *your* eyes open?"

"How would I *know*, if I was *asleep*?"

Izzie groaned as she realized the double image was really the identical faces of her sisters, Cordelia and Imogen. While she was relieved that she was not, in fact, seeing double, the sound of Lia and Genni's bickering was beginning to make her head throb. She turned her head slightly and found the cause of her wet hand. Portia was seated on the bed beside her, her right hand holding Izzie's, her left smashed up against her face. Portia enjoyed sucking on the bottom two fingers of her hand, which left the other three jockeying for space on her tiny face.

Izzie watched, in a sort of disgusted resignation, as Portia removed her fingers from her mouth and reached down to lovingly pat Isabella's hand. It probably meant she was a wretched person, but Isabella was less than comforted by the gesture. As sweet as the intent may have been, the end result still left her hand covered in toddler slobber. Ugh.

"Mama, she's a-wa-ake!" Lia trilled in the hallway outside of the bedchamber. Izzie groaned again. Her mother tended to be a bit, well, overenthusiastic when it came to the sickroom.

"Darling!" Her mother entered the room and dropped a kiss on Isabella's forehead. Olivia trailed in behind her. "How are you feeling?"

Izzie groaned. It seemed to be the only thing she was capable of.

Her mother frowned. "That bad? The doctor told us that you had some bruising where you fell, and that your ankle would be painful for a few days, but he seemed to think that once you were warm and dry, you would feel much better."

"James?" Isabella croaked.

Her mother glanced around, noticing the number of faces gazing up at her expectantly. "Lia, Genni, I'm sure Mrs. Daniels must be wondering where you are. Olivia, why don't you take Portia up to the nursery?"

A chorus of protests rang out, but under their mother's unrelenting gaze, they slowly shuffled out of the room.

Her mother closed the door behind them and came to perch beside Isabella on the bed. "We'll have to speak quietly," she said softly, "since we both know they're all huddled out in the hallway, their ears pressed to the door."

Isabella nodded, smiling a little because she knew it

would make her mother feel better. "Where's James?" she asked. Her voice sounded scratchy, as though it hadn't been used in a long time and needed oiling to work properly again.

Her mother seemed to read her mind, for she got up and poured a glass of water from the carafe on Isabella's nightstand. She helped Isabella sit up in bed, clucking sympathetically each time a little gasp of pain escaped from Izzie's mouth. "My poor baby," she murmured.

Izzie's eyes narrowed. Was her mother referring to bodily aches or those of the heart? Both, she supposed. It was too much to hope that her father would have kept the day's humiliating events to himself. And *where* was James?

She must have voiced the question aloud, for her mother responded, "He sneaked out while I was informing your father that the two of you had returned. I am certain it was only the lure of dry clothing that drew him from your side." Her mother smiled, trying to infuse the words with a cheerful matter-of-factness, but it rang false.

"He's gone, then," Isabella stated woodenly.

"Oh, darling, he'll be back."

"No, Mama, he won't. He—he doesn't love me. He's going to join the army. He said he was going to leave as soon as he could. He would—" She swallowed painfully over the knot of unshed tears closing her throat. "He would rather die than marry me."

Saying the words aloud, acknowledging their truth, sent a wave of grief crashing over her—one strong enough to break the dam. She crawled closer to her mother and wept brokenly, fitting her head against that perfect niche below her mother's shoulder, the spot that seemed designed to comfort all manner of aches and pains. When Isabella was a child, her mother's touch had gently soothed scrapes and bruises; her soft kiss had always promised that she would make everything all right.

When she had finally cried herself out, she lay back in her bed, eyes closed, exhausted to her very bones. The hurt in her body paled in comparison to the ache in her heart, a physical, stabbing pain in the center of her chest. Her mother drew the covers up over her, pressed a light kiss to her forehead, and quietly left the room. As she listened to the silence, Isabella realized some wounds were too deep to be healed by a mother's magic; some situations could not be made right. And the tears she had thought were done began anew.

Chapter 10

*I truly cannot see what the fuss is about kissing!
Yesterday, as I was waiting for my mare to be saddled, one of the stable hands stole a kiss. I probably
should have told Aunt Kate, but in all truth I encour-
aged him because I wanted to know what it was like. I
must say I am sorely disappointed. It seems an unap-
pealing, messy sort of business. It is not the least bit
like what Mrs. Deerehart wrote of in* The Downfall of
the Devilish Duke. *I declare, I do not know whether
to call the woman out as a bald-faced liar, recom-
mend her for Bedlam, or praise her for having such
an extraordinarily vivid imagination!*

From the correspondence of Miss Isabella Weston,
age fifteen

Letter to her sister, Miss Olivia Weston, on the false information imparted by a certain authoress of gothic romance,
much to the sender's disappointment—July 1793

"I hope you don't feel as terrible as you look," Olivia said
when Isabella awoke the next morning.

Izzie turned her head to glare at her sister who had
pulled a chair up beside the bed. She grimaced at the bright
light streaming in through the windows—windows that
would, were it not for her sister, still be covered by heavy
drapes.

"Couldn't you do that"—she gestured to the embroidery in Olivia's lap—"somewhere else?"

"I could," her sister agreed, "but it would be difficult for you to talk to me if I were in another room."

"Since I am not planning on talking to you, there shouldn't be a problem," Isabella said through clenched teeth.

"I really think you should reconsider," Olivia said, bending down to rummage through her sewing basket. She straightened up, a triumphant smile on her face. "I have *news*," she declared, waving about a piece of green embroidery floss.

"One should really consider getting out more," Isabella commented, "when one begins to find a new piece of needlework newsworthy."

Olivia made a sound of pure exasperation. "If I weren't such a good, loving sister—"

Isabella snorted.

Olivia ignored her. "I would get up and leave."

"An excellent idea," Isabella added.

"And then you wouldn't hear the news I have so patiently waited to tell you."

Isabella rolled her eyes. "The news about your embroidery?"

"The news about *James*." Olivia smiled smugly as Isabella bolted upright in bed.

"James! Oh, why didn't you say something sooner?" She held up a hand. "Wait. I know—I didn't ask, right? Well, come on now, out with it."

Olivia began to speak, and then paused thoughtfully. Isabella suppressed the urge to climb out of bed and shake the words from her sister's mouth.

"Livvy!" she barked.

"I'm just trying to figure out the best way to tell you so that you don't get all in a tizzy. Mother said I was not to upset you."

"Not to upset—" Isabella's heart slammed into the wall of her chest and dropped to her stomach. "He's gone," she whispered. All the energy, all the life flowing through her body seemed to vanish, and she shakily sank back against the pillows.

"Gone?" Olivia said in a puzzled tone. Then she laughed. "My word, Izzie, he's not *that* sick. Wait, who told you—"

"He's *sick*?"

"Not everybody has your hardy constitution." Olivia gave a delicate sniff.

"He's sick," Isabella repeated softly to herself. "How positively perfect!"

Olivia eyed her curiously. "That isn't the sentiment one usually expresses upon hearing that another has taken ill."

"But if he is sick," Isabella explained, "he cannot leave. He *is* ill enough to be confined to his bed, isn't he?"

Olivia nodded. "I had it from Mother, who had it from Mrs. Kent, who had it from her nephew who is a groom over at Sheffield Park, who had it from one of the housemaids that James is terribly fevered."

Isabella was tempted to remark that, as of late, "fevered" seemed to be his natural state, but she restrained herself.

"Apparently," Olivia went on, "he keeps raving about having to drown a quilt."

At the mention of the quilt, a tiny gasp escaped from Isabella's mouth. Fortunately, Olivia seemed not to notice.

Her sister continued. "It would be comical if it weren't so serious. So, what do you know about this quilt?"

Drat. Olivia had always been too observant for her own good.

"What quilt?" Isabella asked innocently, even as she felt her cheeks heat.

"Oooh, you're blushing!" Olivia gushed. She shoved her embroidery into the basket and climbed onto the bed. "Isabella Anne Weston, you tell me what is going on right this instant or . . ."

"Or what?"

Olivia exhaled through clenched teeth. "Whatever it is, I promise you won't like it," she ground out.

As a threat, it fell a bit short, but what her sister lacked in terms of punitive creativity, she more than made up for with tenacity. No dog with his proverbial bone could ever live up to the reality of Olivia Jane Weston when it came to private information. In less than a half hour, her sister had wormed the entire story out of Isabella. Well, not the *entire* story, of course, but rather a judiciously edited version of the story—one that made no mention of certain, er, activities involving quilts and only a very limited mention of library sorts of behavior.

"I still can't believe he kissed you," Olivia remarked once Isabella was through.

"Livvy!"

"Sorry, I didn't mean that the way it sounded."

"In any case," Isabella pointed out, "*I* was the one who kissed *him.*"

"Was it enjoyable?"

"Um, er, well . . ." *Enjoyable?* It had been mind-numbingly, earth-shatteringly pleasurable. Just the memory of it was enough to cause her nipples to tighten into small, hard buds, plainly visible through the thin lawn of her nightgown. She shivered and quickly pulled the covers up in front of her chest.

"Did your knees go weak?" Olivia breathed, her sapphire eyes glimmering with excitement. "Did your heart flutter and your insides get all quivery as in novels?"

Izzie grinned widely and nodded. "It was even better."

Olivia clapped her hands in delight, and then abruptly sobered. "What are you going to do?"

"What do you mean?"

"Well, you can't just let him leave!"

"What choice do I have?" Isabella asked wearily. "He refuses to marry me, or any other woman, and he is too proud to accept any sort of charity, however well intentioned, so he must find himself a source of income. For gentlemen of his station, the only respectable option is to join the clergy—or the army."

"The church does seem an unlikely choice," Olivia agreed, "but if he enlists . . ."

"He could die," Isabella finished. The thought took the form of icy fingers, wrapping themselves around her heart, squeezing and clawing, freezing her from the inside. She began to shake. "Oh dear God, Livvy, I don't think I could bear it."

"Izzie!" Olivia gripped her shoulders. "He is *not* going to die."

"He might," she choked out.

"No," Olivia said forcefully, "he won't."

"But how can you be sure?"

"Because we are going to eliminate the need for him to join the army in the first place."

Isabella stared blankly at her.

Olivia sighed. "We are going to make sure he marries you instead. Then his inheritance, and his life, will be safe. Now, what we need is a plan." She tapped her fingers against her chin. "Do you remember Emilia and Jordan?"

"From *The Mysterious Enchantress of Castle Clermont*? The one where she . . . where he . . . But, Livvy, this is real life. It isn't a Minerva Press novel."

"You're right." Olivia gave her a sly look and winked. "It's even *better.*"

As she shimmied down the tree outside her window two days later, Isabella reflected that this just might be the most idiotic thing she had ever done—not climbing down the tree, since she had done that hundreds of times without getting seriously injured or tearing up her clothes, parents and nursemaids none the wiser. She wasn't concerned about navigating her way down from her second-story window. She wasn't even worried about getting back up, although that task certainly required more effort than the former. No, trees had nothing to do with the reason Isabella was questioning her sanity. A certain man named James Sheffield and a certain plot devised by a certain sister, on the other hand, had everything to do with it.

It couldn't be put off any longer, though, since Olivia's chain of informants had reported that, as of today, James was no longer abed, ignoring the doctor's recommendation that he stay there for at least a week. How typically and odiously *male*! Even though James wasn't fully recovered, Isabella had no doubt that he was planning on leaving at the soonest possible opportunity. So here she was, on her way to the seduction.

As she stealthily made her way to the stable and slipped a bridle onto Blossom, her little sorrel mare, Isabella wondered what on earth had possessed her to think that *she* of all people could pull off a seduction? And even if she could pull it off, and that was a very big "if," why on earth was she doing this? *Because you love James*, she told herself. *And in any case, you certainly don't want him going off to war and getting killed because of you!*

She was doing this for him. To save him. Oh, all right, she was lying to herself—or she wasn't being totally honest. She wanted to save James Sheffield, but she also wanted to make love with him. Just plain wanted him.

Isabella's mare stumbled, jarring her out of her reverie. She blinked as she realized she was already on Sheffield land. She shook her head. It was imperative that she keep her wits about her tonight. She had only one chance—one night—in which to succeed. Failure meant the possibility of James perishing on some desolate, bloody battlefield. Failure meant forsaking all of her dreams for the future. Failure meant—no, she wouldn't let herself think about failure. It simply wasn't an option.

She located a small copse of trees where she could tether Blossom out of sight and dug some lumps of sugar out of her pocket. She patted the mare's velvety nose and made for the house, ignoring the occasional twinge in her ankle. She heaved a sigh of relief on seeing that the window to the library had only been partially shut; she truly had no idea how to go about this breaking and entering business.

And really, she thought peevishly, it wasn't as if she had been given a great deal of time in which to formulate a plan. Of course, in all honesty, it had been Olivia who had devised tonight's escapade. Isabella had never been much good at making plans. She had always been more bold, more brash, more impulsive—the one who tagged along on the boys' adventures. But *this*, she thought, grinning ruefully as she hiked her skirts above her knees and clambered over the windowsill, this was outrageous, even for her.

She tiptoed across the room, grateful for the thick Aubusson rugs covering the floor. Isabella held her breath as she slowly eased the door open and silently blessed Mrs. Benton, the housekeeper at Sheffield Park since the dawning of time, for the silence of the well-oiled hinges. Her eyes rapidly adjusting to the darkness, Isabella peered out into the hallway, glancing furtively to her left and right. Once she was satisfied that she was in no immediate danger of being discovered, she hurried down the hallway, heading for the front stairs.

Although they were closer, she didn't dare go up the back stairs. Mrs. Benton's room was right next to the top of the servants' stairs and, despite her advanced age, the woman's hearing was as acute as ever. And, to use one of her mother's favorite phrases, it simply wouldn't do to be discovered skulking about Sheffield Park in the middle of the night. Why, any number of indecent conjectures might be drawn! And most of them would be right, she thought, fighting back a nervous giggle.

Glancing at the wide marble stairs, Isabella gave a sigh and slipped off her shoes and stockings. She bit her lip as her bare feet came in contact with the freezing cold stone, but the marble was too polished and slippery looking to risk keeping her stockings on. Someday, she thought as she hurried up the stairs, she would make James pay for the hardships she was currently suffering on his behalf. She reached the top without incident and hurried toward the east wing, where James's apartments lay. Finally she stood in front of the door to his bedchamber. Her heart was pounding wildly in her chest as the reality of what she was planning finally hit her.

Scenarios began flashing through her mind, each more horrible than the next. Isabella had already accepted that

James would be furious with her plan, but what if he was so angry that she couldn't seduce him? It wasn't as if she were some great seductress, though the past week had significantly broadened her knowledge. It was crucial for him to deflower her, though. If he took her virginity, he *would* marry her. She and Olivia had agreed on that. It was part of the code of honor he lived by as an English gentleman. But she had to get him to ruin her, and what if . . . What if . . .

What if the door was locked? She hadn't considered that scenario. If his door was locked, there wasn't really anything she could do. She was fairly sure she couldn't break down the thick oak door, and even if she could, she certainly couldn't do it silently. And, she rationalized, even if his window *was* open, it wasn't as if she could reach it. Not unless she suddenly sprouted wings or a magic beanstalk appeared, both of which she thought highly unlikely. No, it all depended on the door, on whether or not it was locked.

She drew in a deep breath and stared at the brass knob. There was only one way to find out, she supposed, and there was no time like the present. She wiped her sweaty palm against her skirts and grasped the cool metal in her hand. It was now or never. As if fate had decided it long ago, the knob turned effortlessly and the door swung inward.

Isabella crept forward into the room, lit only by the softly flickering flames of the dying fire. And there, on the bed, she beheld such a sight that her heart, which had been racing and pounding all evening, seemed to stop in her chest. Her entire body sighed, causing her shoes and stockings to slip from her hands.

James was sprawled on his stomach, the sheet tangled and twisted down by his feet, the amber glow of the fire gilding every glorious nude inch of him. Isabella thought she had never seen anything so beautiful in her entire life. He looked like a Greek statue, but those were marble, cold, and untouchable. In contrast, the man before her was alive and warm and oh so touchable.

She wanted to hurl herself on top of him, feel his body pressed against hers, see if he was really as delicious as he looked. James, delicious? She wasn't sure where the thought had come from, but yes, yes, yes, she wanted to kiss him all over, not just his wonderful mouth, and maybe, just maybe, she wanted to bite the spot where the strong column of his neck met the muscled curve of his shoulder. She wanted to *bite* him? A nervous giggle escaped her. Oh dear, she had shocked herself a bit with that one.

She moved closer to the bed and was struck by the sweet, golden smell of brandy lingering in the air. She glanced at the bedside table, noting with displeasure the mostly empty decanter. Apparently someone had been self-medicating.

Come to think of it, perhaps the brandy wasn't a bad idea. In the novels, men always fortified themselves with spirits before engaging in activities that risked life and limb. Not that she was risking either, but then again, a woman's reputation was worth at least as much as a gentleman's limbs. With that logic, Isabella went forward and picked up the crystal decanter, but there didn't appear to be any sort of glass around. Shrugging her shoulders, she lifted the decanter and took a large swallow.

It was, without question, the vilest thing she had ever tasted. She spit about half the liquid down the front of her gown, and gagged and choked on the rest. Her eyes watering, she carefully set the brandy back on the table before sinking to the floor, clutching her stomach. She looked over at James, relieved to see that he was still sleeping soundly. Heavens above, how did gentlemen manage to consume such vast quantities of that devil's brew? Although, she had to admit it wasn't so bad now that the brandy's fiery trail was heating her from the inside out.

Perhaps she ought to try another small sip. She reached out, snagged the decanter off the table, and tilted her head back for a second attempt. It wasn't half bad, she realized, resting the decanter in her lap. It still made her eyes tear up, but it was a small price to pay for the lovely, tingling warmth spreading through her body. How much brandy did one need to drink before one's nerves were fortified? Isabella wondered. She took another little sip and learned that if she held her breath, she could hardly taste it. Much better.

An unknown number of sips later, Isabella set the decanter aside. For one thing, it was empty, though, for the life of her, she could not figure out where it had all gone. For another thing, the room had become unbearably hot. She clambered to her feet, pausing as the room swayed before her, and fanned at her cheeks. It really was overly warm, she thought. And suddenly it seemed the best idea in the world to take her gown off. Then she wouldn't be so wretchedly overheated and, she realized with great glee, it would be an excellent way to begin her seduction.

Olivia had advised her to wear a simple gown that was easy to remove, a statement which, coming from the lips of a younger sister, had made Isabella hideously embarrassed, but it turned out to be a very wise decision since her fingers didn't seem to be working at all properly. After spending the better portion of five minutes fumbling with the three buttons marching down the front of her bodice, Isabella was finally able to wriggle the gown off. As she had eschewed wearing a corset, her chemise was next to come off. She tossed it to join her gown on the floor, leaving her most shockingly unclothed and most shockingly unconcerned about being so.

Loosening her hair from its plait, Isabella danced her way over to the bed. She climbed up and slid herself under the sheets James had pushed aside, delighting in the slide of the cool linens against her naked limbs. Seduction, she decided, felt marvelously decadent. And there was so much more to come. . . .

Chapter 11

At the theater last night, Lord Voxley's antics proved the more interesting performance. The man was so drunk, he clambered out of his box and swung from the curtains, bellowing and beating at his chest like a baboon. Sadly, however, Lord Voxley's rather substantial weight overpowered the poor curtains, and all went tumbling into the crowd below. Fortunately, no one was hurt, but I have realized that people act most ridiculously when intoxicated. By people I mean men, of course, for women are either too sensible to imbibe heavily or wise enough to do so in private. Whatever larks you get up to, I hope you drink in moderation and thus avoid such simian behavior.

From the correspondence of Miss Isabella Weston, age sixteen

Letter to her brother, Henry Weston, on the importance of temperance with regard to alcoholic beverages—May 1794

James Sheffield was foxed. Truth be told, he was more than foxed. Courtesy of the decanter of brandy he'd had the excellent foresight to stash in the bottom drawer of his armoire, he was three sheets to the wind, higher than a fiddler's fist, thumped over the head with Sampson's jawbone—in short, stinking drunk. He was not so drunk, however, that he didn't hear Isabella's voice softly calling his name.

Nor was he so drunk that the sound of her husky whisper failed to bring him to aching, instant attention. He *was* drunk enough that he didn't really question her being in his bedroom, in the middle of the night. Ever since the night of her ball, Isabella visited him nightly in his dreams and indulged him in every hot-blooded, erotic fantasy his degenerate mind could conjure up.

He pushed himself up, propping his head in the palm of his hand, the simple motion enough to make him dizzy. When his sight cleared, he beheld the breathtaking sight of Isabella lying beside him in the bed—an excellent beginning to what promised to be an even more excellent dream.

He stretched out his free arm and wrapped a finger in one of the silky curls draped over her bare shoulder. "I was waiting for you," he murmured.

"You were?" Her pale brows drew together, making her look quite adorably befuddled.

"Sometimes it feels as though I have been waiting for you my entire life."

She sighed and her eyes grew teary. "You must know I have loved you forever," she whispered.

James nodded, able to accept in dreams the truths far too troublesome to be examined in the light of day. He gazed at her, willing himself to memorize her as she was in that moment, soft and loving and *his*. A fantasy she might be, but this exquisite product of his frustrated imagination was all he had to sustain him through a lifetime of lonely nights. A wiser man would refuse her. Why torture himself with these teasing visions that could never come true? But when it came to Isabella Weston, James wasn't particularly wise. Not even in his dreams. He wouldn't—couldn't—completely give her up. Not now, not ever.

"I want to love you *now*," he told her, sliding his fingers down her shoulder to tug at the sheet she had tucked beneath her arms. She caught her lower lip between her teeth, and for a moment she looked as if she would refuse. How fortunate then, that this was *his* dream. As if on cue, Isabella's arms relaxed, allowing the sheet to slither down below her ribs. His hand glided down, the backs of his fingers trailing over the soft curve of her breast. She trembled at his touch, and the knowledge sent a primitive thrill coursing through his veins. But he needed more.

"Come closer," he urged. Although she looked a bit wary, his dream Isabella complied again, scooting over in the bed, closer and closer, until the honeysuckle smell of her hair tickled his nose. As soon as she was within reach, James snaked an arm about her rib cage, pulling her down until she was flat on her back in the bed. The movement, he noted with delight, had also pulled the sheet down to just below her navel. It was a pity she hadn't lost it completely, but perhaps that was all for the best. He wasn't ready to take her yet, not nearly ready to end the fantasy, but it was becoming difficult to control his body's demands.

Need spurred him, urged him to dispense with the bloody sheet and bury himself inside her. To take her hard and fast, then slow and gentle. To lick his way down her body, claim her with his mouth, and drink the musky sweetness of her. He drew in an unsteady breath, reminding himself that there was no rush. She was his until dawn, and he didn't plan on squandering a single moment.

Bracing himself on one forearm, James slid his other hand behind her nape, holding her captive for his kiss. He delved hungrily into the hot cavern of her mouth, recklessly plundering, enthralled and enflamed by her immediate, ardent response. He couldn't get enough of her. He wanted to swallow her whole, to make her a part of himself, to fuse and merge with her in every way possible for a man and a woman. . . . But he was getting ahead of himself again.

Closing his eyes, James began to nibble his way slowly down her neck, savoring the sound of her breathy pants, the salty-sweet softness of her skin, the way she hummed in her throat, purring like a cat, to convey her pleasure. His hand moved, seemingly of its own accord, to settle over one of her breasts. He didn't do anything, but simply held his hand there, letting the heat from his skin transfer to hers and enjoying the feel of her. Her nipple rose up against his palm, and his hand closed reflexively, squeezing gently, wringing a gasp from her lips.

He lifted his head and opened his eyes, grinning wickedly up at her. Then his gaze lowered and his smile fell away, banished by a sweeping surge of lust. He swallowed hard. Truly, she had the most magnificent breasts. They were glorious, even more beautiful than he remembered, and he was sure he had memorized these particular breasts in exquisite, exacting detail—their shape, their weight, their taste—but perhaps he needed reminding.

James lowered his head to her breast. He blew a cool stream of air over the tip, watching the already-puckered nipple draw itself into a tighter, rosy bud.

"James," she pleaded, arching her back, offering herself to him.

"Is this what you want, Izzie?" He drew her breast into his mouth, suckling lightly, then harder, faster at the sound of her moans. Her hands clenched in his hair, holding his head against her—an unnecessary gesture given that he had no particular inclination to move, except to lavish the same attention on her other breast.

He bit and licked and sucked, harnessing his own desire, determined to tease her until she was suffering as he was. Her hands moved down to clutch at his shoulders, trying to draw him over her. He chuckled, sliding his mouth down over her ribs. He wasn't finished tormenting her—not even close.

He reached underneath the sheet, seeking out the soft thatch of hair nestled between her thighs. Her hips jerked as his fingers sifted through her hot, damp folds. Knowing that she was wet and ready for him nearly sent him over the edge. The urge to simply sink into her and thrust himself home had him gritting his teeth, but he knew he wouldn't be totally satisfied until he gave her pleasure—soul-shattering pleasure that would chain her to him forever, ruin her for any other man. That was another nice thing about dreams—a man could be incredibly selfish and not feel the slightest bit of remorse.

Grinning, James felt out the little nubbin of pleasure at the top of her sex and was rewarded with a long, low moan, and he would be damned if that wasn't the sexiest, most erotic sound he had ever heard. He kept his hand there, teasing her with occasional feathery strokes as he worked his way down her body with his mouth, paying homage to every pale freckle, worshipping every inch of her flesh with agonizing slowness. She writhed beneath him when he swirled his tongue into the delicate indentation of her navel, her fingers digging into his shoulders.

When he finally replaced his hand with his mouth, her whole body tensed. She began to protest, but the words turned into breathy cries and throaty pleas. *She wanted more. She couldn't possibly take any more. She never wanted him to stop. He had to stop, or she would die.* Then she was heaving and panting, beyond words, but he continued to hold her hips steady—continued to lick her, to lap up her sweet essence, to thrust his tongue inside her as a hint of pleasures to come.

Her fingers changed into claws that scratched at any part of his flesh she could reach. He had unleashed a wildcat in heat, and the knowledge was incredibly arousing, almost unbearably so. He was so hard, so achingly close, that every moment he denied himself release he remained precariously balanced on that fine, fine line between pleasure and pain. Delicious as the torture was, he had to agree with her. He didn't think he could take much more.

He reached up with his left hand to squeeze and knead her breasts, tweaking and tugging at her nipples. He settled his mouth over the apex of her sex and began suckling strongly as, with his right hand, he thrust two fingers into her waiting passage. Her response was instantaneous. She cried out, arching her back in the air and digging her heels into the mattress, as he felt her inner muscles contract rhythmically, clamping down almost painfully as he eased his fingers out of her.

James had meant to bring her down slowly, but he couldn't wait, not even a second longer. Kissing her with a kind of savage desperation, he spread her thighs and slowly entered her. Although he had readied her as best he could, she was still unbelievably small and tight, though he could feel her body stretching to accommodate him. He caressed her breasts, and she shuddered and convulsed around him. The sensation, exquisite beyond bearing, sent him over the edge. With a primitive cry of triumph and possession, he drove forward, sheathing himself to the hilt.

It was the salty taste of her tears, which had run down her face to mingle with their kiss, that finally jolted James out of his sensual fog. Tears had never played a part in his dreams of Isabella, which meant . . . No. It couldn't be. It wasn't possible. He blinked slowly, shaking his head in confusion, trying to come to terms with the situation. He hadn't been dreaming. This wasn't a damned dream. It was real, and it still reeked of damnation. Isabella, his best friend's little sister, was in his bedchamber—in his bloody bed, actually—and, dear God, he was still inside her.

The blood that had temporarily returned to his head raced back down south. With it disappeared all thoughts of little sisters, best friends, and the burning fires of hell. All that mattered was the incredible feeling of being gripped by Isabella's hot, tight passage.

Just like that, James knew it was all over for him. He thrust once, twice, and then he shattered. He threw his head back as he jerked and heaved and poured himself into her. Utterly spent, he collapsed on top of her, struggling to draw air into his lungs, sated and exhausted by the most explosive climax of his life. And then reality intruded. Again.

"Izzie?"

"Yes?" she said hesitantly.

She was right to be hesitant, James thought. In fact, she should be bloody terrified. He took no small amount of pride in his ability to keep his voice to a low roar as he demanded, "Would you care to tell me what the devil is going on here?"

He couldn't have been any more desperate to get away, thought Isabella, if she had announced she had leprosy. She anxiously bit her lip as James, completely unconcerned by his nudity, leapt out of bed and threw back the covers. The white linen was stained with a spot of crimson, a single red petal against a snowy field. Sacrifice always demanded blood, she recalled. Not that the lovemaking had been a sacrifice, far from it, but the aftermath ... She had expected that he would be angry—indeed, how could he not be?— but it hurt all the same. Somewhere, deep in her heart of hearts, she had cherished the hope that he secretly loved her. . . .

James turned from the bed and strode into the dressing room attached to his chamber. "Get dressed," he called out. His voice was emotionless, chillingly so.

Isabella scrambled off the bed, taking the sheet with her, but instead of reaching for her gown, she followed him. She waddled across the room, stopping in the antechamber's open door frame. He had already put on his breeches and was pulling on his shirt with tight, sharp motions. He certainly didn't look in the mood to talk, but she had to at least try. She drew in a deep breath and said a silent prayer.

"James, I . . . Let me explain."

"There is nothing to explain."

"But—"

"But what?" He turned on her, his blazing eyes revealing the heat of his fury. "You knew how I felt about this, about marriage. You knew, and yet you came here, blatantly disregarding my wishes in service of your own."

"No, please, it wasn't like that. I just wanted—"

"Exactly. *You* wanted. *You*. What I wanted meant nothing." He turned away from her and began to jerk on his boots.

"I couldn't let you die," she whispered brokenly.

He straightened and faced her, shaking his head. "Noble

intentions, my dear," he drawled, "but it wasn't your decision to make. I told you long ago not to try to 'save' me." He gestured toward the bedroom. "I presume you don't need me to act as your lady's maid. You seemed to have no trouble getting out of your gown unaided."

Though every instinct rallied for a fight, Isabella forced herself to retreat. He was too angry to listen to anything she had to say. And he had every right to be angry. She had meddled in his life. She dressed herself quickly—well, as quickly as she could, given that she was attempting to keep herself covered with the quilt. Fortunately, she had herself clothed by the time he emerged from his dressing room. It was most unfair, though, that he was exquisitely attired while she—Isabella glanced down at herself—looked like a rumpled mess.

"Let's go." He gestured to the door.

"Are you taking me home? You needn't. Really. I tethered Blossom just out of sight of the house. I can get back in through the window."

"We are going to announce our engagement," he said.

Isabella nodded. "Yes, but we can do that tomorrow. I suppose you should arrange to have the banns read, but I can do it, if you would prefer."

"You misunderstand me. We are going to announce our engagement *now*."

"Now? But it is the middle of the night!"

"What a pity, then, that you didn't sneak into my bedchamber at some more respectable hour."

He grabbed her arm and steered her out of the room. Once they were in the corridor, his pace increased so that she nearly had to trot to keep up with his long stride.

As James led her out to the stables, Izzie tried desperately to think of some reason why they couldn't go to the manor, but she doubted he would believe any of the myriad excuses running through her mind. She needed something believable, she thought, as James saddled up Samhain, his big black stallion. She considered, but quickly discarded, the notion of running herself through with the pitchfork leaning against the wall. She had already been skewered and roasted enough, thank you.

She was contemplating a resurgence of the Black Plague when James tossed her up on the horse and mounted behind her. He held himself stiffly, as if reluctant to even touch her. It hurt, but not nearly as much as the silence; the only words that passed between them concerned her mare's location.

A conversation from the night of her ball echoed in her head:

"Despite what you say, James Sheffield, you're not past saving, and nothing you say will change my mind. I refuse to believe it."

"Believe it. I'm warning you, Izzie. Don't try to 'save' me. You'll only get hurt."

She couldn't say she hadn't been warned, she thought sadly. She just hadn't expected she would hurt this much.

Once she was mounted on Blossom, Izzie was tempted to run—preferably somewhere far, far away. She didn't know where exactly she would go, but at the moment, any place sounded better than where she was headed. Her cheeks burned with shame as the magnitude of what she had done sank in. Of course, if she had to do it all over again she would, but there was something about the unholy hour that made the entire affair feel so . . . so sordid.

As they rode up the long drive, with only the sound of the horses' hooves to break the early-morning silence, Isabella's dread only grew. She felt physically ill at the thought of having to face her parents. She dug in her heels, both literally and metaphorically, and stopped right where she was. It only took a few moments for James to realize that she was no longer behind him. He looked back at her with an eyebrow raised in silent question, but when she didn't answer and made no move to continue, he wheeled Samhain around and rode back to her.

"Is there a problem?"

"I don't think this is such a good idea," she muttered.

"You thought it was a grand idea when you stripped off your clothes and—"

"Well, yes, but it is the *middle* of the *night*. I thought we could announce our engagement in the usual way. You would ask my father for my hand. My mother would plan an elegant dinner party with some of the local families and then, after the meal, we would call for a champagne toast and officially announce our decision to wed."

He frowned at her, but all he said was, "You thought wrong. We will be married with all due haste." Then he turned and rode up the drive. With a sigh, Isabella followed him to the stables. He wouldn't actually be safe until she married him, she reminded herself. Once that day came, assuming she lived to see that day, *then* she could flee. Perhaps, given the situation, she ought to give serious consideration to a nunnery. Life would be far simpler without men!

They walked around to the front of the house, and James began pounding on the front door, venting his frustration on the thick wooden panels and making enough noise to awaken every last inhabitant of Weston Manor. The door opened to reveal Caldwell; the elderly butler's nightcap was comically askew upon his balding pate, but there was nothing funny about his expression. And when he glimpsed Isabella standing behind James, his bushy white eyebrows rose to new heights. Izzie wanted, quite simply, to crumble into a little pile of dust.

"James!"

Isabella peered past James to see her father descending the stairs, belting his robe as he hurried toward them. Her mother followed a few paces behind him.

"What is the matter? Has something happened?" Her mother's questions started before she hit the bottom step.

James said nothing, just stepped into the foyer, exposing Isabella to two very startled pairs of parental eyes. At that moment, she really wished she had cultivated the feminine art of fainting. It had always struck her as foolish, considering that the cause of distress would presumably still be there when one came to, but Isabella was beginning to realize that a well-timed faint might be a very useful thing, indeed. However, given that a) she had no practice at performing a believable faint, b) the flooring in the entry was marble, and c) in his current mood, James couldn't be counted on to catch her, Izzie decided she had no choice but to brazen it out.

Unfortunately, all her brazenness seemed to have gotten left behind in James's bedchamber. She looked over her shoulder and saw with no small amount of longing that the front door was still open. Perhaps she would bolt after all. James's hand clamped down on her shoulder, and Caldwell hurried to close the door, sealing off her means of escape.

Izzie shuddered.

James pulled her closer and murmured, "Cold, my love? *You?*"

Isabella flinched at his veiled innuendo, his biting sarcasm, but she bit the inside of her cheek and said nothing. It wasn't easy. Not at all.

She raised her eyes to her parents' faces. Her mother looked worried. Her father . . . Judging by the red color staining his face, her father was about three seconds away from exploding.

Three, two, one . . .

"What the bloody hell is going on?" her father bellowed.

"Oliver!" her mother hissed, jerking her head toward the upper levels of the house, not that there was really any chance of anyone still being asleep. Sure enough, the faint sound of crying children floated down to them.

"Would someone," her father ground out, "please explain *this*." He waved a hand toward Isabella and James.

"We-ell," Izzie began, but James cut her off.

"What happened tonight is this: Your daughter, by some means, managed to sneak out of *her* bedchamber and into *mine*. What happened then . . . ? Let us just say she employed some rather persuasive tactics. . . . "

Her mother groaned.

"In any matter, our marriage has become a matter of quite urgent necessity."

Her father was looking a bit purple now. "You!" he barked at Isabella. "Straight to your room. And you!" He turned on James. "My study. Now."

Chapter 12

Here is the latest on dit: *Last week, Lady Chastity Ashworth was found in a compromising position with Sir Edwin Gorsham, a man whose fashion sense leaves much to be desired. I once saw him wearing a mustard-colored waistcoat embroidered with pink polka dots. In any case, the two were found, with Sir Edwin in a most shocking state of undress, though, in my opinion, his undressed state is likely less shocking than his clothed state. I feel quite sorry for Lady Chastity, who, had she been a rose by any other name, might be the subject of far fewer jests.*

From the correspondence of Miss Isabella Weston, age seventeen

Letter to her aunt Katherine, Marchioness of Sheldon, containing nothing of particular importance, yet filled with deliciously juicy gossip—August 1795

James resolutely clamped his mouth shut and followed Lord Weston into the study.

"Sit," he commanded, pointing to a chair.

James remained standing. "Before you break out the dueling pistols," he said, "I would like to point out that I had nothing to do with this."

Lord Weston raised one disbelieving eyebrow.

"All right, I was involved," James admitted, "but it wasn't anything I wanted."

The eyebrow didn't budge.

"Fine! You're right. I wanted it. I wanted her."

The eyebrow lowered to its normal position.

"But," James added darkly, "I did not want to marry her."

Lord Weston's eyebrows drew together in a sharp frown. The sort of frown a man might wear when contemplating murder. A slow, painful murder.

"It was nothing to do with *her*," James explained hastily. "I did not plan to marry. Anyone. Ever," he clarified.

"And now?"

James sighed and sank down into a chair. "And now I have no choice. We will be married by special license as soon as possible."

Long minutes passed in uneasy silence before Lord Weston finally snapped, "You needn't sound quite so put upon. It may have escaped your notice, but there *are* some benefits for you in this arrangement."

"Ah, yes, regaining my precious inheritance."

"I was thinking more along the lines of your having *my daughter* for *your wife*," was the growled response.

Lady Weston's entrance into the room saved him from having to reply. "Well, this is a fine mess!" she huffed, disapproval radiating off her in nearly palpable waves.

James took a step backward, raising his hands in the air like a criminal. He supposed he *was* guilty. He had stolen the innocence of his best friend's little sister. There was probably a special circle of hell reserved for people like him. Then again, perhaps "stolen" wasn't the right word. Isabella had offered herself up to him freely. Actually, he would be damned if he wasn't the injured party in this scenario. Something had been stolen from him, too—his bloody freedom.

Unfortunately, there was something about the situation that made him feel like a naughty schoolboy, which probably explained why he uttered the classic line used in the face of adult displeasure: "It's not my fault." As he said it, James glanced warily over at Lord Weston, who had seated himself at his desk, obviously content to let his wife run the show. Damnation, there went that bloody eyebrow again.

James wondered whether he looked equally supercilious when he did that.

Probably not.

Damn.

Lady Weston began to pace across the room. "Of all the impossible situations." She turned and came back the other way. "I cannot believe—" She stopped right in front of James. *"What were you thinking?"*

"Er," James responded brilliantly.

"Oh, never mind. It is fairly obvious that neither you nor my daughter is capable of acting with any degree of intelligence."

James refrained from pointing out that a man's brain functioned only partly when he was inebriated, barely when he was asleep, and not at all when a naked female in his bed was thrown into the mix. Considering that her daughter was the naked female in question, he didn't think it would go over too well. Still, he couldn't let the insult pass entirely. "*I* was not the one who sneaked into someone else's bedchamber," he said defensively, then added again for good measure, "This was not my fault."

Perhaps, James thought, if he said it enough times, he might be able to convince himself. As it was, the guilt was beginning to choke him. He couldn't escape the fact that Isabella would never have come up with such a ridiculous scheme, let alone have acted on it, if he hadn't introduced her to passion. He had shown her the spark that ignited between them; could he really blame her for seeking more, like a moth drawn irresistibly to the light?

Really, if there was anyone who should shoulder the blame in this debacle, it was his grandfather, who had manufactured the situation, treating people as pawns on a chessboard, to be moved and manipulated as he willed. Of course, at this point it was another game entirely. The die had been cast and there was no turning back.

As if she had read his thoughts, Lady Weston sighed and said, "It doesn't matter who, if anyone, is at fault. What's done is done. All we can do now is move forward and make the best of things." She grimaced, and then gave James a wry smile. "That did not come out quite as I intended it. You know there is no one I should like better to have as a son-in-law, but . . ."

"We would have preferred that the wedding come before the bedding," her husband finished dryly.

"Oliver!" Lady Weston gasped.

James developed a newfound appreciation for the rug beneath his feet.

"Well, it's the truth, isn't it?" he said.

James was relieved that the man seemed to have returned to his usual calm equilibrium.

"Ye-es," she admitted reluctantly. "But you needn't have put it quite so distastefully. Not that a hasty marriage can be seen as anything other than distasteful. Especially while James is in mourning. People are going to think the worst."

"And they would be right," her husband commented helpfully.

She glared at him. "What we need," she continued, "is an unobjectionable reason for an immediate wedding."

"What if one of them—James, for instance—were to suddenly become deathly ill?" Lord Weston suggested, cracking his knuckles.

There was an excited gleam in his eyes that made James worried. Very worried.

"No, that won't work," Lady Weston muttered.

James sighed with relief. Lord Weston, he noticed, was visibly disappointed. James frowned; his relationship with his future father-in-law was off to a decidedly rocky start.

"However," Lady Weston went on, beginning to pace again, "if we let it be known that the Earl of Dunston's dying wish was for Izzie and James to wed, surely no one would find fault with the immediacy of the affair."

Even James had to admit sometimes telling the truth really was the best policy. He looked speculatively at Lady Weston, who had ousted her husband from behind the desk and was jotting things down on a piece of paper.

"Now that *that* is settled, when should we hold the wedding? I suppose it might be done in a fortnight. Hmmm, yes, three weeks would really be better," she said to herself.

"I should prefer something sooner," said James.

"But what about all of the arrangements? The attendants? And the flowers? And the dress? And the wedding breakfast?"

James stood and eyed her dispassionately. "I suppose that they, like the proposal, formal announcement, and engagement party, will fall under the category of things that never were," he remarked.

"One week," she offered. "It will be a challenge, to be sure, but I can do it in a week."

"I am afraid that waiting a week will prove impossible," James said, shaking his head.

"And why is that?" his future mother-in-law asked, her eyes narrowing in suspicion.

"Because," James replied, "by this evening I plan to be on my way to London to obtain a special license from the archbishop. I shall return tomorrow, and we will be married the following morning. I plan to be gone from England entirely by the week's end."

He had to be. He couldn't stay—not when he was going to be leg-shackled to temptation. He had to remove himself. Distance—as much as he could put between them—was the only thing that might keep him sane. Might save him.

"What about Isabella?" queried Lord Weston, though the resigned tone of his voice suggested he knew the answer.

James briefly closed his eyes, steeling himself. "Isabella will shortly be the Countess of Dunston. As such, she is mistress of several properties, including Sheffield Park, a London town house, a Scottish castle, and a sugar plantation in Jamaica. Wherever she chooses to reside, I am sure she will find some way in which to occupy herself."

He strode over to the door as he said, in a voice that he hoped brooked no argument, "Now, if you will be so good as to excuse me, I have an archbishop to visit."

James wrenched open the door. A split second and a startled yelp later, he was on his back on the floor, knocked over by his eavesdropping, soon-to-be wife. The scenario felt far too familiar and—his body began registering the nearness of soft female curves—far, far too enticing.

"Aren't you supposed to be in your room?" scowled James, quickly moving Isabella off himself before his body betrayed him.

"This involves me. I have every right to know what is being said." Her face was stubbornly set as she rose to her feet.

He got up as well. "I hope you heard all that you wanted," he said, "because I was just leaving." He started again for the door, not that he expected to make it through. Sure enough, he hadn't taken three steps before—

"James, wait!" Isabella called out. "I have something I need to say to you."

"Yes?"

"In private," she clarified.

Her father snorted loudly. "If you think we are going to leave the two of you alone—"

"Hush, dear." Lady Weston grabbed her husband's arm and began hustling him out of the room. "I am certain the children have things they wish to say to each other."

"But—"

"They *are* going to be married," his wife reminded him.

"Very well," he huffed as he was dragged out the door. "But this door is to remain unlocked at all times. And there is to be no touching, do you hear? And—"

The door closed, leaving him alone with Isabella, in a room that had somehow shrunk to the size of a broom closet. She took a step toward him. Make that a very small broom closet. She came another step closer. A very small and airless broom closet. And then she was standing right before him, so close that he ached to take her in his arms. Every inch of his flesh tingled with awareness; his skin felt taut and stretched, as if it were physically reaching out to her like a magnet to a lodestone.

He took a step backward and found he could breathe a little easier. "All right, what was it you wanted to speak to me about?"

She bit her lip.

"Look," he said impatiently, "I don't have time for this. Why don't you think on it, and we can discuss it after—"

"Where are you going?"

"I already told you; I have to go see to the special license—"

"No," Isabella interrupted. "Where are you *going*? You said you were leaving England."

"I am."

Before he knew it, she had closed the distance between them and taken his hands with her own. That contact, though ever so subtle, was ecstasy. And agony.

"I know—," she started, staring down at their joined hands. "I know you didn't want to get married because of your grandfather, but—"

"About that," he began, needing to tell her the truth, the full truth.

"No, wait," she said. "This is what I needed to say to you. Of course, I had always thought that someday I would have children, but I want you to know that it—it doesn't matter to me. Well, it *does* matter, but you matter more. You don't have to leave. I promise we won't have children if that is truly your wish. Marriages are built on compromise, aren't they?"

"This one certainly is," James grumbled, dropping her hands. He began to pace around the room. "Isabella, my wishes clearly don't factor into your plans. Don't you realize you could already be pregnant?" he demanded, and then froze.

"Surely not," Isabella said. A frown creased her brow as she looked down at her stomach, clearly perplexed.

"Given the night's events, it's entirely possible." James felt sweat beginning to bead on his forehead.

"You mean . . . from what we did? I know that is how one loses one's innocence, but . . ." Her blue eyes widened, and her mouth fell open in astonishment.

It dawned on him that, had it been a normal wedding, her mother would have explained the intimacies of the marriage bed. As it was, with the wedding night preceding the ceremony, there were apparently some large gaps in Isabella's knowledge—gaps that were now up to him to fill in. Bloody hell.

"A woman gets pregnant from a man's seed," he explained.

"So when you . . . At the end . . ."

"Yes."

"Ah." Her eyes dropped to her stomach once more, her gaze filled with tenderness and awe, as her hand came up to rest reverently there.

James remembered his mother standing in just such a pose when she had been with child. They had all been so happy, so excited, and then . . . He was transported to the day of the funeral. The sky was the same dismal gray, and the ground in the graveyard was still laden with water, spongy beneath his feet, but nothing else was the same. He had revisited this scene any number of times in his mind, but he was always a boy, and his father always stood beside him.

This time, James was alone, and he was a grown man. Confused, he went through the motions he had always gone through in past dreams, reaching down and gathering a handful of muddy dirt in his fist, then stepping forward to the edge of the grave. As he readied himself to toss the fistful of dirt into the grave, he glanced down. There was no lid upon the coffin, which wasn't right at all, so he got down on his knees and peered closer. It wasn't his mother and sister who were being buried, he realized. It was Isabella, pale and cold in death, and a tiny form swathed in white—their babe—was nestled by her side.

In that heart-stopping moment, everything became clear. He didn't know how he knew or where, precisely, the knowledge had come from, but he knew with absolute certainty that if he were to get Isabella with child, it would kill her. And that would kill him. The panic he had held at bay since first discovering her in his bed returned in full force. His heart skipped a beat, two beats, and then began to race. Oh God, no. No, no, no.

Isabella looked up at him, still holding the gentle curve of her stomach, her face filled at once with hope and guilt. Although he had never been particularly devout, James sent up a fervent prayer that no child would result from their lovemaking. He wouldn't ever touch her again, he promised. He would give her the protection of his name, and then he would leave.

James struggled to breathe against the vise squeezing his lungs. He *had* to leave. He had to *leave*. He could still enlist, he reminded himself. He didn't have to anymore, but he could. He *would*. His own death, he could handle. Hers would destroy him. He quit the room without a backward glance. It was much too late for looking back.

Aside from the small number of guests, no one would be able to tell that it was a hastily contrived affair, Isabella thought two days hence, as her father escorted her down the aisle of the Weston Manor chapel. Not that she had ever really questioned her mother's close relationship with the Almighty, but the miracles that had been worked confirmed it beyond all doubt.

The chapel was filled with so many roses, there probably wasn't a single bloom left in the hothouse at either Weston Manor *or* Sheffield Park, for once Mrs. Benton, the housekeeper at the neighboring estate, heard that there was to be a wedding, messages began flying between the two houses as fast as the poor stable lads could carry them.

The soft late-morning light filtered through the stained-glass windows, casting colorful shadows that shimmered and shifted with the changing light. Surreal, Isabella thought. That was the word for it. Everything felt like a dream.

Last night ...

This morning ...

The wedding.

Oh dear God in heaven, she was getting married. To James Sheffield. In the Weston Manor chapel.

It was everything she had ever hoped for, and yet it resembled nothing she had planned. Not that she'd had it planned, per se, but she had expected that people would be smiling. Instead, her mother and Olivia were sniffling into their handkerchiefs, her father was glowering at the groom, who had the definite air of a man facing the gallows, and the vicar's lips were fixed in their usual sanctimonious frown.

She had also expected that her brother would be present, that Henry would stand up with James, but he was off in Scotland. After promising to be on their best behavior, Lia and Genni had been allowed to attend the ceremony but, perhaps taking their cue from the adults, were most unnaturally subdued.

If she had known her wedding was going to be so gloomy, she would have worn black, Isabella thought peevishly, fighting a desire to stamp her way up the aisle. The sunny yellow gown she had chosen seemed distinctly out of place. She defiantly pasted a bright smile upon her face, but it faltered when the vicar asked James, "Wilt thou have this woman to thy wedded wife? Wilt thou love her, comfort her, honor, and keep her in sickness and in health; and, forsaking all others, keep thee only unto her, so long as ye both shall live?"

She turned toward James. In his navy superfine, snowy white shirt and fawn-colored breeches, he was looking far more handsome than any man had a right to. The thought that he would soon be hers left her breathless. Oh, she knew that the laws of church and state dictated that it was the woman who became her husband's property. By that reasoning, she would belong to her lord and master just the same as his horses and hounds belonged to him.

She had never cared much for rules, though, especially ones she couldn't use to her benefit, and when James Sheffield said his vows, he would be hers. Whatever he was in the eyes of God and of man, in her heart she would know he belonged to her just as surely as she had always belonged to him. After an interminable moment of silence, when the awful thought crossed her mind that he might shake his head and walk away, his voice was strong and deep as he finally said, "I will."

Although she cringed when the vicar read the "obey him and serve him" bit, Isabella said, "I will," without hesitation. She tried to convince herself the vows were meaningless, especially as her groom had no intention of adhering to his, but Izzie realized she meant every word. She would be his always and in all ways, forever and ever, until death did them part, amen.

Or, she would be if her father would see fit to release her. The vicar had asked, "Who giveth this woman to be married to this man?" at least twice, and though her father had supplied the proper response, his grip on her arm hadn't loosened. She was beginning to wonder if she was going to have to pry her father's fingers off, when James turned and gently, but firmly took her hand. Her father reluctantly relaxed his hold, but before he took his place next to her mother, he whispered into her ear, "No matter what, your mother and I will always love you, and this will always be your home."

That was when she began to bawl. No delicate sniffles or teary eyes—she was fine one moment, then hysterically weeping the next. And she wasn't even sad, not really. It must be the stress, she thought, weeping all the while. Her father's words had broken some sort of dam, releasing this flood of tears. She had to stop. This was *her wedding*. She shouldn't be wailing like this at *her wedding*. Nonsensically, the thought only made her cry harder.

"Izzie?" Her father's voice was worried and also faintly . . . bemused?

"I"—hiccup—"am"—hiccup—"fine!" she sobbed, the last word emerging as something between a moan and a shriek.

Apparently the ridiculousness of the situation struck the groom as well as the bride, because James began to laugh—huge, bellowing guffaws that had Izzie, the vicar, and all of the guests questioning his sanity. He laughed until he was bent over, with tears running down his cheeks.

"Now we—now—now we're both crying," he wheezed.

The vicar was not amused. "Marriage is a sacrament," he intoned, "a holy estate. It is not to be entered into lightly or wantonly to satisfy carnal lusts and appetites, but soberly and in the fear of God."

"Mama, what is carnal lust?" Genni whispered loudly.

"It's why Mama and Papa started locking their door at night so that you couldn't go in and sleep with them," Lia responded in an equally carrying tone.

"But Mrs. Daniels said they were playing an important game of backgammon," Genni insisted.

"B-backgammon?" James howled.

A strangled groan sounded from the front pew. Isabella couldn't tell if it came from her mother or her father. And just like that, Isabella began to laugh. It started as a tentative smile, and then grew to a giggle before blossoming into a lovely, freeing, joyous chuckle that warmed her soul and soothed the ragged, bruised areas of her heart. As long as there was laughter, there was hope.

Eventually they quieted down—except for Genni, that was. She kept demanding to know why everyone was laughing until Lia, with a weary sigh that made her seem far older than her twin, took her hand and led her out of the chapel. The vicar cleared his throat and began to read loudly from his prayer book.

They each solemnly repeated their vows, but when

James twisted to remove the ring from the pocket of his coat, Isabella saw the telltale wrinkles in the corners of his eyes that meant he was fighting laughter. Mirth bubbled up in her own chest in response, but it died when James slipped the ring on her finger. Neither of them was wearing gloves, and the sensation of his bare flesh on hers sent waves of heat rocketing through her body. From the hitch in James's breathing, Isabella was certain he had felt something similar.

James snatched back his hand as though he had been burned, and Isabella paused to admire her ring, a deep blue sapphire surrounded by a circle of sparkling diamonds. "Thank you," she whispered. "It's beautiful."

He muttered something incomprehensible and male, which she interpreted as "You're welcome," and then they were kneeling to receive the vicar's blessing. Before she knew it, she was married and the vicar was giving James permission to kiss her. Isabella thought she heard her father growl, but then James's lips descended on hers, a brief, firm pressure that had her leaning in for more, but he pulled away.

Very proper, she told her disappointed self. It wouldn't do to give in to temptation in a house of God with her parents and siblings looking on. Dredging up a smile, she took James's arm and walked down the aisle and out of the chapel, where Genni was still badgering Lia, to the Blue Parlor, where her mother had arranged a light, celebratory repast. Once they were out of sight of the chapel, James's pace increased so that she nearly had to trot to keep up with him.

"When the vicar spoke of appetites, I don't believe he meant food," Isabella panted.

Her new husband said nothing.

She tried again. "I am excessively hungry as well," she remarked. "I was far too nervous to eat this morning."

James remained silent, but by that point they had reached the Blue Parlor, and he ushered her inside. As he shut the door, he said, "I wanted to speak with you before the others arrived."

"Oh?" she asked, fanning her hot cheeks.

"I'm leaving," he said, offering no explanations, proffering no apologies.

"Oh." She hadn't known how much misery and dejection a person could pack into a single syllable.

"My man of business will know how to contact me should the need arise." His gaze dropped meaningfully to her stomach.

"Oh!" she exclaimed, startled once again by the thought that she might, even now, be carrying his child.

"Oh, oh, oh," he teased gently. "I hope marriage has not robbed you of your powers of speech."

"Oh no," she protested, then blushed.

He gave her a sad smile. "Good-bye, Izzie," he said, pressing a kiss to her temple.

It was so similar to their previous parting—had it really been only days before?—but there was nothing she could do this time. She had done all the saving she could. Or had she?

"James, you aren't still planning on joining the army, are you?"

His silence was her answer.

She threw her arms around his waist, pressing her face against his chest where she could hear the strong beat of his heart. Tears seeped from her eyes as she asked him for one last thing. She was nearly frantic as she pleaded. "Promise me you won't enlist in the army. Promise me. I won't let you go unless you promise me."

"Damnation, what *is* that?" he asked, setting her away from him and lifting up the heavy gold ball that hung from the chain around her neck.

"It was Henry's birthday present to me." She took the locket from him and flipped the catch, revealing the row of tiny portraits. She watched as his gaze roamed over the smiling faces of her parents and her siblings, observed the flash of grief and longing that crossed his features, felt his loneliness.

"You have me," she whispered. "We could make a family. We—"

"I can't. I—I have to go." He sounded panicked.

She grabbed his coat. "Not until you promise me."

"*Izzie*," he growled, his tone brooking no argument.

That was too bad. "Promise me," she demanded with a choked sob.

"Fine. I promise," he said gruffly, then pulled out of her grasp and left the room.

Isabella left also, first walking, and then running to her room where she could lock herself away and lick her wounds and cry herself dry. James might have missed it, but Izzie had seen the two cakes set out in the room, each bearing an iced message. One had read "Congratulations." The other, the one that gave her pause, read "Happy Birthday."

It was her twentieth birthday, Izzie realized, as well as her wedding day. And she had nothing to celebrate. It was enough to make the strongest heart weep, and Isabella was discovering the hard way that hers was very fragile, indeed.

Chapter 13

I must confess, I do not understand the appeal of taking the waters in Bath. The city itself is quite pretty, the people quite lovely, and the amusements quite satisfactory . . . but the water is beyond foul. It must truly have miraculous restorative properties for people to stomach drinking it in such quantities. Of course, the most common complaint of those journeying here— the elderly, the infirm, even the young, marriage-minded miss— is one of the heart: loneliness. And the only cure I can think of for that affliction is cheery company, and perhaps a cozy shoulder to cry upon. Fortunately, with our ever-growing family, I don't suppose I or any of my siblings shall suffer from it.

From the correspondence of Miss Isabella Weston, age eighteen

Letter to her mother, Mary, Viscountess Weston, considering various types of ailments and their potential remedies— January 1797

Immediately after she locked herself in her room, Isabella began to cry. And cry. And cry. No matter how many tears she mopped away, new ones appeared. It became her mode of existence. The only time she wasn't crying was when she slept, and she only slept when she had completely exhausted herself with crying. She kept the drapes in her room drawn tight, shrouding herself in darkness, and rarely left her bed. She would have lost all sense of time were it not for the trays of food that arrived regularly at her door; she sent them back to the kitchen almost entirely untouched.

The only people she allowed to enter the room were the maids. She shut everyone else out, taking perverse pleasure in their hurt when she refused to see them. Afterward, she always hated herself, but she couldn't seem to stop. Her life had fallen to shambles, and she felt powerless to right it, and while James was out of her reach, her family wasn't. She was hurting so badly, the pain so raw and unbearable, she needed them to feel a touch, some tiny fraction of the grief that swamped her, leaving her vulnerable and debilitated in both body and spirit.

It turned out James had been right all those years ago when he'd told her that loving was a weakness. When she'd protested, he'd called her an innocent. "Izzie," he'd said gently, his voice sad, "I hope you will never find love to be a weakness. But I promise you it can be." She should have known, Isabella reflected ruefully. James Sheffield always kept his promises.

Ten days passed before her mother finally reached the end of her patience. "Isabella," she shouted through the thick wooden panel, "enough is enough. If you do not unlock this door right now, I am going to have it removed and chopped up for kindling! Do you understand me?"

Isabella weighed her options. On the one hand, she really had no desire to get out of bed. Because she had gone so long without eating a decent meal, any movement at all required Herculean effort. On the other hand, the permanent disappearance of her door would certainly spoil the lovely, cavelike atmosphere that so suited her mood.

"Isabella!" her mother warned.

With a growl, Izzie pushed off the covers, slid out of bed, and slowly padded over to open the door. Her mother inhaled sharply as she looked her up and down, but she didn't say anything. She just marched into the room and began pulling back the drapes.

"What are you—aargh! Are you trying to blind me?" Izzie threw an arm over her eyes, trying to shield herself from the blinding rays of sunlight streaming into the room.

"Believe it or not, I am trying to help you. You have wallowed in self-pity long enough. Too long, actually." Her mother started opening the windows, waving fresh air into the room.

"I didn't ask for your help," Izzie replied sullenly, but she said it without heat. Her eyes were starting to adjust to the light, and she found herself gravitating toward the windows, deeply inhaling the clean scent filtering in from outside. Her nose wrinkled as she caught a whiff of herself.

Her mother nodded approvingly. "What would you prefer first? Food? A bath? Something to break?"

Izzie's stomach rumbled loudly.

"Very well, food it is. Then a hot bath. And then back to bed with you, I think. I shall endeavor to find you some things to break for tomorrow."

Izzie shook her head. "I don't understand."

"Now that you have stopped crying—"

"I have *not*." But she had. She had finally stopped crying. Well, fancy that.

"As I said, now that you have stopped crying, I expect you will become angry. Very angry. Furious, even. Men generally take out their frustrations on living things. They pummel one another, or they hunt, or they ride one of their horses into the ground. Women express their tempers in other, far more practical ways."

"By breaking things?"

Her mother's smile was positively devilish. "Believe me, there is nothing so satisfying as breaking things when you are truly outraged, especially those truly ugly pieces that you have always hated but felt you had to keep because they belonged to your husband's grandmother."

Izzie laughed. It was a little bit tentative and somewhat shaky, struggling to stand on its own two feet like a newborn calf, but a laugh it definitely was. She walked over to her mother and hugged her.

"Thank you," Izzie whispered, wrapping her arms tightly about her mother, clinging to her strength and her love. For the first time since James had left she felt, well, it wasn't precisely *happy*, but neither was it sad, and for the moment, that was enough.

The promised food and bath so improved her mood that by the following morning Isabella felt ready to leave her room. She walked slowly downstairs, noting with each step how, although nothing had changed, everything felt different. *She* was different. She was no longer Izzie Weston. She was Isabella Sheffield, the Countess of Dunston, and she didn't feel as if she belonged anymore. Her discomfort grew when the conversation halted as she entered the breakfast room. Several surprised faces turned to look in her direction, one of them so completely unexpected that Izzie blinked to clear her vision.

"Aunt Kate?"

"Darling!" Her aunt rose from the table and enfolded Izzie in a warm embrace.

"What are you doing here? When did you get here? Where is Charlotte?" She looked around for her younger cousin.

Her aunt laughed. "I will answer all your questions, but first you must sit and eat something. You are nothing but skin and bones."

Izzie flushed but complied with her aunt's instructions. She settled into the chair one of the footmen held out for her and bit into a blissfully buttery croissant.

"Very good. Now for my end of the bargain: Charlotte is in the nursery and, I must say, quite eager to see you. We arrived yesterday evening. You were asleep and we didn't wish to wake you. Well, Charlotte wanted to, but your mother and I managed to convince her otherwise."

"For a child not yet five years old, she drives a wicked bargain," her mother said, eyes twinkling with laughter.

Her aunt grimaced. "I had to promise her a puppy."

"But don't you *like* dogs?" Isabella said.

"I like *little* dogs," her aunt corrected. "Charlotte doesn't want a *little* dog. She wants a whelp from the next litter out of my stepson's great Danish dogs. The beast will probably eat us while we sleep. Your mother has already convinced Charlotte that the dog must be named—"

"Hamlet." Izzie groaned.

"Of course!" Her mother beamed with excitement.

"But what if it's a girl?" Izzie countered.

"Ophelia, of course, or Gertrude would work, I suppose. You know, the other day I discovered the most fascinating—"

"Aunt Kate, you still haven't told me what you are doing here," Izzie said loudly. She felt horribly rude interrupting her mother, but the collective sigh of relief that ran through the room made her feel better. It was at times like this that Izzie marveled at her scholarly mother and fun-loving aunt having sprung from the same womb. It wasn't only that their personalities were dissimilar; they also looked nothing alike. Her mother was fair and slender, much like herself, while her aunt had a mane of gorgeous sable hair and more curves than the Serpentine. They had the same expressive blue-gray eyes, though, and the stormy gray cast to her aunt's eyes indicated that, despite her lighthearted demeanor, she was really quite troubled.

"Our purpose in coming would have been far more obvious if we had arrived, as planned, in time to surprise you for your birthday, but our journey was held up by a terrible storm, which turned all the roads into muddy rivers, and then we were further delayed when Charlotte's nurse slipped in the mud and broke her wrist"—she paused for air—"and therefore we have missed not only your birthday, but your betrothal—"

"You didn't miss much there," Izzie muttered.

"And your *wedding*!" Her aunt's voice rose to a wail.

"It's all right, Henry missed it as well. There wasn't really time to send invitations. Believe me, it was not exactly the wedding I had always dreamed of, but I am certain someone has already filled you in on all the sordid details." She shoved her chair away from the table and rose to her feet. Her body fairly hummed with energy, energy that was quickly being converted to something else entirely. "Mama," she said, nearly giddy with anticipation, "did you happen to locate the rest of Great-Grandmother Clorinda's good china?"

"What do you want with my grandmother's china?" her father asked suspiciously, looking up from his paper.

"Izzie thought she might like to have it as a wedding present from us. It has *such* a *lovely* pattern," her mother improvised.

Satisfied by the explanation, her father mumbled something incoherent and retreated back behind his paper.

"Old nursery," her mother mouthed, pointing toward the door.

When her mother had become pregnant with Henry, her parents had decided the nursery, located in the farthest, coldest, gloomiest reaches of the house, was totally unfit for children. They had converted a large suite in the east wing into more suitable surroundings, and the old nursery had been empty ever since.

When she entered the room, the first thing she noticed was that the fire had already been lit. The second thing she noticed was a stack of the most hideous plates she had ever seen. Isabella picked up the top plate and marveled for a moment that anyone would create such a monstrosity— that someone had thought it appropriate to decorate china with not just scenes of a stag hunt, but gruesome scenes of the stag's final moments.

That person, she decided, had needed to have his or her head examined, and the same applied to her relatives for actually purchasing it. As she pulled back her arm and let fly, Izzie felt as close to happy as she had been since Jones had left. With a laugh, she reached for the next plate.

By the late afternoon, Isabella had taken to venting her rage with a fire poker and an old mattress. She found it as satisfying as hurling ugly china, of which there was a sadly limited supply, since her mother had apparently already destroyed most of it.

She had then vowed revenge on those fictional lovers, Emilia and Jordan, for daring to have a happy ending. Since she now knew from experience that scandalous seductions resulted only in misery and heartbreak, she decided the volume was rubbish and deserved to die a slow and painful death.

Many more books might have met the same fate, but after Olivia found her cackling gleefully as she poked at the charred remains of *The Mysterious Enchantress of Castle Clermont*, all novels of a romantic bent were quickly hidden from sight. Thus, Isabella had moved on to mattress beating when her second surprise visitor of the day arrived.

"Take that, you bloody bounder!" she yelled. "I"—*thwack*—"saved you"—*thwack, thwack*—"and you left me"—*thwack*—"on my *birthday*!" Her chest heaving with exertion, she slammed the iron down in a killing blow.

"I always told Mother you were a bloodthirsty wench, but she never believed me," drawled a voice from the doorway.

"Henry?"

Isabella dropped the poker onto the mattress and took a deep breath. She had been dreading this since the moment she and Olivia had begun their plotting. She might be his sister, but he did have four others, whereas he had only one best friend. The odds were not in her favor. Five sisters. One best friend. And she had stolen him. Squaring her shoulders, she turned to face her brother. He frowned at her, and she braced herself for what was to come.

"Bloody hell, Izzie! You look terrible!"

All she could do was stare at him.

"Oh, right," Henry muttered. "I suppose congratulations are in order, but—"

"Hal!" She choked out the childhood nickname and launched herself at him.

He let out a startled laugh, catching her up in a hug. "You know, you haven't called me that in years."

"I was so worried that you were going to hate me," Izzie

whispered against his coat. "But I had to do it. Otherwise, he was going to—"

"Yes, I know."

She pulled away and began to pace around the room; the sudden release of all her Henry-related tension had given her a burst of energy. "I suppose James told you?"

Henry shook his head. "Father told me just now. I'm going to put a bullet in that bounder."

"Hal, you can't shoot him. He married me."

"Yes, between ruining you and leaving you. Christ, what a mess."

She laughed bitterly. "Is that what he called it?"

"Father? No, I believe 'fiasco' was—"

"No. I was talking about James. Did he call me—our marriage—a mess?"

Her brother looked at her askance. "Izzie, I haven't seen or heard from James since I visited him in Ireland shortly after your ball. That was months ago."

Guilt swamped her. James and Henry had always been as close as brothers, and she had driven herself as a wedge between them. A wedge created out of the best intentions, but a wedge nonetheless. "I am so sorry, Henry. He must realize that you had nothing to do with this. If you give him a few weeks to come to his senses and then go to London, I am certain . . ." There was that odd look on Henry's face again. "What?"

"James isn't in London. Once Father's messenger caught up with me, I went straight there to look for him. I asked around at all our usual haunts. No one has seen him. It is possible he has gone to ground at one of his estates, but . . ."

"But you don't think so," Isabella finished.

Her brother nodded, his expression grim. "It seems likely he has left England entirely. He is gone, Izzie, really gone, and I don't think he intends to return."

Despite Henry's misgivings, Isabella still believed James would return to her before too long. She knew that he needed time to come to terms with their marriage, but she assumed that once his anger cooled, he would see reason. She still didn't regret what she had done; no matter what James had said, she hadn't had any other choice. Once he understood that, he would forgive her. And then she, being the magnanimous wife she was, would forgive him for forgiving her when he *should* have been thanking her.

No doubt the entire reasoning process was taking far longer than it should because he was, well, a *he*. Men, she noted, did not think logically, and therefore it took them far longer to puzzle out the "why" of things. She added at least a week for his bruised pride to recover, and another week on top of that because, seeing as James was as stubborn as a mule, he would be that much more resistant to realizing he had been wrong. So, she told herself, she could not expect to see or hear from her husband for at least another two weeks.

After three weeks had passed, Isabella began to make excuses that a letter had probably gone astray, or that foul weather prevented James from traveling. She worried he had taken ill, or some terrible accident had befallen him. When a month had gone by with no word at all, her brother's pronouncement began to echo in her head: "I don't think he intends to return. I don't think he intends to return. I don't think he intends to return."

The words repeated themselves over and over, flapping and beating at her mind like the wings of a flock of blackbirds until she thought she would go mad.

Instead, she began to believe it. James wasn't coming back. He was gone, really and truly gone. There would be no tearful forgiveness, no joyful reunion. He was gone, and where, she wondered, did that leave her?

Apparently it left her drinking tea with her mother and her aunt, she thought wryly. While the activity (or lack thereof) was by no means displeasing to her, it was certainly not how she envisioned spending the rest of her days. It was time for her to grow up, to move on, to *live*.

Quickly, before she could change her mind, she said,

"Mama, Aunt Kate, I think it is time for me to decide what is to come next."

"Next, dear?" her mother queried.

"In my life," Isabella clarified. "I have to figure out what I am to do now. James is not coming back, and I cannot spend the rest of my days waiting for him to change his mind. Neither can I stay here forever, hiding behind my mother's skirts. I am no longer a child; it is time I faced that reality."

Her mother's eyes grew misty. "While I should, of course, like to keep you with me always, you are right. It is time for you to leave the nest. You are a beautiful young woman possessed of fortune and title and, as a married woman, you have far more freedom than you would otherwise. To borrow from Shakespeare, the world is your oyster."

Her mother could always be trusted to pepper the conversation with just such pearls of Bardic wisdom.

"Are you thinking of traveling abroad?" her aunt asked. "Or would London be more to your liking? Or should you like to move into Sheffield Park? I am certain there must be a great many changes you will wish to make."

"I don't actually know what I want," Izzie admitted. "I only know that I cannot stay here any longer. There are too many memories of James everywhere."

"Surely there can be no unhappy memories in London. And with the Season about to start, there will be so many diversions that you will not have time to even think about your husband. And masked balls provide the most delightful opportunities for dalliance."

"*Kate!*" her mother exclaimed.

"Well, if her husband chooses to stay away, then she is well within her rights to take a—"

"I will not have you encouraging my daughter into such—"

"Aunt Kate, Mama," Isabella broke in before the quarrel could escalate into a fight, "truly, I don't believe I am ready for dances *or* dalliance. I was hoping for someplace a bit quieter."

Her aunt clapped her hands. "I have a plan," she said excitedly.

Isabella eyed her warily. So did her mother.

"Oh, don't look at me as if I am some kind of morally defunct corrupter of innocents. What I propose is perfectly respectable. Izzie, you can accompany me to Scotland, and Olivia also, if she likes, and you can stay with me as long as you wish while you decide what you want to do."

Isabella jumped up and went to embrace her aunt. "That would be wonderful. Are you sure Lord Sheldon will not mind?"

A shadow crossed her aunt's face at the mention of her stepson. "Don't be a goose. You are my niece—of course Jason won't mind. Besides, he hasn't left Wales since Laura's death."

"Such a tragedy," her mother clucked. "But that must be at least three years ago. He cannot mean to hide away forever."

"Jason has shut himself off from the world. His son is the only person who can reach him. He is less distant with Charlotte, but I can tell he holds himself back. She adores him, which is only right, I suppose, since he is her half brother, but I fear she will get hurt if he withdraws further."

"I think he sounds quite horrible," Izzie said. "Just imagine shutting out the people who love you, just because . . . Oh."

Her mother reached out and took her hand. "He is in pain, as were you, my love. People do not always behave well when they are hurting. The important thing is that you are healing. Going away for a time will be good for you."

"It will be good for me as well," her aunt added. "Not only will I have the pleasure of your company, but I am almost positive that when Charlotte learns you are to return home with us, she will forget about getting that puppy."

Izzie laughed. "I am not sure whether I should be flattered or offended."

"Flattered, I assure you. Charlotte wants that dratted dog more than anything." Her aunt sighed. "That is not precisely true. She originally wanted a baby brother or sister, but when I finally convinced her of the impossibility of *that* ever happening . . ."

"Well, it isn't *impossible*," Izzie said. "You are five years younger than Mama, and she bore Portia not two years ago."

"It *is* an impossibility because I do not intend to marry again," her aunt said firmly. "For a woman to be married twice is acceptable, but three times . . ." She shook her head. "No, a third marriage borders on scandalous, and were I to be thrice widowed, I should certainly be the subject of pointed fingers and whispered rumors."

Isabella stopped herself from pointing out that her aunt, by the virtue of her beauty alone, had been the subject of pointed fingers and whispered rumors since her debut almost two decades ago.

"So," her aunt continued, "once Charlotte realized she would not be getting a baby to play with, she decided a dog would do just as well. But now, with any luck, the presence of her favorite cousin will cause her to forget that ridiculous promise I made."

"My dear sister, you should know by now, there is nothing in the world capable of coming between a female and a promise made to her, whether she is four or ninety-four. There is nothing so sacred to a woman as a promise."

And that, thought Isabella as she hurried off to tell Olivia of their plans, was the God's honest truth.

Chapter 14

I am writing to inquire whether your store has any books on the subject of the proper care and feeding of great Danish dogs. I should also like to find out if you have a copy of The Mysterious Enchantress of Castle Clermont—*it was published by the Minerva Press. Our copy met with a rather unfortunate accident, and I have promised my sister that I shall do my best to replace the volume.*

From the correspondence of Isabella, Lady Dunston, age twenty

Letter to Mr. John Hatchard, proprietor of Hatchard's bookshop, written to the sounds of sighs and barks, the former emanating from Lady Sheldon, the latter from Charlotte, whose attempts to learn the "dog" language caused her mother much distress—April 1798

Haile Castle, East Lothian, Scotland
April 1798

During the journey to Scotland, Isabella felt cross and out of sorts. She was at once exhausted and restless, alternately ravenously hungry and sickened by the sight of food. She assumed she had caught a touch of something, but it lingered far longer than it should have. She had been in Scotland for a little less than a fortnight when she was struck by a realization at once terrible and wonderful.

Setting aside the book she had been pretending to read, she began to pace about the cozy room in the north tower known as the Queen's Parlor in honor of Mary, Queen of Scots, who had stayed at the castle just prior to her ill-fated marriage to the Earl of Bothwell. Despite the tragic history of the room's royal occupant, Izzie liked the Queen's Parlor; it felt soft and safe, and she and Aunt Kate spent much of their time there.

Livvy was usually to be found in the cavernous library. Once she discovered that the thousands of volumes were shelved randomly, a state of affairs that offended every orderly bone in her body, she had undertaken the daunting task of reorganizing. Izzie doubted she would ever finish, but that was her sister's problem. She had her own problem, she thought with a sigh, and it was going to be far harder to sort out than a jumble of books.

Her aunt, who was seated at her escritoire, had set aside her writing materials and was now watching as Isabella attempted to wear holes in the ancient, and no doubt priceless, carpet.

"Are you planning to do that all day, or will you tell me what bothers you?"

"I have a problem," Izzie blurted out. "A small problem now, but I fear it shall grow into a very big problem."

"All right, out with it. Whatever it is, we shall think of some solution." Her aunt smiled reassuringly. "I am sure it cannot be all that bad."

"Can it not?" Isabella replied shakily, sinking down onto a settee. "I am with child."

She looked on as the words were slowly absorbed, saw her aunt grapple with the unexpected news, watched as joy and excitement replaced astonishment.

"But darling, this is wonderful news!"

Isabella shook her head sadly. "No, Aunt Kate, it isn't."

"But why ever not?"

"I told, I *promised* him, that I wouldn't—we wouldn't— have children."

"Darling, one doesn't always have a choice about these

things. I still don't understand, though. I thought you wanted children."

"I do. Even though it was wrong, I hoped for this child. And yet, with every wish, every prayer, I betrayed him."

"I take it James is opposed to the idea of children."

Isabella nodded, wiping at the tears that sprang up far too often these days.

"First," her aunt declared, leaping to her feet and resuming Isabella's pacing, "let me point out that you cannot be held wholly responsible here. It takes two people to create a child."

"He won't see it that way. I forced him into this marriage or, at least, into what led to the marriage. His pride was injured, but I thought that with enough time, we might have a chance. That was before the babe. But now . . . He will never forgive me for this."

"Nonsense. The second point I was going to make is that many men think they don't want children, but they change their minds when the babe actually arrives. James will come around; you'll see. He was always marvelous with small children. Besides, he needs an heir."

Isabella sighed wearily and sank back against the cushions. "Not according to him, he doesn't. Can you believe, he actually intends for the line to end with him? There is so much anger and hate inside him that sometimes I don't think there is room for anything else."

"Then you must help him make room," her aunt responded wisely. "Surely by now his anger has cooled. Much as I selfishly adore having you here with me, perhaps it is time for you to seek out your errant husband."

Isabella thought for a moment—a short moment. It wasn't very hard to convince herself of what she already wanted. She jumped up and hugged her aunt, happier than she had been in a long time. "Aunt Kate, I do believe you are right!"

"Yes, I usually am," her aunt said, sounding very much like Izzie's mama for a moment.

"Besides, one shouldn't inform a man through a letter that he is to be a father," Isabella added.

"Certainly not! One must impart news of such an intimate nature in person."

"Yes," Isabella agreed. "Only, I haven't the faintest notion where he might be."

Her aunt frowned. "He left you no means at all of contacting him?"

"Oh, yes, of course. His solicitor. A Mr. . . . Mr. . . . Mr. Marbly; yes, that's right. Aunt Kate, you are a genius. I shall write to him at once!"

To say that the response, which arrived nearly three weeks later, was disappointing would be a vast understatement, Isabella reflected. The note read:

Lady Dunston,
 We are regretfully unable to disclose your husband's direction. Any correspondence you wish to have forwarded to His Lordship may be directed to our office.

   Your humble servants,
   Conter, Ellis, Marbly and Stinch

"Well!" Isabella huffed, and handed the note over to her aunt, who quickly skimmed it before Olivia snatched it out of her hands. "Concealing his whereabouts from his own wife! Do I honestly seem so desperate that I would go see the man when he doesn't wish to see me?"

"That *was* the basic plan," Olivia reminded her.

"Oh, go back to whatever it is you've been doing in the library." Isabella made a shooing motion. "Insufferable man! Now I am in the same position I was in before."

"Although it is not ideal, if it is the only way to reach him, I think you should write to James through this Mr. Marbly. Perhaps the news of the babe will bring him running to your side," Aunt Kate suggested.

"Running as far away as he can get, more likely. No, I must tell him face-to-face."

"Very well," said her aunt. "I suppose we must summon Mr. Marbly here."

"And what, pray tell, would be the use in *that*?"

"Darling, I am the Marchioness of Sheldon. You don't think it should be *too* difficult to get the information out of dear Mr. Marbly, do you?" She fluttered her lashes and produced the wicked smile that still caused men to swear their undying love upon first sight. It was no wonder that both her husbands, each man her senior by at least twenty years, were rumored to have died in the bedchamber, beatific smiles upon their faces.

Izzie grinned. "The poor man doesn't stand a chance."

By the time Mr. Marbly arrived almost a month later, Izzie was no longer grinning. Nearly everything she saw or heard brought on a fit of weeping, which was only slightly preferable to the bouts of nausea incurred whenever she smelled or tasted anything. Thus it happened that Isabella's first glimpse of the solicitor was somewhat distorted by a veil of tears. Nevertheless, she could see he was a tall man, probably around her father's age, with a head of copper curls. He was handsome, she supposed, in a distinguished, dependable sort of way, and his clothing was that of a gentleman who insisted that quality and comfort need not be mutually exclusive.

She surmised with confidence that he was that epitome of British masculinity: a confirmed bachelor. The solicitor probably divided his time between his work and his club, disliked having his routine disturbed, and despised weeping females, but here he was, having traveled more than four hundred miles, and he was smiling at her and holding out a handkerchief.

Unaccountably, the action only made her cry harder. With relief, she saw her aunt appear in the doorway. Aunt Kate would take care of Mr. Marbly, Izzie thought, then gave herself permission to sit, or rather, *sprawl* back down on the sofa, where she promptly resumed her crying.

"Lady Dunston?" Mr. Marbly took a step toward her, his expression slightly panicked.

"She has been like this since your letter arrived," her aunt said despairingly as she entered the room.

Izzie watched with a faint glimmer of amusement as Mr. Marbly gaped at her aunt. Though she had seen the same reaction any number of times, the sight of a man looking like a landed fish never failed to provoke a smile.

"I—I beg your pardon." His voice cracked.

Aunt Kate, who knew exactly what effect she had on members of the male species, flashed him a sultry, inviting look. She fluttered her lashes and placed a hand over her heart, drawing attention to the low neckline of her gown, as she said, "I must beg yours as well. It is unforgivable for a hostess to be elsewhere when a guest is shown in and, as you can see, my niece is not quite up to acting the part. Welcome to Haile Castle. I am Lady Sheldon."

He bowed, cool, crisp, and professional. "Timothy Marbly, my lady."

Isabella was impressed at how quickly the solicitor had regained his composure. Thank heavens the "Effective Use of Seductive Wiles" was only the first part of their plan.

"Thank you so much for coming, Mr. Marbly. My poor niece has been in this state since she learned that her husband did not trust her with his whereabouts."

Apparently her aunt had moved onto a new phase of the plan, and it was the "Pity the Abandoned Bride" segment. Isabella sniffled and sighed loudly, throwing in the occasional moan and wail for good measure. Of course, if anyone in the room was deserving of pity, it was the solicitor. The poor man had to be exhausted, but she and her aunt had decided that might work to their advantage.

"I am truly sorry," he began, "but I must respect my client's wishes—"

Lady Sheldon cut him off. "Won't you sit down?" She seated herself and gestured to the neighboring chair.

He took the proffered chair, clearly doubtful that the spindly, feminine piece of furniture would bear his weight. "As I was saying—," he started again.

"Tea?" Lady Sheldon chirped.

"No, thank you. Now, I realize that Lady Dunston is understandably upset by her husband's decision, but—"

"You see, Mr. Marbly," her aunt confided, leaning toward him, "my niece has a rather important piece of news for her husband. News of a rather *personal* nature." She patted her stomach.

He paled. "If Lady Dunston is ill, I must—"

"She is not ill. She is *expecting*."

"Whom?"

"Pardon me?" Her aunt's nose wrinkled in confusion.

Mr. Marbly let out an audible sigh. "You said Lady Dunston was expecting. I asked whom. It is the logical response."

Her aunt gave an unladylike snort of pure exasperation. "A baby!" she exploded, nearly rising out of her chair. "She is expecting a *baby*."

Baby. That was the key phrase to begin the next phase of their plan. Olivia should be standing by with Charlotte. Help, in the form of a four-year-old, was on the way.

"Oh!" he remarked, nonplussed, but he quickly recovered himself. "Be that as it may, I cannot—"

"Maaammmaaaa!"

Right on cue, Charlotte burst into the parlor and, with a dramatic cry, hurled herself into her mother's lap. "I miss Papa," she sobbed.

Isabella watched Mr. Marbly closely. It was working. Her aunt was right. His whole face had softened. After this affecting display, surely he would realize the important role played by a child's father. He couldn't deny her own child the right to a father. The thought trailed off into nothingness as Izzie realized Charlotte's crying had stopped—and a touch too quickly, judging by the solicitor's expression.

Isabella looked on in dismay as Charlotte hopped off her mother's lap and held out her hands. "I said it, Mama, just like Livvy told me. May I have my present now?"

Her aunt groaned and then whispered something in Charlotte's ear that had the little girl practically skipping out of the room. She was probably headed to the kitchen for a treat. Aunt Kate claimed that rather than having a sweet tooth, Charlotte had an entire mouthful of sweet teeth.

Mr. Marbly was trying, rather unsuccessfully, to keep a straight face.

Izzie sighed. "I don't believe the plan is working. We have no one to blame but ourselves. Charlotte delivered her line perfectly. We just forgot to tell her what to do afterward."

Mr. Marbly let loose the laugh he had been holding back. It was a warm, hearty sound that soon had both Isabella and her aunt joining in. He really was attractive, for an older gentleman. From the sideways looks her aunt kept throwing in his direction, Izzie surmised she was not the only one who had noticed the solicitor's charms.

When Mr. Marbly addressed her, his face was full of honest regret. "Lady Dunston, believe me, I wish I could furnish you with your husband's present location, but it is impossible."

Isabella took a deep breath. "I understand."

"You do?" her aunt squawked.

"Yes. It seems I will have to seek my husband on my own." She got up and began to move about the room. Mr. Marbly started to rise to his feet, but she waved him back down. "I must assume," she said, "with circumstances being what they are, that James has gone as far away from me as possible. I must also assume that he will choose to hide out at one of his estates, for convenience, if nothing else. So, the estate that is farthest away? Hmmm. That would be the sugar plantation, if I recall correctly. Tell me, Mr. Marbly, does my husband own any properties farther away from England than Jamaica?"

"Not that I know of, my lady," he said warily.

"Excellent. Then that is where I shall begin my search."

The solicitor frowned. "I don't suppose it would do any good to tell you he isn't there?"

"Not a bit," she responded cheerily. "You might be trying to throw me off his scent, so to speak. No, I am determined to go. I refuse to let this state of affairs continue. As it is, my marriage has little chance of succeeding, but it will have no chance whatsoever if I cannot at least speak to my husband."

"Dearest, you cannot go," her aunt protested. "What if there should be a complication with the babe?"

Mr. Marbly, clearly relieved to have an ally, nodded rapidly, his head bobbing up and down like a parrot's.

Izzie thought for a moment. "I guess that is a risk I will have to take."

Mr. Marbly looked pained. She had seen that expression before on her father's face. It usually meant he wanted to shake her and was lamenting his inability to do so. Presumably, from the way the solicitor's hands were clenched into white-knuckled fists, he felt much the same.

"I must agree with Lady Sheldon. The journey is neither short nor easy nor, I promise you, will you find your husband there. To continue with this plan would be very ill-advised," he cautioned.

Izzie imagined that tone worked quite well for persuading his clients not to invest in risky ventures. But without risk, there was no gain, she reminded herself. Life was a series of gambles, an attempt to play the cards you were dealt as best you could. She just hoped he wouldn't call her bluff.

"Ill-advised though it may be," she ventured, "since you refuse to tell me where my husband is, I have no choice but to search for him myself. If you should change your mind, I might do the same."

She had backed him neatly into a corner, and his expression said he knew it. "Very well, my lady." The words emerged as a resigned sigh.

"Very well? Is that very well, have a safe journey, or very well, I will tell you where your husband is?"

"As I told you before, I believe that providing you with that information will almost certainly cost me my position."

"I assure you, Mr. Marbly, I will not let that happen," she hastened to assure him. "If my husband is angry with anyone, I promise it will be with me."

"Thank you, my lady. As I was saying, though I am convinced that Lord Dunston will dismiss me if I reveal his location, I am just as convinced that he will dismember me if I allow the alternative, your proposed journey, to go forward."

"You will tell me, then?"

"Yes." He nodded, a smile twitching at his upper lip. "Not only because I have no wish to be dismembered, but . . ." He struggled to find the right words.

"What? What is it?"

"Your husband is a fine man, and I have always held him in the highest esteem, but lately he has become somewhat . . . reckless. It is my hope that the news of his impending fatherhood will recall him to his senses."

Isabella was of the opinion that it might send him over the edge, but she kept it to herself. "Mr. Marbly, *where* is my husband?" she demanded impatiently.

"He is serving aboard the HMS *Theseus* which, he informed me prior to his departure, is one of the ships in the Mediterranean fleet."

Serving aboard the HMS Theseus. Blood pounded in her ears. A wave of blackness passed before her eyes, and her entire body began to shake.

"Izzie!"

"Lady Dunston!"

The voices were dim, as if coming from a long way off. Her aunt's gentle hands guided her into a chair and then pushed her head down until her cheek rested on her knees.

"He promised," she whispered.

Fury and heartbreak, fear and despair, and every conceivable emotion in between trampled over her.

"He promised."

All the cracks in her heart, so recently pieced back together, started to open again.

"He *promised*!"

Before, James had only been lost to her physically. Now, at this very moment, he could be lost to her forever. A fresh wave of grief washed over her, and she shoved a knuckle in her mouth, biting down hard, relishing the pain. She didn't know how to exist in a world without him. He had always been there.

The moment she had met him, a piece of her soul she hadn't known was missing had clicked back into place. When she was around James she felt centered and stable; the thought of him was a steady port in the midst of turbulent seas. He was simply a part of her; even when they were separated, the knowledge that he was there, in the world, was simply . . . enough.

All her life, Izzie had believed that James would protect her from any and all bad things. She had always assumed he would keep his promises. She had been wrong, and now she was lost, her moorings gone, adrift in the current. Despair threatened to overtake her, and then she felt it—a tiny quivering sensation in her abdomen. Her babe moved again, as if a delicate butterfly fluttering within her. Her child would be her anchor.

"Perhaps I should be going," she heard Mr. Marbly say to her aunt. "If Lady Dunston wishes to send something to her husband, she need only—"

Isabella raised her head. "I have nothing further to say to him," she told the solicitor in arctic tones.

"But, the child . . . ," he protested.

She rose to her feet, her stance proud and just a touch defiant. "Mr. Marbly, before we were wed, my husband made his feelings perfectly clear on the subject of children. I cannot imagine he has changed his mind. Were I to inform him of his impending fatherhood, he would only run farther away and act in a manner more reckless and rash. I will not chase him, nor will I beg for scraps of his affection, either for myself or for our child."

The solicitor sent her a sad, understanding smile. "Forgive my impertinence, Lady Dunston, but your husband is a fool. Sadly, I fear he will not realize it until it is too late."

"Thank you, sir," Isabella said, an answering sad smile upon her own lips. She waited until her aunt had shown the man from the room before she added, "But it is already too late."

Chapter 15

I have news of a rather delicate, yet most miraculous, nature to impart. You are going to be a grandmother! As there cannot be a great deal of confusion over when the babe was conceived, this happy event should take place in November. Aunt Kate assures me that the midwife who delivered Charlotte will be on hand, but I should like above all things for you to be present as well. I do not wish an accoucheur from Edinburgh to attend, for I wish as few people as possible to know. Please do not tell anyone aside from my father and Henry, and let each of them know, for reasons I shall explain later, that I do not wish James to find out about the child. Bridges have been burned, and I must focus on moving forward.

From the correspondence of Isabella, Lady Dunston, age twenty

Letter to her mother, Mary, Viscountess Weston, informing the recipient that the sender has been, as those vulgar Americans say, "knocked up"—May 1798

HMS *Theseus*
Somewhere in the middle of the Mediterranean Sea
July 1798

He wasn't breaking his promise, James told himself as he stared out at the endless expanse of water. In the seven or so months that he had been at sea, the words had become something of a litany. But, he reminded himself, he had promised Isabella that he wouldn't enlist in the army, and he hadn't. The Royal Navy was an entirely different entity—something he had learned rather quickly. For one thing, there weren't commissions available for purchase as there were in the army; a man rose or fell on his own merits.

And it wasn't as if he had known he would end up in the navy when he made his promise. He had arrived in London without the faintest notion of what he was going to do—other than get roaring drunk, that was, because it was his wedding night. It was his bloody wedding night and he wasn't going to be spending it in bed. Not with his wife, because he couldn't, and not with any other woman, because he wouldn't. Even though theirs would never again be a marriage in anything but name, the thought of going to another woman on his wedding night was repulsive. For one thing, it would destroy Isabella if she ever found out about it, but more important, the truth was that he didn't want another woman. He wanted Isabella.

His wife was the one woman he couldn't have, and the little minx had ruined him for anyone else. It would be laughable if it weren't so damned depressing. So he had headed to White's, and as he was no longer in danger of being left penniless, he had proceeded to order the most expensive bottle of brandy the club's cellars could offer up. It was nowhere near adequate compensation for what he was missing, as his traitorous body recalled all too well, but a man in his situation had to take what consolation he could get.

Then, when he was halfway through the bottle, just beginning to relax, a hand clamped down on his shoulder as a voice from out of the past said, "Well, as I live and breathe, I'll be damned if it isn't James Sheffield."

James glanced up to see Ethan Howe, the second son of Earl Howe, and the first friend—other than Henry— he had made at Eton. Ethan had joined the Royal Navy straight out of Eton, which meant he was rarely home, but time and distance didn't matter in a friendship of such long standing.

And James was in dire need of a friendly face; in fact, he didn't think he had ever been so happy to see someone in his entire life. The amount of brandy left in the bottle had dwindled to almost nothing by the time James had told his old friend a carefully edited and mostly fictional version of all the recent goings-on.

"Sho you shee," James said, gazing mournfully at the empty bottle, "my life ish a living hell. Ish what I deserve for marrying my besh friend's sishter."

"You had no choice," Ethan reassured him. "You were found in a compromising position. You did the right thing."

James struggled to remember what he had told his friend. That was the problem with lies. They were so damnably hard to keep track of.

A companionable silence settled over the two men, and then—

"Good God, man, it's your wedding night!" Ethan burst out.

As if he needed reminding. "I can't bed her," James said, his tone full of regret and resignation.

"Because you see her as a sister?"

"Er . . . yesh. Exactly. A sishter." Since he wasn't about to reveal the truth, James figured it was as good an explanation as any.

Ethan pursed his lips. "Can't you just close your eyes and pretend it's someone else?"

Close his eyes and pretend it was someone else? James raked a hand through his hair. "No," he said, fighting the hysteria bubbling up in his chest. "No, I don't think that will work. I don't think anything will work, really. I wanted to join the army—end it in an honorable fashion, you know, but I promised my wife I wouldn't enlist in the army. But enough about me. What are you doing in London? Aren't you a captain? Shouldn't you be at shea, shaving the Empire from the damned Frogs?"

"Shaving the Empire?" Ethan laughed.

James scowled. "You need more brandy. Makes shense with brandy."

"I think more brandy is the last thing we need. Actually, I am no longer a lieutenant. After the Battle of Cape St. Vincent last year, I was elevated to the rank of master and commander. You see before you the captain of the *Theseus*."

"Didn't that ushe to be Nelson's ship? Congratulations," James said, sincerely pleased for his friend. At least one of them was happy. Damn, he was starting to feel sorry for himself again; the brandy must be wearing off.

"Promotions do tend to fall into one's lap when one's father was formerly First Lord of the Admiralty." He shrugged in self-deprecation. "In any case, I am in town for my brother's wedding—you remember John?"

"Only that he liked mathematics."

"Isn't much else to him. Dullest dog I've ever known, but for all that he is my brother. As the Fates would have it, he found a girl as bloody boring as he is, and they tied the knot at St. Paul's yesterday. With my familial obligations thus taken care of, I will be on my way to Portsmouth tomorrow. From there, I will be on the next ship bound for Gibraltar and the *Theseus*."

"God, what I wouldn't give to be going with you." James sighed.

"So why don't you?"

"I promised my wife I wouldn't enlist."

"You said you promised her you wouldn't enlist in the *army*."

James bolted straight up in his chair. "By God, you're right," he exclaimed. "I'll do it."

The other man grinned, and for a moment James felt as if he were back at Eton, about to pull some sort of prank, all full of nervous anticipation.

"Mind," Ethan pointed out, "life at sea isn't easy. It's blasted uncomfortable at times. You can go for months without a woman, and you won't be ranked higher than a midshipman. The Admiralty has strict rules about that."

"I don't care," James said quickly.

His friend nodded approvingly. "In that case, I would be glad to have you aboard. There will be action before long, mark my words. My father tells me the French fleet is gathered in Toulon. Pitt thinks that damned little Corsican upstart is planning to invade the Mediterranean, but we'll soon put a stop to that."

"Soon," James thought, as the ship's deck pitched beneath his feet, had turned out to be a rather relative term. Rear Admiral Sir Horatio Nelson had arrived in Gibraltar to command operations against General Bonaparte in the Mediterranean, but the French fleet was proving elusive. A month ago, they had learned from a passing ship that Napoleon had captured the island of Malta. Nelson believed that Malta was only a stopping point on Bonaparte's quest to invade Egypt in order to establish a French route to India.

The prospect of the French military in southern India had the British government and the investors in the British East India Company quaking in their boots. Thus, the entire fleet had set sail for Egypt, but they had encountered no sign of the French ships. *Soon*, he reminded himself, his lips quirking into a half smile.

"Woolgathering?"

James turned from the rail and found Ethan regarding him with amusement. The smile faded from his mouth as he replied, "I was thinking about Isabella."

"Again?"

James shrugged, turning back to stare out at the waves. "I can't seem to help it. I don't know why, but no matter what I happen to be doing, my thoughts stray to her."

"Could it be that you miss her?"

The softly uttered question instantly transported James back to the night of Isabella's ball. . . .

"D–did you miss me?"

"I didn't want to."

"B-but you did?"

He *did* miss her. He missed her even more than he missed Henry, his best friend for more than a decade. He missed her more than he could have ever imagined. He absentmindedly rubbed at his chest, at the ever-present ache that hovered there. "I feel as if I left part of myself behind," he admitted in a choked whisper.

Ethan placed a comforting hand on his shoulder. "I think, mayhap, that was your heart. I also think that perhaps you failed to tell me the truth all those months ago in London, hmmm?"

James nodded, not really hearing him. "I can't stop wondering if she is all right. I would have heard by now if she was with child, don't you think?"

"W-with *child*?" Ethan spluttered. "Just how compromising was this position you were found in? And," he demanded, jabbing a finger into James's chest, "how did you come to be in such a position with a girl you see as a sister?"

James smiled weakly. "Did I say that?"

"You most certainly did."

"I might have left out a few small details."

"*A few small* . . . You didn't say you were bedding the chit."

"First of all, the *chit* is my *wife*. Second, I wasn't bedding her," James said tightly. "I slept with her once—*one time*—and—"

"You got caught," his friend finished.

"Er . . . not quite."

Ethan frowned. "She told someone?"

"No."

"Then *you* told someone."

James paused for a moment. "You know, I suppose I did," he said with a rueful grin.

"Whom, exactly, did you tell?"

James took a deep breath and braced himself for his friend's reaction. "Her parents," he admitted with a heavy sigh.

Ethan whooped with laughter. "Her parents? You told her *parents*? You didn't get caught in the parson's mousetrap, my friend. You held out your leg and begged to have the shackles put on."

"Rubbish. Besides, you are mixing your metaphors."

"And you are deliberately avoiding the truth. You wanted to marry this girl."

"Trust me, I did not. Once I took her innocence, though, I didn't seem to have a lot of choice in the matter."

"Come now, if you had kept your trap shut, no one would have been the wiser. She certainly wouldn't be the first girl to enter her wedding bed having cracked her pitcher, nor would she be the last."

"But, even then, she could have been carrying my child," James pointed out.

"Bah. You could have easily waited a month or so to see if that was the case. No, I think that deep down, you wanted to marry her. Don't forget, I know you. I have known you since those early days at Eton, when we were both wet behind the ears. There is not a soul alive who could force you into doing something you really didn't want to do."

"But—"

"No, regardless of what you say, you wanted to marry her. What I don't understand is why you ran after the wedding."

"I slept with her once," James said. "I can't do it again."

"That bad, eh? So keep a mistress. You can bloody well afford it, and most men—"

"No," James cut him off, "that isn't the problem. Far, far from it."

"Then why?"

"Do you believe in omens?"

Ethan halted, thrown by the abrupt change in subject. "An omen as in, 'Red sky at night, sailor's delight; red sky at morning, sailor's warning'? Aye, every sailor knows there is more than a mite of truth in that. Why?"

"I had a vision, a premonition actually, before Isabella and I were wed."

"Go on."

James closed his eyes and raked a hand through his hair. His voice dropped to a near whisper as the awful scene played out in his mind once more. "It was terrible. I was back at my mother's funeral, but I was a grown man, not young, as I should have been. It was a miserable day with storm clouds hovering. I stepped to the edge of the grave, ready to toss a handful of dirt atop the coffin, when I saw that it was missing its lid. It was then I realized it was not my mother and sister being buried. It was Isabella. Our babe was nestled by her side."

"Jesus," Ethan breathed.

James nodded, opening his eyes. Their expression was bleak as he said, "It was a warning. I can't be around my wife without wanting her, but I can't have her. I can't risk it. If she gets with child, it will kill her, just as it killed my mother. I can't—" He drew in a shuddering breath. "I can't lose her."

Ethan was silent for a long moment. "I don't believe it was an omen," he finally said. "If it was a warning at all, it was one conjured by your mind out of fear that you were coming to care for her too strongly. This premonition, as you call it, allows you to justify your distance from her, both physically and emotionally. You can run away and tell yourself that it is for her own good, that you are doing it to protect her."

"I *am* doing it to protect her," James growled.

"Did her mother have any problems bearing children?" Ethan asked. "I recall you said your wife has scads of siblings."

James crossed his arms over his chest and glowered.

"Right, then. There is no reason, other than this vision of yours, to think that your wife would have complications in childbirth. Because of your past, you are scared of ever getting too close, scared of ever caring too much, but it's too late, James. You have fallen in love with your wife, and you have fallen hard."

"I have not."

"Yes," he said firmly, "you have. The question is, are you going to spend the rest of your life running? We could all, any one of us, die tomorrow for any one of a thousand reasons. No one knows how much time he's been given."

James clenched his jaw. "Enough."

His friend refused to heed the warning. "Do you want to spend that time miserable, as you are now? Would you not prefer to be with your wife, to raise children in the loving family you were denied? And what about an heir? Who stands to inherit if you remain childless?"

"Upon my death, the Sheffield line will come to an end, and I presume the title and estates will revert back to the crown." He laughed bitterly. "My grandfather will be rolling in his grave when that day arrives."

Ethan's brow creased into lines of disapproval. "I didn't realize you were so selfish," he said quietly.

"*Selfish?*" James exploded. His outburst attracted the notice of some sailors working on the deck beneath them who looked up, shading their eyes against the sun, to see what the commotion was. James took a few steps away from the railing and lowered his voice. "You grew up in a family. You have a father, a mother, and siblings who all love you. You have no idea what it was like for me growing up, the things I had to listen to."

"Stop thinking about yourself. You hated your grandfather. I understand that. He was a cold, unfeeling bastard, and I don't blame you for feeling the way you do, but you cannot think solely about yourself."

"I—"

Ethan slashed a hand through the air, silencing him. "Every decision you make, every action you take affects others. If all your lands revert to the crown, your tenants will suffer. Instead of having a lord who fairly manages his estates and looks after them, they will be at the mercy of Prince George's greed. Even though your grandfather is six feet under, you are still letting him control you; your hatred is dictating your life."

"Excuse me, Captain," a young officer shouted as he hurried toward them.

"I will be with you directly, Lieutenant," Ethan called out in response. He turned to face James. "All I ask is that you think about what I've said," he told him, and then strode off.

James resumed his position at the rail, staring mindlessly out at the dazzling azure waters of the Mediterranean, his mind awhirl in a chaotic jumble of half-formed thoughts. For the first time since he had been at sea, he was glad for the general inactivity aboard the *Theseus*. It seemed he had quite a bit of thinking to do.

Off the coast of Egypt in the Mediterranean
1 August 1798

The search for the French fleet was over. Four days earlier, Captain Troubrige of the *Culloden* had received confirmation that the French ships had sailed east. Again the British fleet had set off for the Egyptian coast, and they had reached Alexandria earlier in the day. Where it had been empty just weeks before, the port was now filled with French transport vessels. Nelson had directed his fleet to continue sailing along the coast.

The ships had all readied for action; the decks were clear and the guns stood at ready. Dusk had just fallen when Nelson's flagship, *Vanguard*, flew the signal that the enemy was in sight. James was standing beside Ethan on the quarterdeck when the flag was raised. Ethan had been watching the line of French ships through a wooden spyglass, which he offered over to James. Vice Admiral Brueys d'Aigalliers, commanding the French, had his line of battle chained together and anchored in the shallow waters of the Bay of Aboukir.

"It's time, then," James said, handing the heavy glass back to his friend. During the months of searching for the French fleet, Admiral Nelson had made a practice of frequently assembling his captains and discussing plans for the eventual battle. James knew from Ethan that their instructions were to attack with immediacy and aggression. As the last glimpse of the burning, red sun disappeared from the horizon, heavy fire began to rain down from the French batteries on Aboukir Island; broadsides followed from the enemy ships.

Ethan turned to James, anticipation lighting his eyes. "Yes," he echoed, "it's time." He moved into action, every inch the captain of the ship, barking out orders and encouraging his crew. The men were ready for this. They weren't eager, precisely, but after months of waiting, they were ready—ready to have done with it.

James understood completely. He was ready to go home. He had done a lot of thinking since the day Ethan had confronted him. He wasn't sure he had everything quite sorted out, but one thing had become very clear: He was in love with his wife. He was in love with Isabella. And instead of the panicky fear he had expected would accompany such a revelation, he felt only peace. He had spent his life fighting, rebelling against his grandfather, battling his emotions, struggling to keep people from becoming too close.

But somehow, Isabella had slipped past his defenses and breached the walls surrounding his heart. He was done fighting her, done fighting fate. He had lost the battle, but in doing so, he had won something far more precious. For the first time since the day he had arrived at Sheffield Park, James was filled with a desire to *live*, with hope for the future—a future with Isabella. For reasons beyond his comprehension, she loved him.

Oh, no doubt he had fouled things up royally by leaving her, and she would have kittens once she found out about the navy, but he was certain she still loved him. She'd said she always had and always would, and he would hold her to that. He didn't deserve her, but he was going to do his damnedest to be worthy of her. He intended to spend the rest of his life devoting himself to her happiness, but first he had to survive. With a heavy heart, he took up his position at the rail, his pistol primed and loaded. Ethan knew he was a crack shot and had instructed him to take out the captain of the enemy ship once they were anchored alongside her.

With the northern wind behind them, the British fleet, led by the *Goliath* and the *Zealous*, attacked. In a surprise maneuver, the *Goliath*'s captain steered the ship toward the landward side of the line, where he anchored and opened fire. The *Zealous* followed suit, followed by the *Orion* and the *Audacious*.

Ethan also directed the *Theseus* on the landward path, sailing down the line of French ships before anchoring and engaging the French *Spartiate*. James braced himself as the first round of French broadsides shook the ship, tearing through the gun deck. The *Theseus* returned fire, splitting the hull of the enemy ship. James scanned the deck, looking for the French captain. Unable to locate him, he aimed instead for a sailor manning one of the swivel guns. When packed with chain shot, those small cannons could quickly destroy a ship's masts and rigging.

The next round of broadsides came crashing into the upper deck, not ten feet from James. He looked on in horror as men he knew, men he had come to admire, were blasted into pieces. Others were felled by the heavy iron balls, or maimed by the splinters flying up from the shattered wooden deck. He steeled himself against the carnage and focused on reloading his pistol and sighting his next target.

It was impossible, however, to block out the screams of the wounded. Their cries melded into a symphony of pain, a haunting contrast to the faint strains of "Rule, Britannia" coming from the band playing on the deck of the *Vanguard*. Nelson's flagship had entered the battle on the seaward side and was anchored opposite the *Theseus*, attacking the *Spartiate* from the other side.

The fighting raged on for hours. The ship's deck ran red, and the dead were pitched overboard to make room for the wounded. Both ships had sustained heavy damage, but the end was far from near. It was a battle to the death—every sailor there knew it—but James refused to die. Not when he had such a very good reason to live. His clothes were torn and spattered with the blood of his fallen compatriots, but it wasn't for them that he soldiered on.

When his arms ached from the continuous loading and firing of his gun and his legs began to buckle from the strain of bracing himself against the explosions reverberating through the ship, James conjured up Isabella's image to give himself strength. When the heavy clouds of smoke that filled the sky burned his lungs and stung his eyes, he formed Isabella's name on his parched lips to give himself focus. And when despair and exhaustion threatened to overwhelm him and drag him down, he summoned the sweet sound of Isabella's voice promising to love him for all eternity to give himself hope.

He was given a brief respite when the battle paused after the French flagship, the *Orient*, caught fire; anticipating the explosion that would result when the flames reached the ammunition stored in the ship's magazine, all the ships hurriedly tried to distance themselves from the blazing wreck. As an extra precaution, the sailors doused each ship's rigging and woodwork with seawater. The *Orient's* crew began abandoning ship, the men throwing themselves into the water and swimming as if their lives depended on it, which of course, they did.

When the blast hit, it was as if the fires of hell had come racing up from underneath the sea's floor and burst through the water's surface, destruction and devastation following in their wake. Burning pieces of the ship and its crew were hurled hundreds of feet into the air. As sailors of both fleets looked on in shock, all the firing ceased; an eerie silence hung over the scene for seemingly endless moments, and then the debris from the demolished ship began to rain down until the whole bay was covered with the scorched, broken bodies of the dead.

Bile rose up in James's throat at the sight. Although the French were the enemy, every man out there was someone's son, brother, husband, or father. Most of the poor bastards probably hadn't had a clue what it was they were fighting for, he thought, wondering what would become of all the loved ones left behind. So absorbed was he in his meditations, James failed to notice that the fighting had resumed until he felt the searing pain of a bullet slamming into his right shoulder. He grasped the rail, stunned by how badly it hurt.

As he grappled with the pain, a second ball tore into his

torso, just beneath his ribs. He staggered backward, clutching his midsection with his left arm and trying to halt the rush of blood. He slumped down on the deck as blackness began to creep in at the edges of his vision. Ethan's worried face swam before his eyes, and then there was only darkness. He heard his friend yelling for the ship's surgeon, but the sound was growing fainter and fainter.

It was over, he realized. He was going to die there, bleeding to death on a ship in the Mediterranean, far away from Isabella. He had never even told her that he loved her. There was so much he hadn't done, so many regrets that weighed on him, but that was the worst. Mustering what little strength he still possessed, he called out Ethan's name.

"Need you to do something for me," he rasped, each word sending jolts of pain through his body.

"Anything," Ethan said. "But once Wright here patches you up, you will be—"

"No," James whispered sadly. "Tell Izzie—" He fought to draw in one last breath. "Tell her I loved her." As the shadows came to claim him, he thought he heard her husky laughter and smelled the subtle scent of honeysuckle dancing in the breeze.

Chapter 16

*I dreamt of apricots last night. I know the vile
things are purportedly omens of good luck, but given
my utter distaste for them, I fear this dream is a har-
binger of troubles to come. I know it is likely the babe
that has put me in such a superstitious frame of mind,
but I find I have little control over my emotions as of
late. I am certain I do not know how you managed
being with child so often. I have always known that
you are a remarkable woman, but these past months
of misery have increased my respect for you tenfold!*

From the correspondence of Isabella, Lady Dunston,
age twenty

Letter to her mother, Mary, Viscountess Weston, noting
the fearful visions of apricots that danced in the sender's
head—August 1798

At Haile Castle, the month of October was one of arrivals,
both good and bad. With the first week arrived the news
of Nelson's brilliant victory at the Battle of the Nile, as the
papers were calling it, but Isabella felt little like celebrat-
ing. She was frantic with fear for James.

"My dear, you must try to remain calm," Aunt Kate reminded her for the umpteenth time. "All this fretting is not
good for the babe."

"Do you think it would help if we reminded her that

she is supposed to be furious with him?" Olivia whispered loudly.

"Oh, I remember," Izzie said a bit violently. "I haven't forgiven him for breaking his promise to me." In truth, she wasn't sure she could ever move past that betrayal of trust. "But," she admitted, her voice softening, "despite everything, I still love him." And she had finally come to the conclusion that it was pointless trying to figure out why.

"Let's think on something more pleasant," Aunt Kate proposed.

"How about baby names?" Olivia suggested.

"Are you hoping for a boy or for a girl?"

"A girl," Izzie replied without hesitation. A girl she could raise quietly, on her own. If the baby were a boy, though, he would be next in line to inherit the earldom, and he would have to be brought up in a manner befitting his rank. It would also be harder for a boy to grow up without a father.

She had meant what she told Mr. Marbly. She was not going to beg for his love. She had done it before, but never again. Not for herself, and certainly not for their child. She was not going to allow herself and the babe to be weighed against his desire for revenge, because she knew in her aching heart that they would come up short.

She smoothed a hand over the taut mound of her stomach. *You will have more love than you know what to do with*, she silently promised the tiny life growing within her. She already loved the baby so much that it scared her at times, and she knew she would do whatever was necessary to protect him or her. And if that meant shielding her child from a father's rejection, she would do it.

"You aren't planning on naming the child after a Shakespearean character, are you?" Olivia asked abruptly, a look of horror crossing her face at the thought.

Isabella laughed, shaking her head. "I think not. But Mama would love that, wouldn't she?"

"What would I love?"

Both girls turned, wearing identical expressions of disbelief, stunned by the sight of the familiar figure entering the room, like an apparition they had conjured up with their words. The shock only lasted a moment, however, and then both girls were running to embrace their mother. Well, Olivia ran anyway. Isabella waddled as quickly as she could.

"Mama, what are you doing here so soon? We didn't expect you for at least another week," Izzie exclaimed, embracing her mother as best she could, given her huge belly.

"Perhaps we should sit down," her aunt suggested, gently herding everyone over toward the grouping of sofas and chairs. Izzie sank gratefully down onto the sofa, easing the pressure off her swollen ankles. She shoved a fist behind her and began to knead her lower back, which was unusually sore that morning. Her mother sat down next to her and held her hand.

"You look so beautiful," her mother told her. "You are positively glowing. Pregnancy clearly agrees with you."

Olivia snorted loudly in objection and was promptly whisked out of the room by Aunt Kate, who muttered something about seeing to tea.

Once they were alone, Isabella said softly, "It's James, isn't it?"

Her mother nodded, her eyes filling with tears.

An icy numbness enveloped her. "Is he... ?" She swallowed, unable to say the word.

"No," her mother responded, "but he has been badly wounded. The Admiralty sent a messenger to Sheffield Park, but as you weren't in residence, Mrs. Benton directed him to Weston Manor. Once we heard the news, your father agreed that I should come straight to you."

"But he *is* going to be all right?"

Her mother squeezed her hand tightly. "My dear, I wish with all my heart that I could promise you that, but I honestly don't know. The reports the Admiralty received noted that James, along with several other wounded officers, was recovering in Naples. But by now, those reports are nearly a month old." She dabbed at her eyes with a handkerchief.

Isabella lumbered to her feet. "He is alive," she stated forcefully. "I would know if he were not. I would *know*. But

I have to go to him." She realized her hands were shaking violently, and she clasped them together to still the movement. "Yes, I have to go to him," she repeated. The air around her felt thick, and she had to fight to pull it into her lungs. "He needs me. I have to—have to—"

Before her eyes, the walls of the room began to fragment and pull apart; everything around her started whirling about and rearranging itself in a dizzying, kaleidoscopic fashion. She turned jerkily, frantically searching for some point of stability, some beacon of light to guide her out of this nightmarish maze. Her gaze finally fixed on her mother's face, and Isabella reached out her hands in a desperate attempt to be saved. But it was too late. Her body was wracked by a painful spasm emanating from deep in her belly, so overwhelming that it sent her to her knees, and she let darkness take the place of chaos.

Her body ached and felt all heavy and unbearably hot. Isabella blinked, slowly taking in the bed hangings, trying to recall what had happened. She remembered her mother. She had been talking to her mother.... *James!* He was hurt. She twisted on the mattress, trying to maneuver herself into a sitting position, when her body seized up with the most horrible, gripping pain. And then, as quickly as it had come, it was gone. Panting, she flopped back down on the bed.

"That's right, darling, just relax," her mother said, wiping a cool cloth across Isabella's forehead.

Isabella shifted her head so that she could see her mother. "What happened?"

"You fainted."

"How did I get upstairs?"

"I knew there would come a day I was glad to have hired a brawny butler." Her aunt's voice, oddly strained, came from the other side of the bed.

Isabella wanted to turn her head in response to the sound, but at that moment, it seemed far too much of an effort. "Hello, Aunt Kate. Tell me, Mama, is anyone else in the room? Olivia? Charlotte?" she asked jokingly.

"Heavens, no. That wouldn't be at all proper."

"Do you have any idea how much I detest that word?" Izzie muttered under her breath.

"But the midwife should be here soon," her aunt added.

"The midwife? Why would she—aargh!" Another spasm gripped her and then passed, leaving her feeling as if she had been trampled by a stampeding herd of cattle.

"Izzie, your labor pains have started," her mother explained gently.

The implication behind her mother's words slowly sank in, sending Isabella into an uncontrollable terror. The baby wasn't due for nearly another month. Oh God, she couldn't lose her baby. "No. No!" she shouted, then turned her gaze to the enormous mound of her stomach and gripped her belly tightly, as if to hold the babe inside her. She looked back up at her mother with panic-stricken eyes. "It's too soon. The baby isn't ready yet. Why is this happening? What did I do wrong?"

"Nothing. Do you understand me? You did nothing wrong. Sometimes these things just happen, especially during times of stress. If anyone is to blame, it is I. It was likely the shock of hearing about James that brought this on."

"This isn't your fault, Mary," Isabella's aunt said, coming over to put her arm around her sister.

"Will my baby be all right?" Isabella whispered.

"Mrs. Drummond is an excellent midwife, and—" A soft knock at the door interrupted her aunt, who went to answer it. "Oh, Mrs. Drummond, thank you for coming so quickly. I was just telling my niece that she couldn't be in more capable hands."

"Bless ye, dearie. Now let me have a wee look at our new muither ta be. Hello, milady," the midwife said. She set her kit down by the side of the bed, and then moved forward to place her hands on Isabella's stomach. "How are ye feelin' this fine day?"

"I—" Another contraction swamped her body.

"That's it, dearie, jest ride it out and dinna forget ta breathe."

Isabella focused on the soothing sound of the woman's voice. Mrs. Drummond bustled about the room preparing for the birth, pulling various articles out of her case, giving orders for hot water and linens, directing everything as if rehearsing for some sort of performance. According to Scottish custom, she covered all the mirrors in the room and instructed one of the maids who brought the water to check that all the doors in the castle were locked and that every window was tightly closed.

After drawing the drapes and lighting candles, the midwife placed pillows underneath Izzie's head, the small of her back, and her pelvis, which relieved much of Isabella's discomfort. Her entire body relaxed, her breathing deepened, and she was beginning to think that perhaps childbirth wasn't so difficult after all, when she caught the midwife saying, "Och, it's early yet. 'Twill be several hours at least afore her labor truly starts."

"*Hours?*" Izzie croaked. And what was this talk about her labor not having really started? It certainly felt as if it had!

She gritted her teeth as her muscles surrendered to the fast-becoming-familiar brief bout of spasms and cramps. When it had passed, she asked again, "Hours?"

"Walking might speed it up some," Mrs. Drummond suggested.

Izzie groaned, but she allowed the midwife to help her out of bed. Her mother and aunt supported her as she hobbled around the room, while Mrs. Drummond covered the bed with old quilts and linen to protect the mattress.

"With you, I was in labor for only about eight hours," her mother said, trying to make conversation.

"How wonderfully reassuring," Isabella said through clenched teeth.

"I was in labor with Charlotte for twenty-one hours," her aunt boasted in an attempt to lighten the mood.

"T-twenty-o-one?" Izzie wailed.

"Dinna upset the puir lassie," Mrs. Drummond admonished. "She'll need all her strength in jest a little while."

"Or a long while," Aunt Kate muttered under her breath.

Izzie glared at her aunt. "Heard that. Not helping," she ground out.

"Sorry, sweetheart," her aunt said. "I am certain the baby will be born in record time."

"I pray that you are ri-ight," Isabella replied, inhaling sharply as the pains began again. She glanced longingly toward the bed, and the women helped her climb back up, an exercise that left them all somewhat short of breath.

Isabella's prayers fell on deaf ears, though, as the labor continued through the afternoon without advancing. Finally, in the early evening her contractions began to grow longer and more intense. Isabella's thin cotton night rail was soon drenched with sweat, but no matter how powerfully she pushed, the baby stubbornly refused to move. Despite the constant encouragement of the three women in the room, Isabella began to fret that the babe was never coming. Her pains were so close together that there were only scant seconds of relief between them.

When the clock struck midnight, she began to weep. "Why won't the baby come?" she whimpered, nearly ready to give up. "I keep trying and trying so hard, but I'm so tired!" she cried, then started to sob.

"Don't cry, darling," her mother pleaded. "You need to conserve your energy." Then she turned to the midwife. "Do something!" she urged.

Mrs. Drummond ran her hands over Isabella's body. "The fairies have cursed her," she pronounced. "We must break the enchantment."

"The—the *fairies*?" her mother sputtered, but was shushed by Aunt Kate.

Mrs. Drummond began to move about the room, crooning:

> *Broom, woodbine, juniper berries,*
> *Stay the will o' the fairies;*
> *Rowan tree an' this blue thread,*
> *Hold the witches a' in dread.*

As she softly sang the words, the midwife rummaged through her bag and pulled out a length of blue thread, which she proceeded to tie around one of Isabella's fingers.

> *Saint Bride, come, enter this home,*
> *Come, come, an' you are welcome;*
> *Offer aid t' the woman here,*
> *An' keep her babe frae reif an' wear.*

Now, Isabella had never been one for magic or superstition. To her mind, a cat was a cat, regardless of its color, and if the toadstools in the forest happened to be growing in a circular formation, well, she would have been far more perturbed if the mushrooms had spelled out her name. While other girls giggled over omens, the only thing Isabella saw in the leaves left in a teacup was that the drinker had been thirsty.

She might be impulsive, even flighty at times, but she liked to think that at her core, she was a creature of logic and intelligence. That being said, she was ready to swear on a stack of Bibles that Mrs. Drummond was some sort of white witch, because whatever the woman was doing with her chanting and her blue threads, it was working. She could feel the babe start to shift downward, creating such an excruciating pressure in her lower back that she thought she was being split in two. White lightning flashed behind her eyelids, and she couldn't seem to stop screaming, even though her throat felt raw.

Mrs. Drummond took her place at the foot of the bed and guided Isabella into the proper position, spreading her thighs and bracing her feet against the bed's footboard. For modesty's sake, the midwife covered her with a sheet from her shoulders to her knees, but Isabella couldn't have cared less. At that point, an entire regiment could have marched through the bedroom doors and it wouldn't have mattered one whit. The age-old instinct to have the baby was settling over her like a heavy mantle, cloaking her from the distractions of the world around her.

Although she still felt the presence of the other women in the room, she was in some separate, higher realm, consisting only of the intimate communion between her and her baby. Her despair deserted her, replaced by an intense focus and a quiet serenity. She knew what she had to do. When the next contraction gripped her, Isabella listened to her body's demands, bore down with all her might, and yelled loud enough that she was certain people several villages over could hear her.

"Verra good," Mrs. Drummond exclaimed. "Let's ha' another jest like it."

Gulping in a deep breath of air, Isabella pushed again until her face felt quivery and tight and the blood was pounding fiercely in her temples.

"Breathe, darling," her mother reminded her as she wiped a cool cloth over Izzie's flushed face.

"Again," the midwife commanded.

Panting heavily, Isabella complied. Tears leaked from her eyes, mixing with the beads of sweat coursing down her face. How on earth had her mother gone through this so many times? She must have voiced the question aloud, for her mother began to laugh and patted her hand.

"The first child is always the hardest," she said, "though the twins were by no means easy. In hindsight, that was clearly an omen, but"—she shrugged—"trust me, as soon as you hold your baby in your arms, you forget everything else."

"Aye." Mrs. Drummond nodded vigorously. "'Tis always the same. Ye'll soon see when you hold your own bairn. 'Twill be verra, verra soon. Another push now, dearie. Jest a few more."

"I'm not sure I can." She was so tired, exhausted to her very bones; it would surely be impossible to find the strength for even one more. She wondered whether it would be possible for the midwife to shove the baby back up into her belly and leave it there for a few days while she got some rest. It seemed like an excellent solution, and she was just about to suggest it when she heard a voice in her head—James's voice.

You can do this, sweetheart. Our baby needs you. You can do this. I'll help you. We'll push together.

"I can do this," Izzie whispered to herself. Her baby needed her. The thought was a call to action, and she valiantly ignored the awful pain and fatigue, bearing down once again, praying that she would not fail the tiny life inside her.

"I can see the head," Mrs. Drummond crowed excitedly.

Isabella closed her eyes and thought of James. Despite everything that had happened between them, the very thought of him still soothed her.

One more, love.

She pushed with all she was worth and felt the baby slowly emerge from her body. First the head, then the shoulders, and then the rest slid out in a quick, slippery rush. A harsh wail pierced the silence that had fallen over the room. She instinctively reached down for her baby, and the midwife placed the tiny infant on Isabella's chest.

"A beautiful wee lassie," the midwife announced.

"A girl," Izzie whispered, looking down in awe at the precious baby she had brought into the world. They were still connected, she saw, by the dark cord running from the child back into herself. She patted her daughter's head, so small and fragile, marveling at the downy softness of the almost white blond wisps of hair.

She nearly cried when the midwife took her away to cut the cord, but her baby was soon returned to her, having been cleaned up and cozily swaddled in a blanket. Isabella's mother and aunt were each permitted to hold her, cooing nonsense and exclaiming over every miniature feature, but then Isabella grew unaccountably jealous and held out her arms to get her daughter back.

Since they hadn't yet hired a wet nurse, the midwife showed Isabella how to place the baby at her breast, where she happily began nursing, her tiny eyelids fluttering closed in blissful exhaustion. Izzie felt much the same. She was more tired than she had ever been in her life, but she was remarkably content and pleased with herself as well.

"Have you thought of a name?" her mother inquired. "I have always thought Ophelia quite lovely, or how about Rosalind, or—"

"Bride," said Isabella.

"Aye, Bride's a grand name and sae fittin' as it were Saint Bride who helped drive oot the fairies so ye could deliver the wee lassie." Mrs. Drummond voiced her approval.

"Are you sure you wouldn't prefer Bianca, or Beatrice, or how about—"

"Bride," Isabella repeated stubbornly. "Bride Kathleen Sheffield."

Her mother looked pained that not even the middle name was going to be Shakespearean.

"As Mrs. Drummond said, Saint Bride *did* assist in breaking the fairies' spell," her aunt solemnly pointed out, though her eyes glinted with laughter.

"Bride was the name of James's sister," Isabella explained softly, her eyes growing a bit teary. "And Kathleen was his mother. I just want her to have some part of her father with her in case—" Her voice broke.

"Bride Kathleen Sheffield," her mother said lovingly, sniffling a bit as she smiled down at her granddaughter. "Welcome to the family, little one."

Chapter 17

Allow me to thank you once more for all your assistance. I know I told you that I had no message for you to pass along to my errant husband but, as is a woman's prerogative, I have changed my mind. Should my husband contact you, you may tell him this: While penitent groveling, fine jewelry, and any other tokens of apology will be accepted, nothing can change his having broken his promise to me. I shall never forgive him, and I don't wish to see him ever again.

From the correspondence of Isabella, Lady Dunston, age twenty

Letter to Timothy Marbly, Esq., which, fortunately for the sender, was found by a very wise, very loving sister before it could be sent—July 1798

James stood at the ship's railing, a position he had held for the past two weeks, more impatient than ever now that the London docks were visible in the distance. He breathed in the tang of the salty sea air, relishing the grim, overcast, utterly English sky.

"Hard to believe we're almost there. Feels as if I've been away for a lifetime at least," said the man beside him. James turned and nodded at Davies. Both men had been injured at Aboukir Bay and had become friends during their long recoveries in Naples. Despite the difference in their stations—Davies was the youngest son of a country vicar—they were of an age, and they got on so well together that James had offered the man a position in his household as an alternative to going back to sea. Davies had accepted and, without a clear job description, had decided his position entailed taking care of James in whatever ways he could.

"I left in March, and now it's November," James remarked absently. His recovery in Naples had been painfully slow, but the doctors had kept telling him it was a miracle he was alive at all. Had the bullet in his shoulder been a trifle lower or had the one in his midsection been a couple inches higher, he would have been past saving.

As it was, his shoulder was stiff and often ached like the very devil, but it was a small price to pay. By the grace of God, he had been given a second chance at life. This time he was going to do it right. Assuming, that was, that Isabella would forgive him. Doubtful, that. Remembering the bloodthirsty games she had delighted in as a child, he supposed it was more likely that his little hellion of a wife would murder him on sight.

"Do you think the countess will be very angry?" Davies asked, echoing his thoughts.

"I think 'very angry' is an understatement. When I think about the reception I'm likely to receive, I almost envy Ethan and his bachelor life on the *Theseus*."

"You don't mean that," reproached Davies.

He was right. James didn't envy Ethan in the slightest. His wandering days were over. All he wanted was to be with Isabella, to apologize for leaving her, to tell her how much he loved her and admired her. *Soon*, he promised himself. *Soon*.

But two days later, when the carriage finally pulled up in front of Dunston House, James was disappointed to find the knocker off the door and the place closed up but for a skeleton staff.

"Has Lady Dunston lately been in residence?" he asked

one of the remaining footmen, trying to keep his tone casual.

"Lady Dunston?" the man responded, obviously taken aback by the question. "She's never set foot here, far as I know."

James frowned. Where was his wife? Surely she wasn't residing at Sheffield Park. That place was a marble mausoleum. And now that she was married, she couldn't still be at Weston Manor, could she? Why would she, when she had Dunston House to do with as she wished?

"Makes no bloody sense," he muttered to Davies, angry that Isabella wasn't awaiting him in London, even though there was no earthly reason for him to expect her to be there.

Aside from his having been gravely wounded.

Although he'd been told that news of the battle hadn't reached England until the first week in October, it was November now. Surely the Admiralty would have sent a messenger. . . . She *had* to know. He was certain she had been angry when she found out that he had joined the navy, but he had been hurt, damn it. Shouldn't the woman who had professed she would love him forever be in London to fret and fuss over him? Not that he wanted fretting and fussing, blast it. He scowled.

"Er, congratulations on your marriage, my lord," the footman mumbled, and scurried away.

As there was no cook in residence, James left Davies to scavenge and went to his club to eat. His shoulder was bothering him, which put him in even more of a foul mood, so he requested a private room to avoid running into any of his acquaintances. It wasn't lost on him that the last time he had come there, he had ended up in the navy.

After a restless night, James concluded he had no choice but to head for Sheffield Park. First, though, he decided to pay a call to his solicitor. He figured he might as well check to make sure nothing had happened in the months he had been gone, even though he fully expected that all was in order.

"My lord, I see you are alive and well," the solicitor said

archly as he escorted James into his office. From his disapproving tone of voice, though, James suspected the man would have been happier to see him battered and bloody, at the very least. And what was that about, he'd like to know? It seemed the man had conveniently forgotten who paid his quite-generous wages.

"Thank you, Mr. Marbly," James responded curtly. "I trust there have been no problems in my absence?"

The solicitor leaned back in his chair and steepled his fingers, regarding James speculatively. "That depends," he finally said.

"On what?" James demanded, uncomfortable being the subject of such intense scrutiny.

"Well, I suppose it depends on whether or not you would classify the situation with Lady Dunston as a *problem*."

At the mention of his wife, James shot out of his chair like a cannon. Scenarios flashed through his mind, each more terrible than the next, setting his heart hammering violently. "Oh God, what's happened? Is she all right? Where is she?" he asked frantically.

"Calm yourself, my lord. Her ladyship is fine, or rather, she is as well as can be expected, given the circumstances."

"The circumstances?"

"Your leaving, my lord." The solicitor's face was full of reproach. "Lady Dunston contacted me shortly after you left, wishing to know where you could be located. She was most mightily displeased when I refused to impart that knowledge."

James bit back a smile. Isabella hated to be crossed, and she most especially detested not being let in on a secret. She had probably thrown a royal fit. His humor began to fade, however, as Mr. Marbly resumed his tale.

"Lady Dunston then requested that I attend her in Scotland."

"Scotland? What the devil is she doing there? The hunting lodge is hardly fit for a lady."

"Her ladyship is residing with Lady Sheldon at Haile Castle."

"I am sorry you had to go to so much trouble, Mr. Marbly. It must have been a nuisance to travel all that way, only to repeat what you had already told her."

The solicitor shifted uncomfortably in his chair.

"You *did* repeat what you had written in your letter?"

"My lord, I am ashamed to say that your wife completely outmaneuvered me. Faced with the choice of disclosing your whereabouts or booking your wife passage to Jamaica or—"

"Jamaica?"

Mr. Marbly sighed. "Her ladyship was quite insistent about beginning her search for you at the plantation."

James didn't know whether to laugh or to cry. Amusing as it was to think of his little slip of a wife bullying his solicitor, Mr. Marbly's confession meant that Isabella had known about the navy for months. Months and months for her anger to build. Damn, damn, and damn again. He had been counting on her relief that he was alive to outweigh her sense of betrayal. Somehow, he didn't think the technicality that he had joined the navy rather than the army was going to hold up in Isabella's court of law.

"I am sorry to say, my lord," the solicitor said stiffly, "your wife did not take the news well."

James's laugh was bitter. "No, I don't suppose she did."

"I don't think it would be overstating to say she was devastated."

"*Pax*, Mr. Marbly," James said, raising his hands in surrender. "I am more than aware of my failings as a husband, but I am going to do my damnedest to make it up to my wife." The sight of the solicitor's mouth gaping open afforded James no small amount of satisfaction.

"I must say, my lord, I didn't realize you cared so strongly."

"To be honest, Mr. Marbly, neither did I. But facing death has a way of making a man look into the deepest parts of his soul, forcing him to face certain truths long denied out of fear."

"I think you missed your calling, my lord," said Mr. Marbly. "With that silver tongue, you should have been a poet or a politician."

"Someday, perhaps. For now, all I want is my wife."

"Then go get her," the solicitor urged, rising to his feet and shaking James's hand. "And good luck!" he called as James headed out the door.

You are going to need it. Though neither man voiced the words, they hovered in the air, echoing in each man's mind, as each wondered whether it was too late after all.

With every mile that brought him closer to Haile Castle, James's enthusiasm waned and dread began to take its place. As eager as he was to see Isabella, he was beginning to have some doubts about his grand plan to declare his love and sweep her off her feet. He had a feeling she might prove a bit resistant. Then a horrible thought occurred to him—what if she refused to see him at all? Given all that had passed between them, he wouldn't have been surprised to find his likeness pasted near Lady Sheldon's front door, with the butler given orders to shoot on sight. Forget the butler, his wife would insist on doing the honors!

Struck by an all-too-clear vision of Isabella pointing a pistol at his black heart, James concluded that a peace offering was most definitely in order—something to at least get him through the front door. *Flowers*, he thought. Women always loved receiving flowers. Pleased with his own ingenuity, James instructed Davies, who was serving as his coachman, to stop at Haddington, the county town of East Lothian. He was fairly well acquainted with the town since it was a convenient stopping point on the way to his hunting lodge, which was farther north. As it was already midday, he decided he might as well pass the night there. If he remembered correctly, the George boasted an excellent kitchen and cellar in addition to comfortable accommodations. Surely he was deserving of the condemned man's last meal.

When they pulled up alongside the front of the inn, a young lad ran over to investigate the new arrival. The boy was reverently eyeing the matched bays when James stepped down from the carriage. He smiled as the boy, a charming little scamp who couldn't have been more than six or seven, reverently ran a hand along the nearest horse's nape, saying, "Aye, they be rum 'uns. Right beauties."

The lad clearly had an eye for fine horseflesh, James thought appreciatively. He reached out without thinking and tousled the boy's hair, surprising himself with how natural the gesture felt. "Thank you, er?"

"Rory, yer lairdship."

"Right then. Thank you, Rory. This pretty lady is Lucy," he said, laying a hand on one of the horses, "and that is Adele, and they are both prodigiously fond of apples. I am sure you have chores to do, but once they are finished, I don't suppose you would like to help my coachman see to them?"

A brilliant smile spread over Rory's face, and he nodded vigorously. James only wished everyone else were so easy to please. He waved the beaming boy toward the front door and watched as Davies led his horses away to be stabled. Not for the first time, James wondered how foxed he had been when he had decided to name the bays after his former mistresses. He grinned as he wondered how many apples Lucy and Adele, who were as spoiled as their namesakes, were going to get. They would be very happy ladies. As he set off down High Street, James chuckled to himself as he wondered if Isabella and Lady Sheldon liked apples.

He located a flower shop fairly quickly and ordered for two lavish arrangements to be delivered to the inn the following morning. For Isabella's bouquet, he requested nine white roses, one for each month they had been married, surrounded by fourteen yellow roses, one for every year they had known each other—for every year she had brought sunshine into his life. Damn, but he was becoming a sentimental fool.

With that errand accomplished, he walked on, peering into the shop windows and amusing himself by imagining Isabella in this bonnet or that gown. He considered himself fortunate that it was unacceptable to display unmentionables so publicly. He hadn't had a woman since Isabella's premarital seduction, and the sight of a woman's stockings or a lacy chemise just might drive him over the edge. Mentally and more than a bit physically uncomfortable with the direction of those thoughts, he forced his mind back to the far less arousing and far more likely notion of his wife wielding a pistol.

That was, of course, if her aunt didn't beat her to it. If Lady Sheldon's protective instincts were anything like her sister's, he had probably been safer fighting the French at sea. As he walked past a toy shop, he paused, suddenly struck by an ingenious idea. Lady Sheldon had a child—a girl, he thought—and Isabella, as well as her aunt, would surely be pleased if he brought some sort of a toy or doll for the little one.

Of course, a little one of her own would please Izzie more than anything. She had promised him that they wouldn't have children if he didn't wish it. He was so tempted just to accept her sacrifice, but he couldn't. It was the coward's way out, and it wouldn't be right. She was meant to be a mother. He was still scared—terrified, actually—especially now that he had figured out how much he loved her.

The hole in his heart left by the tragic loss of his mother and sister was a constant reminder of the risks women faced in childbirth. And try as he might, he couldn't shake that haunting omen. The nightmare lingered with him, burrowing insidiously through his mind, causing him to wake in the middle of the night, his heart racing and his body drenched with sweat.

He would keep trying for her, though. As his wife had said, marriage was built on compromise; with Isabella's help, James thought he could lay the demons of his youth to rest. Together they could face all the future dangers and past devils. And, of course, there was the making of the babe to take into consideration. He rubbed his hands together in anticipation. That would be his pleasure—and hers. He would make sure of that. He grinned. It was going to be his very great pleasure, indeed.

As he entered the shop, the woman sitting behind the counter lumbered to her feet, exposing the fact that she was clearly with child. James began to protest, but the woman cut him off.

"Dinna fash yerself. 'Twill be good fer me to stand awhile. Now, how can I help ye?"

"I need to buy a doll," James said offhandedly, trying to mask his embarrassment by pretending that a doll was the most normal thing in the world for a man of his age to be buying.

"And what kind would ye be wantin'?" The woman gave James an encouraging smile.

Kinds. There were kinds? "Er, well, whichever one is most expensive. It's a gift, you see," he hastened to add.

The woman retrieved a doll in full court dress, white ostrich feathers and all, and held it up for his inspection. James had no real idea what he should be looking for, but presumably Izzie and Lady Sheldon would, and even he could tell that the craftsmanship was exquisite.

"Yes. Fine. Perfect," he said, nodding.

The woman didn't even bother asking whether he wanted to know the cost, but given that he had asked for the most expensive doll, she must have assumed, correctly, that he had the blunt to afford it. As she made her way to the counter she asked, "Will ye be wantin' it wrapped?"

James had a vision of himself strolling down Haddington's High Street with a doll tucked in the crook of his arm. "Yes, please," he said hurriedly. There was no bloody way in hell he was going to be caught carrying a doll in public.

While the woman busied herself with wrapping the doll in tissue and brown paper, James perused the other items on the counter. He picked up a little wooden horse, which he decided to buy for the boy at the inn, and then his eyes came to rest upon a small blanket, obviously intended for a baby or young child, made of what looked to be the softest wool imaginable. It had been dyed pale pink, embroidered with delicate ribbon roses, and trimmed with fine Brussels lace. His imagination conjured up an image of an infant, with Isabella's fair hair and aquamarine eyes, swaddled up in this confection of a baby's blanket.

He was an idiot. It was women who were supposed to have these daydreams of babies. Men weren't supposed to daydream or, if they did, it should be about something manly, such as food, or hunting, or sex. *No!* he thought, as his body instantly responded to the thought of sex. He was *not* going down that road, not when his breeches were finally starting to feel comfortable again.

The shopkeeper caught him eyeing the blanket and smiled, patting her rounded stomach. "Me, I'm hopin' fer a lass. Callum, me husband, is wantin' a lad, but such is the way of things, I'm thinkin'. I brought the blanket here since Callum canna stand seein' it in the house. Keeps insistin' it's goin' to be a lad. With the way the bairn's been kickin' me lately, I'm startin' to think he might jest be right."

She scowled, so obviously chagrined at the thought of her husband besting her that James had to laugh. He reached out and ran a finger along the edge of the blanket; it was as soft as he had suspected, and although it might damage his reputation as a sterling specimen of masculinity, James knew that he had to have it. Still, there was enough of the rake in him to be embarrassed over his desire for a baby's blanket.

"It's exquisite," he murmured. "Might I ask where you purchased it?"

"Purchased it?" The woman gave a little laugh. "Bless yer heart. It's jest somethin' ta keep me hands busy an' pass the time in betwixt customers."

James's face fell. A baby blanket would have been the perfect gift for Isabella. Flowers were all well and good, but a present for their future child would show her how much he had changed and how hard he was trying to be the husband she deserved. But he had time. The flowers would be a start.

"I am certain you must be terribly busy," he said, "but would you consider taking a commission for a similar blanket? I would pay you quite handsomely for it."

"Och, it warms my heart to see a man sae excited to be a father. If ye like it sae much, ye can have this one."

"Oh, I couldn't take this one," he protested. "And besides, I'm not . . ."

He had been going to say that he wasn't going to be a father, but given that once he got Isabella in bed, he didn't plan on letting her out for at least a month, there probably *would* be a babe arriving in the coming year. His stomach pitched as he fought off the vision of a coffin being lowered into the ground. It wouldn't happen, he told himself, hoping that this time he would believe it. He swallowed hard. If and when the time came for his wife to give birth, James would see to it that London's finest accoucheur—no, a team of England's finest accoucheurs—stood at her bedside, ensuring nothing went wrong. But still . . . James forced the thought from his mind, and focused instead on the words issuing from the shopkeeper's mouth.

"Och, Callum will be glad to see it go, and I can easily make another. Besides, I ken it sounds a bit daft, but it seems like ye should have it. Let me wrap it up for ye, and the toy horsie as well, aye?"

"Oh, yes. There is a boy back at the George who was rather taken with my horses. He's helping my man care for them, and bringing him a small gift seems the least I can do."

She gave him a searching look, and James suddenly felt as if her warm brown eyes could penetrate his flesh and see to his very core.

"Ye've a guid heart, milord," she told him softly. "Yer wife is a lucky woman."

James chuckled as he collected the packages and paid the woman several times more than the price she had given him. "I doubt she would agree with you, but thank you. As for my heart . . ." He sobered, then said quietly, "I'm working on it."

Chapter 18

*I fear I have inherited our mother's tendency to
cry at the slightest provocation. Whether I am happy
or sad, angry or glad, the tears stand at the ready. I
suppose it could be worse. I might have ended up
with her Shakespearean obsession instead!*

From the correspondence of Isabella, Lady Dunston,
age twenty

Letter to her brother, Henry Weston, on the sender's alarm-
ing propensity to burst into tears at the drop of a bonnet—
September 1798

James got an early start the next morning, despite Rory's
insistence that the horses were still tired and needed to
be fed more apples, and Haile Castle was in sight before
noon. It was an imposing mass of gray stone spread across
the grassy hillside; its twin towers, rising five stories high,
were separated by a long, three-story hall. Even more intimidating were the gun ports and pistol loops decorating
the exterior, but James consoled himself with the knowledge that if Isabella was indeed going to shoot him, she'd
want the satisfaction of berating and insulting him first.
Oddly reassuring, that.

Social protocol dictated it was far too early to be calling, but James figured it was a man's right to call on his
wife at whatever damned hour he chose. Although his

wedding day was a bit of a blur, he was quite certain something to that extent had been mentioned in the marriage service.

Davies dropped him off at the front entrance to the castle before proceeding to the stables. Squaring his shoulders, James marched up to the door; however, with a huge bouquet of flowers in each hand and packages tucked under each arm, he realized he had no way of knocking. After a moment's hesitation, James lifted his booted foot and gave one of the massive, ancient doors a hard, satisfying kick. He was getting ready for another when the door swung open to reveal a man as solid and massive as the portals he guarded.

The butler eyed James up and down for a long moment; he must have passed muster, for the man bowed. His lips twitched as he rose and said, "You kicked, my lord?"

Impertinent bastard, James thought. "I have come to see Lady Dunston," he stated, and moved to enter.

The butler blocked him and folded his arms across his chest in a menacing manner. "Lady Dunston is not at home."

James frowned. "What time do you expect her to return?"

"From where?"

From where? "From wherever she has gone, of course." Obviously the man had not been blessed with brains proportional to his brawn.

"She hasn't gone anywhere."

The conversation was so ridiculous, James began to wonder if he wasn't still asleep at the George, tucked under the blankets, trapped in a bizarre dream. He would have pinched himself, but as his hands were occupied, he had no choice but to continue with the farce.

He took a deep, calming breath. "If Lady Dunston has not gone anywhere, how is it possible that she is not at home?"

The butler looked thoughtful, but James could have sworn he saw a satanic glint in the man's eyes as he responded, "Perhaps I should have said the lady in question is not receiving visitors at present."

James seriously considered dropping everything in his arms and lunging for the man's throat. It was tempting, so very tempting . . . but his shoulder was sore from jouncing around in the carriage. And in any case, he doubted he could even fit his hands around the behemoth's thick neck. So he took several more of those deep, calming breaths, enough for the red haze to clear from his vision. Isabella was there. He was moments away from seeing her. Or was he?

"Is Lady Sheldon also not receiving visitors?" he inquired.

"Lady Sheldon is not at home right now."

James gritted his teeth. "If that is your obtuse way of saying—"

The butler had the audacity to grin. "No, Lady Sheldon is truly not at home. She is out for the morning."

James heaved an inward sigh of relief. At least that would be one less person trying to shoot him. On that happy thought, James drew himself up and, imitating his grandfather at his most imperious, demanded to be shown into the castle.

To his surprise, the butler stepped back and allowed James to pass by him into the cavernous entryway.

As he closed the heavy doors, the butler said, "If you will give me your name, I will inquire if Lady Dunston wishes to receive you."

"She'll see me," James stated with far more confidence than he actually felt. "I'm her husband."

As the butler gaped, James thrust Lady Sheldon's bouquet at the man. "Have those put in water for your mistress," he ordered, "but first tell me where my wife can be found."

"Of course, my lord, but you must be weary from your travels. May I get you—"

"My wife? Yes, but you needn't bring her to me; only tell me her present location."

The butler sighed, unhappily resigned. "She is probably in the nursery."

"With her cousin?"

"No, my lord. Lady Sheldon took Lady Charlotte with her."

"When they return, see Lady Charlotte gets this." James shoved the parcel containing the doll into the butler's free hand. "Where is the nursery?"

"Shall I show you the way, my lord?"

James shook his head. "Just tell me how to get there." He didn't want the butler announcing him and ruining the element of surprise.

As he climbed the winding stairs to the top of the south tower, James wondered what his wife was doing alone in the nursery. When he reached the open threshold, though, it became apparent that she was not, in fact, alone. Her back was to him, but he could see the downy fuzz of an infant's head settled into the curve of her neck.

"Hello, Izzie." His voice felt thick in his throat. She didn't respond, but he knew she had heard him from the way her body stiffened. She gently laid the baby down in its cradle, and then turned to face him. Her face was deathly white, her mouth a thin white line—not, he supposed, the greeting he had hoped for, but it was the one he had expected. In any case, she was the most beautiful sight he had ever seen.

"I didn't realize that Lady Sheldon had remarried," he said conversationally, nodding his head at the cradle.

Isabella's eyes widened in disbelief.

Hmmm. Perhaps "I love you" or "I was a fool to leave you" might have been a better choice.

"She didn't."

Maybe he should have just swept her off her feet and kissed her. He wondered if it was too late to implement that plan.

"She didn't what?" James asked distractedly.

"She didn't remarry," Isabella said, a hint of impatience in her tone.

"Whose baby is it, then?"

Isabella looked at him as if he were fit for Bedlam. "Yours!" she exclaimed. "I mean, mine." Then, in a softer voice, she added, "Ours."

The addition was, in his opinion, rather unnecessary. Just because he had fallen out of her good graces didn't mean he was a complete idiot. And then he realized what she was saying, and—

"Oh Jesus Christ," he whispered to himself, dropping the package so as to brace a hand against the wall for support. He sank down to the floor, and then, when the room had stopped spinning, he looked up, dazed.

Isabella moved to stand in front of the cradle, her stance reminding him of the way female animals fought viciously to protect their young; only the bared fangs were missing.

"You're alive!" he blurted out.

She eyed him oddly. "James, are you all right? You don't look very well."

Was he all right?

Was he all right?

Once he recovered from the shock, he would be bloody marvelous! He held up his shaking hands and found he was still clutching the flowers in his fingers.

"These are for you," he said, holding out the bouquet. She made no move to take it, so he laid it on the floor alongside the parcel with the baby's blanket. "The present was to be for you as well, but now you'll have to share it with h—" Bloody hell, he didn't know the sex of his own child. "With the baby."

She looked supremely uninterested in his offerings, but she did give him the answer he sought. "You are fortunate; the demise of the earldom still remains within your grasp."

A girl. He, or rather, *they* had a girl. He was a father. It hadn't been a premonition, or even if it had, it didn't matter, because both Isabella and their child were alive. They were *alive*. He rose to his feet and walked over to the cradle. His heart rose up in his throat at the sight of her and, watching her little stomach rise and fall, he sent up a prayer, thanking God for every breath that passed through her tiny body. "May I . . . May I hold her?"

Isabella bit her lip, but she picked the baby up and gently placed her in James's arms. He looked down at his daughter as he cradled her warm, sweet weight in his arms.

Just like that, James Sheffield fell in love again.

"What did you name her?"

"Bride," she murmured lovingly, her gaze straying to the tiny object of her affection. "Lady Bride Kathleen Sheffield."

"After my sister and my mother?" he asked, his throat tightening.

"I was extremely exhausted and feeling sentimental," she snapped. "You were naturally on my mind, but it seemed unfair to burden a child with some of the names I was calling you."

He ignored her jabs. His mind turned to his baby sister who had died before she had taken a single breath or felt the caress of sunshine on her face. He had always imagined her at various stages of her life, wondering what sort of child she would have been, and although he had never really known her, he had grieved for the life she should have lived. Now it felt as though she had a second chance. The burden of loss he had carried with him for so long eased. It wasn't gone completely—he knew it never would be—but it was lighter.

"Thank you," he rasped out, his eyes burning with unshed tears, completely overcome as he was by the gesture. Apparently it was the right thing to say, since it took the wind right out of her sails.

"Why are you here?" she asked wearily, holding out her hands for Bride.

Reluctantly, James gave the baby back, but he couldn't stop looking at her, couldn't tear his gaze away as Isabella laid her back down in the cradle. "Why am I here?" he repeated automatically, memorizing his daughter's face: the golden crescents of her lashes and brows, the button nose, the pink bow of her mouth. . . .

Then Isabella's words penetrated his thick skull, and James jerked his head up to regard his wife. The question was so ridiculous that a choked laugh escaped him. She wanted to know why he was there? There were so many words and phrases that rose up in his mind, but all he said was, "You're my wife."

"Nice of you to remember," she muttered.

James's expression darkened and the muscles around his mouth grew taut. This was not exactly the reunion he had been imagining. Then again, he would be more than happy to impress on her just how much his wife she was. A lusty gleam lit his eye. "I remember perfectly. I think you are the one who needs reminding," he said, reaching for her. "Come here, wife."

She backed away from him. "No! Don't touch me!"

The vehemence of her reaction surprised James. "You liked my touching you well enough before," he muttered sulkily.

"Yes, *before*. Before you left, before I had Bride, and before I realized that you don't need me—won't ever need me—as I thought, as I hoped you did." She drew in a shaky breath and exhaled, battling for composure. "But that was before. And now, I don't need you, either. *We* don't need you. We were fine—I mean, we *are* fine, but you can't be here. We've learned how to live without you. No. No, no, no. Just go away. Please. Go away."

James made a move to grab her, and Isabella threw up her arms, warding him off. He ignored her and quickly gathered her in his arms, holding her tightly against his chest. He rubbed a large hand up and down her back as she collapsed against him, all the fight suddenly gone out of her. "What's all this about, sweetheart?" he murmured.

Isabella felt tears gathering in her eyes. She was so tired. Her body had healed from the birth, but she still hadn't regained all of her energy. That was why she was crying—because she was exhausted. It wasn't because of this impossible man who held her so sweetly in his arms, as if she belonged there. And it certainly wasn't because she felt she belonged there.

She drew in a shuddering breath. And it had nothing to do with her simply having missed his smell—that subtle mixture of outdoors, horses, warm male flesh, and something that was uniquely James. Having a baby made a woman emotional, Izzie told herself, and that was why she was prone to all these ridiculous feelings and longings.

She didn't know how much time passed as she stood there, held in the circle of his arms, her head nestled against his shoulder, simply breathing him in and out. In those dreadful first weeks after he had left, and then again when she had realized she was with child, she had dreamed of him like this. Holding her, comforting her.

But the hope of his returning to her and professing his undying love had been crushed when she had found out about the navy. Once the shock had worn off, a fierce burning anger and resentment had set in. Her fury had, in turn, been supplanted by grief and a bittersweet longing for what might have been.

As James continued to soothe her, murmuring endearments against her hair, stepping back into her life as if he had never gone away, Isabella's rage returned in full force. *How dare he?* Her fingers itched to slap him. She wanted to rain down blows on his chest, inflict just a fraction of the hurt he had caused her. Instead she tore herself away from him.

"Get out," she hissed, pointing at the nursery door.

If she hadn't been so furious, she would have laughed at the dumbstruck look on James's face. She stamped her foot. "I. Said. Get. Out."

He looked at her in complete befuddlement. "What in God's name is the matter with you? A moment ago you were soft and willing in my arms, and now you're acting like some sort of virago."

Isabella crossed her arms over her chest. "I remembered that you broke your promise to me, that's what."

"Technically, I didn't break my promise." He crossed his

arms over his chest, mimicking her angry stance. "If you will recall, I promised you that I would not enlist in the army, and I didn't. You never said anything about the navy."

"That is complete rubbish! You knew perfectly well what I meant when I asked for that promise, and you just chose to ignore it."

James released his arms and tapped a finger thoughtfully against his chin. "Hmmm," he mused, "you know it's rather like when you chose to invade my bedchamber, even though you knew perfectly well that you were acting against my express wishes."

"The difference being that I acted to save your life," Izzie hissed. "You tried to throw it away."

"I know, but I didn't. I'm alive, sweetheart, and I'm here now. Can't we just start over?"

She looked up at him with huge, sad eyes. "I don't know. No matter what you say, you broke your promise to me, and I don't know if I can forgive you for that. How can I trust you again?"

A mottled flush crept up James's neck and into his face, and he began to pace about the room like a caged beast. "If I can forgive you for seducing me, you should damned well be able to forgive me for breaking a promise that I didn't really break in the first place," he growled.

"But you haven't," Izzie cried. "You haven't forgiven me. If you had, you wouldn't keep throwing it back in my face."

James stopped abruptly, one hand sliding up to massage the base of his neck. His hair was longer than he usually kept it, she noticed, and there were golden highlights from the months he had spent outdoors. The sight of those strong fingers sent a rush of longing through her, left her insides quivering and her knees feeling weak.

Isabella stumbled over to the chair by the cradle where she often sat and rocked Bride late into the night. She sank into it and gave in to the flow of tears that had begun to leak down her cheeks. "Go," she choked out. "Please, just go. The longer you stay, the harder it will be when you leave.

The days after you first left were torturous, but they were nothing compared to how I felt when I learned you had been wounded, when I thought I had lost you for good." She began to cry in earnest. "Losing you a third time would kill me. So please, I am begging you, just go away."

She buried her face in her hands and waited. For a long moment the room was silent, and then came the heavy fall of James's footsteps. For a moment she thought he was walking toward her, that he was somehow going to make everything right between them, and then she remembered that he had to move past her to reach the door. Each step echoed loudly in the silence, and each one crushed her heart a little bit more. It was better this way, she told herself. This was what she wanted, what she'd asked for. It hurt, of course, that he could walk away so easily, but that had never been a problem for James.

Running away was what he did best, but this time she wasn't going to chase after him. This time she was going to do what was best for all of them—for Bride, for James and, though it was difficult to admit, for her. She was going to do what she should have done long ago. . . .

She was going to give him up and let him go.

And then she realized he had stopped moving. Puzzled, she raised her head, only to see him drop to his knees before her, his face filled with remorse. The sight of the naked pain in his eyes didn't leave her feeling vindicated.

That was the problem with trying to wound someone you loved, she supposed.

In the end, you were only hurting yourself.

She was breaking his heart, tearing him up inside. James felt every sob that broke from her throat like a fist in the gut. He lifted her hands from her tearstained face and tenderly wiped away the salty drops coursing down her cheeks. "Izzie, I am not going to leave you. Never again. I learned my lesson the hard way. When I thought I was going to die, I went through hell knowing I had never told you—"

He was cut off by what sounded like a thundering stampede of elephants making their way up the stairs. Huffing and puffing from their mad rush, still in their bonnets and spencers, Lady Sheffield, Lady Weston, and Olivia exploded through the door frame. Three pairs of eyes noted the tears on Isabella's face, and then turned in unison to fix James with angry, accusing stares. As for him, his gaze fell to their hands: not a pistol in sight. There was a God, and he was on James's side.

As he sat in the parlor facing his trio of accusers, feeling uncomfortably like a victim of the Spanish Inquisition, James was having second thoughts about his standing with the Almighty. After the women had burst into the nursery, they had clucked over Isabella, declared she was far too pale, and sent her off to rest in her room. He, on the other hand, had been marched downstairs to face "Torquemama" and her acolytes.

"Am I allowed the chance to defend myself, or am I to be sent straight to the rack?" he asked jokingly.

Lady Weston frowned. "Don't be ridiculous. No one here is going to torture you."

Lady Sheldon's face fell.

"You have just given all of us something of a shock, turning up so unexpectedly. Not that I'm not delighted to see you, of course," she hastened to add.

"Could have fooled me," James muttered.

"And you look so well," she continued. "You gave us quite a scare, you know."

Obviously displeased with her sister's kindness to the enemy, Lady Sheldon noted, "It was, in fact, the news of your injury that sent your wife into premature labor—"

"Kate!" Lady Weston elbowed her sister. "We can't know that for sure, and in any case—"

"It was an extremely long and difficult labor," Lady Sheldon went on. "Had the midwife been less competent, we could have easily lost them both."

James buried his face in his hands. He would have preferred the rack to this hellish, emotional torture.

"Stop, Aunt Kate," Olivia said softly. "We are not the only ones who have had a shock today."

Personally, James was of the opinion that finding out he was a father trumped his unannounced arrival at Castle Haile by a hundredfold, but he kept it to himself.

"Fine," Lady Sheldon huffed, "but I still want to know what he is doing here."

Isabella had wondered the same thing. *Wasn't it bloody obvious?* "I have come for my wife."

"So now you have decided you want her?" demanded Lady Sheldon.

"Kate," Lady Weston murmured in warning.

"No. Don't 'Kate' me. He abandoned Isabella on their wedding day, and we have all been nursing her broken heart ever since. I need to make sure he won't hurt her again, and I don't really care if his feelings get hurt in the process."

"Lady Sheldon, I have no intention of hurting Isabella. I never wanted to cause her any pain. In retrospect, I realize I should have handled things differently, but I can't undo the past. And even if I could, I am not altogether certain that I would. Neither can I promise that Isabella will never be hurt again. We both have tempers, and it seems quite probable that we will disagree on any number of things over, oh, the next fifty years or so."

Lady Sheldon tried to keep a straight face, but she couldn't keep her lips from twitching up at the corners. A moment later she began to laugh out loud.

"What?" James, Olivia, and Lady Weston chorused in varying tones of annoyance, confusion, and bemusement.

"I was just thinking that if you are to be married for such a long time, my wedding present to you will be a second set of china."

"Why? Does it wear out?" James wanted to know.

The general mirth in response to what had been an earnest question left him feeling somewhat miffed. He was a man, after all. Men didn't know about things such as whether china wore out.

Lady Weston wiped at her eyes. "In most households, the answer would be no, but in your case . . . Knowing Izzie . . ." She started laughing again. "I predict that you and my daughter will go through a great deal of china."

James nodded, though he still hadn't a clue what they were talking about or why it was so bloody funny. Fortunately, they were distracted by the butler's entrance into the room and the huge display of flowers he carried before him.

"Oh, Dimpsey, how gorgeous!" Lady Sheldon exclaimed.

Dimpsey? The giant's name was *Dimpsey?*

"Whom are they from?" asked Olivia.

"Me," James answered, quite pleased with himself. "I have a present for Charlotte as well. Had I known there were more ladies in residence . . ." He shrugged.

"Seeing you alive and well is more than enough for me," Lady Weston declared. "Although I wouldn't mind a proper hug from my favorite son-in-law."

"I am your only son-in-law," James muttered, but he happily obliged. He glanced at Olivia over Lady Weston's head and raised an eyebrow in silent question.

"I am sure I can find some way for you to make it up to me," she pronounced cheerfully, grinning at him.

"Thank you, James." Lady Sheldon's voice was only slightly grudging. "The flowers are lovely, and bringing a gift for Charlotte is most thoughtful. Despite the inauspicious start to your marriage, I believe you will make Isabella a very fine husband."

"Thank you, Lady Sheldon," he said earnestly.

"If, of course, she deigns to forgive you," she added blithely. "And call me Katherine, or Aunt Kate, if you like. We are family, after all."

A sense of peace settled over James at her words. Partly because he felt something of the relief Hercules must have known when he wrestled the monstrous, three-headed Cerberus into submission, but mostly because Lady Sheldon—Aunt Kate, he reminded himself—had said a magical word: "family."

Isabella would forgive him. She *had* to forgive him. He would sacrifice his pride and grovel if he had to; he would even crawl on his knees if necessary (though he really hoped it wouldn't be), because no matter how fiercely he had fought against the idea of his own marriage and children, there was nothing more precious, nothing more sacred to James Sheffield than family.

God knew he hadn't planned it, but it was too late for that. He had a family. And he was in love. With his wife. With his daughter. With the knowledge that, through them, he now belonged to as big and loving a family as he had ever dreamed. By some miracle, the innermost wishes of his heart had been granted.

Excusing himself on the pretext of needing to make sure his man had got settled in, James went off in search of Dimpsey, his new and entirely unexpected ally. He found the butler waiting for him just outside the room. Without a word spoken, the two men walked down the corridor until they were safely out of earshot of the parlor.

"I must thank you for bringing in the flowers when you did," James said. "Your timing was nothing less than inspired."

The butler shrugged his massive shoulders. "In a household full of women, men must stick together for survival."

"Yes, how very true." James nodded, beginning to wonder if Dimpsey wasn't actually much smarter than he let on. "I say, do you know if my things have been brought in yet?"

"They have already been placed in a room for you, my lord. And I offered your man lodging in the main house, but he preferred to bed down in the quarters alongside the stables with the grooms."

"Excellent, excellent. So, about this room I have been assigned to—how near is it to my wife's chamber?"

The butler winked. "Directly across the hall, my lord."

"Brilliant. Bless you, Dimpsey. You are a butler among butlers. I don't suppose I could lure you away from Lady Sheldon's employ? No, I didn't think so. Now, if the ladies ask, my war injuries are acting up and I have gone to my room to rest." He started for the stairs, and then stopped as he realized he had no idea where his room was. He turned around and saw Dimpsey waiting patiently by the base of the stairs.

"Shall I show you to your chamber, my lord?"

"I should be lost without you," James responded dryly.

Dimpsey left him at the door to his room, but instead of going in, James waited until the butler was out of sight, then crossed the hall to peer inside Isabella's bedchamber, needing to see her again. She had fallen asleep atop the bed, fully dressed except for her shoes. He unfolded the quilt by her feet and gently covered her. Then he shrugged off his coat, yanked off his boots, and took a seat near the bed, content simply to watch over her as she slept.

She looked like one of Botticelli's angels. The drapes had been only partially drawn, and soft light filtered into the room, casting a golden glow around her. Her face was peaceful in slumber, making her appear so young and vulnerable, it seemed unbelievable that she had borne a child—his child.

She was far from innocent—it hadn't been an immaculate conception, after all, but a planned seduction—but it was so damned difficult to remember that when she looked like this. He knew he shouldn't be there, wasting time looking at her. He needed to come up with a plan before she woke up, to think of some way to convince her that he was back for good. It wasn't going to be easy. She was an angel who had tangled with an all-too-mortal man, a man with none of her light and goodness, and her wings had been broken. Now he had to figure out how to mend them, how to heal her heart and give her the strength to believe in him again.

God, how could he have been such a fool to throw away her trust without a backward glance? He stopped himself from going down that path. The road of regrets and recriminations ran to eternity and beyond. He needed to look forward, to act before it was too late. He had hammered the wedge between them into place; it was up to him to pry it out and close the gap he had so thoughtlessly created out of fear and frustration.

He really ought to leave and formulate his plan of action, but to a man who had been wandering lost in the desert, she was the cool, sweet water of deliverance, and he couldn't stop drinking in the sight of her. His breath caught as she turned over onto her side, nestling her cheek into the pillow, her hand reaching out to search beside her.

"James," she murmured drowsily.

He froze, then rose to his feet and turned toward the door. He wasn't ready to face her; he hadn't come to terms with everything yet. He forced himself to turn around, opening his mouth to respond to her, and then abruptly shut it when it became apparent she was still very much asleep.

"James," she sighed again, burrowing her face deeper into the pillow.

She dreamed about him? The very thought of it instantly had him harder than the wooden bedposts. Then again, her dreams about him probably had very little in common with his dreams about her. They were both usually naked in his dreams. With a sigh of his own, he sank back down into the chair and buried his face in his hands, trying desperately to force his mind away from thoughts of Isabella naked.

Of course, she needn't be naked. There was something naughtily arousing about making love to a woman with all her clothes on, something extremely erotic about having to burrow beneath all those skirts to reach the hot, secret heart of her.

He stifled a groan, half ready to explode, lust clawing at him, gripping him with sharp talons. The fact that Isabella was lying in bed only steps away wasn't helping things. He took a deep breath, counted to ten, and then counted to ten again, trying to get himself under control. He wondered whether there was an icy Scottish loch nearby. Dimpsey would know. That man seemed to know everything.

Stiffening his spine, and ignoring other uncomfortably

stiff parts of his body, he raised his head and pushed himself up out of the chair. Much as he would have liked to sit and watch Isabella all day, James forced himself to leave the room and make his way downstairs.

He wanted to be sure he'd have every day of the rest of his life to look at her, and the germ of a plan was forming in his mind. He was going to woo his wife. And three meddlesome women and a hulking giant of a butler were going to help him.

Chapter 19

I understand from Mama that you are quite impatient for us to travel to Weston Manor, though I am not sure which excites you more—the arrival of your new granddaughter or the return of your wife—though I have my suspicions. You will be happy to know that even though our motley crew will be traveling slowly, in deference to the baby and the weather, we shall certainly be back well before Christmas.

From the correspondence of Isabella, Lady Dunston, age twenty

Letter to her father, Oliver, Viscount Weston, regarding travel plans and the painful absence of loved ones . . . and the activities one can engage in with them—November 1798

The knowledge that James was just across the hall kept Isabella tossing and turning all night, and once the sun started trickling through the curtains, she gave up trying to sleep. Deciding to let her maid stay abed a bit longer, she donned a heavy flannel wrapper and went upstairs to check on Bride.

"I was just aboot to bring her to ye, milady," the nurse-maid said, jouncing the crying baby in her arms. "She's up early this morning, and fair hungry by the sound o' it."

Izzie settled down with her daughter and, calmed by the

sweetness of her baby at her breast, she let herself relax. Her eyelids started to feel unbearably heavy, and it soon became harder to keep them open than it was to let them close. She was still distantly aware of the baby's suckling and the rhythmic creak of the rocking chair, but after a while she let go of those moorings as well and drifted off into oblivion.

She awoke sometime later to find Bride asleep in her arms, and her heart swelled at the sight of the tiny fists clutching the fine linen of Isabella's night rail like a lifeline. She dropped a kiss on her daughter's downy head and settled her back in her cradle.

Much restored by her brief repose and feeling ready to confront the day, Izzie headed back to her room to get dressed. When she entered her chamber, though, she found that her maid was several steps ahead of her: The entire contents of her wardrobe were strewn atop the bed.

"Becky?" she called out.

"Coming, milady," came the huffed reply as her maid emerged from the dressing room, dragging one of Isabella's trunks behind her.

"Whatever are you doing?"

Her maid frowned. "His lordship came looking for you, and I told him you were probably with Lady Bride. He said he'd find you, and that I was to start packing all your clothes and such and then see to the little one's things. Did he not speak with you, milady?"

Isabella drew a deep breath and slowly released it. "No, Becky, he did not, but I intend to remedy that directly. In the meantime, you may leave off packing. As far as I am concerned, *he* is the only person leaving here in the near future."

She strode across the hall and rapped on the door. No response. She knocked again, louder this time. Nothing.

"The earl is taking breakfast, my lady."

Isabella whirled around, heart pounding, to find her aunt's giant butler not three feet away. "Heavens, Dimpsey, you startled me!"

"I beg your pardon, my lady. It certainly wasn't my intention."

"No, no, of course not, but how a man your size can creep about so quietly is a mystery. There's an interesting explanation, no doubt, but at the moment I've another, more pressing explanation to demand. He's eating breakfast, you said? Well, I hope he is prepared for some serious indigestion!"

Isabella barged through the castle and stormed into the dining room like an Amazon ready to do battle. James sat alone at the head of the table, reading a newspaper. He glanced up briefly at her entrance and then, as if he hadn't noted anything—or any*one*—of interest, went right back to his paper. If she'd thought she had the slightest chance of succeeding, Izzie would have seated herself next to him and eaten her breakfast while ignoring him as splendidly as he was ignoring her. Since she lacked that sort of reserve, however, Isabella marched over to her husband, tore the paper out of his hands, and threw it aside.

James just sat back in his chair and gave her a lazy smile that made Izzie's heart skip a beat. Longing filled her in a heady rush and her own lips started to turn up and—no! She was angry with him, she reminded herself.

"Good morning, wife. I say, you're looking a bit peckish. Has something happened?"

His eyes twinkled with merriment, and Izzie had to fight the urge to throw something at him. She eyed the stack of plates on the sideboard longingly. No, it wouldn't do to break her aunt's china. Well, maybe just a saucer . . .

"Izzie? Has something happened?" James repeated.

As if he didn't know.

"Not something," she ground out. "Someone. You. You ordered my maid to pack up all my things."

"Is that what has you so overset? I apologize, my dear. I shall tell her to stop at once."

"You will?"

"Of course."

Izzie eyed him suspiciously, mistrusting his easy capitulation. He didn't disappoint her. After a moment's pause he continued. "But were I you, I should instruct her to resume the task directly, as I mean for us to leave once the second carriage arrives from Edinburgh. I sent my man to hire it yesterday afternoon, so I expect it shall be here tomorrow or the next day."

"I have no intention of accompanying you anywhere."

"There are matters I need to attend to at Sheffield Park."

"Go on, then. Bride and I have managed fine without you thus far."

He winced. "Please, don't make this difficult, Izzie. You and Bride are coming home with me, and there's an end to it."

"No."

"I don't recall giving you a choice."

"Bride and I are staying here."

"Oh dear." Her aunt swept into the room. "I am afraid that won't be possible."

Izzie frowned. "What won't be possible?"

"Staying here. You see, Charlotte and I always spend the holidays with my stepson, and since he insists on residing in the most remote part of Wales, I need to pack up the household and be on the road within a fortnight."

"Bride and I will travel home with my mother and Livvy, then."

"Didn't I tell you, darling?" Her mother entered the parlor, Olivia right behind her.

"Tell me what?"

"Well, as you know, I have been here far longer than I originally intended, and I am most anxious to get back home. You won't be able to travel quickly with an infant, so James has offered to take your sister and me to Edinburgh and see to hiring a post chaise for us."

"Actually, I'm not all that anxious to get home," Olivia spoke up.

Bless her, Izzie thought. A sister could always be counted on to—

"If it is all right with Aunt Kate, I should like to travel with her to Wales. I've always wanted to see the area, and I can help take care of Charlotte."

"Olivia Jane Weston, where are your manners? You cannot just invite yourself along on other people's journeys! Certainly not to someone else's house! Charlotte has nursemaids to look after her, and if this is your notion of how a young lady of good breeding acts, she's better off without your poor example. Furthermore, such behavior is not at all proper."

There it was, Isabella thought, her mother's favorite word.

Proper.

She shuddered. She really, really loathed that word.

"But then my children"—she looked pointedly at Isabella—"seem to delight in this sort of reckless impropriety."

In *all* its forms. She shuddered again for good measure.

"But I haven't finished with the library yet," Livvy countered. "I didn't mean to be rude, Aunt Kate, truly I didn't, but I would so like to see Wales. Once I have my Season, I may never have the chance, so I must go before it's too late."

Aunt Kate moved forward and drew Olivia into her arms. "Darling, I had no idea you wanted to accompany us. Of course you must have a last adventure before you settle down, and I shall be very glad to have someone to help entertain Charlotte on the journey!"

"Fine." Lady Weston rolled her eyes. "Go ahead and reward her bad behavior. You'll regret it when Charlotte is old enough to follow her example." With that dire prediction, she swept out of the room, Olivia and Lady Sheldon following cautiously in her wake.

Izzie turned to face James. "I suppose I have no choice but to go with you. I hope you're pleased with yourself."

"I would be happier if you were not so put out by the arrangements. Come now, it won't be so terrible, will it?

We've never lacked for things to talk about, you and I. You might even find yourself enjoying my company."

"Unlikely."

"Careful, sweetheart. I might take that as a challenge."

"Do you live to vex me?"

"Certainly not. Men don't like to upset their wives."

"Is that so?"

He nodded and gave her a conspiratorial wink. "It tends to give them headaches."

It took a moment for her to comprehend his meaning. "If you think that I—that you—," she sputtered.

James threw back his head and laughed.

"I can't begin to guess what you find so amusing."

"You. The way you think we can keep our hands off each other." His voice deepened, and his eyes darkened with desire.

His words sent a liquid thrill of excitement racing down her spine, and she started toward him. She was within arm's reach of him when the satisfied smile on his face gave her pause. She'd taken his bait and let him reel her in like the veriest gull. Her nails dug into her palms as she struggled to regain control of the conversation . . . and of herself.

She uncurled her fists and placed her hands on her hips. "As you can see, I have no problem keeping my hands to myself. Now, if you will excuse me, I have packing to do." She flounced out of the room, the grating sound of his chuckle ringing in her ears.

"I cannot talk to that man. There is just no reasoning with him," Isabella muttered to herself. "He twists around everything I say, so I clearly can't say anything. But I'm going to be trapped in a carriage with him for hours each day, and I don't think I've ever managed to go more than an hour without saying anything. Except when I'm asleep. But I can't possibly sleep the entire journey."

"No, and unless something has changed drastically in the past decade, you're not very good at pretending to be asleep, either." Her mother's voice intruded on Isabella's ramblings. "Come, I would like to speak to you for a moment." Lady Weston gestured for Isabella to follow her into the drawing room across the hall.

"Did you want to apologize for abandoning me?" Izzie muttered.

"No," her mother said, shutting the door behind them, "I did not. I acted as I thought best."

"Just whose side are you on?"

"That's just it, Isabella. Marriage isn't a competition. It isn't about winning and losing. Relationships require each partner to give and take, and there will be many days when you feel you are giving far more than you are getting. But you have to learn to compromise. You cannot give up or start a fight each time you don't get your way.

"It's time to grow up, my dear. Marriage is never easy. Every day takes work and patience and understanding. You have a responsibility to your daughter to try to make this relationship work. Look, I know you love James."

"I don't know if I do anymore. Love shouldn't be so difficult."

"It isn't love that's tough. It's all the emotions that come with loving someone. Love doesn't mean that fear or anger or hurt will disappear. If anything, they will be magnified. Loving someone, opening your heart to him, always carries that risk."

"Is it worth it? Truly?"

"I think you know deep down that it is. But if you want James to trust you with his heart, you must be willing to do the same."

"I just . . . I'm not sure . . . That is . . . What if I let myself love him and he leaves again? I don't think I'm strong enough to bear that."

"*If* he should be so foolish, your aunt and I will draw straws to see who gets to hunt him down, but I doubt it will come to that. What the two of you need is time alone together."

"Mama, James and I have never had any problems in *that* capacity."

Lady Weston looked pained. "I meant for you to talk to each other. Passion is a key element to a happy marriage, but desire alone is not enough to sustain a lasting union. Communication is the most important element of any such partnership, and until you and James can express your feelings toward each other with words, I would urge you to abstain from more . . . physical means of expression."

"Considering we'll be spending all these hours alone stuck in a coach, I hardly think that will pose a problem."

Lady Weston said nothing, but her face turned a most astonishing shade of crimson.

Isabella's eyes widened. "Oh dear. Really? In a *carriage*? But how—"

"I really must see to packing now. I think we've said all that needs to be said, don't you?" Her mother edged toward the door.

"No, I—"

But Lady Weston had already made her escape, leaving Isabella alone to ponder the intricacies of intimacies in confined spaces. Of course, as she had no intention of participating in such activities, such conjecturing was, she eventually decided, unproductive. She needed to think of something to occupy herself on what promised to be a very long, very tedious trip.

Oh, if only Olivia hadn't deserted her with this trumped-up excuse of wanting to visit Wales. She'd like to know what *that* was about! She headed to the library to pry the truth out of her sister, and on the way she realized she'd found the perfect solution.

"Books," Isabella said, bursting into the library. "I need books. Lots of books."

Olivia looked up from the dusty pile of books she was examining. "Oh, you'll get them."

"Beg pardon?"

" 'Thank you' would be more appropriate, but unless you've developed psychic powers of premonition, I suppose your gratitude would be a bit premature. Besides, I wouldn't wish to ruin the surprise."

Isabella stared at her. "I would say you just did," she said slowly, "only I haven't the faintest notion what you're talking about."

"That's as it should be." Livvy shook her head. "You can thank me when it is revealed because, I assure you, James would not have thought of this on his own."

Isabella kept staring, unable to make the slightest sense out of her sister's pronouncement. Olivia could be incomprehensible at times, but this . . .

"What, have I grown a second head?"

"Hardly. I'm wondering what's happened to the one you have. But back to my original purpose in coming here . . . books!" Isabella picked one up from a nearby table. "*A General History of Scotland: From the Earliest Accounts to the Present Time* by William Guthrie." Her face screwed up with distaste. "Not exactly what I had in mind."

She set the book back on the table and moved to investigate one of the stacks of books scattered about the room, rising up from the green Axminster carpet like the massive standing stones strewn about the Scottish countryside.

"Is there nothing readable here?"

"Given that you're currently picking through the volumes I sorted as religious, I shouldn't think you're likely to find anything appealing. Instructive, perhaps."

"Oh, very funny." Isabella moved to the next pile of books. She hefted the top tome into her arms and opened to the title page. "*English Etymology, or, A Derivative Dictionary of the English Language* by George William Lemon. Enticing, to be sure."

"When life hands you lemons, or in this case, a Lemon . . ." Olivia started to laugh.

"Livvy, I already had that lecture from Mother. The only thing I am tempted to do with *this* lemon is chuck it at your thick head."

"Right. Why make lemons into lemonade when you can throw them at people instead?"

"Do you *want* me to hurt you?"

"I'd prefer you didn't. Please remember I *am* the loving sister who traveled all the way to Scotland with you...."

Isabella set the heavy volume back down, enjoying the loud thud it produced. "You have been spared the Lemon for now," she warned, fighting a smile. "But only for now." She moved past her sister to the far end of the library where the conglomeration of books resembled more a mountain than a megalithic monument.

"What are these?" Izzie gestured broadly toward the mound.

"I don't know. Those are the books I haven't sorted yet."

"I thought you said you were almost done," accused Izzie.

Olivia shrugged. "It's all relative."

"If you say so." Isabella shifted several thick, and thus likely boring, texts aside and pulled out a slim leather volume. "Aha! An old journal ... well, not that old, judging by the dates of the entries. Let's see, are you going to be dull or full of juicy secrets?"

She opened to a random page and began to read. "Juicy secrets, it is! Finally, some decent reading material," she told Olivia. "Listen:

Rec'd letter from J. His father is recovering slowly, but the doctor is afear'd of a relapse. J plans to stay in Scotland, esp. as his stepmother is nearing her confinement. Again he entreats me to join him & writes how he has hidden a treasure for me at Haile Castle. I shall receive my first clue as soon as I arrive. He is full of remorse over our quarrel & I long to end this wretched distance between us. I awake at night, restless & fevered, aching for him & the closeness we once shared. Would I were packing to go to him, but I must go to London instead. Though it goes against my husband's wishes, I cannot—I will not—desert C. I pray this business may be resolved quickly, for I do not know how I shall mend matters with J should he learn of my deception. . . .

"Well!" Izzie fanned herself. "Finally something interesting after all those—"

"Give it to me!" Olivia snapped.

Isabella frowned. "I'm the one who found it. Don't fuss, I'll give it to you after I've finished—"

"No!" Olivia lunged forward, grabbed the diary out of Isabella's hands, and clutched it to her chest like a priceless relic.

Izzie eyed her sister speculatively. "You're acting quite odd, even for you. It's not as if we know these people. . . . Wait, you know whose diary that is, don't you? You know who 'J' is?"

Her sister nodded. "The 'J' is Jason, Aunt Kate's stepson."

"I remember her saying he was a widower. This must be his wife's journal. Oh dear, I hope they resolved their quarrel. I wonder whether she ever found that treasure he hid for her."

"She didn't," Olivia said softly.

"How do you know?"

"Because I did."

"Olivia Jane Weston, what have you gotten yourself into this time?"

"Oh, Izzie, it's like something out of a novel!" Her face glowing with excitement, she seated herself on the carpet amidst the towers of books.

Isabella settled down beside her, a frown creasing her brow. She had no idea what her sister was about to tell her, but she felt certain she wasn't going to like it. Not when the story involved Olivia's fascination with a reclusive widower. "So that's why you were always skulking about," she mused aloud. "I wondered when you'd developed such an interest in the history and architecture of Scottish castles."

"I have always been interested in old houses, and furthermore, I resent the term 'skulking.' It implies I was up to no good."

"If what you were doing was good, why the need for such clandestine behavior?"

"If you were a pirate, would you want to split your plunder?"

"Olivia, you are *not* a pirate."

"Maybe not, but I still found the treasure." She lifted the hem of her dress and fumbled under her petticoats. After a moment, she handed Isabella a tiny brooch no bigger than her thumbnail.

Closer examination revealed a finely rendered man's shadow portrait set in a gold frame surrounded by garnets. Whatever else she might have to say about the Marquess of Sheldon, Isabella was forced to admit the man had a striking profile. She expected to find the customary lock of hair on the back, but instead, engraved into the gold, were words so tiny she couldn't make them out.

"You need a magnifying glass to read it," Olivia informed her, "but it's a quote from Donne: 'So we shall be one, and one another's all.' Tell me, is that not the most romantic thing you've ever heard?" With a dreamy smile, she plucked the brooch from Isabella's fingers and pinned it back in place, then shook out the skirts of her dress, hiding it from sight.

"Oh, it's romantic all right, but it's not *yours*."

"I found it, didn't I?"

"Livvy, regardless of your having found it, that brooch is not yours. I don't know what your purpose is in going to Wales, but life doesn't work like one of your novels." She stood, adding softly, "I should be proof enough of that."

Olivia got to her feet as well and pointed an accusatory finger at Isabella. "No, your happy ending is in sight, but you're too afraid to take the final steps."

"I hardly think you're in a position to tell me how to live my life."

"Then don't try to tell me how to live mine."

They were nose to nose, circling and hissing like a pair

of tabbies, when the absurdity of the situation struck them both at once. "I'm sorry," they burst out in unison, then laughed at their timing.

"I shouldn't have said you were scared," Olivia apologized. "I just want for you and James to be happy."

"I am scared. Terrified, to tell you the truth, but that's no excuse for snapping at you. I just don't want you to get hurt."

"Don't trouble yourself about me. I'm simply curious to meet the man. I hardly think I should suit with someone brusque and brooding, no matter how dashing he looks pacing the misty Welsh moors. However, if that diary is anything to go by, I wouldn't mind a few kisses."

"Be careful. A few kisses can lead to a lot more."

"Is that so?" Olivia looked far too interested for Isabella's peace of mind. "More kisses . . . or *more*?"

Izzie groaned.

"I see." Livvy's broad grin could only be described as anticipatory.

Isabella shook her head. "That's what I was afraid of."

Chapter 20

I realized I forgot to impart a most important piece of sisterly advice: Whatever else you do, make certain you never find yourself alone in a closed equipage with Lord Sheldon. It is difficult to believe, I know, but I have been told—you do not wish to know by whom—that any number of improprieties, including the most improper of them all, can be committed in a carriage. Pray remember this is meant to warn and inform, not to inspire!

From the correspondence of Isabella, Lady Dunston, age twenty

Letter to her sister, Olivia Weston, slipped to the recipient at the breakfast table, on what may be set in motion once one is, in fact, in motion—November 1798

The morning they were to leave, James stood outside and watched the trunks being loaded onto the carriages. "Does everything look to be in good shape?" James asked his manservant, Davies, who was supervising the process.

"Indeed, my lord. It won't be an easy journey, seeing as it's November in Scotland, but we'll get through."

It wasn't going to be an easy journey in more ways than one, James thought, recalling Isabella's expression at the breakfast table. She had pasted a pleasant smile on her face, but it was clear to anyone who knew her that she was seething inside.

"Davies, please, tell me you were able to get the books."

When James had gathered his troops to plot Isabella's courtship, Olivia had declared that her sister would love nothing so much as having the latest gothic novels to read on the long journey back from Scotland. She'd even told him the titles, but he hadn't bothered to write them down.

When he'd sent Davies to hire the traveling coaches, James had asked him to stop in at one of the booksellers in Edinburgh to purchase the books, but he hadn't been able to remember the titles. "I know at least one of them had something to do with ghosts and ruins," he'd told his manservant. "Or perhaps it's ghosts and ruination."

"I got the books, but I don't know whether they're the ones you wanted. When I asked for gothic novels as you told me, I was shown huge stacks of these books. I tried looking at a few, but every last one seemed to be about ghosts and ruins *and* ruination."

Lots of ruination, eh? No wonder women devoured them, James thought. He might have to read one himself.

"You told me to get as many as I could, and once I gave them your card . . ." He sighed and motioned to a large crate.

"Good God!" James exclaimed, just as Olivia flew out the front door.

"Is that entire box from Creech's Bookshop?" she asked excitedly, dancing her way over to where the grooms were lifting down the wooden container.

"What's going on?" Isabella called out from the front door.

"Come see!" Livvy yelled back. She pulled at the top board, straining with all of her might, but it refused to budge. Irritated, she kicked the side of the crate, which promptly split apart. A pile of books poured forth like gems from a broken treasure chest. The sight certainly seemed to evoke a marauding instinct in the women.

Isabella lifted her skirts and rushed over to Olivia, who had already begun piling books in her arms.

"What is all this?" Izzie asked James, waving an arm in her sister's direction. "Why are there books spilled all over the ground, and why is Livvy pecking away at them like some sort of demented chicken?"

"In answer to your first question, I thought you might like some reading material for the journey. As to the second, there are books all over the ground because your sister was too impatient to allow someone to properly open the crate and therefore decided to demolish it. As to Olivia's farmyard antics . . ." He shrugged. "Ask her yourself."

Isabella turned to her sister, who had set aside one towering stack of books and had begun gathering more. "Livvy," she said sweetly, "what do you think you're doing with my books?"

"Even if you spend every hour in that coach between here and Sheffield Park reading, you still won't be able to finish all these books. I see no reason why I shouldn't help myself, especially since they wouldn't be here at all if I hadn't suggested it."

"Yes, you are the epitome of modesty and selflessness."

Izzie faced James again, ducking her head as if embarrassed. Was it possible his wife was softening toward him? By damn, he'd buy Olivia her own bookstore.

"I want . . . That is . . ."

She flushed, looking every bit as delectable as a ripe peach.

"Thank you. While a tad extravagant, this was very thoughtful."

"Why are you thanking him?" Olivia looked up from her book hunting. "If anyone was thoughtful, it was me. He was just the blunt. *I* was the brains!"

"Olivia," James warned, "if you wish to take those books you've set aside—you know, the ones purchased with my blunt—I would advise you to take them and go. Now."

That demented chicken was not getting a bookstore from him. She did, however, take the hint and retreated to the house with her spoils. Saucy chit—she'd be some man's downfall, poor sot. His downfall stood before him, fresh and fair in the clear, crisp morning air. He reached out and brushed the backs of his fingers against one soft, rosy cheek.

"You're cold," he murmured. "There are heated bricks and blankets in the carriage. We should say our farewells and be on our way."

James watched as Isabella kissed her aunt, sister, and cousin a fond good-bye, and then they went together to make certain Bride was settled in the second coach with his wife's maid and Thora, the nursemaid who had been hired to look after Bride, whose services James had managed to retain with the offer to triple her salary. Thora was a smart lass; she loved Scotland, but she loved sterling more and, most important, she seemed genuinely fond of his daughter. As he'd said, she was a smart lass.

Finally James assisted Isabella into his carriage and seated himself next to her.

She looked pointedly at him, then at the vacant bench opposite.

"I dislike riding backward," he claimed.

"Then it is fortunate I have no such problem," Izzie responded, moving to the empty seat.

James sighed. "We would be warmer sitting together."

"I am perfectly comfortable, thank you."

And with that, she buried her face in one of the novels he'd bought her. Perhaps they hadn't been such a wise purchase after all. He wanted Isabella focused on him, not on some ruined castle wherein ruinations took place. Well, the ruination bit was all right. He considered picking up a book himself, but he didn't particularly want to read. He wanted his wife.

After five long, torturous minutes of silence, James could stand it no longer. "What book are you reading?"

Without looking up she replied, "The third installment of *The Orphan of the Rhine*."

"Oh."

He let another small eternity pass.

"What's it about?"

Her face tightened with annoyance. "The plot is quite complicated. I'm certain the first and second installments are around if you wish to read them."

"Is there ruination? I won't bother unless you assure me the novel contains some truly good ruination."

"Is there such a thing as 'good ruination'?"

"If memory serves, you enjoyed yours thoroughly. As did I."

James let Isabella brood on that until they reached their first stop. While the horses were being changed out, he arranged for a private parlor so Izzie could nurse Bride and, remembering how his wife had picked at her breakfast, he had food sent up as well. The party was back on the road in just over an hour, which he considered making fairly good time, considering the number of females involved.

Again, nearly as soon as the wheels on the coach began to turn, Isabella stuck her nose back in a book ... and again, James found he couldn't let her alone.

"Are you still reading *The Orange in the Rind*?"

"Something like that."

"And has our poor, dear orange been ruined lately?"

Isabella slammed the book closed. "Yes. It was painfully eviscerated and ingested by the *orphan* of the *Rhine*."

"Quite right, quite right. Have you given any further thought to your own ruination, my dear?"

"I don't wish to speak on it."

"What would you like to talk about?"

"I don't want to talk. I want to *read*!"

Lord, but it was fun twitting his wife. Besides, an exasperated response was better than no response at all.

"Why don't you read aloud to me?" he suggested. "Then you can talk *and* read."

Oh, if looks could kill ...

"I am actually rather sleepy." Isabella made a great show of stretching and yawning. "I believe I shall take a nap. You should do the same. You must be tired after all those nights spent plotting against me with my family." She let down the shades, nestled against the plush squabs, and closed her eyes.

"Don't be such a spoilsport," James chided.

She pretended not to hear him.

"Isabella, there is no way you could have possibly fallen asleep so soon."

She attempted a snoring sound, but the noise she produced sounded more like a wild boar snuffling for truffles.

James grinned. "Was that a growl I just heard? My, you must be having some interesting dreams!"

Isabella's jaw was clenched so tightly that James had to fight to keep from laughing. His wife had many talents, but acting was certainly not among them.

"Come, Isabella, enough of this farce. We both know you're not sleeping."

She squeezed her eyes closed more tightly in response, and James had to wonder whether she had ever actually observed a sleeping person before.

"Perhaps I was wrong, my dear, and you truly are asleep," he murmured.

Her body relaxed against the squabs. Did she really think he was going to give in that easily?

"But," he continued, "as the sound of my voice doesn't seem to bother you, there doesn't seem to be any reason why I shouldn't continue amusing myself."

She tensed right back up, stiff as a board again.

"I guess it would be selfish to entertain only myself, though," he went on. "Perhaps you can hear me in your dreams. In that case, I should try to make your dreams as pleasurable as possible. It is my duty as your husband. Ah, I know just the thing! I will recount one of my dreams—one of my very pleasurable dreams—to you, my dear, sleeping wife. Now, how does it begin? Oh, yes, it starts out with the two of us alone in a carriage—a carriage much like this one, in fact—but rather than sitting opposite each other as we are now, you are next to me, no—not next to me—you are perched upon my lap."

From the utter stillness of his wife's body, James could

tell she was listening intently. How far would she let him take this little fantasy?

"You can feel me beneath you, and know exactly how much I want you, so you wiggle your bottom just to tease me. I pull you close for a kiss, but it's not enough. I need to be able to touch you all over. To taste you all over."

James noted that Isabella's breathing had grown shallow; her hands were fisting restlessly by her sides.

"I kiss my way down your neck and fondle your breasts through the fabric of your gown. You arch your back, silently asking for more, and I can tell you want my mouth on you."

A little whimper escaped from Isabella, and the sound shot straight to his already-aching cock. He'd meant to torment her with his words, but he'd gotten tangled in the web he was spinning—hoisted with his own petard, as Lady Weston would say. James stopped himself. He was fairly certain that thoughts of one's mother-in-law did not belong where seduction was in play. So, back to the game . . .

"Fortunately you are wearing a gown with a drop-front bodice, so it is a simple matter to undo the buttons. Your petticoat is easily pushed aside, and the front-lacing stays that are in fashion right now suit my purposes admirably. I have your breasts bared to my gaze in less time than it would take you to object.

"You don't object, of course, but cup your breasts together and lift them up like an offering of some divine, exotic fruit that I am all too eager to taste. As my lips close over one taut nipple, I shift your body and hike up your skirts so you're sitting astride me. I feel your damp heat through the barrier of my breeches, and the knowledge that you want me as badly as I want you drives me mad."

His voice was rough with desire and longing. Every muscle in his body was tensed and primed for action. His body thought the time for words had long passed, that it was time to pillage and conquer and plunder until Isabella belonged to him. But he had to tread carefully. . . .

"I take your mouth again, wondering how you always

taste faintly of berries—sweet as sugar, but with a hint of tartness that keeps me wanting more. Each time I taste you, I know a lifetime of kisses won't be enough to satisfy me. And all the while the swaying motion of the coach is rocking us together, pressing your soft flesh up against my hardness, again and again."

Her low moan was the end of him. "Open your eyes, Izzie," he commanded.

She did more than that. She launched herself at him and grabbed his face, pulling his mouth down to hers. His chuckle at her eagerness dissolved into a strangled growl as he tasted the hot, luscious cavern of her mouth.

Delicious.

From the moment her lips had touched his, there had been a sort of divine alignment, like the unique pairing of a lock and key, and something had shifted in the universe, fitting them inextricably together. And fit together they did. He remembered all too well how sweetly her tight passage had gripped him . . . and how much he wanted to be inside her again.

He settled her on him just as he'd described in his fantasy, straddling him, with her skirts rucked up about her thighs, allowing him to slide his hands down and cup the soft, firm flesh of her posterior. He gently urged her forward, pressing them together at the spot where their bodies longed to join. The action wrung gasps from them both, and Isabella's arms tightened around his neck as if she never wanted to let go. He hoped she never would.

How could he have ever thought anything—revenge included—tasted sweeter than her love?

How could he have believed he could stay away when he needed her to survive?

How could—

How could the bloody coach have stopped?

"Izzie?"

"Mmm-hmmm."

She nipped his earlobe and Christ, if he didn't nearly come in his breeches right then and there.

"Oh God," he groaned. "Sweetheart, you have to stop."

"And why is that?" she purred. "I don't think we're nearly done here."

James wanted to weep. "I know, my love, I know, but the coach has stopped, and I believe we're about to be interrupted."

He watched as she processed his words, then saw the dawning horror on her face. She scrambled off him and flung herself into the opposite corner of the carriage just as there came a rapping on the door.

"Yes?" James bit out.

"Begging your pardon, my lord, but the other coach just pulled off the road."

"Bride!" Isabella gasped.

James bolted out of the carriage and began to run, Isabella close on his heels. They slowed as the occupants of the other conveyance disembarked and a squalling Bride was handed down to Thora, who grinned and waved.

"I thin' this wee lil' piggie is hungry again," she shouted.

James didn't particularly like hearing his daughter referred to as swine, but as long as she was safe and sound, he was willing to overlook the matter. He went to consult with Davies, who had been driving the second coach.

"We hit a rut," the man explained, "and though it was a fair jolt, I didn't think too much on it, but then the carriage started to feel different beneath me and I got uneasy-like. I figured it was better to pull off and check that everything were sound."

"When the contents are that precious, one cannot be too cautious," James agreed. Together they checked the vehicle for damage and found a crack in the rear axle. Had Davies driven much farther, or had he hit another bad spot on the road, the piece would have broken clean apart and the carriage would almost certainly have overturned. His guts twisted.

"There's no use fretting over what-ifs, my lord. What's important is no one got hurt."

"Ever the voice of reason, Davies. Tell the postillion to

walk the carriage to Ayton. The axle should hold up that far; it can't be more than six or seven miles. We may as well rack up there for the night."

With the addition of Becky, Thora, and Bride to the coach, James's visions of a romantic interlude were again relegated to the status of dreams. Three-quarters of an hour later, he wondered if he hadn't somehow stumbled into a nightmare.

Bride would not stop crying, and nothing Thora or Isabella did seemed to comfort her. She couldn't possibly be hungry, because Izzie had fed her while he'd been inspecting the other coach. Thora swore her diaper was dry, so that wasn't the problem. Izzie rocked her, bounced her, sang to her, swaddled her, unswaddled her—none of it made a difference. Bride screamed till she was red in the face and then shrieked some more.

James was at his wits' end. "Can't you make her stop?"

Isabella looked at him through narrowed eyes. "If it's so easy, why don't you try?" She shoved the squalling bundle at him.

James warily took Bride into his arms. The wailing stopped. James smiled smugly at Izzie. "See, that wasn't so—"

Bride resumed her howling with renewed gusto.

"You were saying?" Isabella sneered.

James drew Bride closer to his chest. "Just give me a moment and—Jesus, what is that smell?"

"Oh dear!" Isabella put a hand up over her nose. "She needs to be changed, and there's not enough room with all of us in the carriage."

James nodded, handed a now-whimpering Bride over to Thora, and rapped on the roof of the coach to signal Davies to pull off the road. As soon as they had stopped, James threw open a door and jumped to the ground, gulping deep breaths of fresh air. "How can someone so little," he gasped, "produce such a horrendously foul odor?"

"Welcome to the joys of parenthood," Izzie grumbled from inside the coach.

"I believe I'll ride the rest of the way on the box with Davies," James said quickly. "That way you will all have more room."

Isabella muttered something James felt certain was desultory. It was difficult to believe that an hour or so earlier she'd been moaning in his arms. Events, and his mood, had definitely taken a turn for the worse.

Matters declined further when they reached Ayton. James was able to secure two rooms for the night, and he'd planned to use one of them to pick up where he and Isabella had left off in the carriage. Unfortunately for him, Isabella seemed to have come back to her senses and insisted on rooming with Bride and the female servants.

James was in a foul temper the next morning, which wasn't helped by learning that the repairs on the second carriage might take several days. Then Isabella announced over breakfast that after the previous night's near mishap, she planned on riding with Bride the rest of the way back. Having had a brief taste of what *that* would be like, James decided for the sake of his sanity—and his ears—to hire a horse and let the women take over his coach.

Becky and Thora set about repacking the trunks, and James arranged to have the remaining baggage sent on to Sheffield Park. It was ironic, but for the first time in his life he was actually looking forward to seeing the damned place.

By the time they reached Sheffield Park, Isabella was thoroughly sick of traveling. The journey back from Scotland had not only felt twice as long as the trip there, but by her calculations it had actually taken twice as long. Between the rotten weather and the demands of an infant, their return had taken more than a fortnight. Fifteen days, five hours, and forty-eight minutes, give or take a few.

Not that she had been counting.

She was more familiar than she wished to be with the various inns and posting houses along the Great North Road, including their lumpy mattresses, inferior cooking,

tepid bathwater, and in several cases, their rodent population. Sheffield Park was an impressive estate by even the
highest standards, but given her accommodations of late,
passing through the gates and up the long, curving drive
was like approaching heaven.

James had ridden ahead to alert the staff of their immi-
nent arrival. Izzie hoped Mrs. Benton wasn't going to round
up all the servants to introduce them to their new mistress.
There would be time enough for that tomorrow; right now
all she wanted was a hot bath and a decent night's sleep in
a comfortable bed.

Alone.

She didn't know what arrangements James had seen fit to
make, but she had a feeling she wasn't going to like them—
or that she might like them too much. Their moments in the
carriage kept her awake at night, but she hadn't forgotten
her mother's warning.

As much as she yearned for his touch, as much as she
loved him, there was still too much left unresolved between
them. She just hoped she had the strength to resist him and
to keep from giving in to her own desires.

When the coach pulled up in front of the house, James
was waiting on the stairs to meet them. He escorted Izzie
into the house, where Mrs. Benton (and only Mrs. Benton,
thank heavens) was waiting to fuss over everyone.

"Welcome, my lady. I couldn't be more delighted to finally have you here at Sheffield Park. His lordship decided
that the formal introductions could wait, seeing as the hour
is late."

"Thank you, Mrs. Benton. I confess, I am likely to fall
asleep where I stand."

"You poor dear. I ordered a hot bath drawn the moment
I heard the clatter of the coach coming up the drive."

"Bless you! I trust my husband told you I would need
rooms near the nursery?"

"Indeed. Quite convenient it is, what with his lordship's
chambers being so near there."

"I beg your pardon?"

"The nursery is in the east wing," James explained. "My rooms are there as well since my grandfather's apartments are in the west wing and he preferred that we have as little contact as possible."

"Your old rooms, you mean. Now that you are the earl, you have moved," Isabella clarified.

James shook his head. "I still use my old rooms. I have some fond memories there." He had the audacity to wink at her.

Izzie tugged on James's sleeve. "Excuse us, Mrs. Benton. I need to have a private word with my husband." She dragged James to the far end of the entry hall. "I don't know what notions you've got into your head, but we will not be sharing a bedchamber," Isabella hissed.

"Where do you expect me to sleep, then?"

"Sleep in the earl's apartments."

"No."

"Then sleep in the stables for all I care. You are not sharing a bed with me."

"Fine." James sighed. "I'll take the earl's chambers, but only because I'm too exhausted to debate the matter."

"Now for the rules . . ."

"There are rules?" He looked amused.

"Yes, I think we should set some basic rules. Namely that, with the exception of visiting Bride, you will not set foot in the east wing unless I have expressly invited you."

"Very well, then you will not set foot in the west wing unless *I* have expressly invited *you*."

Izzie rolled her eyes. "What, are you worried I'll sneak into your bedchamber and seduce you?" She spoke without thinking, then clapped a hand over her mouth when she realized what she'd said.

James burst out laughing, curse his black heart. "Let's just say it's happened before."

Chapter 21

*We are finally arrived home to Sheffield Park. I
cannot help feeling odd calling this house my home,
but I hope in time the word will come naturally.
I shall bring Bride for a visit in a few days' time,
once we are suitably recovered, so she may meet her
grandfather, her uncle, and her gaggle of aunts. Please
assure Lia and Genni that I have not forgotten their
recent birthday. I have had little time to shop, but it
just so happens I have come into a vast library of
books that I believe will make an excellent present for
girls of thirteen. They shall be excessively diverted,
and I have always believed the sign of a good gift is
its ability to delight and amuse.*

From the correspondence of Isabella, Lady Dunston,
age twenty

Letter to her mother, Mary, Viscountess Weston, proposing possible, if potentially improper, presents for a pair of
already-precocious poppets—December 1798

A day passed in relative peace with Isabella settling in
and exploring her new home—at least, the half she had
claimed for herself. She didn't see James, but she figured
he was closeted in his study, tending to all those urgent estate matters that had necessitated their precipitous return
from Scotland. Even Bride was quiet, though that probably

had more to do with the sugar teat Mrs. Benton had made for her than anything else. As with all good things, though, it was not to last. The air of calm dissipated early the following morning when a veritable army of tradespeople descended on the house.

Isabella went to the front hall to investigate, but all she managed to see was Mrs. Benton pointing the last man in the direction of James's rooms. As she'd claimed no interest in her husband's affairs, Izzie sent her maid to the servants' hall to see what gossip she could glean.

"Redecorating, my lady, and some renovations," Becky told her, relaying the limited information she had been able to gather. "That's all anyone would say. They're a close-mouthed bunch here, I must say." She shook her head in disappointment.

Isabella quite understood how she felt. It wasn't that she cared what James was doing, she told herself, but redecorations should really fall under the province of the lady of the house. Not that she didn't have plenty of issues with which to occupy herself. Sheffield Park hadn't had a mistress since James's grandmother had died, which she reckoned had to be at least fifty years ago, and the house clearly needed a woman's touch. Mrs. Benton was a more than competent housekeeper, but she was getting on in years.

Her mood was improved in the early afternoon when Davies arrived bearing gifts. It was difficult to remain down in the mouth when there were presents to be opened, and even harder to stay sullen when a glittering diamond and aquamarine necklace entered the picture. Enclosed in the velvet case was a letter from James requesting her company at dinner that evening.

"May I take back your reply, my lady?" Davies queried.

"You may tell him I would be delighted to dine with him tonight."

Isabella dressed with care, choosing a pale blue silk gown that complemented her new jewels. She entered the drawing room promptly at seven and found James waiting for her, looking splendid in his formal evening wear.

Before her courage deserted her, Izzie quickly kissed his cheek. "Thank you for the necklace. It's beautiful."

"So are you."

Izzie blushed, feeling more like a maiden than a married lady. Then again, she reflected as James led her into the dining room, in many ways she was closer to being a virginal miss than a woman of experience.

They enjoyed an elegant repast, and James proved a most diverting companion. He kept up an easy conversation throughout the meal, skirting any potentially uncomfortable subjects. They reminisced about childhood adventures, and James kept her amused with tales about the scrapes he and Henry had got up to at Oxford. She, in turn, regaled him with anecdotes from her time in London and Bath, until he was roaring with laughter. She stayed at the table while he drank his port, their conversation having dwindled to an easy silence. When one of the candles sputtered and burned out, Isabella forced herself to stand. The evening had been so pleasant, she wished it wouldn't end.

James rose when she did. He took her hand and walked back to the drawing room. Without warning he drew her close and took her lips in a kiss so tender, her knees nearly buckled.

"Invite me to your chambers," he urged, playfully nipping her lower lip.

Isabella reluctantly drew away. "Not yet. Not tonight."

He sighed. "Pleasant dreams, then, Izzie. Until tomorrow."

"Good night," she replied, hurrying off to her room before she changed her mind.

That night established a pattern. James kept to his wing of the estate during the day, and Izzie spent her mornings playing with Bride and overseeing the household. Every afternoon, Davies arrived with some sort of present: a bonnet trimmed with yellow and white silk roses; beautiful, enameled trinket boxes; tortoiseshell hair combs; an exquisitely painted fan; a pair of lovebirds; delicately scented soaps and bath oils. . . . And accompanying each gift was a note from James inviting her to dine with him.

Each occasion proved more pleasurable than the last. Isabella learned more about her husband, reveled in his company, and began to crave his presence during the day. Every night he walked her to the drawing room and kissed her. Sometimes he was slow and gentle; other times he was rough and demanding, but each kiss fueled the fire he had carefully built within her.

He always asked to be invited back to her room, but Izzie remembered her mother's advice. They had yet to discuss any of the serious issues at hand, and until they did, she would keep him from her bed. It was increasingly difficult, though, and she felt her resistance weakening.

She tossed and turned every night, and when she finally fell asleep, she dreamed of James. Needless to say, the dreams were not restful. She always awoke sweaty and aroused, with the quilts tangled in a heap at her feet. She tried touching herself, but that joyful release hovered just out of reach, as elusive as her dream lover.

After a fortnight had passed, Izzie's nerves were stretched to the breaking point. James consumed her every waking thought, and most of her sleeping ones. She knew she would have to be the one to bring up any touchy subjects, but dinner had turned into a perfect, magical time of day, and she was loath to break the spell.

That night, James didn't stop at kisses. He cupped her breasts through her gown, and with the fever that raged through her blood, that simple caress nearly caused her to explode. He pulled her close, cupping her behind and pressing her against his erection. She was dizzy with desire, and he knew it.

"Let me take you to your room," he said, in between hot, openmouthed kisses down her neck. "Tonight, Izzie, before we both go insane."

How was she supposed to think when he kept touching her like that?

"I—" Her brain refused to function. All the blood that

belonged there had raced to the spots where James's lips met her bare flesh.

"I—"

"*Yes*," he said, encouraging her. "Say *yes*."

"I can't." She wrenched herself away from him and saw the disappointment in his eyes. "I'm sorry," she whispered, then fled.

Back in her lonely room, Isabella wondered if she had made the right decision. Would it have really been so terrible if she'd given in and said yes? What was she gaining by denying him—and herself—the pleasure they both craved?

Nothing, her body screamed. *Go to him*. She contemplated the thought for a moment. She knew he would welcome her into his bed, but she couldn't break the rules she'd been the one to insist on in the first place.

She called Becky to help her undress, but once she was in bed, she couldn't sleep. She needed some distraction to keep her from running to James's chamber and ravishing him. . . .

Ravishment—that was it!

Even with all the gothic novels she had given to the twins for their birthday—much to her mother's horror— there were still a great many Minerva Press books left over. She donned her wrapper and padded off toward the library. If her own ruination was out of reach, she would settle for living vicariously through an enterprising heroine . . . and perhaps she'd even pick up some pointers along the way!

When she reached the library, Isabella found she was not the only one who couldn't sleep. She stared at the man silhouetted by the light of the dying fire. He was her husband; he was *James*, and yet in some ways he was a perfect stranger. She needed to know what he was doing there, not in that particular room, but in her life. *Why had he come back?* Everything would have been so much simpler had he stayed away.

"Because I need you," he said, and she realized she had

voiced her thoughts aloud. It was amazing, really, how he could devastate her with three simple words. How long had she waited, how many times over how many years had she prayed to hear him say those words? But hearing them now, rather than any sort of triumph or exultation, all she felt was a vast emptiness.

She had needed him once. She wasn't sure if she still did, and the fact of the matter was, she didn't really *want* to know. It would mean looking into places in her heart and sections of her soul that she had closed off and locked up. She had learned to cope without him, had found a measure of contentment that she didn't want to risk. Besides, she had Bride to fill her heart.

That organ began to thump erratically as he got to his feet and walked over to her. He reached out a hand and tenderly traced one of the curls at her temple. It was too much. She turned her head away from him, but not before she saw the flash of hurt in his eyes.

"Don't you need me even a little bit, Izzie?" he asked softly.

"Don't. Please, don't," she begged him, hating the wobble in her voice. Then again, she had cried so many tears over this man, what were a few more?

"Do you know what I was thinking about before you came in? I was thinking about that morning in Scotland when I found you and Bride asleep together in the nursery. You looked like an angel, so beautiful and good, and Bride looked just as heaven-sent. I wish I had been here when she was born."

Isabella gave a watery sniffle. "Mrs. Drummond would probably have sent you off with a bottle of brandy and instructions to stay away."

"I would have stayed with you the whole time," he promised solemnly, brushing away the tears as he turned her face toward him.

The genuine regret she saw in his eyes was impossible to ignore. "You were with me," she whispered. She brought her hand up for a moment to cover his, wordlessly imploring him to maintain the contact of his palm pressed to her cheek. "When I had lost the will to push, I heard your voice, felt your arms around me, lending me your strength."

"When I was shot, when I thought I was going to die, I felt you with me, easing my pain, and all I could think about was how I had never told you how much I love you. You must understand—"

"You love me?" she exclaimed, totally dumbfounded.

James was so startled by her shocked outcry that he stumbled backward, tripped over an ottoman, and landed heavily on his behind. He smiled up at her sheepishly. "Do you honestly mean that I still haven't told you?"

She shook her head, her heart beating wildly in her chest, filled with a hope so wondrous, so gorgeous, she was scared to breathe.

"Oh dear. How terribly remiss of me," he clucked.

Her breath whooshed out of her, and she fell to her knees beside him. "James Sheffield, if you don't tell me right now . . ."

He pulled her into his lap and held her tightly in his arms. "I love you," he said roughly into her hair. He pulled back so that he could look into her eyes. The depth of emotion she saw there staggered her. "I love you," he repeated. "I love you more than I have ever loved anyone. More than I thought it was possible to love someone."

"And Bride?" she asked.

"I won't deny that it has taken some getting used to, this notion of being a father, but how could I not love her?"

Isabella pulled away and sank down on her heels. "What if she had been a boy? Would you still feel the same way?"

"I cannot imagine not loving any child of ours, but perhaps we should test it out to be sure. Bride ought to have a little brother to play with, don't you think?"

"But what about your determination that the Sheffield line end with you?"

"My love, my grandfather ruled my life for far too long. Even from the grave he's kept his claws in me, and I will not give him that power any longer." He rose and took hold of her hands, pulling her to her feet. "Seeing you again, holding our daughter in my arms, everything has become clear."

Isabella snatched her hands away from him so quickly that he toppled back onto the floor.

"What in God's name was *that* for?" he demanded, picking himself up and rubbing his sore backside.

And a mighty fine backside it was. No, no, no. She had to focus.

"Am I honestly to believe that you have had some sort of miraculous revelation? That you no longer care about your plans for revenge and the end of the earldom?"

"Er, uh, well . . . yes?"

She glared at him.

"Do you know why I left?"

Isabella sighed. She thought they had moved past that. "You were angry at me for tricking you into marriage, and also for forcing you to bend to your grandfather's plans."

"That isn't why I left. Well, that was part of it, but that wasn't the real reason."

"Which was?"

"I was scared. Partly for myself, but mostly I was scared for you."

That definitely was not what she had expected to hear. Her legs felt wobbly, so she stumbled over to the nearest settee. "You were scared for *me*?"

He nodded and began to move restlessly about the room. "When I explained to you about how a woman gets pregnant, I had a vision. I don't know if that is truly what it was, but it no longer matters since, thank God, it didn't come to pass. But at the time, I truly thought it was a premonition, and there's enough superstitious Irish blood in me that I believed it."

"What did you see?"

He turned and stared at her, the pain and sorrow in his eyes almost more than she could bear. She patted her hand beside her, motioning him to sit. She moved over to make space for him, taking comfort in his nearness and hoping he would do the same.

Slowly, haltingly, he began to explain his fears, and then it all began to spill out of him, the words tumbling over one another in their haste to get out. "I thought I would lose you," he choked out, "and I was so scared. Scared of loving, and scared of losing. I told myself that it was only lust, and that all you felt was infatuation. I thought that if I could just stay away from you, I could keep myself from falling in love, and then I wouldn't be hurt again. Everything was tied up together, all the anger and the fear and the sadness intertwined, and I didn't want to unravel it. It was easier, safer, that way.

"After my father died, when I was on the ship coming to England, even in my darkest hours I retained some spark of hope. After not two minutes in my grandfather's presence, hope turned to hate. I was so angry with everyone—not only with my grandfather, but also with my mother for dying and even more with my father for not loving me enough to have the courage to live. But then, when I had that vision, I finally understood my father. How he felt that life without my mother wasn't worth living. Because that was how I was beginning to feel about you. It terrified me. And I was certain you would die if I got you with child. But I knew I wouldn't be able to keep my hands off you if I stayed.... So I left. I could bear being away from you, I could bear your hatred, but your death would destroy me."

"Oh, James!" She wiped at the tears running down her cheeks. "That was the way I felt when I went to your room that night. I thought if you enlisted, you would die. I thought if you married me, you would be safe. I knew you would hate me, but I could bear it as long as you were alive. I was so scared when Mr. Marbly told me you had joined the navy." She placed her hand on top of his, needing the contact, the feel of his warm skin beneath her fingertips.

"I'm so sorry, Izzie," he said, turning his hand so they were palm to palm, their fingers interlaced.

It was unexpectedly sensual, the movement of their

fingers sliding past one another, the brush of skin on skin. She wondered if the simple motion had affected him as well. She tilted her chin up to look at him, noting the slight hitch to his breathing, the almost imperceptible flare of his nostrils, and the heavy-lidded slant to his eyes—eyes that watched her with a burning intensity.

His gaze never leaving hers, he lifted their joined hands to his lips and lightly nipped one of her knuckles, his tongue darting out to taste her flesh. The feeling of his wet, warm mouth on her skin flipped some sort of mechanism inside her. Without thought, out of control, she raised her free hand, tangled it in his hair, and drew his mouth down on hers.

It was a kiss made of the frustrated longings of lonely nights, a kiss forged from the heat of anger, a kiss born of the aching need to comfort and be comforted. But mostly it was the kiss of lovers whose bodies had been too-long denied. The fires of passion raged brightly, igniting their blood, driving them into a fever of lust and desire.

The very small, logical part of Isabella's brain that was functioning tried to intercede. It was too soon. There was too much unresolved between them. Sex was not the solution; it wasn't the answer to their problems. It would only muddy already-cloudy waters. But her body didn't care. After all the tears and the pain of the previous months, surely she deserved this one moment, this perfect pleasure.

Her mind made up, Isabella slowly trailed her fingers down through James's hair and around his nape, where she employed both hands in undoing his cravat. She hadn't had the chance to undress him before, so she lingered over the novel task of taking off a man's clothing. She took her time with his neckcloth, stroking her fingertips along the rigid lines of his jaw, dropping light, fleeting kisses on his forehead, his cheeks, his nose, and then longer ones on his mouth.

He sat like a statue, so still she could barely see the rise and fall of his chest, as if he were afraid to move for fear it was all a dream, but she could feel the pulse hammering away at the base of his neck. Tossing the cravat to the floor, she leaned forward and placed her lips over that rapidly beating pulse, breathing in the scent of him. She splayed her palm over the hard planes of his chest, thrilled by the way his heart was racing like a stallion at full gallop.

"Izzie," James groaned, reaching for the ties to her wrapper. Then, abruptly, he stopped and jerked his hands back to his sides. "You need to tell me if this is what you want," he said raggedly. "If I start touching you, I don't know if I'll be able to stop."

"I want you."

His breath released in a slow hiss. "Is that an invitation to your room?"

She nodded, and he scooped her up in his arms and took off at a near run. He wasn't going to give her time to remember all the reasons why this was a bad idea. Thank God.

As if he had read her mind, James pressed a quick, hard kiss on her lips. "Don't," he said. "Don't think, Izzie."

And she didn't. They had reached her bedchamber, and once she heard the bolt shoot home, Izzie closed her eyes and gave herself up to him and all the amazing feelings he aroused in her.

He slowly set her down, sliding her down the length of his hard body until her feet touched the floor. She clung to him, but he held her at arm's length, untying her wrapper at an infinitesimal pace, teasing her as she had done to him. He kissed and laved her nape, gently raking the tender spot with his teeth, an action that caused each hair on her body to stand on end, and then he slid the garment off her shoulders, letting it fall to the floor.

"God, Izzie," he breathed, his eyes widening at the sight of the lace-trimmed lawn chemise her aunt had insisted was the proper nighttime attire for a married woman. His gaze fixed on her chest, and her breasts swelled and peaked in response, straining against the thin fabric, hungry for attention, hungry for *him*.

She wriggled her shoulders, and the gown slipped off,

puddling at her feet. Reveling in her nakedness, Isabella threw back the coverlet and climbed onto the bed, expecting James to pounce on her at any second. When she finally turned to look at him, he stood frozen beside the bed.

She crawled over to him and rose up onto her knees so they were face-to-face. She pushed his waistcoat off the broad slope of his shoulders. Her fingers moved to loosen the button at his collar from its hole.

"Your shirt," she commanded breathily. "Take it off."

He yanked the white muslin out of his breeches and lifted it up, revealing inch after delicious inch of golden skin. Her breath caught when she saw the scarred flesh on his torso where he had been wounded, and a little cry escaped her throat when his shoulder came into sight.

Heavens above, she had come so close to losing him. *Too close.* She didn't want to think about it. She didn't want to *think.* She flung herself against him, molding her curves to his hardness. She needed to feel the steady drum of his heart in his chest, needed the way he could make her forget, needed *him.*

As if he could hear her thoughts, he asked again, "Do you need me, Izzie?"

This time she couldn't deny it. She couldn't deny him, and she didn't want to deny herself. "Yes," she whispered fervently, planting an openmouthed kiss at the base of his throat. "Oh God, *yes!*"

Chapter 22

Now that we are back in England, I suppose you will inevitably see James. I asked you once before not to shoot my husband, but I am not certain you ever actually agreed. Remember, he is my husband and the father of my child, your niece. If ever he deserves to be shot, surely the honors should fall to me.

From the correspondence of Isabella, Lady Dunston, age twenty

Letter to her brother, Henry Weston, containing a reasonable argument for the precedency of mariticide over fratricide—December 1798

At her words, James felt something raw and broken inside himself heal. At her kiss, something primitive caged within him broke free. One of his hands fisted in her hair, angling her to receive his kiss. As his mouth descended on hers, his other hand captured one of her breasts.

They were bigger now, fuller, and her nipples had deepened to a dark plum color. They were more sensitive, too, he thought, when she inhaled sharply as he plucked one of the hard buds, rolling it between his thumb and forefinger.

When she tugged him closer, James felt his heart stop beating, then resume in double time. He eagerly stripped out of what remained of his own clothing and joined her in the bed, and then they were both reaching for each other, touching each other.

Lord, how he needed this woman. She was like a fire in his blood, making him fierce and wild in his desire to conquer her, to brand her as his own. And yet he knew that even if he possessed her in every way, it wouldn't be enough. He would still want more of her. She was an addiction he would never truly be free of, a craving he would never quite fill. He knew that every struggle for release, every attempt to sate the hunger would only make it worse, but underneath his proud armor, he was a willing prisoner, and she was a feast of which he would never tire.

He raked her naked body with his eyes, devouring each delectable curve so magnificently laid out before him on the bed. Her breasts. Her hips. The gentle swell of her stomach—a sweet, lingering reminder of the tiny blessing that lay upstairs in the nursery.

Her beauty overwhelmed him, humbled him, and gave him the sensation that he was a lowly supplicant in the presence of a goddess. And then she held out her arms to him, a sultry, inviting smile on her lips, the spark of passion and longing lighting her eyes. He went up in flames.

He fell on her like some sort of ravening, rutting beast, frantically running his hands over her body as he drew her breast into his mouth. He was rewarded with the sound of her moaning his name and the feel of her nails digging into the muscles on his back as she clutched him to her, silently urging him to take her.

He reached down between their bodies and found her wet and ready for him. He felt light-headed, knowing she was as desperate for the joining as he was. It was a good thing, too, because he wasn't going to be able to love her slowly and tenderly, the way she deserved. He had spent too many sleepless nights and had been celibate far, far too long for that. There would be other times when he would cherish her. This time he was going to take her. . . .

And when he was done, she would know she belonged to him.

He stroked her cleft, circling his index finger around the bud at the peak of her sex. She moaned and arched her back, lifting her hips to give him better access. Keeping his thumb pressed against that button of pleasure, James slid a finger into her.

"Now!" she panted. "Please. I'm almost there. I want you with me." She brought her hands up to frame his face. "I want you in me."

He groaned. "Tell me again," he said, flexing his finger.

She gasped, her hands falling away from his face to clutch at the sheets. "Oh, James! Oh God!"

He began to withdraw his finger.

"I want you inside me. Please. Now."

Sweat was beading on his forehead and every muscle in his body was painfully tense, but erotic as her words were, they weren't the ones he wanted to hear. The reins on his control were frayed and quickly slipping from his hands, but he started working a second finger in beside the first. "Tell me you need me."

"I need you," she pleaded.

He pressed deeper into her, gently rocking his hand back and forth.

"I need you," she yelled, bucking up against him. "*Need you, need you, need you, need you, need you,*" she wailed as he brought her to the peak, then withdrew his fingers before she could tumble over.

James positioned himself against her entrance, swallowing hard at the feel of her soft, slick flesh. He nudged forward, sheathing the tip of himself, fighting the urge to thrust all the way in.

Her hips rose as she tried to draw him deeper. "Yes," she whispered. *"Yes."*

He pressed forward another inch. "Tell me you love me."

"James!" she begged.

"Say it."

"I love you," she cried brokenly.

The reins snapped as he surged forward, claiming her

mouth in a rough, wet kiss as he drove into her velvety warmth. He closed his eyes and threw his head back, savoring the way she clasped him so tightly, her inner muscles clenching around him, drawing him deeper with every stroke. Again and again he pounded into her, spurred on by the sound of her throaty cries of desire, the musky scent of their mingled, mutual arousal, the taste of ripe strawberries and golden honey that was uniquely Isabella, and the feeling of her fingers tangled tightly in his hair. . . .

She was a feast for his senses and, having been denied this particular delicacy for far too long, James gorged himself like the hungry beggar he was. He took everything she had to give and demanded more. More from her, more of her. He pushed her ruthlessly, higher and higher, using whispered words of love and the commanding tempo of his hips. She followed where he led, lifting up to meet him, her nails digging into his flanks, her body making its own wordless requests. *Deeper. Harder. Faster.*

He gave her what she wanted . . . and more.

"James," she groaned in protest when he withdrew from her.

"Trust me," he rasped in response, as he turned her over onto her stomach.

"But—"

"Hush," he ordered, grabbing a couple of pillows and positioning them under her hips, preparing her to receive him. *Perfect.* His erection throbbed with anticipation. Shaking and trembling with need and excitement and desire, he guided himself into her, delighting in the resulting symphony of needy whimpers, harsh moans, and frenzied gasps.

He pumped into her over and over, each stroke making his body more desperate and frantic for release. Guided by some primitive instinct, he leaned over her and lightly bit that sweet, vulnerable spot where her neck and shoulder met. Her inner muscles clamped tightly around him, caressed him intimately, and James knew he didn't have long. Reaching beneath her, his fingers sought out that secret, sensitive nubbin of flesh that crowned her sex, praying that the additional stimulation would send her over the edge.

"*Now*, Izzie!" he directed her. "Come for me *now*!"

Her entire body went tense, and her head lifted off the bed, her mouth open in a silent scream. As the first ripple of contractions radiated from her core, squeezing him in unbearable rhythmic bliss, James let himself go. He thrust once, twice, three times, and then he was gripping her hips, shuddering and jerking violently as he spilled his seed deep within her womb. For all he knew, he had just planted another babe there. Surprisingly, he felt only pleasure at the thought. And then he stopped thinking entirely and gave himself up to feeling and pleasure.

He was sprawled on his back, lying in a state of sated bliss, his breath still rushing in and out of his lungs, happier than he had ever been in his life, when James realized the bed was shaking. Then he heard a low moan. He grinned. He was a lucky man to have married such a lusty wench. Even if his body still needed time to recover, he could pleasure her again with his fingers and mouth.

He felt a stirring in his groin. Perhaps he would be ready sooner than he'd thought. Smiling, he rolled onto his side and was met with a sight that hit him like a fist to the gut. Isabella had curled up into a tiny ball, facing away from him, and her shoulders were heaving—but not with pleasure. She was crying—sobbing, actually, with her fist pressed to her mouth to stifle the sound.

He felt hurt and helpless, completely adrift, and the place within himself he'd thought was healed split open again, leaving him raw and vulnerable.

"Izzie?" he said cautiously.

"Leave. Please."

Her words pierced his heart, but he kept his tone light, pretending to misunderstand. "I shall oblige you, my dear, but only because my bedchamber is quite on the other side of this house and I fear sleep is upon me. You have quite worn me out."

"No. I need you to go away from here, away from me. I need space, time to think."

"Away from you," he repeated slowly. "And away from my daughter?"

She rolled over and sat up, clutching the sheets to her chest. "She is *my* daughter. I am the one who wanted her, carried her inside me, brought her into this world, while you—"

"Forgive me, my dear," he said, a hint of sarcasm creeping into his voice. "I didn't mean to belittle your part in the process. I was just uncertain whether you actually thought I would walk away from our child."

"Why shouldn't I believe it? Walking, or rather, running away, is what you do best, isn't it?"

A hit. A palpable hit. "I have changed. As, apparently, have you. Because instead of the courageous woman I was foolish enough to leave, all I see is a coward. In this case, by asking me to leave, *you* are the one who is running."

"I am not *asking* you to leave. I am *telling* you to leave."

James raked a hand through his hair. "I don't believe this," he muttered. "I don't bloody well believe this. A few minutes ago we were making love, and now you are asking—no, pardon, *telling*—me to leave. You will understand if I am somewhat confused."

"I'm sorry."

"For what, exactly? Because if you are filled with regret over our lovemaking, I don't particularly want to hear it."

"It's just . . . I just . . ."

"You wanted it. Don't you dare try to deny it."

"I'm not. What just happened was as much for my comfort as for yours."

"For my comfort," he repeated slowly, trying to reassure himself that she didn't mean it the way it sounded. It didn't work. "*For my comfort?*" he roared, his pride bruised and battered. He flung himself out of the bed and began pulling on his clothes. It was damnably reminiscent of the last time they had made love, and he felt equally betrayed.

"Comfort!" He let out a derisive snort. "I'm tempted to climb back into that bed and prove just how much of a liar you are. Tell me, Izzie, what are you really scared of? Are you more afraid of my leaving or of my staying?"

"I don't know," she whispered. "I don't know what I want anymore."

"You love me. I know you do." Even had she not admitted it, he would have known. A woman didn't give herself to a man like that unless her heart was involved.

"I do love you. That's not the problem."

"Then what exactly *is* the problem?"

"I don't *want* to love you."

James swallowed and nodded tersely, masking the painful wounds her words wrought. He'd exposed his soul to her, told her his most private fears and secrets, and he had come up lacking. She didn't love him; she loved the fantasy of him she'd created in her head. No man could live up to that.

He'd finally pieced his heart together, and he had thought he could trust her with it. He'd been a fool. He gathered the rest of his clothes and headed to the door, then turned to look back at her, his heart clenching. He'd be damned if he'd let her have the last word. "I'll be gone by the morning," he assured her, because really, nothing else remained to be said.

As soon as the door closed, Isabella began to cry. She didn't understand herself sometimes. How long had she dreamed that he would return to her and profess his love? Now that he had, she sent him packing.

He was right. She wasn't brave anymore. She was terrified. She had fallen back into his arms so quickly. Had fallen back into the habit of *him*. And it wouldn't matter if he left within the hour, or in a week, or even in five years. Whenever that day came, he would take her heart with him.

She knew it as surely as she knew that day *would* come— the day when he would leave her.

Because he didn't love her. Not really. It was his sense

of duty that had brought him back to her, and that, along with his pride, would keep him by her side. But one day it wouldn't be enough for him, and it certainly wouldn't ever be enough for her.

And even if he did love her, was that really enough to sustain a marriage? How could she know whether it would grow and strengthen under the inescapable stress of family life, or collapse like a flimsy house built of cards under the strain? She was lost and confused, more so than she had ever been. She wasn't used to the feeling, and she didn't particularly like it. She had more than liked the feelings James had roused in her, though. Her body hungered for that sweet release again, and her mind craved a return to that glorious place where she didn't have to think, only feel. And her heart, her very soul, longed for *him*.

But she had sent him away, stupid, scared creature that she was, and she had no idea if he would come back. Miserable and filled with doubts, Isabella bawled and blubbered and sobbed and sniveled until she finally exhausted herself and fell asleep.

When she awoke, it was morning. She allowed herself to hope that her words hadn't chased him away, that this time he had stayed because he loved her too much to leave, but a visit to the housekeeper's rooms disabused her of the notion.

"He left early this morning, my lady." Mrs. Benton clucked disapprovingly. "Didn't say a word as to where he was going, neither."

Isabella burst into tears.

Mrs. Benton laid a hand on her shoulder. "So the two of you have had a falling-out, have you?"

Izzie bobbed her head. "I said the most awful things," she confessed.

"He knows you didn't mean them, dearie. It's plain to anyone who sees you that you're in love. He'll likely go and get soused with that brother of yours and spend a few days feeling sorry for himself, but then he'll come home. You'll see."

"You think he's gone to London, then? Not to"—she drew in a shuddering breath—"to Jamaica?"

"Jamaica?" The housekeeper's brows rose in amusement. "Seeing as I saw Mr. Davies carry only a small portmanteau out to his lordship's chaise, I think it highly unlikely that he planned on traveling quite that far."

"He wouldn't leave Bride," Izzie repeated to herself.

"Of course he wouldn't. He dotes on the pair of you."

"He may dote on Bride," Isabella said, "but not on me. He doesn't love me."

Mrs. Benton crossed her arms over her chest. "Honestly, child, do you have eyes in your head?" she scolded. "Of course he loves you. Why else would he be letting you live in your own wing so he could court you like a proper suitor?"

"I never thought about it like that."

"Perhaps it's time you start. While you're here, though, perhaps you can help me. I've sorted through everything in the trunks that arrived earlier this week, and there's an unmarked package. . . ."

She went over to a cabinet and pulled out a paper parcel that looked somewhat the worse for wear. "Do you recognize this, my lady?" she asked, handing it over to Isabella.

"I know I've seen it before." Izzie cast her mind back, trying to recall where.

"Well, it can't have been for you or you would have opened it."

The housekeeper's pragmatic observation triggered Izzie's memory. "No, it was, I mean, it is for me. James had it with him the day he came to Haile Castle. There was so much going on; I suppose it got left in the nursery. One of the maids must have found it and set it aside. It probably got packed along with Bride's things."

"That mystery is solved, then," Mrs. Benton remarked. "Now all that remains is what's inside."

"If you don't mind, I think I'll open this in my room," Izzie told Mrs. Benton.

"Of course, dear."

Isabella hurried to her chambers. Once inside, she pulled at the strings and the paper fell away, leaving her breathless. James had bought her a baby blanket—the loveliest, most perfect baby blanket in the world—and he'd done it before he had known of Bride's existence.

He had told her of his awful past—a past she feared he would never be completely free of—and he had still bought the blanket. *For her.* To show her that he was willing to face his past and fight his demons . . . *for her.*

He'd told her that he had changed, but she hadn't believed him. He was such a strong, virile man, and even though she'd known he was capable of love and tenderness, she hadn't been certain he was capable of making the sort of compromises marriage required.

She had been wrong. It wasn't as hard to admit as she'd thought. If she could go back in time to the previous evening, Isabella would have run after him, fallen on her knees, and begged his forgiveness for the awful things she'd said. Then she would have kissed him and never let go.

He would be back, she told herself. He wouldn't stay away from Bride, and once he was back, she would convince him to stay. He'd said he loved her; the blanket was proof. And she couldn't stop loving him even if, as she'd stupidly said, she wanted to. They were perfect for each other in so many ways, she mused, fingering the soft wool of the baby blanket. They would complement each other and complete each other. Oh, they would have their fair share of fights, she had no doubt, but in the end they would always be drawn back together by a force greater than themselves: love.

Now she just had to wait.

James regretted leaving Sheffield Park almost as soon as he set off, but his pride drove him on to London. On James's fourth night in London, Davies confronted him.

"My lord, would you say you are a man of your word? That you keep your promises?"

"I would, no matter what my wife has to say."

"When we were sailing back to England, you told me that on the day of the battle you made a promise, to yourself and to God, that if you survived, you would spend the rest of your life devoting yourself to your wife's happiness."

James scowled. "She told me to leave. I am making her happy in my absence."

"Do you truly believe she's happy? Are you happy?"

"No." James sighed. "But what am I to do? She doesn't believe I've changed, and it's damned difficult to convince her otherwise if she doesn't want me near her. For Christ's sake, I bared my bloody soul to her. I explained why I went away—to protect her—but she thinks I left rather than deal with—"

He stopped and raked a hand through his hair.

"Lord, I've done it again, haven't I? I did just what she said I would do. I ran away like a bloody coward. I gave up without a fight."

"Don't be so hard on yourself, my lord. Sometimes it is more difficult to battle ourselves than a warship full of brigands."

"What do I do now, Davies?"

"Why don't you go to your club, my lord? You will seem much less pathetic if you're surrounded by other unhappy husbands seeking solace in liquor."

"You are an impudent bugger, Davies."

"Yes, my lord."

"Perhaps you are right. Very well, tell Cook I shall dine at White's tonight."

"Very good, my lord. I expect it will do you good."

"Thank you, Davies. I expect it shall."

What James didn't expect when he entered his club was to see his best friend, or rather, the man who had been his best friend until he'd taken his sister's innocence. He figured that pretty much violated the sacred rules of friendship, regardless of who had been the actual seducer.

A man could have only one *best* friend, though, and after so many years James really had no inclination to find another. As with Isabella, he wasn't prepared to let the relationship go without a fight. With Henry, however, James suspected that the fight would be an actual bout of fisticuffs. His bad shoulder ached at the thought, but if that was the only price he paid, he'd consider himself as having gotten off lightly.

Henry was devouring his dinner with single-minded devotion, so it took him a moment to register James's presence. When he did, his expression was hard and unwelcoming.

"You should leave. My sister asked me not to shoot you, but I never actually agreed," Henry said, then turned back to his food.

James winced, but he wasn't giving up. As his friend shoved another forkful of food into his mouth, James dropped himself in the neighboring chair. "The French already did," he replied. "Twice. And it was a pretty damned near thing with your aunt, let me tell you."

Henry unbent a fraction of an inch. "You do realize that I'm still going to pound you into the ground at Jackson's?"

"Just as long as you realize that Isabella will pound *you* into the ground when she hears about it." Actually, James thought Izzie might applaud her brother, but Henry didn't know that.

Henry grimaced. "Damn it, you're right. When I think about her with that poker . . ." He began to laugh.

James raised an eyebrow.

"Trust me, you don't want to know. But next time you anger her, I suggest you do it someplace out of arm's reach of the fire irons."

Henry was right, James thought. He didn't want to know.

"And how is my niece? I suppose any child of Izzie's is bound to be trouble."

"Not Bride. God, Hal, she's so beautiful and little and perfect and good." He thought back to some of the days on the trip home. "Most of the time," he amended.

Henry's lips twitched. "Are Izzie and the baby here with you in London?"

James sighed. "Your sister sent me away. She claims she

needed space, time to think. She doesn't believe that I've changed, that I love her."

"Do you?" Henry asked. "Love her, I mean."

James met his friend's gaze. "With everything I am," he said solemnly.

Henry clapped him on the back. "Well, it took you bloody long enough to figure it out."

"Just you wait," James muttered. "When you fall in love, you'll soon realize it's a hell of a lot more confusing than you ever could have imagined. And when you get married—"

Henry shook his head. "I don't plan on entering that state anytime soon, but when I do, it will be to some pretty young chit with nothing but fluff between her ears. My little sister may have your ballocks in an iron grip, but my marriage is going to be very, very different."

"Just you wait," James repeated.

"I will. I intend to wait a good, long time. What's your excuse?"

"For what?"

"Why are you sitting here waiting? It's obvious you miss her."

"I told you, she sent me away. She said she needed time to think."

"Ah, but what she thinks she needs and what she really needs are two different things."

James didn't think he was drunk, but damned if Henry wasn't starting to sound profound.

"Wait, repeat what you just said."

Henry gave him a funny look. "I never thought the day would come when *I* would be explaining something to *you*."

"Neither did I," James admitted, "but it's the first thing that's made any sense since I came to London, so say it again."

"Very well. My sister thinks she needs space, but my guess is that she's been miserable since the moment you left. Her asking you to go was a test; she told you to leave to see if you would. I have to say, coming to London was not the smartest move you've ever made."

"You're right. I realized that earlier tonight."

"As for needing time to think, Izzie has never been one for long, thought-out deliberation. She makes up her mind in an instant, and then it's impossible to get her to budge. You're lucky, though, because she decided she loved you long before she decided she wanted to kill you, so chances are love will win out in the end."

"Hal, I don't know what to say."

"You don't have to say anything. Just go home and make my sister happy. Tell her I'm growing wise in my old age."

"I'll be off first thing in the morning, and I plan to spend the next fortnight making her very, very happy."

Henry groaned. "That's my sister you're talking about."

"Sorry." James's grin was completely unapologetic. "Now, just so I know that all is right and the end of the world isn't approaching . . . 'To be or not to be . . .' "

Henry frowned. "To be or not to be *what*?"

"That is the question. Perfect answer, Hal."

"How could I have answered correctly? I asked you a question."

"Your question was an answer in and of itself."

Henry shook his head. "Now you're just confusing me. Off with you. Leave me to my meal and my brandy—them I understand perfectly."

Chapter 23

I have been most negligent in thanking you for all of the presents you have showered upon me. There is one gift in particular that remains most dear of all, and that, my beloved, is your heart. Mine was in your possession before you were even aware of it, but you had to work to give me yours. There were cracks to be mended, raw edges to be smoothed, missing pieces to be found, and a tough outer shell to break through. I know you believe these scars and imperfections to be offensive, but to me they are beautiful, for they have made you the man you are today. Our path has not always been smooth, but I would rather travel a bumpy road with you (preferably in a closed carriage) than walk an easy course with anyone else. I have made many decisions in my life, some admittedly better than others, but choosing you for my husband, recognizing you as the other half of my soul even at our first meeting, was the best one of all.

From the correspondence of Isabella, Lady Dunston, age twenty

Letter to her husband, James Sheffield, Earl of Dunston, concerning gratitude, flaws, and decisiveness—December 1798

"He's back! My lady, he's back!"

Although Isabella had been sound asleep, her maid's words jolted her awake. Her heart started pounding.

He was back, and it suddenly didn't matter why.

He was back.

She had another chance at happiness. He had overcome his fears for her; this time she would be brave enough to defeat hers. She would fight for him.

No, she would fight for *them.*

The pirate queen was headed into battle once more, and she planned to seize the day and conquer. There was a captive to ensnare, and once she had him, she was going to captivate him and bind him to her so tightly that there was no telling where she left off and he began.

But first she had a crucial decision to make. . . .

"Oh, Becky, whatever am I to wear?" she wailed.

"Keep calm, my lady. We'll start with the essentials. Shift, stays, stockings, and garters."

Isabella scrambled out of bed and followed Becky into her dressing room. She shook her head at the plain cotton shift her maid held out. "What if I have to resort to seduction again? No, I must wear one of those lacy silk gowns Aunt Kate gave me. I suppose there's nothing to be done about the stays. They're meant to be sturdy, not salacious. And I will wear the clocked stockings with the pink roses and the garters that match."

"I'll set everything out, my lady, while you see to Lady Bride. I expect we'll be hearing from her soon enough."

Becky was right, and by the time Izzie had nursed the baby, donned her prettiest undergarments, tried on four gowns, and had her hair styled two different ways, the clock tolled the noon hour. A maid brought up some sandwiches for luncheon, but Isabella had no appetite. Her stomach was too fluttery with anticipation.

Surely he wasn't going to make her wait until dinner! After an hour had passed with no communication of any sort, Isabella began to eat, contemplating which piece of china she was going to throw at her husband's head when she finally saw him. She picked up a novel, but found she couldn't focus. After reading the same page five times without taking in a word of it, she gave up.

She would have gone to confront him directly, but she was brought up short by her own ridiculous rules. She couldn't enter James's wing of the house without an invitation. Impatient, she began to compose a letter asking James to come see her as there could not possibly be a more pressing matter than the state of their marriage. Sometime, and many crossed-out lines later, she was interrupted by a noise at her door. It sounded as if something heavy had bumped against it. Intrigued, she turned the handle and discovered it was not something, but rather some*one*, two someones to be precise—Becky and Davies—both looking far too flushed and happily embarrassed to suit Izzie's mood.

"Begging your pardon, my lady, but Mr. Davies wishes to speak with you."

"I think he would rather speak with you, Becky."

Her maid turned crimson.

So did Davies, but he quickly recovered his equilibrium. "No, my lady, for I am only here on behalf of the earl, and his message is for you. He requests that you allow me to escort you to the west wing. He thought you might like to see the renovations."

"Am I to see him as well, or am I simply to be taken on a tour of my own home?"

"Certainly not. His lordship wishes to see you. Indeed, I believe he has a great deal he wishes to say to you, my lady. Now, will you come with me?"

Isabella nodded, unable to speak. Davies's words sounded ominous. What if James had changed his mind during their time apart? She knew he adored Bride, but what if he had realized he didn't love *her*, too? What if she couldn't convince him to give her a chance to make things right? A flurry of doubts attacked her, crumbling her confidence. Isabella trailed Davies through the house to the main hall, then down a long corridor and up two sets of stairs. When they reached the second landing, Izzie heard James's strident tones ring out. "No, not there. *There*. A little to the left. Yes, perfect. By all that's holy, John, I think it's finally finished. And just in time, too. Davies should be here with her any moment."

"I think I can take it from here," Izzie said softly.

"Very good, my lady," Davies replied, turning to head back down the stairs.

Isabella squared her shoulders and set off in the direction of James's voice. It was time to face her husband.

She tiptoed down the hallway until she spied an open door and cautiously peered into the room. Her breath caught as she took in the loveliest nursery imaginable. The sunny yellow walls were adorned with murals of sweet woodland animals. A rocking horse occupied one corner, and dolls and toys covered nearly every available surface.

Standing in the middle of the room, with his back to her, was James. He was gazing up at the something above the fireplace that Izzie supposed must have been the subject of the conversation she'd overheard. A painting, she figured, but she couldn't see it from where she stood.

Another man, John, she presumed, was kneeling on the floor, putting away his tools. He looked up and caught sight of Isabella. His eyes widened and he opened his mouth to speak, but Izzie quickly put a finger to her lips. He closed his mouth, jerked a nod in her direction, and got to his feet.

With one hand he gripped the handle of the leather case, and with the other he took hold of a short ladder that must have been borrowed from the library. "I'll just be returning these to their rightful places, my lord."

James murmured his thanks, never looking away from whatever was above the fireplace. Isabella used the covering noise of John's departure to slip into the room. And then she saw what held James so captivated.

Above the mantel was a large portrait of her and Bride. The pose was informal; the artist had captured the two of them in a moment of play. Bride's chubby little hands clapped in delight as she looked up at Isabella, who held her on her lap. Isabella gazed down at her, her expression a mixture of laughter and maternal tenderness.

She wondered how he'd had it done, as she certainly would have remembered sitting for a painting, and then she remembered how Henry had used Olivia's sketches to have the portraits done for her necklace. Livvy had sketched her with Bride several times in Scotland; James must have asked her to paint a watercolor before they left, which meant he'd been planning this for some time. A rather thought-out, complex scheme, but a successful one, executed by a rather complex, successful, and very thoughtful man.

Her throat closed with emotion as she looked at herself in the painting. Her face was familiar, the image she saw each morning in the looking glass, but it was different, too. Perhaps she was different. He had changed her in so many, many ways—mostly for the better, she thought. She had been forced to learn some hard lessons, made to weather rough storms, but she had survived. At her ball, she had thought herself grown-up, but her actions had still been those of a child.

It was sobering to look back on that time, the person she had been. It wasn't that she had been bad, precisely, since there had been nothing evil or malicious about her actions, but she cringed to remember how she had recklessly pursued what she wanted without any thought to the consequences. She had been so certain that she knew what was best for others, that her way was right. She had spoken but not truly listened, touched but not really felt. Everything had been black and white, and there had been no middle ground, no compromise. Actually, there *had* been compromise—her own.

Yes, she was a different person now—a woman, not a girl; a mother, not a child—but no amount of time would ever alter some things.

Like her love for James.

Unchanging and immutable.

She had ordered him away in a desperate grab for control, but even then she had known she would never willingly give him up. She just hadn't wanted *him* to know it. Grown-up behavior, indeed!

Tantalizing visions of true grown-up behavior flitted through her mind and, as if he'd heard them, James turned to face her. His face was calm, but there was an air of tenseness about him.

Slowly, cautiously, Izzie walked toward him, suddenly unsure of her reception. She chewed on her bottom lip, trying to decide her next move when, suddenly, James held out his arms to her.

She ran into them with a happy cry, and then he was holding her so close, wrapping her tightly in his warmth and his strength and, yes, his love. She wanted to laugh, she was so giddy with all the emotions bubbling up inside her. She would burst if she couldn't somehow release them. She wriggled up higher on his body to cup his face in her hands. Stroking her fingers along the hard edge of his jaw, she gazed into his eyes. Without warning, tears welled up and began running down her face.

James frowned, obviously confused by her crying. "What is it?" he asked gently.

"I just wanted to tell you how much I love you."

"I love you, too."

"Lord, but you scared me, leaving like that. I was certain you weren't coming back."

"Goose. How could I stay away? Your brother is not nearly as scintillating a conversationalist at the dinner table. I only left because I thought that was what you wanted, but I was miserable every moment. I also hoped the portrait might help convince you of the truth of my feelings where the other gifts failed."

"It's beautiful," she sniffed.

"It doesn't hold a candle to the reality," he murmured, tracing a finger down the side of her face.

She gave a watery chuckle. "I must say, you've rather outdone yourself with this one. I am almost reluctant to let Bride have it—perhaps I will move in here."

"Your place is beside me," James growled. "The only

chambers you will be moving into are mine. In any case, I have an even better present still planned for you."

"You know, you don't need to give me presents. All I truly needed was you." She tightened her arms around him. "I've missed you so much. It scares me, sometimes, how much I need you. Even if you told me you would break my heart, I fear it would still be yours. Forever and always, *I* am yours."

"And I am yours." He kissed her temple. "Always and in all ways. More than just the three ways you once told me."

"What are you talking about?"

"The night of your come-out ball, you told me that you had loved me in three ways. First, you said, was the sort of love a girl feels for her storybook prince. Then, if I recall correctly, you loved me as the fantasy of a young girl's dreams. Finally, you told me you loved me the way a woman loves the man she knows she is meant to be with."

"I can't believe you remembered that. I didn't think you were even listening to me."

"I tried to forget. God knows that I tried. But those words were seared onto my brain, into my heart."

"I love you," she said again, pressing her body even more closely against his and lifting her head for a kiss.

"And I you." He bent and dropped a quick kiss onto her mouth. "I have always loved you."

Isabella rolled her eyes. "James, it's very sweet of you to say it, but we both know that isn't true. It doesn't matter, though. Not now."

"It *is* true. I just didn't know it for a long time. Women are far more perceptive in affairs of the heart than we thickheaded men."

She smiled. "No arguments here."

"Good, because as much as I adore fighting with you—"

"What?"

"Come to think of it, it isn't the fighting bit I like so much as the making-up part."

She huffed in amused annoyance. "You are utterly ridiculous."

"Ridiculously in love."

She snorted.

"See," he said, "I even love it when you do that."

"When I do what?"

"When you make that funny little snorting sound."

"I do *not* snort!" she insisted furiously, but it was hard to be outraged when she knew she did. But wasn't love supposed to be blind or, in this instance, deaf to such things?

"*And* I love your breasts."

"What's wrong with *them*?" she demanded, her arms reflexively rising up between them to cover her chest.

"Oh, nothing is wrong with them. In fact, you have the most exquisite pair I have ever seen, er"—he coughed loudly—"not that I have seen a lot. I just felt like saying it. And you blush so delightfully whenever I mention certain anatomical parts. A month or so spent in bed ought to have you cured of that."

"*Men*," she muttered under her breath.

"In any case," he continued, "I was telling you how I have always loved you."

"And I was replying that it was total rubbish."

"Now who is being ridiculous? My love grew and matured over time, just as yours did." He brought a hand up to cup her face, rubbing his thumb over the pad of her cheek. "I first loved you as a child, probably from the first day we met." His voice grew deeper, huskier, weaving a spell about her senses. "You were such a precocious little imp. You brought sunshine into the darkest days of my life. The first night I spent under my grandfather's roof, I wanted to die. Literally. Death seemed preferable to spending a lonely life in this marble mausoleum."

"Oh, James!"

"Your family made life bearable, more than bearable, really. I almost felt a part of it—that Henry was my brother, and that you were my little sister. It was difficult for me to imagine you in any other way, but on the night of your ball, you and that damnably low-cut dress you were wearing forced me to see you as a woman."

"Oh, James." She sighed, nestling her head against his chest.

"The problem was that I wasn't ready to see you in that light. I had always been able to protect my heart from other women, see, but you were already in there. It terrified me. I didn't want anyone to have that sort of power over me. At least, that was what I thought. My heart had already accepted you in this new guise, had determined you as my life's mate."

"If all that is true, how come *I* was the one sneaking into *your* bedchamber to seduce *you*?" she demanded, poking a finger into his chest.

"Well, I do have my pride," he admitted with a rueful smile. "And I felt a tremendous amount of guilt."

"Guilt? Over what?"

"Izzie, you are my best friend's little sister. As I said, I was used to thinking of you as a sister. Compromising you, having any lustful thoughts about you at all, just seemed utterly wrong. It not only felt like a betrayal of Hal, but I came off feeling like the worst sort of lecher."

"I recall rather enjoying your *feelings* that night."

He playfully swatted her bottom, gave a gentle squeeze, and she couldn't prevent her body from arching up against him.

"Here I am, pouring my heart out to you, and all you can think about is sex!" he reprimanded.

"Mmmm . . . It's rather remarkable how the tables have turned," she said with relish.

"Quiet, wench, and listen up. You'll not get another declaration like this for at least a year. A man can only store up so much romance in his soul, and I am exhausting it all here."

"If you think telling me you love my"—she paused, then dropped her voice to a whisper—"my *breasts* is romantic . . ."

"Trust me, the best is yet to come. I was just warming

up. Now, where was I? Oh, yes, I started loving you as a woman the night of your ball, but I didn't realize it until I was at sea. You were constantly in my thoughts. I remember telling Ethan it felt as if I had left a piece of myself behind."

"Ethan?"

"An old school chum from Eton. He captains the *Theseus*. No, don't look so sour. The man saved my life in more ways than one. It was he who suggested I had fallen in love with you even before I left. He made me see that I was letting fear and anger dictate my life, and that I was selfishly refusing to take the wondrous gift that had been offered to me. You. The warrior queen who fought for me when I wouldn't fight for myself. My savior."

The lump in her throat had grown so large, Isabella could hardly swallow. "You were right," she choked out. "It got much better."

"And I haven't even finished yet," he teased.

"There's more?" She laughed, producing that sort of odd gurgling noise one makes when laughing while trying not to break down into sobs. "Just give me a moment to prepare myself."

She relaxed against him, her ear against his chest, calmed by the rhythmic beating of his heart. A heart that beat for her. Because he loved her—really *loved* her. Yes, he had given her the words that night in the library, but she hadn't truly believed he loved her in the way she loved him.

She took her own love for him for granted, but just as she had changed over the past year, the way she loved him had changed, too. When she had married him, there had still been that impossible, storybook expectation of perfection, but his uncertainties and vulnerabilities only made him dearer to her now.

Before, he had merely completed her heart. Now, he swelled it until it was nigh bursting from her chest. She felt light-headed and deliriously happy. She had a husband she loved with her whole heart and, miraculously, he seemed to feel the exact same way about her. It was a forever sort of love—exactly what she needed from him but had scarcely allowed herself to hope for.

"Are you ready?" he asked.

She was. Whatever life had in store for them, she was ready for it.

Isabella lifted her head and met his gaze. "Ready," she responded.

"Good. Because once I finally get this out, when I have exhausted my supply of romance, I am sweeping you off to a sweet little love nest I've created, and I am keeping you there until the *rest* of me is exhausted!"

Izzie groaned. "I shouldn't have stopped you. I should have known you would become sidetracked. What *was* I thinking?"

James lowered his head until they were eye to eye. "When you're bawling," he said, "just remember you asked for this." He took a deep breath. "I fell in love with you all over again in Scotland. You are the mother of my children, our darling Bride and all the unborn ones to come.

"You are the love of my heart and my hope for the future. Your face is the last thing I want to see when I go to bed each night, and I want to wake every morning knowing you are cuddled beside me. You are the missing piece of my puzzle, the only person who can make me whole.

"I learned the hard way that without you by my side, I am a lost, broken man, never truly happy, never quite complete, wandering aimlessly through a gray mist. You are the sunlight that warms my soul, and you helped me grow into and become a man I never dreamed I could be."

"Are you done?" she asked, her voice wavering.

"Ye-es." The warily voiced word was more a question than a statement. "Why? Did I leave something out?"

She shook her head and flung herself against him, sobbing uncontrollably.

"I did warn you," he noted, dropping a kiss on her head, "but no more crying, my love." He gently wiped the tears from her face. "I have another surprise for you." He pulled a piece of black silk from his pocket and began to tie it around her head.

"You're blindfolding me?"

He paused. "Are you objecting?"

"Not if I may do the same to you someday."

James chuckled and swept her up in his arms. "Anytime, my love, anytime," he responded, and began heading downstairs. Izzie closed her eyes and rested her head against the muscled plane of his chest. Wherever he was taking her, she was more than happy to go.

When the blindfold was finally removed and Isabella realized where they were, her jaw dropped. James had completely transformed the folly— their folly—making it over into an exotic sultan's den. Swags of jewel-colored silk flowed out from the center of the ceiling and ran down the walls to form glimmering puddles on the floor. While she stared in amazement at his efforts, her husband lit the candles scattered about the room. Quilts and pillows were heaped in a cozy pile before the softly glowing fire. It was exactly as he had said—a sweet little love nest.

"Well?" he asked, coming to stand before her.

"It's perfect." She sighed. "But . . ."

"But?"

"But"—she poked his chest, and then trailed her finger slowly down to the top of his breeches—"you must have been awfully sure of yourself."

"I told myself it was impossible to love someone so much without being loved in return."

"You were right."

"And I had your maid send me daily reports detailing how you were pining away in my absence."

"She did not!"

"No," he admitted, "she did not, but it's nice to have it confirmed that you missed me as much as I missed you."

"Did you know she and Davies are sweet on each other?"

"I did, and I think it's a fine thing, but do you *really* want to talk about your maid right now?"

His eyes had taken on the heavy-lidded slant she had come to associate with his arousal. His desire ignited hers. "No," she whispered huskily, her pulse beginning to pound. "I don't want to talk about Becky."

"What *do* you want, then?"

"You." She looped her arms around his neck and pressed her body against his. "Just you. Make love to me, James."

Wordlessly, he led her over to stand before the fire and began to undress her. She closed her eyes, the action heightening her other senses. Her tongue tingled with the sharp taste of anticipation. She felt lightning bolts every time his fingers brushed against bare skin; inhaled the mingled smells of him, and her, and their need for each other; heard the crackling and hissing sounds of the logs in the fireplace . . . and the hitch in his breathing when he reached under her skirts and discovered that she was already wet for him.

He quickly unlaced her stays so she was clad in only her shoes and stockings. "Are you warm enough, my love?"

"Mmmm . . . Positively feverish," she replied, kicking off her slippers. "And from the look of you, I fear the condition is catching." She reached for the buttons on his waistcoat. "We must get you unclothed posthaste."

With four frantic hands at work, the task was completed in record time. Naked, he knelt before her and set about untying her garters and removing her stockings. The amber light of the fire gilded his skin, and Isabella marveled again that he was hers. Determination clearly paid off.

James settled himself down into the nest of blankets and cushions and then drew her down on top of him, guiding her into position so that she was straddling his hips. The stance opened her to his view in a way she found wildly exciting. She reached up and drew the pins from her hair, tossing them aside until the heavy mass of curls tumbled down her back. Now she was a lusty pirate queen . . . a pagan princess . . . a seductive siren. Now—and always—she was *his*.

Isabella gasped with pleasure as James caught her breasts in his hands. He teased the tender globes, kneading her flesh and tweaking her nipples, causing her to squirm about on him. The movement pressed her sensitive, exposed flesh against him; they groaned in unison, and Isabella felt his shaft, throbbing and insistent, against her buttocks. She cried out as he circled a finger about her wet entrance.

"You're ready for me," he said with satisfaction.

"And you," she remarked, boldly reaching down behind her to touch him, "are ready for me."

"Always," he rasped. "God, do you have any idea how much I need you?"

She smiled slyly and ran a fingertip along the length of his erection. "Oh, I think I have some idea."

Grasping her hips, James lifted her up. Their eyes met and locked. "Take me inside you," he commanded.

Still trapped by that green-gold gaze, Isabella felt around blindly until she captured him. She couldn't resist stroking him a bit.

"Now, Izzie!" he said through clenched teeth.

She guided him to her aching opening, then slid the tip of him inside her. She waited for him to push into her, but he just held her there, poised to receive him.

"More," she insisted.

He lowered her another inch.

"More," she pleaded, wriggling her hips. Her muscles gripped him tightly, trying to draw him in farther.

Another painful, pleasurable inch.

"More, more, more!" she yelled, lifting her hands into her hair and thrusting her breasts forward, utterly wanton and loving it.

"*Yes*," James growled. He pulled her hips down at the same time as he thrust upward, coming into her so hard and fast and deep, she nearly swooned.

"Are you all right?" he asked in concern.

"Even better," Isabella assured him. Instinctively, she began to rock against him, and he lay back, folding his arms behind his head, allowing her to discover what she liked.

After a while, she found a glorious, primitive rhythm that soon had them both panting. James cupped her behind, his strong arms supporting her and urging her on, quickening her pace.

Isabella leaned over him, dangling her breasts like ripe fruit before his face. He eagerly drew one into his mouth, suckling strongly, swirling his tongue about her nipple. Isabella felt an echoing response down below, as if the hard bud in his mouth shared some invisible connection to the one at the apex of her sex. She was close to coming undone. Close to coming. *Close.*

"More," she demanded.

It was apparently the signal he had been waiting for. James surged up into her, grinding her hips down on his. He thrust into her over and over, his hips bucking beneath her. She rode him, raced him, reached with him for heaven, and then rejoiced with him when they exploded together and landed among the stars.

They clung to each other afterward, sweaty and sated, happy simply to hold and be held.

"I love you," Isabella murmured against his shoulder.

He lifted his head and met her eyes. "I love you, too."

"Promise me?"

"Always."

She arched up and kissed him, her soul filled with the knowledge that this man and this love—and these kisses—were hers forever. He had promised her "always," and she believed him with all her heart.

Epilogue

Holding up a hand to shade her eyes from the sun, Isabella slowly made her way down Haddington's High Street until she finally found the establishment she was looking for. In the three weeks they'd been in Scotland visiting her aunt Kate, this was the first opportunity she'd had to execute her plan. When James had mentioned over breakfast that he planned to spend the day alone with Bride—now two years old and as feisty as her uncle had predicted— Isabella had seized the day.

She had some very wonderful news for her husband, and she knew just how she wanted to tell him. Filled with giddy anticipation, Isabella pushed open the door to the toy shop. But as soon as her eyes adjusted to being indoors, she realized she was too late.

"Mama!" Bride shrieked, pulling her thumb out of her mouth and waving wildly over her father's shoulder. Clutched in her other hand was her baby blanket, though it looked more like a tattered rag and had faded to an indeterminate gray color. Isabella liked to say it was "well loved."

James turned around to see what his daughter was fussing about. When he saw her, though she could tell he was as shocked as she, a smile lit his face.

Izzie frowned. "I thought you were spending the day with Bride. What are you doing here?"

"I *am* spending the day with Bride. She wanted to see about having a special blanket made for her little brother or sister."

"You know," Isabella whispered. Then her voice rose. "You *know*?"

James laughed and pulled her to him with his free hand. He dropped a kiss on her mouth, which was still hanging open in shock.

She gathered her wits back around her. "How long have you known?" she demanded.

"About a fortnight."

"Why didn't you say something?"

"Why didn't you?" he countered.

"Because," she huffed, "I had this ridiculous notion of surprising my husband with a gift, for once!"

"I appreciate it, my love, but I shall tell you what you once told me. I don't need presents." He rested his hand over her abdomen. "For the rest of my life, you and our children are the only gifts I need." He kissed her again, long and slow and sweet, drawing away only when they heard the shopkeeper's soft chuckle.

Isabella gasped and raised her hands to her burning cheeks, mortified at being caught sharing such intimacies in a public space. "I am so sorry—," she began.

"Och, lassie, never be sorry fer lovin'," she said, and then turned her attention to James. "This is yer wife?"

He nodded.

"I was right. Yer wife is a lucky woman."

"That she is," James replied, drawing her even closer against him. "But I am an even luckier man to have such a wife."

Isabella sighed. Was it any wonder that she loved this man? Then she grinned like the minx he often accused her of being. She intended to remind her husband just how lucky he was every night—and some mornings and afternoons—for the rest of their lives.

Turn the page for a sneak peek at Olivia's story,

Tempting the Marquess

Coming from Signet Eclipse in June 2010

*O*livia stood before the castle's thick wooden portal, inwardly bracing herself against what lay in wait on the other side. Freezing rain had plastered her shabby traveling gown to her body, and the biting wind whipped at her sodden blond ringlets. She thought wistfully of her blue velvet pelisse with the ermine trim, but she had left the garment—and the elegant, easy life it represented—behind when she had chosen to run away rather than marry the lecherous Duke of Devonbridge. And now she was a lowly governess, dependent on the kindness and goodwill of her employers—and her new master was purported to have little of either.

A lone wolf howled somewhere out on the misty, moonlit moors that stretched for miles around the isolated edifice. She shivered with cold and fright, wondering whether she might not be safer with the wolves than inside the castle's walls. A different sort of beast lay within that impenetrable stone fortress. A caged beast, confined not by chains but by his own despair.

The villagers called him the Mad Marquess, for he had been crazed with grief since the death of his wife some four years prior. He eschewed all company—not that there were many eager to subject themselves to his foul humor. In the past year alone no fewer than eleven maids had resigned their posts at Castle Arlyss. She'd heard rumors, too, of a centuries-old curse. . . .

Olivia raised her face to the heavens, searching for a sign that this was indeed the path she was meant to travel—that she was meant to save this tormented soul and show his son *a mother's love. Lightning flashed and crackled through the night sky, setting her hair on end. The angry rumble of thunder followed close behind.*

Stiffening her spine, Olivia raised her fist to knock. Then, all of a sudden, a strong gust of the wind snatched at her sleeve, as if trying to stop her. The air swirled around her, rustling through the dead leaves underfoot.

It seemed to whisper a name.

Livvy, it murmured.

Livvy . . .

*A Carriage Bound for Castle Arlyss
Pembrokeshire, Wales*

December 21, 1798

"Livvy!"

Olivia opened her eyes and stared unseeing out the coach window. She blinked at the few rays of sunlight that dared penetrate the winter gloom lingering over southwest England. She shook her head. The wild, stormy night had vanished, and she was back in her aunt's well-sprung carriage.

A wistful sigh escaped her. The dream had been so real . . . but now she was back to being ordinary Olivia Weston.

She turned her head to look at her young cousin Charlotte, who was tugging rather insistently at her sleeve.

"Livvy!"

"What is it?" Livvy asked in as understanding a tone as she could muster. The journey from Scotland to Wales had already taken close to a fortnight, and though she loved Charlotte dearly, the boundless energy of a five year old was ill-suited to the close confines of a carriage. Not that Olivia was any stranger to small children. As the third of seven siblings, she knew all about them.

The little girl frowned, pulling at one of her glossy dark ringlets, then shrugged. "I forget."

Livvy bit back a groan and stifled the urge to tear at her

hair which, to her everlasting disappointment, was neither curly nor dark. Neither was it blond and straight. Olivia's hair was a very ordinary, indeterminate shade of brown, and it had just enough of a wave to always look unkempt.

"Livvy?"

"What, Char?"

"I remembered. I had a secret to tell you." Charlotte crossed her arms over her chest and flopped back against the plush squabs with a satisfied smile.

"And ... ?" Olivia prompted. She waited for further elucidation, but none was forthcoming. "Did you wish to tell me this secret you remembered?"

Charlotte thought a moment before shaking her head. "I'll tell Queenie instead."

Queen Anne, a doll in lavish court dress, was Charlotte's most prized possession, a distinction held since being unwrapped a few weeks past. Yes, Livvy thought, she had been replaced in her cousin's affections by an inanimate object. How distressing! She consoled herself with the knowledge that her conversational skills far surpassed those of Queenie. Then again, so did a squirrel's. As was her wont, she began composing a list in her head:

Ways in Which I Am Superior to Queenie
1. I can read.
2. I can write.
3. My head is not made of wood.
4. I can breathe.

Hmm, perhaps that last should have been first on her list; it seemed a fairly important distinction. Of course, squirrels also breathed. Maybe she ought to list the ways she was superior to squirrels instead. . . . She stopped herself, wondering whether it was possible to go mad from boredom.

Aunt Kate looked up from her book to address her daughter. "Charlotte, I do believe Queenie looks a bit peaked. Perhaps you should both try to rest for a time and let your poor cousin alone."

Charlotte was disgusted by this suggestion. "Mama, Queenie is a *doll*. How can she rest when her eyes don't close?"

Aunt Kate sighed and peered out the window at the passing scenery. "At least we are getting close to the end. We should arrive tomorrow, provided the weather doesn't change. . . . That child will be the death of me!" she muttered.

Livvy glanced at Charlotte, who had apparently decided to take her mother's advice. She was curled into the corner of the carriage with her feet drawn up under her and her head pillowed against one hand. Her eyes were closed, a beatific smile on her face. Queenie lay in the crook of her free arm. Olivia smothered a laugh as she realized the reason for her aunt's proclamation.

As the doll's eyes did not, as Charlotte had pointed out, close, her enterprising mistress had contrived other means by which Queenie might rest. Raising Queenie's gown up over her head *did* shield her face from light, but this action also exposed the doll's lower half. And while Queenie's ensemble boasted exquisitely detailed garters, stockings, and shoes, it did not apparently run to petticoats.

Ha! Petticoats! There was another way in which she was superior to Queenie *and* squirrels, too, for Livvy had never encountered a petticoat-wearing squirrel and very much doubted she ever would. The closest she was ever likely to come was the stable cat her younger sisters had caught long enough to dress in a bonnet and christening gown.

Aunt Kate leaned forward and spoke quietly, so as not to disturb Charlotte. "I feel I ought to warn you about my stepson."

"Warn me?" Olivia's cheeks grew warm. "I hardly think—"

Her aunt waved a hand dismissively. "Heavens, child, I'm not suggesting anything of *that* nature. No, I only mean to caution you about the welcome we are likely to receive."

"You mentioned Lord Sheldon keeps to himself a great deal of the time. I am not expecting to be met with a grand parade. I wish to inconvenience the marquess as little as possible."

That wasn't precisely true.

If all went to plan, she would put the man to a great deal of trouble.

But that was her secret—one she didn't dare share with present company. Not with Aunt Kate, certainly not with Charlotte, and not even with Queenie, who was by nature most admirably closemouthed.

"Jason—," Aunt Kate began, then sighed. "I suppose I should call him Sheldon, but I can't seem to get my mind round it, no matter that he's held the title for five years now. He has always been Jason to me, or Bramblybum, though few have called him that and lived to tell the tale."

"B-Bramblybum?" Olivia burst out laughing. She caught her aunt's sharp glance at Charlotte and lowered her voice. "Surely you are joking."

Aunt Kate shook her head. "The marquisate was created for the ninth Viscount Traherne who was, I gather, a great personal favorite with James the First. The viscount's son, who went on to become the second Marquess of Sheldon, openly disapproved of his sire's, ah, proclivities. The viscount begged the king to disregard his son, and joked how the boy had been born with nettles stinging his backside. The king's revenge was to bestow a marquisate *and* an earldom upon the viscount. While his father was alive, the second marquess was known by his courtesy title."

"The Earl of Bramblybum," Livvy whispered, torn between horror and hilarity.

"Earl Bramblybum, actually, but I wouldn't suggest you let that pass your lips once we reach Castle Arlyss. Jason always gets fussed on hearing it. He certainly doesn't use the title for Edward. I have told you about Jason's son, Edward, haven't I? He's nearly seven now and such a dear, sweet boy."

Olivia nodded. She wasn't sure whether Aunt Kate had told her about Edward, but she knew about him all the same. But that was part of her secret.

Unconsciously, she bent forward, reaching for the hem of her dress. Her fingers sought out the small bump of the brooch she had pinned to her chemise.

"I'll stop nattering on and let you rest." Aunt Kate's eyes twinkled. "You needn't go take the same drastic measures as poor Queenie and cast your skirts over your face."

"I wasn't—I mean, you weren't—," Livvy stammered out in protest.

"Calm yourself, my dear; I'm only teasing. I know I have a tendency to ramble, especially when I don't have to mind my tongue." She winked, nodding in Charlotte's direction.

A rush of pride swept over Olivia at her aunt's words. In the eyes of society she was an adult and had been since her eighteenth birthday, close to a year earlier. Girls her age, and even some younger, had already had their come outs this past Season. She should have come out then as well, but her sojourn in Scotland with Aunt Kate, Charlotte, and Livvy's newly married (and freshly abandoned) older sister, Isabella, had lasted longer than expected.

Nine months longer, give or take a little.

Olivia hadn't minded putting off her come-out. She wasn't overly eager to put herself on the marriage mart, and besides, her sister had needed her. That last trumped everything else as far as Livvy was concerned.

Aunt Kate reached forward and patted Olivia's knee. "I've grown accustomed to having you and Izzie around. I was so pleased when you asked to come along with us to Wales. I would have invited you had I known you were so interested in this part of the country."

"I must confess, some of my interest stemmed from wanting to avoid spending countless hours trapped in a carriage listening to Mama expound on some Shakespearean heroine or other."

For as long as Olivia could remember, her mother had been writing a critical work about Shakespeare's heroines. Life in the Weston household was all Shakespeare, all the time, at least when her mother was present. The rest of the family bore it with equanimity—mostly because they tended to ignore her—but over the years her mother's obsession increasingly grated on Livvy's nerves. She adored her mother, really she did, but she could easily have done without hearing, at least once a week, as she had for her entire life: "Be not afraid of greatness: Some are born great, some achieve greatness, and some have greatness thrust upon them."

Lady Weston particularly enjoyed tailoring her recitations so that each of her children would be familiar with the plays from whence had come their names. Olivia resented having Shakespeare's greatness constantly thrust upon her, but not for the world would she have hurt her mother's feelings by telling her so. All in all, she felt lucky to have been named for a character in *Twelfth Night*, which, in her opinion, was one of Shakespeare's more tolerable works, and not only because it was relatively short.

"What's caused that long face?" Aunt Kate asked. "Have I scared you off with this talk of my stepson? You mustn't let him upset you. He is very changed since the accident, and grief affects us all in different ways. Perhaps, given time . . ." She trailed off, her hopes for the future unspoken but entirely clear.

Olivia wanted to say she knew, or at least had an inkling, of what the marquess had been like before his wife's death—but she could not. Instead she smiled brightly and said, "Then we must do our best to bring some cheer to both Lord Sheldon and his son this holiday season. If you don't mind, Aunt Kate, I think I'll read a bit while Char is quiet."

Her aunt laughed. "Yes, living with Charlotte, one does learn to seize those rare moments of peace. They certainly don't last long."

Olivia nodded distractedly, already absorbed by her book. Or rather with the piece of paper hidden inside. In bold, scrawling script were the words that had prompted her seemingly impromptu journey to Wales—words penned by none other than the Mad Marquess of her dreams.

Author's Note

On Savage Heathens, Nelson's Navy, and Shakespeare's Women

First, a disclaimer . . . As a lifelong bibliophile currently studying to receive my degree in library and information science, it should come as no surprise that I love to research and to share the information I find. Though the historical romance genre obviously presents a romanticized version of history—and I, for one, am happy to ignore the less pleasant aspects of life in the past—I have tried, wherever possible, to faithfully depict the sociocultural climate of the late eighteenth century.

The anti-Irish sentiments expressed by James's grandfather were, unfortunately, quite widespread in England, especially in the upper classes. While the Normans established settlements in the twelfth century, systematic colonization of Ireland began under the Tudors. When Henry VIII broke with the Catholic Church, the common link between the two countries was also broken. The Irish were depicted as savage heathens who were, according to English soldier Barnabe Rich, "more uncleanly, more barbarous, and more brutish in their customs and demeanors, than in any other part of the world" (*A Short Survey of Ireland*, 1609).

Consequently, the English justified depriving the Irish of their civil, religious, and land rights; by the mid-eighteenth century the Protestant English and Scottish settlers—though only a small fraction of the population—controlled more than ninety percent of the land. Tensions between the English and Irish were especially high in the years leading up to the Irish Rebellion of 1798. James had already left Ireland at the outbreak of the rebellion in late May, but he probably wouldn't have been involved in any case, as the fighting took place in the northern counties, far away from County Kerry and the charming miscreants of Belmore Hall.

As much as possible, the events of the Battle of the Nile are depicted faithfully. Nelson's decisive victory established the superiority of the British navy for the rest of the French Revolutionary Wars. There was an Earl Howe who served as First Lord of the Admiralty, but he had no sons. My thanks to the real captain of the *Theseus*, Ralph Willet Miller, for allowing me to commandeer his ship—I made certain Ethan took good care of her.

In a twist sure to please Lady Weston, the Battle of the Nile brought the term "band of brothers" into popular use. The phrase, originating in Shakespeare's *Henry V*, was repeatedly used by Nelson in reference to the fifteen captains with him during the Nile campaign and battle.

Lady Weston and her critical work on Shakespeare's heroines developed from my own feminist tendencies and love of the Bard, but Lady Weston is far from an anachronism. The first critical essay on Shakespeare, dating from the mid-seventeenth century, was authored by a woman, and the first detailed study of Shakespeare's female characters by early feminist Anna Jameson dates to 1832, five years before Victoria ascended to the throne.

To learn more about Georgian history, the next Weston novel, or (far less interesting) your devoted authoress, please visit me at www.saralindsey.net.

Best Wishes,
Sara

From
JO BEVERLEY

The Secret Wedding

At the age of 17, Christian Hill impulsively
defended young Dorcas Froggatt's honor—and
found himself forced into marriage. That didn't stop
him from pursuing his military career abroad,
where he swiftly put his young bride out of his
mind—until the past came back to haunt him...

Not long after her traumatic marriage, Dorcas heard
that her new husband Hill had died in battle. She's
shocked to discover that he's not only still alive,
but searching for her. She's determined not to
sacrifice her independence, not expecting the true
dangers she'll soon face, and even less, the true
love she'll discover with the man who rescued
her all those years ago...

New York Times Bestselling Author

Jo Beverley

**Available wherever books are sold or at
penguin.com**

From
BARBARA METZGER

The Scandalous Life of a True Lady

Spymaster Major Harry Harmon's latest assignment requires him to serve as a nobleman at a house party attended by his enemies. To play the part convincingly, he needs an intelligent, beautiful woman to act as his mistress. A woman like Simone Ryland.

Simone and Harry both have their reasons for going along with the ploy, but they both also have secrets—and desires...

<u>Also Available</u>
The Wicked Ways of a True Hero
Truly Yours

**Available wherever books are sold or at
penguin.com**